GLO

Ac
Brother of Agravaine, elder son of Urien of
Gwynedd

Agravaine
Younger son of Urien of Gwynedd

Ambrosius Aurelianus
Former King of Dumnonia (before Uther)

Arienwen
Priestess of Avalon, Seren's mother

Arthur Pendragon
High King of Britannia

Balan
Twin of Balin, a warrior in Arthur's army

Balin
Twin of Balan, a warrior in Arthur's army

Bishop Elwyn
Bishop of Cymru

Brochwel
King of Powys, Cymru

Cai
Childhood friend of Arthur, a warrior in Arthur's army

Caireann
Priestess of Avalon

Ector
Foster father of Arthur and Morgan

Elinor
A princess of Elmet, elder daughter of Leodegrance

Fila
Serving maid at Caer Arthur

Gaheris
Eldest son of Morgause and Lot, a warrior in Arthur's army

Gareth
Youngest son of Morgause and Lot, a warrior in Arthur's army

Gawaine
Middle son of Morgause and Lot, a warrior in Arthur's army

Gorlois
Former King of Kernow, Igraine's first husband

Gruddieu
Village woman, wife of Meurig, mother of Naw

Guinevere
A princess of Elmet, younger daughter of Leodegrance

Igraine
Former Queen of Dumnonia, Uther's widow

Illytd
A warrior in Arthur's army

Isolde
Wife of Mark of Kernow, lover of Tristan

Lachlan
A warrior in Lot's army, slain in battle

Lancelot
Bastard son of King Ban of Benwick (Gaul), a warrior in Arthur's army

Leodegrance
Co-ruler of Elmet, father of Elinor and Guinevere

Lot
King of Caledonia, north of the Wall

Lumiel
Son of Guinevere and Arthur

Mark
King of Kernow

Merlyn
Archdruid of Britannia

Meurig
Village man, husband of Gruddieu, father of Naw

Mordred
Son of Morgan the Fay and Arthur

MORGAN THE FAY
BOOK TWO:

BLACK MORGAN

WOMAN. WITCH. GODDESS

SHANI STRUTHERS

MORGAN THE FAY
BOOK TWO:

BLACK MORGAN

ALSO BY SHANI STRUTHERS

Morgan
Daughter of Viviane, princess of Dumnonia

Morgause
Wife of Lot, sister of Igraine, Arthur's aunt

Mynyddog
King of Gododdin

Naw
Village boy

Nesta
Priestess of Avalon

Nimue
Priestess of Avalon

Óengus Mac Airem
King of Demet, Cymru

Pellinore
Co-ruler of Elmet

Peredur
A warrior in Arthur's army

Priscilla
Foster mother of Arthur and Morgan

Rhianinfelt
Agravaine's mother, Urien's first wife

Sagramor
A warrior in Arthur's army

Seren
Priestess of Avalon

Taliesin
Former Archdruid of Britannia

Teg
Morgan's Serving Woman

Tewdric
King of Glywysing, Cymru

Tristan
Son of Mark of Kernow, lover of Isolde

Urien
King of Gwynedd, Cymru

Uther Pendragon
Former King of Dumnonia, Igraine's second
husband

Uwaine
A warrior in Arthur's army

Viviane
High Priestess of Avalon

Vortigern
Former King of Powys, Cymru

Wenna
Priestess of Avalon

Saxons (the Sea Wolves)

Aelle
Saxon leader

Cerdic
Saxon leader

Hengist
Brother of Horsa, Saxon leader

Horsa
Brother of Hengist, Saxon leader

Octa
Son of Hengist, Saxon leader

CALEDONES **

DÁL
RIATA *

MAEATAE *

DAMNONIA

MANAW
GODODDIN GODODDIN

BRYNICIA +

R
H
E
G
E
D
(?)

DEIRA *

ELMET

LINDSEY +

EIRE

GWYNEDD

CEREDIGION

DEMET *

POWYS

BRYCHEINIOG *

GLYWYSING

PENGWERN

BRITONS

ERGYNG

a
u

BRITONS

MERCIA +

MIDDLE
ANGLIANS +

SOUTH
ANGLIANS +

EAST
ANGLIA +

GEWISSE -

EAST
SEAXE -

Kingdoms of

KERNOW

DEFNAINT

BRITONS

DUMNONIA

BRITONS
(DORSET)

MARA ***

LEON ***

SAXONS -

SUSSEX -

KENT ***

Britain, c. 540
in the time of Gildas

Based on *The Anglo-Saxon Chronicle*
and LLoyd's *History of Wales, Vol. I*

ANGLES **+**   IRISH origins ***** PICTS ******
BRYTHONS   JUTES ******* SAXONS **-**

PROLOGUE

The lifeless body of the lacewing lay before me. Crushed.

"You've an affinity with animals," Priscilla, my foster mother, once said to me when I was a child, or words like it. "With all living creatures."

Would she think that now?

My fist comes down again, not to harm the delicate creature further, but because I can't help myself. The storm inside me needs release.

Again and again, I slam the table, and if I hurt my own bones in the act, so be it. Let them break, let them splinter, the skin there reduced to pulp.

In truth, I should wreak more damage. I should have torn myself to shreds long ago, for despite what's been said, Britannia would have been better for it.

There is so much that might have been.

I've become the enemy, as much as the Jutes, the Angles, the Saxons, or the Romans ever were. Worse, I may have *bred* an enemy.

I am cursed, and in turn, have cursed another.

This chamber I call my own is a dark one. Blackened.

When first it was shared with me, I'd been thankful. My heart had *sung* for it.

Now, my heart plays a different tune.

But here it is – the chamber. And here I am, within it.

This so-called sanctum.

Two walls are lined with shelves, and each shelf is filled with jars of herbs and plants. Some are innocent, meant for healing – following the teachings of my foster mother, Priscilla. Remedies for all ailments, from the common flux – with its fever and watery bowels – to more insidious sicknesses that tighten the lungs like a noose.

There are wounds too, of course. Mostly household ones – scalded hands from boiling water; Elen, the clumsy kitchen maid, is often guilty of that. But also wounds from conflict, gaping and raw. These must be cleansed, then stitched – a bronze needle piercing flesh, horsehair or sinew drawing the skin tight, a rag clamped between the teeth to muffle screams. Afterwards, a little honey to soothe.

In my years here on this rock, this…*barren* rock, far from everything I once knew, I've done it all. And despite killing the lacewing, I've saved animals too.

I am Morgan the Healer.

A *great* healer.

Regarded as such.

Revered.

But not by all. Oh, not by all. To others, I am something else entirely.

My eyes drift along the shelves to jars filled not with remedies, but poisons. Wolfsbane, to paralyse the heart, to induce a long and lingering death. Coat an arrow tip or blade with it, and should it find flesh, none will survive – or are meant to. Hemlock works much the same. And Belladonna, which does more than kill. It warps the mind first, twisting sight into horror – men made hideous, ghostly forms, and the monsters of legend, all rising from a swirling mist to hunt the afflicted down. Death follows, but not before convulsions wrack the body, the mouth so dry they claw at their lips, desperate to taste even their own tears.

A terrible thing to witness! Unforgettable.

Priscilla would say it should *never* be used. That on warm days, when riding through the countryside, one should steer clear of places where it grows in clumps: the woodland clearings, the hedgerows, and hillsides. But its flower – bell-shaped and purplish-brown – is so very pretty. It catches the eye, and keeps catching it.

I've nothing but love and respect for my foster mother, but why – *why* – would the Great Mother, the goddess of all, create such a plant if we weren't meant to use it?

Some people…*deserve* a cruel death.

That's how I've justified it.

But now – now I can justify nothing.

All seems ruined.

All is…desperate.

There are those who don't deserve death at all.

Plants and herbs. Potions and lotions.

There are scrolls here too.

In this remote corner of the world, I've learned to read and write in fuller measure. Not in Latin, nor in the speech of the Christian priests, those robed creatures who sit in their holy houses, scribbling by candlelight until the wicks burn low, preaching of their One True God. This tongue is older by far, the words of gods and goddesses, committed to parchment and, I'm certain, on flesh as well, though I've never been permitted to touch such relics. It is arcane. Mystic. Symbol-bound.

Wrought with power.

But power demands a price.

I know that. Have *always* known it.

5

Oh, what have I done?

What have I done?

This room! So often, I've thought of it as cavernous, but now the walls close in, pressing tight, and in the corners, they wait: the shadows. Vague at first, then taking shape – one, two, three of them – arms outstretched as though lovers calling. As a child, when I lay in bed beneath the roof of the villa I shared with Priscilla, Ector, and Arthur – that Romanesque house we held in such pride, deep in a shaded valley – even then, they called to me. *Legions* of shadows.

And sometimes – *sometimes* – I'd answer.

The lacewing is dead.

And my heart – unless I can save it – is dying too.

But how do I even *begin* to undo the damage?

The scrolls hold no answers. Written by the gods, yes – but which gods?

They have only led me deeper into darkness.

Rage and despair, like the moon, wax and wane. I should *never* have killed the lacewing, when once I'd loved the creatures so. I'd often coaxed them to come closer, and willingly they had, perching on my hand in a shaft of sunlight so I could admire their gossamer wings, the impossibly intricate patterns etched there.

A small death, some would say. It shouldn't grieve me as it does, not when my hands have wrought slaughter on a far grander scale.

But it is *this* death – the smallest of all – that reveals what I've become.

Again, how do I set right what has gone so terribly wrong?

How?

A scream erupts in the pit of my belly, forcing its way out

through the hollow of my mouth. It echoes through the chamber. Reverberates. Enough to cause a disturbance elsewhere? No matter. Who it brings is of no consequence anymore.

Those of consequence have gone.

My fists clench again. This rage… Ah, but the sea is easier to control!

Remember what Merlyn said: 'There's such fire in you, Morgan.'

He was right. A fire that *burns*.

Though I run towards the shadows, it's the shelves I strike, tearing down what was once so carefully curated. Glass shatters, and contents spill.

So much commotion, but no one *dares* to come. It is night – the *dead* of night. They'll stay in their beds instead, clutching their blankets beneath their chins.

The scrolls…

If I destroy them, there *will* be consequences. A godly rage to eclipse my own. *Sacred* scrolls, yet profane in equal measure. They teach, but not for the better. My hands itch to tear them apart, imagining them cold and leathery beneath my touch as fingers curl into claws, and nails into talons. I *could* do it. Destroy them. I *should*.

But scrolls like these…they sing with a power of their own. They whisper too…

Do it, Morgan.

Do it!

And see what happens…

I can't. All I can do is escape them, or try to. Magic comes in many forms, and not all of it is natural; not all of it is condoned. I must put distance between them and me.

For my quest begins soon.

Though I've returned to these shores, it was only to put to the test what Merlyn had so recently claimed. Now that I have, I must leave this enclave – this place like Tintagel in Kernow, poised at the world's edge, gazing out over a broiling sea.

I can hear the waves right now, how they lash at the shingle shore without respite, each one carrying the howls from that nearby isle – Ynys Môn.

There were times when Ector, his voice low and steady, would tell Arthur and me of that mystical place, once a Druid stronghold, until the Romans came. The Romans had feared the Druids. *Hated* them. Saw them as a threat to their power and pride. So what did they do? They hunted them there, herded them, onto the very ground they held dear, then followed – swords drawn and blades sharp. They didn't stop until the earth was slick with Druid blood, and the sea about it churned red.

As hallowed as Avalon once, but now a place of madness.

And it is close. So close.

Perhaps therein lies the answer.

The madness here – threaded now through me – cannot be blamed on the scrolls alone, nor the worship of dark gods. It stems too from what history forced on this land. A madness that clings, refusing to fade.

Air. I need air, no matter how infected.

At the window, I wrench open the shutters. The cold hits me like needles.

I gulp it in, feverishly trying to form a plan. Where might those I seek have gone? Anywhere! They could be anywhere – lost in the mists, as I so often am. The Fay guiding them, having renounced me, those who are malleable, when I am not.

I rub at my eyes, drag my hands through my hair. No mist hovers tonight, but I'm lost all the same. I *must* form a plan! Take back what is mine. What is *ours*.

Arthur… How does he fare in Dumnonia? And Guinevere too? Bright Guinevere – who has lost her shine, who blames me for everything. As well she might.

My despair for her, for the pain I've caused, must be set aside. I have to master my emotions. And encourage obsession. A *righteous* obsession, this time.

For my son – my son may yet be a saviour if I can find him, as great as Arthur.

Or a destroyer, like me, if I don't.

So much depends on fate, and fate, I've learned, is fickle. Given to whimsy.

The shadows don't just surround me, they don't just whisper, they're *screaming* my name now. I must fend them off, if only for a while longer.

"Mother," I beseech. Not my birth mother – my lip curls at the thought of her. Not my dear, sweet foster mother either, but the mother of us all. The Great Mother. If my hands have become claws, then I will claw my way back to her.

Will she let me?

"Great Mother, help me. *You*, not Brigid, nor Arianrhod, Ceridwen, nor the Fay. You alone." And not the demons, either. For they're here as well as the shadows. Always watching. Always waiting. "I turned from you once, sullied your sacred ground, and for that, my heart is heavy. But don't turn from me too. Show me the path, the one that leads to what I seek, no matter how crooked, how perilous it is."

A howl on my lips again, to match the sea, for it will

surely be perilous.

Then, I quiet, grow deaf to everything but her.

I wait, and I wait – my hands by my sides, perfectly still – until I hear it.

Another whisper.

The Great Mother is not like the Christian's One True God. I begged Him for help too, long ago, kneeling at the altar in a chapel newly built for Him, with my hands wrung tight. There were no whispers then, only silence. Colder than stone.

But the Great Mother answers.

Her voice is in my head, in my heart, and all around me, light, ethereal, strong.

"*Go,*" she says. "*Go,*" and then again, "*Morgan…go.*"

Her urgency floods me with purpose.

But again, go where?

No answer. Only *GO!*

For *everything* is at stake if I don't. Her fate as well.

I step back from the window, my feet crunching over broken glass. The smell of herbs and plants is acrid and stings my eyes. Good. Let the tears come. Before I leave here tonight, I will have wept enough to create a second sea, just as turbulent.

But after that, let the well run dry.

The chamber is in ruins. Only one thing remains: a mirror of black quartz, hanging on the wall. Not meant to flatter, but to scry. A looking glass in which to peer long and deep, to see beyond its murky surface, to divine what is yet to come.

A mirror of prophecy.

I shouldn't pick it up. I should destroy it too.

But…

One more time.

That's all.

Just...one more time, *then* I will smash it.

I approach. Nothing greets me, not even the ghost of a reflection, though I can picture it well enough: a woman who was once a girl, so full of innocence, radiant with joy and love. But now... Now, that woman is far more besides. She is a mother.

The mirror darkens.

Ah, this is the moment. When Sight begins.

I swear an oath: whatever it reveals, I will trust the Great Mother, that she might wield this vision as a tool, to guide me, to reassure me.

For I'm afraid, and though I've been afraid before, never so much as now.

Yes – something stirs.

Something straining to break free.

Fire!

Sudden. Vicious. Flames climbing higher and higher.

Is it mine – the fire Merlyn spoke of?

Or another's?

Unquenchable.

I seize the mirror, no matter how jagged-edged, wrench it from the wall, and hurl it down, certain that as I do, I hear the flames hiss.

Illusion.

What I saw was illusion.

I shake my head, tangled black hair tumbling past my shoulders.

It is *not* illusion.

But I will go regardless.

Arthur... *Oh, Arthur.*

You know this wasn't meant.
Not by me, at least.
I'm sorry. So sorry.
How many times must I say it!

PART ONE

CHAPTER ONE

Five Years Earlier

"Quick! Someone approaches. A woman? I think it's a woman, she's so slight."

A voice. I could hear a voice. *The Great Mother be thanked – I'm still alive!*

"That's it. That's it. Take her arm. Carefully now. Oh, but look at her – how cold she is. She's half frozen, poor thing. Yet she's found her way here…in weather like this, through such thick mists." A pause, and then the voice again. "*Who* is she?"

"My horse," I croaked, surprised I could do even that. "Taran…does she follow?"

A hand touched mine, warm and steady.

"The dapple? She's here. She came ahead of you, out of the mists. It was because of her I searched further. Hush now, though. Save your strength. We'll stable…Taran, is it? And take you to Wenna's cell, fetch you something to drink."

Taran…

Relief broke through the numbness.

I remembered losing her, in the mists the woman spoke of, somewhere out there in the swamps. Her hooves had trod so carefully before, but then…then she was gone, and I was alone. On my hands and knees, wading through the murky waters that surround this place, clutching at tall reeds to drag myself forwards.

The speaker was right – I was cold. Cold before I'd even left…

Left where?

Caer Arthur.

Of course Caer Arthur! The place I'd lived for nearly three summers. And yet now it felt like something I'd only dreamed of, slipping from me so quickly.

"Wenna. Wenna! Does the fire burn well enough in your cell?"

Another voice, softer, answered. "Yes. Yes. It's freshly stoked."

"Good. The hour is late. We must get her into dry clothing and warm her blood. This kind of cold can fell an ox. Great Mother, but look how she trembles!"

The world shifted as I was lifted between them, arms braced beneath mine, guiding me towards shelter. Once inside, I was laid on a bed, careful hands peeling away my sodden garments and brushing the snow from my hair. As they worked, the mists closed in again, but this time I welcomed them, aching for sleep.

Avalon.

That's where I was – despite the weather.

Winter still held the land in its fierce grip, one of the harshest I'd ever known. Ice and snow smothered all, and the sky sagged low, heavy with white or sullen grey.

It came to me more clearly now. In our chambers at the caer we'd shivered constantly. The fires, though their flames had leapt high, could barely take the edge off. I'd *confined* myself to my chamber, and, ah, my body had trembled indeed.

The warmth of *this* fire, the press of *these* blankets – they lent no comfort. Not truly. They stirred the ache of memory instead.

I'd left Caer Arthur.

I'd left because of Arthur...

Arthur *and* Guinevere.

He'd married her. He'd had to. Her dowry fifty horses fit for war – enough to form a cavalry and sorely needed if we were to triumph in a second war against the Saxons, those who threatened our shores without cease. I'd thought it so many times, but what *determination* they possessed, the Sea Wolves, to come as they did, wave after relentless wave, braving the tumbling, treacherous seas. What must their homeland be like to make such a risk worthwhile? How wretched?

There was no doubt – Britannia was blessed. In winter, spring, summer, and autumn alike, it was bountiful. And Dumnonia, where I was born and raised, was a jewel among kingdoms. The Summer Country, they called it, where, when the sun shone, it shone the brightest. A place where fields yielded crop after crop, and birds trilled sweetly from the treetops. The meadows blazed with gold and crimson: buttercups and poppies, the dusky purple of knapweed too, and the pale haze of cow parsley. There were woodlands, vast and ancient. Forests where you could still find refuge from the world of men. Where *I'd* found refuge once.

A pool there.

A silent pool...

The West had long held strong against invaders – first under Ambrosius Aurelianus, then Uther Pendragon, and now his son, Arthur Pendragon. It was no longer just the West; the entire land lay in his hands. The fate of all Britannia.

Not just a king.

A High King.

My brother.

My…*alleged* brother.

My lover.

He was nothing to me now. He couldn't be.

"She's waking again," I heard a voice say. "She's murmuring…"

Should I try harder to surface? Spare myself the pain of these memories? I could still hear those others speaking – the women of this sacred isle. Priestesses.

"But who is she, to have found us like this? And on such a night too?"

"Someone…special?"

"I know you've said the hour is late, but should we rouse Viviane?"

"No. Let her sleep. Dawn isn't far."

"But what if…Viviane *angers* if we don't?" There was fear in the speaker's voice. She tried to mask it, cloaking it in reverence, but it was still there.

"She…won't. But she may anger if we disturb her for nothing."

For nothing?

Twice they'd asked themselves who I was. Perhaps they'd decided that even with a horse as fine as Taran to my name, even though I'd braved the mists and the swamps and survived, I was still not special enough. Mad. Only that.

Priscilla was the last person I saw at Caer Arthur, pleading with me to stay, though she knew she couldn't stop me. My will is my own. My path is too.

I'd left because of betrayal, though I'd betrayed as well. Not Arthur. Never Arthur.

It was Lancelot.

We were to be married. He loved me, and I believed I loved him.

At least, he...*used* to love me. Until he saw Guinevere, walking down the aisle to wed Arthur. From that moment, his heart was hers. Entirely.

But before he turned from me, I turned from him – to Arthur.

And then Arthur...Arthur saw Guinevere too.

In that infernal chapel, he stood at the altar with Bishop Elwyn and Merlyn opposite him – each of them representing their gods, each giving their blessing to this new reign, this so-called bright beginning meant to drag us from the dark. He wore his wedding finery, his golden curls gleaming, yet he was forlorn all the same.

Until she joined him.

Guinevere – adorned not in jewels or silks, not painted like a gaudy doll – but a girl, simply that. A beautiful, radiant girl. In that moment, capturing his heart.

I could have wept to see it!

I *have* wept, over and over.

And now, perhaps I wept without knowing it, as fingers brushed my cheek.

Arthur and I had been together, when so many said we couldn't be. Ours was a hidden bond, conducted in secrecy, but if secrecy was the price for love, and for uniting Christians and pagans under one rule, we were willing to pay it. He'd married Guinevere because he had to, because of what her hand secured: not just horses, but the allegiance of a kingdom – Elmet, stretching wide across the Middle Lands.

What a prize that was.

But it paled beside Guinevere.

I'd wager she stole every heart in the chapel that day, that so-called simple girl, for it wasn't only Lancelot who'd gasped when he saw her.

But his gaze had been the most intent, and Arthur's only a shade less so.

Could they be rivals for her love – Arthur and Lancelot, his warrior, yet also his closest friend? Rivals, even though Arthur and Guinevere were already wed. Because I'd seen it – at the altar – when Guinevere's eyes shifted from Arthur to Lancelot as she spoke her vows, her gaze *drawn* to him, the gasp that left her too…

Ah, Guinevere and Lancelot. I didn't care about them. Not truly. Only Arthur.

He'd told me that, for him, mine was the face of the Goddess. *Always.*

And Arthur did not lie.

His soul was the purest I'd ever known, one bound to mine, the two of us entwined through the mists of time. Surely he knew that? He felt it too? He'd sworn it! Those times we'd lain together by the silent pool, the moon above us and the night birds quiet rather than crying out, he would turn to me, brush the hair from my brow, and pledge it – Arthur, a man of honour. "I will not love another, Morgan. I *cannot.*"

And yet…when last we spoke, he could barely lift his eyes to mine. All he managed was a whisper, "I still love you."

Still?

Still!

Even now, those words rang as loud as bells in my ears.

"Hush! Hush, now! You must try to rest. Don't babble so. Don't thrash."

The woman speaking to me – the one called Wenna...was it true what she said? That I was babbling? Throwing my arms about?

"Please, please, calm yourself. Oh, Nesta, we *must* wake Viviane."

Nesta. So that was the other one with me tonight. A name I'd heard before – perhaps one of the ladies at Arthur's court bore it as well. It meant *pure*, or *holy*. I was certain Wenna's name carried meaning too, chosen to reflect her path. They sounded young, both of them, younger than me even, who would soon see twenty-one summers. Twenty-one! A woman grown. A woman with child.

They couldn't know that. Despite being slight of build, nothing showed yet, nor did I know when it would. *If* it would. I'd survived the journey from Caer Arthur to Avalon, but perhaps what grew inside me hadn't. The weather had turned so quickly, first a snowstorm, then the eldritch mists that ever shroud this isle.

Had I truly understood the dangers when I set out?

Was that why I'd pressed on, rather than seeking shelter?

For there *had* been shelter – signs of several homesteads, though I'd kept mostly to the back roads, the ones Merlyn claimed to know so well. Fires had burned in their hearths, as told by the smoke that curled from their chimneys. It wasn't as if my arrival would have caused alarm, I was only a lone woman. But I'd passed them by.

Viviane... It was she who drew me to Avalon – or the thought of her. The woman whose body had borne me, who had nearly died in the act.

I was delivered during a great storm, or so I'd been told. A night when thunder shook the sky and lightning split it. When Avalon's holy thorn was cleft in two.

They say the gods cried out that night, the Bean Si too – that harbinger of doom. But even so, I was *born*. I drew breath. Was I held in her arms? I must have been. Was it she who'd named me – not Morgan, but Morgana, *she who comes from the sea*? A name not unlike the Morrigan – another omen-bearer, another face of wrath.

And then, when still so young, I was given away. Fostered.

But now I was back.

Perhaps it was just as well Wenna and Nesta didn't know who I was. If they did, they might not have rushed to help me. They would have barred their doors instead, leaving me to the snow, the ice, the swamps – to certain death. Me *and* my child.

My…boy.

For I can feel he is safe enough, the energy that stirs, *masculine* energy.

We will both survive, and I will have what I came for: an audience with Viviane.

But tonight – ah, tonight – I continued to drift, and the women tending to me fretted still. One of them might even be weeping, the one whose cool hands had brushed away my own tears while she murmured, "Hold on. Don't leave us just yet."

Once, I believed this holiest of places *unholy* – this famous bastion of the old ways. The ways of Britannia before the Romans named it so – when it was Albion.

Mythic Albion.

But Wenna – and Nesta too – kind and gentle, inspired

hope. It *was* the right choice coming here. I might yet find refuge. A welcome. Open arms.

A comforting thought.

I wanted to tell them not to worry. Though I was drifting, it was only a little further.

The mists weren't always fearsome.

Was someone calling my name within them? As the shadows used to…

Morgana.

Morgana.

She who is sea-born.

If that were so, then yes, I could find my way when so many couldn't.

The seas will part for you, Morgana. You have only to command them.

Such a lofty promise – but oh, how sweet the voice was. Low and lyrical.

Convincing.

I was power*ful*, not power*less*. Found, not lost.

This was a holy place…and yet…who'd made me doubt it?

Seren.

She'd been here once. Was she still?

Something as black as her…

As black as you, Morgana.

A whisper that almost halted me, as I sank deeper.

Almost.

Because the voice wasn't finished with me yet.

But there's power in that. Power that's owed.

Remember that.

It is power that's owed.

CHAPTER TWO

"She has a fever. She's weak. Wenna, Nesta – you should have roused us earlier!"

Don't blame them, I wanted to say, but my throat was thick, swollen, and no words would come. My eyelids stayed sealed shut, so I willed them to hear my thoughts instead. *I'm not weak. Someone has said otherwise. I...I'm far from weak.*

Those whispers had faded now. *Enchanting* whispers, crooning like a mother at a cradle. As gentle as they'd been, though, their truth now blazed through me – I was *owed* power. The daughter of a High Priestess, and perhaps a king as well.

Yet there I lay – wretched and fevered, a creature dredged from the depths.

Who was it chastising those who'd come to help me?

Someone leaned over me.

Mother?

As she did, there was another voice – an apology, heartfelt, anguished.

"We're sorry, Eda, but the hour was so late, and...and... We've tended to her, done everything we could, everything we were taught, by yourself, and by others. She calmed eventually and slept well. Her cheeks cooled. But then...this morning..."

The fever, that's what they meant. It had returned.

And it wasn't my mother so close to me, but another priestess – Eda.

My already muddled mind spiralled further. This was Viviane's domain. Surely word had reached her by now of the newcomer. And even if it hadn't…couldn't she *sense* me? Her daughter. So near. Flesh of her flesh, blood of her blood.

I hadn't heard Seren's name – and for that, at least, I was grateful. It reminded me that these women still couldn't know who I was, so why do it, why disturb Viviane?

"Caireann," Eda decided. "Fetch her. She'll know what to do."

Caireann – another name familiar to me. Tribal. *Little dark one.*

It was her they needed to tend me – another like Priscilla, perhaps. A healing woman, her knowledge of herbs and plants likely just as extensive.

If I could have spoken, I'd have told them what to do – for I was a healer too, or aspired to be. A Morgan so at odds with the one they whispered of in the mists. She who could become fearsome, wilful, and something more dangerous still: entitled.

Meadowsweet or willow bark, brewed into a tea, would ease the fever. They'd also do well to burn mugwort to clear the air. Simple remedies, but effective. Their stores must be well-stocked, surely? Ah, but why continue to worry? They'd called for Caireann. That was enough. Thanks to her, I might surface more fully soon, be well again, *introduce* myself. I might be able to think clearly, plan what to do next.

If my mother were to come…would she even recognise

me? She hadn't laid eyes on me since I was a bairn. Not once in all my years of growing had she reached out. She was a woman devoted to other pursuits: the worship of the Great Mother, keeping Her spirit and Her teachings alive. But had it never occurred to her I might become curious? That one day I'd be *driven* by that curiosity?

Of course she couldn't sense me. We were nothing but strangers to each other…

Oh, where was Caireann? Even half-awake, I was so tired! Someone was sponging my lips, gently coaxing my mouth open to trickle water down my throat. I was grateful for the relief, but it was all too fleeting. My thirst returned. It *raged.*

And the mist was back. Just when it had almost cleared. Swirling.

Perhaps…*stronger* medicine was needed. More than meadowsweet or willow bark. A combination of several would have more effect: yarrow, elder, and horehound, the white variety. Having almost surfaced, I was pulled back under, but this time I tried to resist. What if I was drifting too far now?

Others had entered the chamber. It seemed to *heave* with movement. Voices rose and fell, sometimes hushed, but at other times quite normal, speaking in ordinary if somewhat brisk tones. There was a strange smell. Not mugwort, but perhaps a resin, drifting in soft, persistent waves, both dreamlike and cloying. Now and then, a breath of fresh air reached me, and when it did, I tried to gulp it down, desperate for it to be the thing to revive me. My chest tightened with each attempt until I nearly choked.

Taran… Did she still fare well?

Someone had said she'd been stabled. I missed her, my loyal steed, so sure-footed under clearer skies, but entry into

Avalon had been precarious, what walkways there were slick with moss and mist. Yet I hadn't taken pity on her, I'd urged her on. If anything should happen to her while I lay so inert...

This burning in my chest! And the terrible, terrible weakness that accompanied it! I prayed for it to ease as someone spoke again, words I could barely capture.

"...with child...see there...belly...swells. Heartbeat...hers...faint...faint."

And what of the child's? Was his faint too?

He'd been strong once! Days ago. It was just *days* ago, wasn't it?

I couldn't tell. Time had become something strange, as though suspended. There was no night, no day, only this mist and the chorus of voices that came and went.

I was worried about my horse, but what of the baby?

The silent pool... When so much was vague, what I'd seen there remained vivid – a place deep in the woods near Caer Arthur, revealed to me by none other than Arthur's mother, Igraine. A sanctuary bequeathed. It had not been my reflection in the rippling waters when I'd peered into them, but another's. A boy who'd *exploded* into life, and all the blood there was because of it. *Just* the blood of childbirth?

The Bean Si howling... She did so at my birth. Would she at his?

"Heart...faltering."

Mine still? *Who* were the priestesses talking of?

The truth was that I didn't know how to feel if he was in danger! It was all so new to me. I didn't even know whose child he was – Arthur's or Lancelot's.

At the pool, when I'd seen him, he'd had dark hair and

grey eyes, so a blend of them both. I'd done this! Put myself in the same position Viviane had been in with me. She'd claimed not to know who my father was either – Uther or Taliesin. Was that why I'd come? To ask her? To see her face when I did? *Test* her?

It was said she'd lain with both around the time of my conception. Yet Merlyn had stood before Arthur's court and declared I was another child of Uther's, and therefore Arthur's half-sister. He'd said it even after admitting to me, in private, that I might well be Taliesin's – the Archdruid before him. If that were true, if Taliesin was my father, then it could have been me with Arthur in his mixed court of pagans and Christians.

Not her.

Not Guinevere.

As the king's sister, I was a commodity, with plans being made to marry me off to Urien. Old, old Urien, the King of Gwynedd, who'd seen more summers than even he could count. If I'd done it – placed my hand in his – Arthur would have held nearly all of Cymru. Only Demet would have remained an outlier, ruled by Óengus Mac Airem and his Blackshields, those who'd crossed the wild sea from Éire to these shores, fleeing the spread of Christianity, more rampant there than here.

But I'd refused, *ruining* Merlyn's plans. I hated him for it – for trying to force my path. And I think…I think I've hated Viviane too. Merlyn told me he was at Avalon the night I was born. He and Viviane both could have devised a use for me – one that deepened further when Arthur was born two years later.

And yet…even if there was hatred, even if there was resentment…I still wanted to see her. Perhaps to gauge if something else could bloom between us, the love that was missing. Yes, *that's* what I longed for. Not destruction of any kind, for me or my child to be the architects of it. But what I'd seen that day at the silent pool couldn't be dismissed as fancy. It was a vision. Goddess-sent. An omen of the darkest kind.

A warning.

His eyes… I remembered his eyes. How hardened they'd been.

A baby. Not even born. An innocent – surely?

A mother should never wish death for her child.

I didn't!

Yet…

There it was again – the two halves of me. Morgan the Healer, and that other Morgan – the one more blackened. How could a woman be both?

Ah, but what would the Fates decree? Who would survive the journey I'd undertaken – and who wouldn't? I was unmoored. Cut loose…cut loose.

And so very tired.

I needed to escape the mist. Escape *everything*.

Sleep. Just sleep.

There…that was better.

All thought was fading. All voices. All whispers.

And perhaps now…the ceasing of not just one heart, but two.

"Ah, you stir. Good. Aye, 'tis good. I'm Caireann. I've been tending you. No, no – still yourself. Don't rise. Not yet.

You've been sorely unwell. We nearly lost you to the mists…
But hush now – no need to dwell on shadows. You're awake.
You're here. As the Great Mother wills."

Hands were helping me to sit, though even that simple
task was enough to set my heart racing, draining what little
strength had gathered in my limbs.

Another woman stepped forwards, a sweet smile on her
face.

"There," she said. "There, that's it. What a blessed day
to see you recovered!"

It was a maiden and a crone who stood before me, both
clad in long, loose robes – the maiden's the green of spring
leaves, Caireann's the blue of river water.

The younger woman was barely more than a child, no
older than fourteen or fifteen summers. The crone was
stooped with age, her hair wispy and nearly all grey. She was
a small woman, bird-like, yet as she moved around me, I
could imagine, if the years were to fall away, her hair being
as dark as mine and her eyes bright instead of rheumy. It was
clear the blood of the Fay ran through her veins, as it did
through my mother's, and mine. She was a crone, yes – but
one with the gentlest hands. As she eased me back against
the pillows, and as the girl passed her a bowl of broth to
bring to my lips, I understood it was to this woman I owed
my life.

My life.

But what about my son's?

She noticed as my hands went to my belly.

"Your baby lives too," she said. "Don't fear."

Was it fear? Or was it hope, no matter how wretched? I
still didn't know.

She spooned some broth into my mouth, a little at a

time, barely a sip, but it was all I could manage. When my eyes went to the window, she noticed that too.

The shutters stood open, yet there was no icy blast to chill the bones. The sky framed beyond was blue, and the trees – those that I could see – were in leaf. And yet…when I'd left Caer Arthur, it had still been winter, the trees mere spindles, most of them. And now? Winter had fled at last? Another season taking its place.

My hand flew to my mouth, pushing the spoon aside as more broth was offered.

"How long was I lost for?"

"Don't fret, little dove—"

"How long? It's spring out there. It is! Not winter."

Caireann lowered the spoon and nodded. "Aye, you're right. It is. The sacred feast of Imbolc has passed. Spring is well underway now."

My mind tried to grasp it. "Then…then I've been lost for some time."

"Child—"

"That's what it felt like! Like…I was drifting. The mist was everywhere, and in it, so much lay hidden, but I could hear voices… I could hear whispers."

The old woman set the bowl and spoon down, then reached out, seeking to comfort me. "If you were lost," she said, "you're now found."

They were words that held an echo of something, a resonance. But I couldn't fathom it, not yet. I was still in too much shock.

"So much time has gone by! I… I…"

I don't feel found, was what I wanted to say. Though the world had come back into focus, I was still adrift. Tears sprang to my eyes, the sting of them.

31

Caireann gathered me to her. "There, there. 'Tis all right, Morgan. All is well now."

I jolted at her words, but didn't pull away.

Morgan. Not little dove, not child, she knew my name well enough. That could mean only one thing: Viviane *had* come! She was here, and she'd recognised me!

I was in a priestess cell, possibly the one I'd first been brought to.

It was a small chamber, its walls not built of timber or wattle and daub but rough-hewn rock. A cave, then? Was this truly a room carved from stone?

It was dim, but candles burned softly. Beside the narrow window stood a door so low even I'd have to stoop to pass through. The air was faintly damp, but the fire kept the chill at bay. The space was sparsely furnished. Other than the bed I lay in, there was a small table, a stand with a basin and folded cloths, and an array of jars – tinctures, likely the very ones administered to me.

"It's my chamber," the girl said, as if reading my thoughts. "And I'm Wenna."

"Wenna?" I repeated. "There was another…Nesta."

"Nesta is busy elsewhere now."

"Ah," I said, nodding.

If this was Wenna's chamber, then where she slept, I couldn't say. The only other piece of furniture was the chair on which Caireann sat. It was bleak in here, yes. Barren, even. And yet a quiet serenity prevailed, one I clung to as I did the crone.

She knew my name, so I had to ask, had to find the words, *make sure of it.* Had Viviane come? Had she done more than that – tended to me, as a mother might?

The thought of it…

The thought of...*missing* it. Of being unaware. Oblivious.

Before I could form the words, Caireann laid me back down, covering me with a woollen blanket. "Hold still now," she said. Turning to Wenna, she added, "Keep the fire stoked. 'Tis a fair day outside, true enough, but we mustn't let her catch a chill now, must we? Aye, come sundown, the cold creeps in despite the season." She shivered as she said this, even though I sensed it was early still, the night a way off yet.

What energy I'd summoned had been spent. But I had to know.

"Viviane...did she—"

I got no further.

The door to the cell creaked open, dragging against the packed mud floor.

Caireann and Wenna both turned, Caireann seeming to know who was there, even before a figure appeared.

"Ah," she said, and her voice sounded even enough. "Here she is, the one who knew you. Come in. Come in. Oh, she's been fair beside herself with worry."

I held my breath, though even as I did a heart that had beat slow – that had very nearly stilled altogether – *two* hearts – was quickened, wholly alive once more.

This was the moment I'd waited for all my life.

Caireann rose, smoothing the folds of her robe – a gesture of respect, surely?

The figure, a woman, stepped fully into the chamber.

A *young* woman.

"Seren," Caireann greeted. "Come again to check on our little dove, have we?"

CHAPTER THREE

Viviane had *not* come to see me. Not in all the days I'd lain there, through the last of winter and into the first breath of spring.

But Seren had.

She'd been *devout* in her attention.

My strength was returning. I could sit upright now, even take a few steps around the cell, at first leaning on Wenna, but gradually managing alone.

I *had* to grow stronger. For Seren, though she smiled, though she greeted me with the warmth of kin, though she made *such* a show of concern and empathy for my plight, even offering to help Caireann and Wenna in any way she could – there was something in her eyes. I saw it there. What had *always* been. If I was something dark, then so was she – darker still, able to harbour resentments every bit as much.

We'd been seven summers when we first met, when she'd come to stay with us at Ector and Priscilla's – fostered there too, though only for a short while. Her mother, along with many of the priestesses of Avalon, had fallen ill with the winter flux.

From the first moment, I'd known to be wary. Seren the Spiteful, I'd called her then, but she was more than that.

She was dangerous.

She'd disliked me, certainly, but Arthur? Arthur she'd

hated.

Little Arthur – then only five summers old. Sweet, bright-eyed, and sunny in disposition. It had mystified me then, as it did now, what she could possibly have found in him to despise, yet she had. So much so that one day, when all were occupied, she'd led him to the river near our villa with the intent to drown him.

It was I who'd noticed her absence, who'd run to the water's edge and found them. And then…the fury that had gripped me! My fists had pummelled her into the ground, pressing her deep into the muddy bank. I'd wanted to bury her there – alive.

I couldn't lie – I'd *enjoyed* it. I'd relished every scream that tore from her mealy little mouth, but truly – ultimately – I'd wanted only to silence her.

No one was to hurt Arthur. No one.

They'd have to get through me first.

"You are ever his protector," Priscilla would say, and she was right. I had been since he was two and I was four, since that morning I'd first found him bouncing on Priscilla's lap in the villa's kitchen, laughing with such unfettered joy. A boy fostered, as I was fostered. Our true parentage a mystery until we grew.

My assault on Seren had been stopped, of course. Ector and Priscilla had found us and dragged us apart, Seren spouting such nonsense in her defence, claiming *I* was the evil one – an abhorrence, an insult to the Great Mother.

We'd been hauled home, sent to separate rooms, and by morning she was gone – sent elsewhere. All I'd felt was relief. Relief that I hadn't been cast out as well, that Arthur lived and breathed still, safe among us. The river near our villa could be perilous, its current swift and unforgiving. Had I arrived even moments later...

I suppose I'd always believed I might see Seren again – unless illness, or someone else she'd crossed, claimed her first. It had long been my intent to return to Avalon, to meet my mother, the woman so many spoke of with reverence. Before Seren, my only wish had been to gaze upon her face, to see if my likeness dwelt there. In her absence, Priscilla had been a wonderful mother to me, but perhaps it is something innate in fostered children, that yearning to seek their true parentage.

But *after* her – even before Merlyn – that yearning had changed.

There were *many* questions I needed to ask Viviane, if everything Seren had whispered to me all those years ago was true. Those things she'd said when we were forced to share a bed about the circumstances of my birth.

Should someone have died? Me?

And having lived, was I indeed an affront?

This darkness in me – this force that could erupt so spectacularly – whose was it? Viviane's? Or my father's? And of my father, was it truly Uther, or more likely Taliesin? I've wondered before, but could a man like Uther, a warlord, really have been to her taste? Surely Taliesin, an archdruid, as wise and veiled in mystery as she was, would have suited her better? Had there even been love between them?

Imagine that – to be born of love!

There was so much I longed to uncover. The duality of my nature left me confused. If I could grasp even part of the truth, perhaps I could still the storm within.

But still she hadn't come. Only Seren had.

She, who now clasped my hands and said with such sincerity, "Oh Morgan, Morgan, *friend* – it is a blessed day

to see you looking so well. The Great Mother be thanked."
She'd gestured towards Caireann and Wenna, standing
nearby. "What fine work they've done in tending to you.
You know, Morgan, we thought you were lost. *Many* times
we feared it. You and…" Her gaze slid to my belly, and I
saw her eyes narrow, just as they used to when she looked at
Arthur. "…the baby."

But just as swiftly, she was all smiles again.

"It's so good you're here! To wonder – is it the path of a
priestess you'll choose? What a boon for Avalon if you do!"
A wave of her hand dismissed the thought as quickly as it
had come. "Consider it when you're stronger, when you've
had time to see where it is you are, *truly* are – the
magnificence of it. Avalon is at once humble and a seat of
power. I know you'll love it. You, the daughter of the High
Priestess." She stepped closer and quickly embraced me
before adding, almost casually, "She'll visit soon, I'm sure.
Ah, but she's kept busy, though…hasn't she been resting of
late, Caireann?" Feigning mild confusion, she then nodded
faintly. "Yes, resting, but she'll come in time. All that
matters is you're better." Still she wittered on. "I look
forward to spending time with you again, like when we were
children. How fare Priscilla and Ector? And Arthur…oh,
what he's become! The High King of all Britannia! That
little boy. There's *so* much for us to talk about, *dear* friend."
Only then did she step back, her eyes narrowing once more.
"Interesting times, now you're here."

Wenna's cell lay at the base of Avalon's green hill, the Tor.

At its summit stood what the priestesses called the Dream Tower – a weathered stone construction, ancient, its roof long gone – if it ever had one. It was a place, Wenna told me, where those among them with the Sight would go to meditate. They would gaze up at the stars, reading not only what had passed, and what was unfolding, but what was still to come.

"Is it true?" I'd asked her. "There are some here who can do that? *See?* Can you?"

Wenna had laughed, a sound as gentle as the rain that fell at Avalon in springtime.

"Not me! But some, yes. Those who have the ears of the gods and goddesses."

"Like Merlyn, then," I'd muttered somewhat darkly.

Wenna was oblivious. "Those with the Sight – Viviane among them, of course – have the ears of the kings of this land. And the High King too, no doubt. Though, yes, I've heard it's Merlyn whom Arthur prefers to consult, who never leaves his side."

"Not if he can help it." I'd even rolled my eyes at that, but still she smiled. That was the thing with Wenna, I was coming to realise; she only saw the good in people. And instead of resenting that, as I might have once, I *liked* it, her simplicity, the light that shone in her eyes. I wanted to bask in it. To heal further.

Was that what being here would give me? Healing, when I felt so broken.

Wenna was a pretty girl, not beautiful like Guinevere, though she reminded me of her. She was how Guinevere *presented* herself, as wholesome, but not, I think, how Guinevere truly was, not on the inside. Not that I'd find out, for I wouldn't go back there, to Arthur's court. I'd already decided. I'd go *anywhere* but there.

I was grateful to Wenna, too – for just as Merlyn never left Arthur's side, she never left mine. Whenever Seren visited, Wenna was there, always keeping busy but hovering close. At night, she even slept on the floor beside my bed, swaddled in blankets. I protested, offered to give her her bed back, but she refused.

"It is my honour to serve you," she said. "The *Lady* Morgan."

Even here, in Avalon, I couldn't escape the title that had haunted me at Caer Arthur. There I'd been the High King's sister, and for that alone, granted deference. Here, I was the daughter of the High Priestess, and once again held in high esteem.

But where was *I* in all this? How did I see myself? Deserving – or not?

Whatever I felt, I didn't correct her. I had to cease fighting battles I couldn't win. But yes, above all, I was grateful – for the buffer she placed between Seren and me, the help she gave me to grow ever stronger, and, in turn, the child I carried.

But today – ah, today was not a day to allow thoughts of Seren to haunt my mind. She was at worship this morning, as were Caireann and Wenna. I'd insisted they both go, assured them I would manage well enough in their absence, and so, at last, I was alone. Free to explore more of the place I now called my own.

A cave at the foot of the Tor, but it wasn't the only one. There were *several* such cells tucked into the hill, in which priestesses-in-training, those who wore the green robes – symbolising their bond with the earth, with fertility, and nature – inhabited. Caireann wore blue, as did Seren – a mark of a higher tier, of wisdom earned, and deep intuition. Caireann I could understand. But Seren? That baffled me. And then there was me, among them, yet apart. Still in plain clothes. The *un*initiated.

When I'd first been able to step outside and breathe the fresh air, I'd only managed a few steps – and even then, only with Wenna's help. Now I could wander further, eager to fully immerse myself in the splendour, to absorb it.

The green hill rose steeply. I couldn't climb it – not yet – though I spied a pathway winding to the top, well-trodden but, for now, empty. The grass surrounding it was the greenest I'd ever seen, kept short rather than allowed to grow tall, though I saw no animals grazing nearby, nothing that could detract from it.

Cells had also been cut higher into the hillside – cruder than the one I'd just left, more turf huts than dwellings. Harsh places so at odds with the beauty here, but a priestess must know *all* facets of life, not merely the content and bountiful.

As I stepped back, I saw it, and my breath caught.

The Dream Tower. Rising against the open sky, it was so ancient no one knew when it had been built. Perhaps before the Romans, even. It seemed to *touch* the sky, bridging the gulf between earth and the great above, a very pathway to the stars.

I'd never seen a building like it – stone from foot to crown. The Romans had favoured such buildings, but when they withdrew from Britannia, the people returned to older materials: wattle and daub, and timber. And so this…this was extraordinary. A miracle, even. It stirred something deep within me. Awe. Reverence. Peace?

The longer I stood there, gazing upwards, the more that

sense of peace settled. What turmoil there was within me –
the raging waters, the baby that would soon kick and kick –
became quiet. The feeling was so profound that tears
pricked at my eyes.

Home. I'd come home. And though I'd never wish away
my time at the villa with Arthur, Ector, and Priscilla – no
matter all that had happened since – in some ways, it might
have been easier had I never left Avalon. *Been cast out.
Banished.*

No! Just like thoughts of Seren, such stubborn musings
had no place today. I had to follow Wenna's example, and
hold fast to the good. Embrace it.

And explore!

Wrenching my gaze away, I turned from the Tor. *Taran.*
I must find her.

A cluster of buildings lay on the flat plains below the hill.
I had to tread carefully as I approached them, for though
some said Avalon was an island, it wasn't, not in the strictest
sense. The illusion came from the marshes that ringed it,
glassy waters that caught the light just so, making it seem as
if it *hovered* above the surface. Even where I walked, the
ground was spongy in places, quickly covering the slippers
I'd borrowed from Wenna in mud. Yet still, excitement
tugged me onwards.

Because of the marshes, this place could not be found
without a guide – or at least, not ordinarily. It was secret. So
secret. And yet there I was, at the very heart of it, with a
sound drifting my way: chanting. There must have been a
hundred voices or more, carried on the breeze, rising and
falling – sweet, melodic…*purposeful.*

Ask the Great Mother, and the Great Mother shall provide.
It was my own prayer, but here, in this realm, it would surely

prove true. How could the Christians believe their so-called One True God could ever replace Her? She who'd birthed all this – creation itself.

The chanting came from a house of worship, what the Christians might call a chapel. It stood at the centre of the clustered buildings, overlooked by the Dream Tower and the Tor, though neither cast a shadow. Built from timber, rather than stone, it was no less impressive, its oak door wide and arched.

I longed to climb the Tor, and I longed to enter that building too, but again, I couldn't. I was not a priestess, and my desires must be bridled.

The smaller huts nearby must be bakehouses, I decided, bread being the staple of so many lives. There would be a brewhouse as well, and a cookhouse where other foods were prepared. Likely not meat – not even fish. I couldn't imagine any creature being slaughtered here. This was a haven for all, a sense that grew ever stronger in me. Perhaps the priestesses ate only what the earth gave freely: fruits and nuts, grains and vegetables. Already I'd passed orchards in bloom, their boughs heavy with blossom, but come Mabon, there'd be apples instead, in abundance.

Other buildings, long and narrow, must have been dwellings for those who had completed their training, or the elders who'd earned a degree of comfort. Then I saw them: two more buildings, set apart. One was grander than the other, attracting me to it. Again, its door stood out – not oak, though oak was used freely here.

Rowan? Was the door made of rowan? Its reddish-brown hue and fine swirling grain suggested so. If I was right, then it would serve as a ward against magic – but of the malevolent kind. I frowned at such a notion. I couldn't imagine anything evil *daring* to enter these grounds either – even though travellers surely came and went. Kings, even, Uther supposedly among them. When he'd lived.

Was this…Viviane's dwelling? One so grand? It had to be. She *was* the High Priestess. And clearly, she was cautious. *Very* cautious. Charms were carved into the wood – the crescent moon among them – and bundles of herbs hung nearby, dried rowan berries bound with thick thread, as well as garlic and mugwort.

I leaned closer, catching a scent other than herbs, faint yet persistent, as though incense burned inside – *perpetually*. I breathed deeper. Juniper. Priscilla had burned it at the villa, on her altar to Brigid – the goddess of healing, fertility, and wisdom.

I looked down. Something was scattered across the threshold. Salt?

As I was trying to discern it, words crowded my mind, unbidden: *May no harm pass this door. May only truth and light cross the floor.*

The strangeness of them made me flinch, take a step back even, then another. Had something brushed against my hand as they were spoken? Something cold?

My breath turned ragged.

Who was speaking to me?

Great Mother? Is it you?

Despite being such a fine spring day, with the promise of summer in the air, sweat pricked my brow. The peace I'd felt earlier was gone.

Should I be here? Or far, far away – seeking my home elsewhere?

Viviane's house – if this was hers – could I cross its threshold, even if invited? Or were those charms set here for

43

me? *Against* me?

I retreated still, even though I was sure the dwelling was empty. The voices continued to rise from the temple – not a chapel, never a chapel. The sound was as sweet as ever, joined by birdsong, warm enough to stir the heart. It *had* stirred mine. Began to thaw what had long been frozen. But now…ah, now it was cold again.

How could I swing so quickly between such states – one so blissful, the next bewildered? The baby within – was that a kick I felt? Too soon, surely. But if I was in distress, he was too. He sought comfort, and so I laid a hand on my belly.

But I needed comfort as well. Something more familiar than the scent of juniper.

At last, I turned. Another long building stood nearby. I ran towards it, my feet pounding the ground, my heart beating as it so often did, wildly.

The doors faced away, so I rounded the corner until I found them, gripped the iron-ring with both hands, and pulled.

What greeted me was the sight I'd hoped for.

A reminder of other homes – the villa and the caer. Both lost to me now.

She whinnied. Reared up. Called to me.

"Taran," I cried, closing the distance and flinging my arms around her neck.

CHAPTER FOUR

"Viviane has sent word she will see you now. We're to prepare you first, then accompany you there."

It was Caireann who told me this. Wenna stood beside her with a delighted smile on her face, clearly *thrilled* for me. But Caireann…she was more subdued. Her gaze shifted to just beyond me as she spoke, never quite meeting my eyes.

I'd just come from my wanderings, and from Taran, from clinging to her as she nuzzled her face against my neck, stamping her feet slightly, restless, as if eager to be away, though the stable was spacious enough, the hay plentiful. She even had companions, several other horses in stalls beside her, but she remained unsettled.

"Soon," I'd assured her. "I'll be able to ride you soon."

But when that time came, where would we go? And how far? Would we remain in Avalon or once again brave the land beyond it? *Could* we?

The thought crossed my mind then, to do it, regardless of my health, or any dangers, saddling Taran and fleeing. Heading further west, perhaps.

At Arthur and Guinevere's wedding, Mark of Kernow had attended, his son Tristan on one side of him, his wife, Isolde, on the other. His *new* wife, brought across the waters from Éire to be his bride. She was so much younger than him, much younger even than Tristan. A beautiful girl with creamy skin, dark hair, and darker eyes. But it was Tristan she loved – not Mark. One glance between them had made that clear enough. Yet Tristan had come not only to witness the wedding of the new High King and High Queen, but to stand among Arthur's warriors. Isolde would return with Mark alone – smiling on the outside, but inwardly bereft.

It was there I thought of going, to Kernow, for she would offer the High King's sister refuge, surely? We would understand each other, she and I, *help* each other, there at the end of the world, for I would let her know I was heartbroken too. We could exchange words of comfort as the sea lashed the rock Mark's fortress stood on. A pagan court, not a Christian one, where I might raise my son without reproof for who his father might be. He and I, we could live and die there, never to be heard of again, eschewing power of any kind. Gone from history. Vanished.

I did no such thing. Instead, I'd kissed Taran goodbye, promising to return soon, and, for a while, went elsewhere on the grounds, calm again. I'd skirted the temple of chanting, passed more buildings and orchards, and came to another hill, one that stood opposite the Tor, and was less steep. The hill where the thorn grew. Even from below, I could see it, encircled by a ring of flat stones.

The thorn was said to have been planted by Joseph of Arimathea, the uncle of Jesus, when he came to this isle after the crucifixion. Jesus – the Son of the One True God, according to the Christians. Joseph had travelled to this isle to spread word of Him, to convert – that was his mission. And what a journey it must have been, across land after land, sea after sea. Wearyall Hill, this place was called, buttercups and daisies scattered across its slope. Here Joseph had paused, thrust his staff into the earth to lean on, and it had taken root, becoming the thorn.

The very same that had split in two on the night of my birth.

I'd approached it warily. The skies were clear, but what if they should darken suddenly, if thunder rolled? All because I – *I* – was there. I'd come back. Would lightning strike again, this time intent on finding its true mark?

Absurd! And the thorn seemed…pitiful rather than magnificent, unable, perhaps, to recover fully from the onslaught it had endured.

I'd gone only so close – my breath laboured from the climb, however gentle – but near enough to see how spindly it had become. And still it grew, refusing to wither entirely, a few new leaves pushing through.

Why was it revered here? This thorn. Here was where the Great Mother was worshipped, all things to do with Her not Him.

I'd shaken my head. Who was I to question it? To *keep* questioning? The Great Mother was not like the One True God. She had, after all, spawned an entire pantheon. She was all-encompassing. Ever benevolent. She'd welcome even someone like me, when Viviane hadn't. I was her daughter. Her *only* daughter, for I hadn't been told there was another, either before me, or after. Yet still she kept her distance. Viviane, who had woven protection around her dwelling.

Recently?

"Morgan?" Caireann's voice pulled me from thoughts that were always trying to carve their own path. "Will you come with us so we can prepare you?"

I tilted my head, curious. "Come where?"

Though Wenna had looked happy at the prospect, Caireann had been solemn, but now – now she smiled.

"The White Spring," she said, and her eyes lit up with a girlish delight, a spark that easily matched Wenna's. "We've been permitted to take you there."

This place! Of all I'd seen here, it was the most magnificent.

The White Spring lay hidden in the caves beneath the Tor, deep within the hill. The darkness there would have gathered quickly, if not for the dozens of candles set in hollows along the walls, their flickering flames drawing us further inwards.

The air was not as cold as I'd expected, and the ground beneath my bare feet was damp from two small streams that ran gently on either side of me.

Everything here was gentle – the air, the silence itself. A balm to the heart, even one such as mine, Avalon whispering its solace around me.

With Caireann leading and Wenna behind me, we continued. *How* far beneath the hill were we going – into its very heart? It felt as though we'd left one world behind and stepped into another, where a different kind of magic existed. *True* magic. That of the Great Mother – She who was everywhere: outside, around us, and within.

The tunnel, wide at first, began to narrow, a first flicker of unease stirring in my chest. How much closer would the walls draw in on us? We were scraping through when – suddenly, almost impossibly – a chamber opened before us. A vast hollow, tall and wide, and not just one pool there, as in the forest near Caer Arthur, but several, tier upon tier, water spilling from one to the next in a continual flow.

I heard the breath Caireann released as she turned to me, yet more wonder in her eyes. This was a place she'd rarely been, if ever. As for Wenna, she was trembling beneath the robe she wore, though trying desperately to keep composure.

Caireann gave a small nod, reaching out to unclasp the robe I'd been given before I came here. It slid to the ground, leaving me as bare as a newborn before them. Wenna then left us to fetch something, returning only moments later. My hands longed to cradle my belly as I stood there, some mother's instinct, perhaps, though why my child should be anything other than serene in a place like this, I couldn't say.

It was a bowl Wenna had brought, beaten bronze, and filled to the brim with water, its surface shimmering with candlelight. Though heavy, she bore it steadily, bending to set it at my feet. A cloth lay draped over the polished rim, which she wrung out before rising again. Without a word, she took my arm and began to wash me.

I needed no explanation. This was ritual. A rite. Before entering the pool, I must be cleansed by water drawn from this exact place, from the Great Mother's womb.

Wenna continued, using long, deft strokes. My body tingled with each one as I continued to stand there, entranced. None of us had spoken since entering the cave; it felt like sacrilege to do so, an unwritten rule.

I closed my eyes under Wenna's touch. When I opened them again, it was to find Caireann's hands on me, guiding me towards the largest of the pools. She nodded for me to ascend the steps there, those that were carved into the rock, and leading to the water's edge. I was to enter the pool, and once in it, submerge.

I did so willingly. Eagerly. I longed for the water to rise

up and cover me, to float there forever if I could, far removed from the world of men and the hurt they could so casually inflict. Here was a hidden place indeed, free of war, conspiracy, betrayal. No schemes or poisoned love. A dark world, yes – but one lit with unceasing flame.

Behind me, Caireann and Wenna stood side by side, with their heads bowed. Though I could no longer see their faces – nor they mine – I could feel their awe, and how it mingled with my own. Like a rising mist, it *filled* the cavern.

It was a silent pool like no other, and an honour to stand before it.

The waters lapped first at my feet, and then my ankles as I lowered myself further, covering my knees, my thighs, my belly, and shoulders. They cradled me as I leaned into them, the black of my hair fanning out. A raven's wing, as Priscilla would say.

It was water that stole my breath, but quickly I grew used to the cold, and my eyes closed again, silence in my mind as well as all around me, the voices in my head – forever arguing, forever challenging – falling quiet. We were buried essentially – beneath the Tor. Sealed in a tomb of stone and water. And I didn't mind one bit. If death should come for me here, I'd welcome it, for it would be a peaceful end.

Utter, utter silence.

And then a prayer began to form, a plea.

Great Mother, let me stay here with you, in whatever form you see fit – my son and I both. Cradle us in your arms. Rock us. Let us feel your love, the all-encompassing magnificence of it – here, now, and in the time beyond, in a world *beyond even, far from the stars, but where there is light. Only light.*

For there we can do no harm.

Harm?

The word struck like a crack in glass. The silence rippled.

Harm? my mind repeated, but not in prayer, in alarm.

I was floating no longer, but flailing, the water not soothing but suffocating. My arms sliced through it in panicked bursts, splashing wildly, shattering the calm I was so enjoying. Where there had been serenity, now came confusion. Like Wenna earlier, I had to fight to regain composure, to cleanse not just what lay on the outside, but inside too. That peace I'd felt – why was it always so fleeting? Even here.

Especially here.

As I continued to struggle, I remonstrated with myself.

Be at peace, Morgan. Be at peace! You, who are a lady, a warrior, an…an abomination. You – and what you carry inside…carry inside…carry inside…

Again, hands were on me, and this time firm. They dragged me towards the side as I coughed and choked, water entering my mouth, my throat on fire.

"Get her out! Get her out!" In a chamber such as this, the command echoed, but none more so than her next words. "The spring…it does not suit her."

Was that Caireann speaking? Wenna?

It wasn't true! The spring *had* suited me – at first. I'd loved it. I'd felt serene, as I should. But then the thoughts came, the doubts, rising up to tear it all apart, to sabotage. The silent pool; the White Spring…there *was* no silence. None! Nowhere!

Not for one such as I.

Serenity was not my destiny.

Nor his. My son's.

The stone was no longer smooth against my skin, but jagged as I was hoisted out of the pool. It scraped me, bruising me, and then I was lying on the cavern floor, still coughing, still retching, but able to see who'd saved me, who'd just spoken.

It was Seren.

She too had entered the cave and it was her, not the Great Mother, who cradled me now, her touch repellent, exactly as she meant it to be.

Such a strange look on her face! She was at once snarling, but so, so gleeful.

Had she come to fetch me? Been given orders to take me to my mother?

If so, would she tell her the truth that echoed? *The spring… it does not suit her.*

CHAPTER FIVE

Arienwen – that was the name of Seren's mother. Born on the isle of Avalon, just as her daughter was, and perhaps even her own mother before her. Generation after generation of the initiated. A true child of Avalon, living and thriving here, learning the ways of the Great Mother, worshipping Her, absorbing all the mysteries She embodied. Here was a seat of knowledge, a seat of power – a place not wholly of the physical world, but with one foot in the world beyond, *worlds* even. Where time was of no consequence and nothing stood between.

Arienwen had been devout. *Not* the High Priestess, but held by many in equal esteem. She was someone pure and learned, who taught freely, bringing all into the fold, elevating them to higher purpose. They came to her willingly – they loved her. She may have named her daughter after a bright, shining star, but her own name meant 'silver fair' – and she, unlike her daughter, deserved it.

All this I learned while in Avalon, as told to me by Caireann and Wenna. Both of them could talk endlessly of Arienwen. Even Wenna, who had never known her – only the legend. Oh, to be remembered like that! Their voices held not only love for her, but something else – though I wondered if they realised it. A *preference*.

She hadn't been the High Priestess, but perhaps...she could have been. Perhaps some had hoped for it, for someone more...relatable. Had my birth killed Viviane, then perhaps it would have been Arienwen who rose in her place, taking the mantle with grief, with grace, but above all, with the best of intentions. For the Great Mother was everything to her – as the Great Mother should be.

But it was Viviane who lived, and Arienwen who died. The illness that took her, the one that led to Seren's temporary fostering with Priscilla and Ector, was a winter flux. It had swept through Avalon, affecting many, and it had claimed her.

After being dragged from the White Spring by Seren, to lie naked, cold, and coughing on the cavern floor, Caireann and Wenna – who'd hesitated at first, it seemed, rooted, perhaps, by shock at the disturbance – rushed over to me.

It was they who helped me to my feet, who dried me, who dressed me, both with hands that trembled for reasons *other* than awe.

This initiation – this *cleansing* – had not gone as expected. A sacred ritual was meant to be joyous. We'd entered the cave in awe but left it feeling bewildered.

Why – *why* couldn't I master this battle in my head and in my heart? Win it? Just as the land teetered on chaos, so too did I.

We left the springs behind. As we walked, I fought the urge to turn for a parting glimpse, one that might well be my last, for I couldn't keep denying what had happened, the reality of it: the waters *didn't* suit me. Didn't...want me.

Seren, daughter of Arienwen, walked ahead of us in her blue robe. Caireann followed, her robe the same shade, and Wenna, who was behind me, in green. The robe given to me was green too – but I wondered if it should have been a colour *not* pertaining to a rank at Avalon, for what had I achieved there yet? Nothing. There was no doubt Seren thought that, she who'd held me with such contempt earlier that her lip had curled. Caireann, perhaps, felt more sorrow than scorn. But Wenna…

I couldn't bear it if Wenna thought ill of me.

If I were to stay here, I had much to prove. Just as Arthur had, that day when Merlyn rode into our lives at the villa and revealed his true lineage. He was not merely the son of a nobleman, but the son of a king. The great Uther of Dumnonia.

But Merlyn had named him more than that – High King of *all* Britannia. One man to unite the kingdoms, the faiths, the peoples. The Picts, the Christians, even the wild tribes beyond Hadrian's Wall in the far North – the Caladones, forever untamed.

Until now?

Some welcomed the news – petty kings of petty realms, weary of endless squabbles with their neighbours, who saw the advantage of extra protection from the mighty army Merlyn promised – *Arthur's* army. But some – Lot of the North among them – hadn't been so enamoured. And that was where Arthur had had to prove himself first, battling against one of our own before we could face the Saxons: Aelle, rising in the lands above Londinium, and Cerdic, by the coast that overlooks the southern sea towards Gaul. There was much I disagreed with Merlyn about, but when he spoke of kingdoms standing together as the only hope against the Sea Wolves, the only way to save Britannia, and the Britons' way of life that had endured for centuries – despite the Romans – I couldn't argue with him.

At just fifteen summers old, Arthur had marched against Lot, and won.

Then came the battle at the River Glein, against Aelle, and he'd won that too.

I'd been with him for both victories, standing at the edge of the battlefield, loosing arrow after arrow. His good luck charm. His talisman.

But I wouldn't be there for future battles. Guinevere was his token now.

His…*wife*.

My place lay elsewhere. Avalon? Where else? Not Kernow as I'd thought. Isolde and I would only keep breaking our hearts together. And my son…did he deserve a shadow of a mother, or one more present, who could love him properly?

Avalon was a place of girls and women, but while he was young, how could they object? Still I convinced myself of it; this was the best place for him as well as me – for while there may be unholiness here indeed, in the form of Seren, and as Seren would say, in the form of me, it had also spawned the likes of Arienwen too, a mortal akin to a goddess. It had Caireann and Wenna, who I knew were good, good people. The kind I'd need around me, that my son would need. Who could turn the tide…

Just for a while we would stay, and in that time seek our peace. Not only seek it, but keep hold of it. With no Arthur to distract me, I could learn how to do just that.

Despite what had happened at the spring, what Seren had said, Avalon remained the perfect home.

If I could prove myself.

I'd forgotten it was still daytime when we'd entered the cave. And so, emerging now, the sun – *the light* – stung my

56

eyes, and I had to lift my hands to shield them.

Seren turned to me, and I was surprised. She se\
suffer no such reaction.

Before speaking, she looked me up and down – *appraised*
me – then reached out and tugged at my robe as if to
straighten it. It was a far from caring gesture.

She sighed. Deeply. "Are you ready for this? To meet
your mother?"

"I've waited a long time," I said. *My whole life.* "So yes,
I'm ready."

Her nostrils flared, as though I'd given the wrong answer.
But what else could I have said? Here, in Avalon, the truth
was expected.

"I'm ready," I repeated, even though she hadn't asked
again.

Beside me, I could feel Caireann and Wenna tense.

Seren kept staring, and I realised why.

She didn't *want* to do this, take me to my mother. Every
bit of her resisted. In contrast, every bit of me longed for it.
I will see her! She is my *mother. Mine!* And if I was owed
anything, it was this. Even if I barely saw her again all the
while I remained at Avalon, even if she never acknowledged
my son, I was *owed* this – one meeting with her, the woman
whose body had carried me from conception to birth. There
may have been silence between us for years, but I was still a
part of her. We shared the blood of the old, those who'd
inhabited this isle since the dawn of time, now in danger of
becoming the stuff of legend too, existing only in the mists.

Just as Viviane herself did, to some extent, here at
Avalon.

"I'm ready," I said again, taking a step forwards, and then
another.

If Seren didn't move, our noses would touch. Stubborn creature that she was, she held her ground, until we *were* nose to nose.

"I'm ready," I said a third time, my tone sharpening as I added, "*friend*. Either you take me to her, as you've been instructed, or I'll walk there on my own."

CHAPTER SIX

I was right about which dwelling belonged to Viviane. It was indeed the one with the rowan door, with symbols of protection carved into it, herbs hanging there too, also protective, incense that burned, and grains of salt scattered at the threshold.

It had been empty before, my mother likely away at worship, the door barred against intrusion. Now, though, it swung open – Seren pulling it wide and stepping through ahead of me. I followed, with Caireann and Wenna close at my back.

Despite my love for Priscilla and Ector, I'd wanted this – more than anything. *More than Arthur?* No…*not* Arthur. But this meeting was something I hoped would complete me – that first glimpse of the one who'd delivered me, who may have felt at least a flicker of love for me then, when I was so small, so helpless. Who might love me still, for look what she'd done – the foster parents she'd entrusted me to.

She'd be as magnificent as Avalon itself. I'd always imagined her that way – regal, reverent, among the greatest high priestesses remembered.

The door closed behind us, and inside, the air was thick; it was hazy with the scent of juniper, mixed this time with other herbs, those I couldn't quite place. They were a curious mixture, though, burning…*furiously*. The curling smoke was enough to choke us, with only a little managing to find an escape through the vent above. It stung my eyes as harshly as daylight had when I first emerged from the cave, and again I was forced to lift my hands to ease them, blinking rapidly. How I wished the door behind us had remained open, if only a crack, allowing us to breathe easier, to clear the air so I could *see*. I'd come so far, and now, now I felt thwarted. Denied.

A voice drifted towards me. "Morgana. You have come to Avalon."

Immediately, I stilled, my hands dropping back down to my sides. I focused on breathing instead – slow and rhythmic – just enough to steady myself.

Shapes moved within the haze – shadows shifting up ahead in a room that seemed as vast as the cavern which housed the White Spring.

Someone...moved towards me.

Mother?

When at last the figure grew clearer – as though the mists parted at her command – I saw it wasn't my mother who'd spoken, but a girl. Young. Nine or ten summers at most.

I tried to look past her, to where Viviane might stand. But I couldn't.

She...*held* my gaze.

A girl, as I've said, but there was something ageless about her, as if truly she were an old head on young shoulders, carrying a wisdom beyond her years.

Merlyn was like that. One moment ancient, with his flowing white hair and long beard, his back hunched beneath his black cloak, but then he'd straighten, lift his head, and smile. And when he did, the years fell away as though they'd never been.

It was the girl who'd welcomed me, not Viviane, her voice soft, lyrical almost, and filled with such calm. She was the very opposite of me, or at least, in this moment, appeared to be. Someone who was *always* calm – nothing wild or stormy about her.

As she moved closer, I noticed something else.

She…flowed, as though made of water, as though not truly human, but a sprite.

She was before me now, Seren having moved to one side of the dwelling, and Caireann and Wenna to the other. Viviane *was* here, for there was another shape just beyond the girl. Was that where she meant to stay?

I remembered the words that had echoed in my head the first time I stood outside this dwelling while exploring. When I'd paused before the rowan door and wondered at it, the need for such protection. *May no harm pass this door. May only truth and light cross the floor.* Not my words; they'd been cast into my mind, like dice thrown upon a table. I tried to remember too what the voice had sounded like. Had it been hers? This child in front of me.

"I am Nimue," she continued – pronounced *nim-oo-ey* – the name itself fluid too.

Though the room was hazy, with candles flickering but barely casting any light, I noticed the robe she wore. Not green – the colour I might expect for one so young, a novice. It was red, and not a dim shade either, but bright.

Symbolic, clearly. But of what?

Her hair was as dark as mine, fully braided to frame her face. As for the colour of her eyes, I couldn't quite tell, but I imagined them to be as light as water.

Some might call her pretty, I supposed, with the promise of greater beauty yet to come, but there was something about her that made me...shudder.

She'd spoken, so I must too.

"I...I am glad to be here. To have...returned. My mother—"

Before I could say anything more, Nimue *touched* me. My belly. Uninvited. A smile crept over her face while she did so, not wide, not a grin, but small and secretive.

"He flourishes," she said, a statement rather than a question.

She then took my hands in hers, and her touch – flesh to flesh – was cold, reminding me of something else, an accompanying sensation of someone brushing against me when those strange, strange words had appeared in my head. Yet when I'd turned to look, there'd been no one there.

Who was this girl? This...magical girl. For I sensed that about her, such power. Her body was *riddled* with it. Nimue, who *hadn't* been at the dwelling when I'd first visited, when I'd stood outside it, who had likely been at worship too, yet...had she been aware of me? Had she...warned me? *Don't go any further. Not yet.*

If so, then she was the greatest protection of all, one all-seeing, all-knowing.

"This child," she said, looking deep into my eyes. "This...boy. You will foster it?"

"No!" The word burst from me, which I again admonished myself for. I must be like her, as calm. "I will keep my baby. He will grow to manhood beside me."

"Here?" she asked.

"Here," I replied.

"*If* you stay?"

I started at that, but knew I must answer in kind. "If I stay," I repeated.

She nodded, neither in agreement nor dissent; it simply seemed to be a gesture.

We stood, still holding hands, mine growing colder, then she smiled again.

"Ah, but I apologise. You have waited long. You must be impatient, I understand," she then added. "Come, Morgana. Come closer now."

She gave a gentle tug of my hand and the haze parted again.

I'd waited a long time indeed, but I found my gaze dropping.

The woman I was about to meet – if not for the first time, then for the first time I could remember – what if she had never truly recovered from my birth? What if, like the thorn, she was still weakened by it, her body plagued by illness ever since?

If so, it was because of me. I'd *ruined* her – the High Priestess of Avalon.

Could I bear the guilt?

Then came another thought, sharp and sudden. What if my son did the same to me when his time came? Would that be atonement enough? Like for like? But no, of course not. It would never be equal. I was *not* the High Priestess. In truth, I was no one, not even a princess now, if I'd forsaken my courtly role at Caer Arthur.

How could a nobody ever atone for the destruction of one so great?

"Lift your eyes."

Nimue's voice cut through me – firm, commanding, impossible to defy.

She'd released my hand, and moved further, taking her place beside Viviane.

I obeyed, and the baby inside me, if not yet able to kick, began writhing.

Viviane. Ah, Viviane.

"Mother!"

The word burst from my lips the moment our eyes met – hurled forth with the same force as my refusal just a short while earlier to surrender my child.

She was…*everything* I thought she'd be, yet at the same time, *nothing* like it.

A woman, a *living* goddess, sat before me – not on a throne, but a plain wooden chair, though it might as well have been the former. She was dressed in white, the purest of colours at Avalon, denoting divine connection. A woman who was mortal, yes, but at the same time *im*mortal, rendered so by the extent of her devotion.

She was small, as I was small-boned, as Caireann was. Her loose hair, once surely as black as mine, was now threaded with grey but still abundant. Her skin, milky and flawless, glowed even in the dim haze, as if lit from within. Unlike her hair, her eyes had retained their darkness, taking me in with the same intensity that mine offered her.

I leaned forwards. Was that a mark upon her brow, similar to what I'd seen carved into the doorframe? A crescent moon tattooed there. Strange, but as I stared at it, I yearned to have a mark of my own – something that would set me apart too.

So many emotions surged through me at the sight of her! Merlyn had once said I should feel proud to call her Mother, and I was – never more so than in this moment. However good and kind Seren's mother may have been – despite what she'd raised – so too was Viviane, for the Great Mother would allow nothing less.

And yet...the darkness of her eyes held not coldness, exactly – but aloofness?

Mine brimmed with awe, with reverence, with love – anyone in the room could have seen it, if they'd cared to look. But hers gave nothing away. It was impossible to tell what she was feeling, whether there was any awe in her whatsoever for the daughter who had grown from a child to a woman.

More words wanted to follow my single utterance. So many questions gathered on my lips. *Do you love me? Did you ever? Have you thought of me as often as I've thought of you? Why did you choose Priscilla and Ector? Was that at Merlyn's behest or your own? Did you know Arthur would be placed with them too? And if so, couldn't you see what might come of it? Mother...who is my father? Do you truly not know? You, the High Priestess. A seer. The voice of the Great Mother. Her chosen. Her vessel. You* must *know! Taliesin. It has to be Taliesin.*

The smoke in this room – her shrine – if it had been cloying before, was suffocating now. Had I spoken aloud? Or were those questions still swirling in the confines of my head? I was unsure suddenly, lightheaded, intoxicated even.

I couldn't keep looking at her.

Instead, I turned to Nimue. I was so near to my mother when I felt so far. It was as though a chasm yawned between Viviane and me, invisible, but immense.

I pleaded with Nimue, silently – or so I thought.

Why doesn't she speak to me? Why doesn't she come to hold

me?

But Nimue was as mute as Viviane now, though her face was not in repose as Viviane's was. There it was again, a faint smile, meant only for the two of us, though I was far from alone in that dwelling. For besides Nimue and Viviane, there were Caireann, Wenna, and Seren. And there was the unborn child.

Whose is he? I was now asking that of myself, not Viviane. *He will have dark hair, but grey eyes. Is he Lancelot's or Arthur's? And if Arthur's, then he is the son of a High King. A true-born. A firstborn. The blood of the old in his veins. Whose is he?*

Perhaps that was what Viviane's silence meant, that she *couldn't* answer, *couldn't* help. Because if Arthur *were* my half-brother, perhaps even that knowledge might not be enough to douse this burning love I had for him, as I prayed it might.

The haze curled tighter, creeping into my mind, a shroud that would settle over everything, leaving me more confused, scared, and vulnerable.

Why couldn't I think clearly? Why couldn't I tell what was real and what wasn't? If words *had* spilled from my lips, how had I spoken them? Had I asked plainly? Calmly? It was only natural I should want answers.

Or had I – and my legs nearly buckled at this – *demanded* them? An *accusatory* edge to my voice. Disbelief that she'd tell the truth even if she knew it. An inference she'd condemned me to ignorance – because it served her as well as it did Merlyn. It didn't matter to them whose daughter I was. What mattered was whose I *could* be – for I was useful then. I'd lived, so there might as well be purpose to it.

Had I not only demanded answers of Viviane

but…raged at her? The High Priestess of Avalon? *Dared* to? *Tell me everything. Now! The truth! I want the truth.*

I didn't know! And the smoke was giving rise to nausea now, rendering me as weak as when I'd first crawled out of the swamp.

I was falling. The juniper – did they really need to burn so much? It was acrid!

Mother – I could no longer see her, a blackness overwhelming the haze. Could she still see me? *You know everything. You do. You saw a plan before you, one that took no account of how I might feel about it, that couldn't care less if I loved Arthur as more than the brother you decided he'd be. You only ever cared about your aims. A holy person? What is holiness without compassion? Purpose without love?*

I should stop. These words…these accusations…these *fantasies*. I should hang my head in shame and beg forgiveness. *I don't know why I say such things.*

If I did, she might come to me still, even as I lay on the ground.

I'm sorry! I'm sorry!

But she only sat there, unsmiling…no pity in her. None. And Nimue…Nimue only smiled.

Satisfied. So very satisfied.

CHAPTER SEVEN

A vow of silence – that's what Caireann told me later, as I lay in my chamber, still reeling from the meeting with my mother, still choking on the incense. Even in Wenna's cell, with the shutter at the window drawn back, the residue clung to me. It coated my throat, and filled my nostrils, beginning to unfurl, to lift – but slowly.

Viviane had taken a vow of silence. It began the night I was born – the screams that tore from her throat the last sounds she would ever make.

"Why didn't you tell me this before?" I asked.

If I'd thought Caireann might look abashed because she'd failed to, I was wrong. She simply gave a shrug of her shoulders. "It wasn't mine *to* tell."

Wenna was there along with Caireann, but more shadow than presence, letting her elder see to me. Though a fine spring day, they'd stoked the fire, ensuring a mix of both fresh air and warmth.

"That night," I murmured. "That…terrible night."

The older woman leaned back in her chair. "I was a young woman then, Morgan." At this, a wry chuckle slipped from her lips as she briefly studied her hands, weathered by sun and time, the veins rising like tree roots beneath her skin. "Nigh as young as you are now, if you can believe it. And aye, the tales you've heard – they're true. I remember the storm well enough, how it tore through Avalon like a beast unchained. It was as though Lugh himself rode the thunder!"

I swallowed to hear it, as well I might.

"It made us shudder, that storm," she continued.

"And the thorn was rent in two?"

"Aye. But it grows again now. Or at least tries to."

"Why do you revere it so much? The thorn. You, who are pagan?"

"Because it's woven into legend," she replied with a simple shrug. "And at Avalon, we know the value of such things. Joseph of Arimathea – aye, the Christ's uncle, so the old tales say – was a good man. He came to spread the word, but not with the force of iron. Never once was it said he raised a hand against those who would not heed him." She paused then, as though weighing her words. "As for Jesus – what I've heard through the turning of the seasons is that he was gentle too. Kind of heart. A healer. Whoever they were, Morgan, wherever they were born, in distant lands, so far from ours, they were sons of the Great Mother still, beloved of Her, as all true-hearted souls are. So, aye, we show our respect, for the Great Mother is gentle too…though Her ways are older than the Christ. So much older."

The Great Mother was as boundless, as encompassing, as I'd always thought. She who reigned without judgement… *My* mother, though?

"So that's why she didn't speak to me," I said instead, not a question, but a statement, simply…confirming it was so. The *only* reason.

"It is. It is Nimue who speaks for her," Caireann replied.

"She who wears red."

"Aye, and gifted, that one. Just as the Great Mother

69

whispers in Viviane's ear, so She communes with Nimue too." Caireann gave another small shrug and chewed at her cheek. "And the red the girl wears? It's a colour her spirit leans to, I suppose."

"Strange for someone so calm."

"Calm?" Caireann echoed, curious. "Aye…I suppose she is."

"You…suppose?"

"Nimue keeps close to Viviane," Caireann explained further, "more often than we do. Mayhap the red is her mark – her sign to the world she walks a path apart."

Another High Priestess in training? I almost asked, but bit it back. One was more than enough to contend with right now.

A sigh left me. "There was so much I wanted to ask her," I said, not realising how faint my voice had become.

Caireann leaned forward. "What was that, child?"

I cleared my throat. "I said…there was so much I wanted to ask her." And then, "Did I, Caireann? Did I say anything else – anything…besides *'Mother?'*"

It took a few moments to realise I'd leaned in too, was clutching at her hands.

"You spoke no more than that, little dove," she said, sounding so like Priscilla in that moment that my heart ached further. "You mustn't trouble yourself about it."

"But—"

Her dark eyes fixed on mine. "Enough now! Let that be enough. Aye, you're troubled – I see it plainly. You've questions that burn. I know. Those only a daughter can carry for her mother. But Viviane *cannot* give you those answers. Her first duty is to the Great Mother; that is where her devotion lies, as it must, it must. In silence, she hears

Her clearest, follows Her will, and in doing so, allows us to as well."

"So much devotion there's no room for devotion to another?"

Again, she hesitated, perhaps sensing just how deep-seated my bitterness ran. Shaking her weary head, she tried to explain yet more.

"Morgan, the Great Mother is gentle, as I've told you, as you surely know, but to hear Her exacts a toll. You must understand, child, the Great Mother feels *all* that we offer. Our love when we worship Her, our reverence – it feeds Her as surely as the moon pulls the tide. But She feels more than love. She feels our pain as well – our sorrow, our struggles, the very warring of our spirits. Every wound, every cry, every conflict is Hers. She bears it all. And so too does Viviane."

I knew her words were true and I was chastened by them, silent too for a moment before speaking again. "She was magnificent, Caireann. And I expected nothing less, but I thought she might also be…"

"Wizened?" Caireann suggested with a lift of her brow. "Similar to me, is that it? Aye, but there are days when the weight of Avalon rests heavily upon her. And on other days…you would never know it. She *is* magnificent, even in weariness. The glamour, Morgan – have you heard of it?"

I hadn't.

"It is a gift only the truly wise, the deeply seasoned, can summon. It's how they choose to be seen – like a veil, a cloak they cast about themselves."

I gasped. "So that's what Merlyn does!"

"Merlyn?" she repeated, the awe in her voice obvious. "I've yet to meet him."

"Truly? But he says he visits Avalon. Often."

71

"Then perhaps he does," she conceded. "But even so, I've never met him."

Count yourself lucky. Again, I only just refrained from saying it. "This glamour," I said instead, "Viviane used it during our…encounter?" I didn't know what else to call the meeting we'd just had. Certainly, it couldn't be deemed a reunion.

"Aye. But the face she showed was near enough the truth."

Tears filled my eyes. That face was *not* a loving one.

"I'm sorry for what I did. The harm I caused by being born."

This small woman before me, with so much of the Fay about her, squeezed my hands tightly. "Morgan, she lived. And you lived. There's no more to it than that."

"But Seren—"

"Seren be cursed!"

Even as she said it, she glanced around, as if expecting Seren to materialise from the shadows. But no – it was still only the three of us. Her outburst and the wary glance that followed, though, both startled and reassured me. I wasn't alone in my dislike of Seren – my *hatred* of her. Even Caireann was cautious of her. Wenna's eyes had widened too, with something akin to fear. Again, if so, then perhaps my feelings weren't so monstrous after all, but justified. Seren's mother had graced this place with holiness. But her daughter, as I'd long believed, did not.

"Seren be cursed," Caireann repeated. "*Thrice* cursed." Then her tone shifted, for to speak ill of another was not something encouraged at Avalon. It lightened as she sought to weave warmth into her words, becoming more genuine the longer she spoke. "Avalon…how shall I speak of it? How may a simple soul like me put into words what lives beyond speech? Let me try. Aye, let me try. Avalon is…*everything*. All that is, all that was, and all that shall ever be. The Great Mother is everywhere. She is in all places at all times, in the world of men – *especially* there – for that's where She's needed most. But it's here She *dwells*. Not in secret, not in shadows, but just as She is: in the blossom of the trees, in the breeze that stirs the leaves, in the sun that warms the earth, in the rain that feeds the soil and grows the food to fill our bellies. But most of all, She is the flame within the breast, the whisper in the blood." Releasing one of my hands, she pressed her own to her chest and patted it. "Let Her dwell in you, Morgan. Let Her take root in your soul. Let Her be your balm. For She will be, She will be – if only you let Her."

I reached for my chest too. "I don't know. I just…don't know."

Her gaze searched mine. "But you can feel it, here at Avalon?"

"Feel what?" I said, my eyes glistening.

"The peace. In the cave, at the White Spring. You felt it then. Before…before…"

I spared her the pain of finishing. "Yes. And when I've wandered too, when I've lifted my eyes to gaze at the Dream Tower. There is *much* that is good here."

Her smile bloomed. "Aye! There *is*. Hold fast to that. Steep yourself in that knowledge. The path of the priestess is no small thing."

"But…" How could I shape this? Caireann loved Avalon, as she should, as *I* should, both of us born to it. And yet…Seren aside, there wasn't just the light here.

Perhaps it was the Fay in us, that ancient thread that tied

us to a deeper knowing, but I didn't have to elaborate. Caireann knew.

"This world moves in balance," she said. "Where there is good – *great good* – you may well find its opposite. Such seems to be the way of it. No place is *wholly* good, but Avalon…" She paused, her gaze turning distant. "Avalon comes closer than any place I've known." Her eyes returned to me. "And no place is ever wholly lost to darkness either. You'd be wise to remember that too. Even the blackest night bears stars. Ah, I love it here indeed. 'Tis my soul's resting ground. I *belong*. And you – you and the life within you – may yet belong as well. There is learning to be had, plenty of learning, work for your hands, and food for the spirit as well as your belly. It will steady you, give your heart an anchor, and your thoughts shelter. The Mysteries—"

"The Mysteries… What are they?"

She was amused again by the eagerness of my voice, and she turned to glance at Wenna before beckoning her closer. "The Mysteries are many, Morgan. Many! Aye, Wenna? Too much to grasp in one lifetime. Even ten. Even twenty or more."

With tears drying, I blinked. "We live again?"

"Aye! We do!"

"*That's* one of the Mysteries?"

"Put simply, yes."

If that were so, then I'd known it, deep in my bones, from the moment I'd first coupled with Arthur. He and I had lived beyond this life, in other guises, perhaps, but always together. Now, though, the thread that bound us so tightly had frayed. I'd ensured it when I left him that cold winter's day. Our paths no longer ran side by side, but they would again – surely. In time. In another life. Elsewhere.

For now, though, I'd come to Avalon, not just to meet Viviane, but for something more, because my child and I needed a home. And this sacred isle, as Caireann said, as I longed to believe, might yet be it. A place to learn, to change, to reach for the light. To strive for it, and keep striving. To turn peace into something lasting.

A world of balance, and Avalon was of that ilk too. That there was great good here, I believed with all my heart. For *she* was good, Caireann, as wise and as steady as the earth on which we walked. And Wenna – ah, Wenna – who had indeed drawn nearer, who was smiling down on me – goodness *flowed* from her.

I closed my eyes for a breath, letting such goodness wash over me, lost in its sweet embrace. Caireann and Wenna had tended me, nursed me back to health, through the waning grip of winter and into the first bloom of spring. But they were more than healers; they'd become friends – kin. *True* kin. I counted them as such.

Ours. My son's and mine.

"I want to learn," I said, though again my voice barely stirred the air. I took a breath and spoke more clearly. "I want what is good here. And I will hold to that – I swear it." Priscilla had begun to teach me about the healing arts, but there were the divine arts too, or the Mysteries as Caireann called them, and in the learning of them, it was possible I could become whole again. Through them, not Arthur.

As Caireann beamed at my words, and Wenna too, a gentle breeze entered the cell and warmed my bones, cleansed me, more so than the waters at the White Spring had, no matter how sacred. I found I was smiling too, my hand drifting from my chest to my belly, to Arthur's child…or Lancelot's. Perhaps I would know when he came into being, when he grew, the traits that would characterise him. But even so, Arthur and Lancelot – they were shades now. Distant. Faded.

They had to be.

What name would I give this child? What name would *suit* him – carry him through the years with strength and meaning?

Ah, but that could wait. Now was not the time for pondering such things, only for rejoicing. We'd come home – he and I – and home was where we would find our rhythm, and realign ourselves. The Dream Tower…I'd visit it one day, climb the steep hill it sat so majestically on. When I'd earned it. When I was ready.

And I *would* be ready.

Viviane, Nimue, Seren…

They didn't matter either in this moment. I would pay my respects, of course, but otherwise it was to Caireann and Wenna I'd look, allowing their example to guide me.

The child… Was he stirring again? And if so, was it a sign? Was it his way of letting me know I should stop fretting? It was just a flutter, but I imagined his limbs, no matter how tiny, moving contentedly, our happiness shared.

Our excitement.

The sun's rays entered through the window too, and I welcomed them for the blessing they were. When they reached me, and bathed me in their gold, every trace of weariness – every doubt, no matter how deeply it hid within me – would dispel.

From this moment on, I would be a different Morgan.

One any son would be proud of.

CHAPTER EIGHT

Avalon – Island of Apples, Island of Glass, the Fortunate Isle. Blessed.

A place as old as the Fay, once theirs, now they dwelt in the mists that so often surrounded it. Thick mists, rolling in from every side to cloak or to shield us. Even in spring the mists came, and in summer too, perhaps. The skies might be blue, the air clear, but come sundown, the veil returned – a breath from the Otherworld, hovering close. By morning, it would be gone again, the sun shining down on the waters that encircled us. Hence one of its names: Island of Glass – for they shone like mirrors.

After speaking with Caireann, *listening* to her, I wasted no more time in settling in. I opened my heart to Avalon, welcomed the life there, with no more looking back.

I wondered: did the sun always shine on Avalon? It seemed that way. Whatever the weather was doing elsewhere – at Caer Arthur, in the Middle Lands, or as far north as Hadrian's Wall, even further west to wild Kernow – on this isle we were graced with long hours of sunlight day in and day out. It was hard to believe a storm had *ever* touched this place – harder still to remember I'd been born during one.

They were simple days at first, and for that I gave thanks. I would take myself to the kitchens, to help prepare roots and greens for the evening broth – thick stews to warm us when the sun dipped low. At dawn, I kneaded dough for the morning bread – loaves we'd break together with the returning light.

I tended to Taran, and sometimes the other horses. It was quiet, steady work, for Caireann would have it no other way.

"You still have to gather your strength," she said, ever firm, ever kind. "Heed me well, Morgan – slowly, slowly does it. Aye, for your sake…and the bairn's."

Strangely, it was easy to avoid Viviane, and by the same token, Nimue, moving as they did in each other's shadow. Or perhaps…it was *they* who avoided *me*.

If so, I refused to care. I'd known love in full measure – from my foster parents, and now from Caireann and Wenna. It was perhaps asking too much to expect the same from Viviane as well. I'd been blessed already, and should not press for more.

As for Seren…she was not so easily avoided. Wherever I walked, there she was, lurking, either with a smile on her face – void of warmth – or narrowed eyes tracking my every step as though I was a puzzle to solve – or a threat to be weighed. But again, I made sure to shrug it off. Let her watch, if that was her pleasure. If, in all of Avalon, she could find no better pursuit – no scripture to study, no wisdom to drink from – then let her waste her time on me. Again, in this regard I remained true to my vow, to seek the good, to dwell on it. And Seren – she was far from that.

The days slipped by and my belly swelled further, red marks appearing as the skin stretched. The fluttering became stronger too – kicks now, sure and quick.

Sometimes I laughed when they came.

"You're a restless one, aren't you?" I'd murmur.

At other times, I wished he would still. Especially at

night, when weariness weighed heavy, and all I longed for was sleep.

I'd shouted once. "Enough! Stop now! I need rest – we both do. Why do you move so? What troubles you? *Is* there something wrong? Is there? I've told you, stop it!"

How harsh my voice had sounded – raw and unbecoming. Caireann said the child within could hear the mother, that her voice would echo in his ears. That night, I believed her, for if he'd been restless before, my anger only roused him further.

Even so, my mood, on the whole, erred towards calm, and my bond with Caireann and Wenna deepened. With Wenna especially, I spoke more freely of the Mysteries.

"What are they?" I would ask. "How might I approach them? Is there an initiation process? A rite to be undertaken? Trials to prove myself, to show I'm worthy?"

No such thing had been mentioned to me. No further summons, no ceremony, though I was allowed to wander at whim, breathing deep the air of Avalon, counting down the days until I might climb the Tor – alone, or in procession.

"Have you been initiated?" I pressed her again one morning as we walked, not to the sacred well of the White Spring, but to another in the grounds, to replenish the water we'd used in the cell we shared.

She looked so pretty that day, the green of her gown a match for the green flecks in her eyes, her brown hair catching gold.

I was surprised when she said no. "For me, there was only willingness."

"Willingness?"

"Yes. That was all that was asked. A willing heart. A spirit devoted to serving the Great Mother. As Nimue speaks for

Viviane, so we must speak for Her."

"To carry Her voice far and wide?"

"Some will do just that – leave Avalon, if the Great Mother wills it."

"For that is their fate."

"Their *path*, Morgan. Yes."

I mused on her words. Were some paths truly so clearly marked – lit like torches in the dark? If so, how fortunate. For others – for me – it was much less certain.

"I wonder how the outside world fares," I murmured, briefly likening Avalon to a fortress, its walls unseen but just as high, every bit as confining.

A trill of birdsong pulled me from such thoughts, along with the merry sound of laughter, coming from just ahead, two young women walking together, as Wenna and I were. One I recognised: Nesta, who had first tended to me. They were replenishing their pails too, water sloshing over the edges of one to soak the hems of their gowns.

Wenna smiled and waved, and so did I, but then she shrugged.

"The outside world? I cannot tell you. Some days I forget such a world exists at all. But of these matters, Viviane would keep the measure well enough."

"Viviane *and* Nimue," I said, perhaps scathingly, but if that were so, Wenna shrugged it off, allowing nothing to mar this bright day, as was her way.

As we approached the well, my thoughts turned again. Wenna was right – it *was* easy to forget what lay beyond Avalon's mists: a world of crowns seized and wars brewing. What of Aelle in the east, or Cerdic in the south? How many had flocked to their banners since Arthur's victory at the River Glein? Aelle's *first* attempt, there could be no doubt about it, demanding his warriors retreat when it was clear the tide was turning in Arthur's favour. *Testing* him, it seemed to me now, the boy king and his legions, merely that, a probing of strength. Then regrouping indeed, just as we ourselves had, to plan again, strike again, with fresh forces and greater knowledge.

The outcome of those battles – the fates of Lancelot, of Cai, of *all* Arthur's companions, and Arthur himself – I played no part in anymore. All that remained to me now was to pray they'd stay safe, and I would, fervently. I'd beg the Great Mother to hear me. She must. For if Arthur was at stake, then all of Britannia was.

But first – the Mysteries.

If Wenna could guide me, if Caireann too would share what she knew, if I could show my willingness, my good intent to follow the path of a priestess – a path some might say I was born to – then perhaps the learning would come. And with it, the power to *use* that knowledge. To keep Arthur safe not with bow and arrow, sword or shield – I was far from a battlefield now – but in ways more hidden.

Like Wenna, I wore green, was still permitted to, but in time, it would be blue.

I could climb the Tor, to the Dream Tower, and weave dreams of my own.

For every ailment, for every wound, the Great Mother provided a remedy. Hers was the power to heal, but if She chose instead to reclaim your soul, She would, then no remedy in the land could save you, not if it was Her will.

We, the people of Britannia, though not gods and goddesses, were Her children still, and so we returned to Her embrace, there to rest awhile before returning. Birth, life, death, and rebirth – these were the great Mysteries, Wenna told me, but Caireann gave them further shape.

"Aye, some of us are born into greatness, and others are humble, or lowly, as the world might call it," she said, touching on the role of kings and queens, of seers like Merlyn, of priestesses like Viviane. "And there is deep mystery in that too…why such burdens, such sacred callings, fall to some and not to others. But I've told you this before, haven't I? There's mystery in *all* things, Morgan. All unfolds as it must, even when our hearts cry out that it should not, that it *cannot*. And that, little dove, is often the greatest mystery of all." As she so often did, she reached for my hand. "We must trust in this unfolding, even when our trust is worn thin. We must hold fast to our faith. Aye, this, more than anything, is at the heart of what we do here in Avalon, learning how to live with the mysteries that guide us – in our world, the world of the Fay, and the Otherworld – *Annwn*, as we call it. We learn to walk between them all."

"*Annwn?*" The name left my lips in a whisper. "We can…visit the dead?"

"Those who've passed," she corrected. "And aye, we can, if only for a short while."

"How?"

"There are many ways. Most often we walk those paths through dreamwork…and, though rare, through shapeshifting – an art only the truly gifted may ever wield."

My curiosity tightened. "Shapeshifting? What is that?"

Caireann's gaze lingered keenly on me. "You've heard of the Morrigan?"

I told her I had, that she was called the *Phantom Queen*, and how, when seen on the battlefield, often as a crow, she was an omen of doom. A goddess of Éire, from across the water, yet one we'd adopted here as well.

"Aye, she comes as a crow," Caireann said, nodding, "but that's not all. She is the raven too – the watchful one. She is the maiden, beautiful and beguiling, seducing a man with ease. She is the crone by the river washing bloodied clothes – approach her with care, for it may be your death she foretells. She is of the water, too – an eel, slippery and clever, a trickster who drags the unwary below. She is the wolf that roams the wild places, fierce and cunning – a hunter, but also a guardian of the land. And she is the cow – a symbol of life's abundance, of fertility, and sovereignty."

"But she's also a goddess," I pointed out. "*All* gods and goddesses can change form. But us? We're not made for that!"

"True, she is a goddess," Caireann said, with a small smile. "And it's true, we *cannot* do all that the gods can. But if our gifts are fewer, it's only because we *believe* them to be." She lifted a hand and tapped at her temple. "It's this that limits us. We can do more than we think – always. And when we falter, when the path is hidden, we may call upon the Morrigan – or Danu – for wisdom, for guidance, for…prophecy." She paused, then added with warmth, "There is also Brigid."

Ah, Brigid, I knew of her well. The one whom Priscilla held dearest, as any healer might. It was to Brigid that Priscilla gave her prayers, her work, her quiet devotion.

"And there is Arianrhod," Caireann went on, "she whom *I* favour – the goddess of the moon and stars, and of destiny. Morgan, she is a *perfect* teacher for one beginning a journey such as yours. Her power runs deep, yet she is gentle too."

"Arianrhod." I tried the name on my tongue. It was strong, yet soft, as Caireann said. "If she is the goddess of destiny, will she help me to see?"

"If that's what you desire, Morgan. And if you use the Sight with good intent."

"I would. I swear it."

Caireann gazed at me, her expression thoughtful. It reminded me of how Priscilla had looked when I'd first asked to learn the healing arts – a quiet scrutiny.

Was it doubt? Did she, like Priscilla, hesitate to believe me? Or was I misreading her silence? For just as the thought came, she smiled, pushed back the stool she'd been sitting on, and rose to her feet before helping me to stand too.

"You're looking well today, Morgan. There's a bloom in your cheeks that becomes you. You're feeling well too, aye?"

I nodded. "Yes. Yes, I am."

She smiled again. "Good. Then perhaps…you're strong enough to climb a hill?"

I gasped. "A hill? You mean…the *Tor*?"

I thought that such a journey might come later – after the birth of my child, rather than before it. Though the Tor stood near, it also felt distant – unreachable. Like the mist-strewn land of the Fay itself. A path might lead there, but I hadn't believed it was mine to walk. Not yet.

Caireann had reached another conclusion.

"Come," she said softly. "Come with me to the Dream Tower."

CHAPTER NINE

Even my tumultuous heart had known peace before – not only here at Avalon, but at the silent pool near Caer Arthur, and certainly in childhood, with my foster parents and with Arthur. But recently, that peace had grown elusive. All too often, my thoughts would intrude upon it – my fears, *the shadows* – and sweep it all away.

But atop the Tor – a steep climb that forced me to pause more than once to catch my breath – it was different. There, at the summit, I felt I might *drown* in peace.

I was so close to the sky – closer than I'd ever been! Closer, too, to the Great Mother, to Priscilla's Brigid, Caireann's Arianrhod, and the Morrigan – not always an omen of doom, not if she chose otherwise, but a guardian, a blessing even.

On that famed hill, I experienced not only peace, but something more. It was as if the fragments of my heart *and* soul – fractured by all that had come before – were slowly drifting back together. The healing I'd longed for beginning at last.

That first time we visited we didn't stay long, but it was enough to deepen my sense of belonging. In me, as in Caireann, there was a love for Avalon, a sense of true homecoming, even if it hadn't unfolded as I'd once imagined. To feel whole here – when I never had without

Arthur – was the greatest blessing I could have received. It meant I could *hope* to let him go, in ways beyond merely fleeing his presence. Not forgetting him, but carrying his memory gently, no longer bound in sorrow's chains.

Even if my child was his too.

If.

Ah, that first time… That first time… We'd simply stood there, Caireann and I, in front of the Dream Tower, gazing out at the vista. It was breathtaking, the mirror-like stillness of the waters below, the lone thorn on Wearyall Hill, the wooded glades that unfurled in every direction, the land that rose and fell in soft, green swells. Follow them far enough, and they'd lead to Caer Arthur, the seat of Dumnonia.

There was no going back, though. Not for me. My life was different now. And rather than mourn that fact, I spun around – suddenly, *wildly* – my black hair flying. Much to Caireann's surprise and delight, I laughed. I wanted to embrace it all: the land; the White Spring that flowed with sanctity; the humble cells carved into rock and turf; the temple of the priestesses; and the almost daily chanting.

It was slowly, and with some reluctance, that we made our way back down the hillside, but I knew I'd return, and soon, wondering too when I could *enter* the Dream Tower. A place of vision, I would need training first to make sense of what I might see or hear, to understand rather than fear it, as I once had at the silent pool.

With so much to learn, I no longer spent my days in the kitchens, chopping fruits and vegetables or kneading dough, but at the side of the priestesses instead – attending worship, and listening to their discussions of the divine. I never raised my voice, but remained as silent as Viviane herself.

I witnessed rituals too, ceremonies honouring the Great Mother, invocations of the goddesses, and prayers for guidance. At such times, a small group of us would gather in a circle within the temple – that hallowed place whose roof, like the Tor, seemed to stretch all the way to the sky – bathed in the thick, sweet smoke of incense. With our hands lightly touching – just the fingertips – we drew breath as one: in and out, slow, and deep, until the stillness between heartbeats grew vast.

In that calm, in that utter silence, heads would bow, one by one, especially among those in blue, but sometimes among the green-clad initiates as well. Then – suddenly – those same heads would lift. Eyes would snap open, though only the whites of them showed, ghostly in the dim light. This was the trance-like state Caireann had told me of, when the wisdom of the goddess poured through them.

When one of the women spoke – an elder in the crone stage of life – her voice was different to before, huskier, lower, though able to pierce skin and bone.

"I am the first flame," she whispered. "And even after the last breath is taken, I will burn still. I walk in the tides and speak in the wind. I am of your blood, and you are of mine. *All* women are goddesses. We are as one. Remember that. We are as one."

Others followed – each carrying the voice of a goddess.

"Yours is the courage to bloom," said another. "The laughter before the fall. Trust your hunger. Trust your fire – for it was I who gave it to you."

It was a priestess called Lheanna who'd said that, and when she did, I jolted.

Merlyn had spoken of the fire in me once. *It's a glorious thing to behold,* he'd said. *Truly.* His words had surprised me, for I'd thought it was something he despised – feared even. Delusion! The great Merlyn, afraid of me? Delusion too, to think the goddess had singled me out through Lheanna, but I persisted in believing it.

I had to trust the fire within.

And trust the fire in my son, too – the restless child who kicked and kicked.

As in the outside world, seasonal festivals were celebrated in Avalon. Imbolc, the year's first, had come and gone, but more would follow, the next being Beltane.

It marked the turning of spring into summer, when the earth grew warmer still, the sacred element of fire in use again, burning on every hilltop as far as the eye could see while drums pulsed through the night. People would come from all over – the villages and the countryside – to join together, to be as one too.

It was at Beltane that a younger Arthur and I had stolen from our home, intending to unite, bodies as well as souls, still innocent of the possibility we might be true brother and sister, not just fostered kin. We'd never reached those hilltops. Never danced around the fires. Never loved in the way we thought we might.

At Avalon, we would celebrate this festival too, and I wondered how. In truth, I felt a little…apprehensive about it, something Wenna picked up on.

"Not in *that* way," she said, barely suppressing a giggle. "Not for all of us, anyway – only for those who desire it. But that comes later on the eve of Beltane. First, there's the ritual. And, Morgan," a sigh escaped her as she said it, "it is magnificent."

A ritual? Another one? But of course.

"I look forward to it," I said. A night once ruined, once

the death of dreams, was now becoming something else. Yet another marvel to behold. I was…excited for it, that excitement growing, the *healing* continuing, as the festival drew closer.

Beltane would take place on the Tor – those gathered on distant hills turning their heads towards us in awe. It was a true celebration of the Great Mother, with both Viviane and Nimue in attendance. *All* of us would be there, even the older and frailer, aided by younger, sturdier hands until they too reached the summit.

The procession along the Tor's winding path would begin at dusk, and, as had been the custom at the villa in my childhood, the night before was spent in the silence and darkness of our cells, with no light at all. It was a time for reflection – Wenna lost deep in her thoughts and me trying to ignore mine.

The night came and went, sleep only found in fleeting snatches, and the day that followed also passed quietly, given over to the cleansing of our bodies and the adorning of our garments. I still happily wore the green, and on this day, it came with yet more greenery: ivy fastened to the front of our gowns, and then woven through our hair, with blossoms tucked among the leaves for further blessing – the hawthorn this time, when once, with Arthur, I'd worn violets.

When we'd finished dressing, Wenna held me at arm's length.

"Ah, Morgan," she said. "You're beautiful. Quite beautiful."

It wasn't the first time I'd heard those words – Priscilla had said so, and Anwyn, my childhood friend. Even Lancelot had. And Arthur… Arthur most of all. *Yours is the face of the Goddess, Morgan. Always.* Words that had once quickened my heart.

There was a time – another age, it seemed – when I could never have believed Arthur capable of betrayal. And so, how could I trust such a compliment now?

Perceptive as ever, Wenna caught my hesitation, and gave me a small shake.

"Morgan! You are. Truly."

"I…"

Curse it, but tears filled my eyes – unbidden, and yet I truly was excited for this evening, to witness Beltane celebrated in this holiest of places.

Wenna's concern deepened. "This night…it holds memories for you, doesn't it?" Her gaze dropped to my belly. "You had a lover. Was it at Beltane you met him?"

If only it had been. Some stranger, unbound to me by history. Or blood.

"No," I said simply.

"But this lover…he hurt you? Morgan, is he the father of this child?"

A low murmur escaped me. "I don't know who the father is."

She pulled me to her. "Whoever he is – whatever brought you here, by choice or necessity – you *are* beautiful. Believe that. And he? He was a fool to let you go."

Arthur – the High King of Britannia – a fool? Or something else? *Bewitched.*

Enough with tears! Summer was coming. In Avalon, the kitchen gardens were in bloom, and soon the orchards would follow. We should celebrate. Give thanks.

And we would.

A time of renewal. Nothing had changed since that Beltane long ago – three summers past. Could it be so long already? And yet…*everything* had.

If more change was coming, would I welcome it?

Or, for me, was change always something to dread?

CHAPTER TEN

At dusk, Caireann, Wenna and I left our cells and stepped outside, making our way to the foot of the Tor to join the others who had gathered there. Like us, they were dressed for celebration – some wore leaf crowns, more elaborate than ours, while others were draped in cloaks woven entirely from greenery. Again, spring flowers added welcome bursts of colour: bluebells, primroses, and the bright yellow of gorse.

We joined a neat, orderly procession, those around us clearly accustomed to the practice, for Beltane was one of four great fire festivals, albeit the most widely celebrated. But perhaps to some extent the other three were honoured in a similar way: Imbolc at the year's start, Lughnasadh, following Beltane, marking the height of summer, and Samhain, as winter neared, ushering in the darker, colder half of the year – a time of remembrance and deeper communication with the spirit world.

We would seek communion with the spirit world tonight as well, that was our intention, as Caireann and Wenna had told me. Four fires were already lit on the hill, one at each cardinal point around the Dream Tower: north, east, south, and west.

Where Viviane and Nimue were, I didn't know – already at the summit, perhaps. I'd glimpsed Seren earlier, near the front of the line. She'd kept glancing back, as if searching for me, too. Her eyes, whenever they caught mine, had looked more flint-like than usual, her mouth a white line, but I dismissed the unease they caused.

We began the climb, up a path worn smooth by many but new to me. I'd visited the Tor several times since my first ascent with Caireann, but had never entered the Dream Tower, though it wasn't something closed off, but open to the elements. Arched at the front and back, it had no doors, no rooms, no levels, was instead more akin to a threshold or a passageway, its floor untouched by any attempt at comfort.

What would it be like to lie there, I'd wondered – to gaze up at the stars, to dream, to see? If I could find answers there, I'd lie for hours if I had to.

From up ahead came giggling – two priestesses in green nudging each other – until one in blue turned to hush them. I glanced at Wenna, who smirked. This was a joyous occasion, yes – but sacred, too. There was a balance to be struck.

I was becoming a little out of breath as we climbed, though not the only one by far. Wenna patted my arm as if to reassure me we'd be there soon.

When, finally, we reached the summit, the priestesses fanned out, forming three circles around the Dream Tower, as though it were a Maypole. No ribbons fell for us to grasp, though, and we didn't dance, not at first. Instead, hand in hand, we *stepped* around it at a slow and measured pace, our feet quickening little by little as the chant rose. "From mist to flame, from dark to dawn... Great Mother, Great Mother, guide us on! Between the worlds, the path is shown. Let it be, and be unknown."

The words gathered strength, spilling into the night,

until the Tor pulsed with them. Smoke swirled, thick with burning juniper and vervain – both gathered at dawn, when dew still clung to the leaves, mead poured back into the soil in thanks. Tonight, it was only us who moved in the mists it created, though there was a sense we were becoming something other – transformed, as magical as the Fay. Whether young or old, the priestesses spun faster, our voices rising, and skirts flaring like wings.

Then we stopped. So abruptly I almost stumbled, Wenna having to catch my arm. I was breathless again, expecting the baby to stir, but he didn't. He was quiet this night, unusually so, and I was grateful. I wanted no distractions, only to surrender to the moment, to do as was intended – learn from it, grow.

Why had we stopped?

Two rows of priestesses stood just before me, so I couldn't see, not until they stepped back and widened the circle.

They'd stopped for Viviane, the High Priestess.

She'd appeared inside the Dream Tower, standing between the arches. At her side – just as Merlyn was always at Arthur's – was Nimue, in her customary red.

The sight of them – the girl especially – made my jaw clench. Something stirred in me, and it wasn't my child. Not hatred, for how could I hate someone I didn't know? Resentment. She was the chosen one, whereas I – I'd been discarded.

Nimue may be gifted indeed, and we might well witness those gifts tonight, but there was something about her that reminded me so much of Seren. She was too composed. Sly. Why else would she smile at me the way she did?

A hush fell. There was barely even the sound of

breathing.

From her stance inside the Dream Tower, bathed in the glow of the fires, rendered otherworldly by them, Viviane stood motionless, her head tipped back. In contrast, Nimue's gaze was fixed on us – the priestesses – watching closely as we waited.

I watched her too, just as intently.

Then it began. Viviane's head lowered, and her lips parted – but the voice that spoke was Nimue's.

My breath caught as the mist curled round them. Whatever Nimue spoke, I couldn't understand, not at first, and I wondered if anyone truly could. Yet all remained as rapt as me. Perhaps this was another of the Mysteries – a language not grasped by the mind but felt by the spirit. The tongue of the Great Mother, rising from the deep heart of the Tor, the hollow beneath our feet, the womb as I'd likened it to.

Around me the others began to sway, Wenna and Caireann too, their eyes closed, their faces serene. Then Nimue's words shifted, slowly, steadily, becoming familiar.

"The Great Mother's will be done," she said. "We, Her children – Her instruments – walk in Her will. Such is our path, our reason for being." Her voice deepened, no longer a child's, perhaps emulating the richness of Viviane's tone as well. "Yet a threat arises against Her reign – greater than any before: the Christians' One True God, He who suffers no other to be worshipped but Himself." She paused as her gaze swept the circle. "And men – ah, men, so often they are but children. They run to the lap of this God, believing Him stronger, that He alone can shield them. Fools! It is *She* who breathes life into all things – and She who may draw that breath away."

Nimue's small body cut through the mist like a blade.

"If the Great Mother should perish – if even the *memory* of Her should fade – then all is lost. Our task is set: to keep Her alive. To open the eyes of men, to make them see what we already know – that She is the path to peace, to redemption. Any who threaten Her – *any* – are a threat to us. It matters not what their name is, nor how high they stand. Before the Great Mother, we are *all* children."

How high they stand?

The highest in the land...was Arthur.

Was it possible...could she be...*threatening* him?

Arthur, son of Uther. Meant to unite the warring kings. To unite the tribes too – Pagans and Christians alike. If we were to stop the Saxons, we had to stand as one.

That was all he wanted to crush: division. *Not* the Great Mother.

But Guinevere – daughter of King Leodegrance – he who'd insisted a chapel be built at Caer Arthur as a condition of their marriage. Ah, Guinevere...

From the moment Arthur set eyes on her, she'd held such sway over him. Was she as devout as her father? Or *rabid*, as Priscilla preferred to call it?

As these thoughts raced through my mind, I lowered my gaze, afraid Nimue might catch them. Soon, though, my eyes were back on her – and hers on me.

There was that smile again – subtle, knowing. Hidden from Viviane.

Then her mouth opened, just as Viviane's did.

"But from ruin springs the making – born of the very *source* of it. Thus speaks the Great Mother this night! What is torn down will rise again, made stronger than before. The fields are ploughed, the soil turned, and fresh seeds sown.

We know this. We claim this. The seed flourishes – and so, too, shall the Great Mother."

Her gaze was no longer on my face, but my belly.

And I remembered. At our first meeting, Nimue had touched me there. *He flourishes*, she'd said. That same word. She'd known he was a boy, just as I had. She'd spoken tonight of Arthur – and of my child, too?

I wanted to cry out loud: *Arthur is not a threat to the Great Mother!*

And my child – who would *he* threaten? His father?

Again, no! I'd told no one who his father might be, and nor did I intend to. Perhaps he was Arthur's son – his firstborn – but would it be better if he were never acknowledged? Half of me rebelled against the idea, of denying him the power *he* was owed, while the other half fervently agreed, my dual nature at war again. Whatever choice I made, one truth remained: so far, I could craft any story I wished. I could say his father was indeed little more than a stranger – someone I'd known in passing, never even learning his name. The choice was mine, just as the choice had once been Viviane's.

Before I could think further, the sound of drums rose from afar, travelling swiftly towards us – the low thunder of wood and leather, rolling across the hilltops before erupting into the night. Viviane and Nimue had spoken with the Great Mother, and a cheer rose in answer – deep, resounding, like the roar of a feasting hall in a caer, or in the Otherworld itself, Annwn. Then, as if a spell had been broken, the women scattered into smaller groups. They talked, danced, laughed – a celebration indeed.

I searched for Viviane again, for Nimue. I *willed* the crowd to part, and when at last it did, the Dream Tower stood empty.

I turned my head from side to side but I couldn't see them anywhere. I was fretting about it, about what had been said, what had been *meant*, when Wenna appeared.

"Morgan!" she said. "Come, let us celebrate the words of the Great Mother, for She is great indeed. She will endure. She will! Can one such as Her fade from memory? Of course not. Impossible!" She took my arm. "This land is ours because She wills it, and so it shall remain. There's cider, Morgan, and apple wine."

Wenna – bright, hopeful Wenna – pulled me towards a long table where drink flowed freely. She poured two cups and pressed one into my hand.

"Drink," she urged.

"But the baby…"

"The apple wine is pure, from our orchards. It won't harm him."

There was such joy all around, the women's faces gold and crimson in the firelight. Though the Great Mother's message was still an echo in my mind, I was swept along on the tide of it. This was what I'd longed for – a true Beltane.

The apple wine, when raised to my lips, tasted just as Wenna had promised – sharp, fresh, and clean. Realising how thirsty I was from the exertion of climbing the Tor, I gulped it down greedily. Wenna then pressed another cup into my hand, and another.

Soon, and despite the weight I carried – though I would grow heavier still – I danced with Wenna, our hands entwined, the smoke from the fires billowing around us.

Lost in the haze, my arms rose above my head, the ivy in my hair slipping loose. This was how I'd danced before, with Igraine, when I'd first gone to Caer Arthur, drunk on wine for the first time, moving with that same abandon.

It took some time to realise it, but Wenna was gone from me now, and I was dancing alone, though there were shadows all around me still, the sound of laughter ringing out. So much laughter! Loud and raucous at times, with an abrasive quality to it, but cries of another kind too, just as I'd cried out with Arthur, with Lancelot, *ecstatic*.

I moved on, lighter; freer; a smile spreading across my face. For a while all worry fell away – so much so that I even forgot I was with child!

When once there'd been others, now I felt alone in the smoke, on top of the Tor, but in that solitude, there was contentment. Perhaps *this* was how it was meant to be, from now, until the end of my days: I was to be alone. If so, it didn't mean I must leave Avalon, only that I should remain…untangled. Even from my own son. I'd raise him, nurse him, then when the time came, let him go – free to walk his own path too.

That notion sat more and more comfortably as I drifted further, until I heard something beyond the laughter and cries of pleasure – a voice, soft as a whisper, brushing my ear. It was my given name again – *Morgana* – spoken like the distant chime of bells, melodic and alluring, threaded with the promise of pleasure.

I made my choice. Whatever the bearer of that voice desired, I would yield. This was Beltane – a sacred night – and what passed between us would be sacred too. I was made for solitude, yes, but not always. I could briefly belong to another.

The whisperer drew closer.

Closer still.

As my eyes closed, I tilted my head, and parted my lips.

But it was not a lover's kiss I received.
It was the kiss of a blade.

CHAPTER ELEVEN

I fought to break free, my hands clawing for purchase – cursing myself for leaving my sickle knife behind. But why would I carry it, and on tonight of all nights? This was Avalon. Holy ground. A place of peace. *No one* wore weapons here.

Or so I'd thought.

I was wrong.

The blade that found me wasn't meant to kill, though. It didn't plunge into my side or try to spill my guts. No – it *carved*, slicing into my brow.

Confusion swelled. Was this real? Or a waking nightmare?

I *had* drunk a great deal of apple wine earlier. Had it affected me more than I realised, clouding my thoughts in this bewildering way, skewing truth from illusion? I *could* be dreaming – my eyes were open, but all I could see was mist, engulfing me.

"Morgana, Morgana…stop fighting. This must be done."

The voice was low, as smooth as silk. So at odds with what was being done.

Despite the terror, something in it lulled me and I went limp, cradled in someone's arms. Whose? Shadows swam in the mist, resolving into three figures – neither wholly human nor entirely other. They were radiant, so beautiful even Guinevere would dim beside them. One gazed at me with golden eyes beneath lashes pale as frost, her skin shimmering like morning dew, her hair a fall of silver rain.

The carving continued. It had hurt at first, but the pain was now distant, softening into something I could endure. Another of the trio turned her eyes on me, and within them I read kindness and something else: an unshakable resolve. No words passed between them, yet they worked in perfect accord, and I realised then: it wasn't they who'd called to me earlier. That voice, though melodic, had borne a childish lilt.

"Nimue," I whispered, as at last, with their work complete, the three withdrew.

Only she remained – Nimue, who was shimmering too, the shape of her not something rigid, but swaying as I had swayed earlier. She wore her customary red, the colour that set her apart, just as white distinguished Viviane.

Colours of rank. Of power.

Where was everyone else? The Tor had been full before, yet now it was just us.

I felt something drip from my brow.

Blood.

"What's been done to me?" I asked – part plea, part demand.

"It's a sigil," Nimue said. "You wanted one, didn't you?"

"What?" My confusion deepened.

"You envied your mother's crescent moon."

"But…how did you know?" For I'd never voiced it.

No answer, but this instead: "It will remind you of your path…lest you falter."

"My path? My path is here!" Wasn't that what I'd fought so hard for? "But you – you don't want me here, do you?

You don't…trust I'll stay? Not if you've done this."

Nimue simply shrugged. "I don't *care* where you are. Here or elsewhere. I only want you to remember this: those who held you are your people."

"The Fay?" I breathed.

She nodded. "Yours. Viviane's. And mine."

"They…they're beautiful."

A small smile from her? If it was, it was as devious as those she'd given before. "They can be," she said. "Beautiful *and* savage. Savage because they have to be. Because savagery is sometimes the only way to protect what matters most." She softened – barely. "I'm sorry if the sigil hurt. Truly. But you can't forget."

That word again – *sigil*.

"What does it mean?"

"A sigil is your seal. Your promise to us."

I swallowed. "What does it say?"

"It forms your name – what you will be known as from here on. Morgan the Fay."

All I could do was repeat it. "Morgan the Fay."

"We are your people; we want you to fight for us. But—" she pointed to my belly, "it may be that *he* will fight most of all. We've marked you, and you now know what that mark means. He will be born with his own sigil – *Mordred the Fay*."

"Mordred?" The name caught in my throat. This had to be a dream, one I was trapped in. I hadn't named my son yet, hadn't even *thought* of a name.

"Why Mordred? Does it mean something?"

How quickly she told me. "His name means ruler – and so it shall be. His name is defender, righteousness itself. The Great Mother will *not* be cast aside for a God who would place Her beneath Him. Mordred is the name She has spoken. He will walk the true path, unswerving. Our saviour."

The mist was on the rise again, juniper and vervain pungent. The blood from my brow stung my eyes, having dripped down my cheeks to reach my lips, and no doubt staining them too, as red as Nimue's robe. Watery, willowy, *gifted* Nimue – my eyes seeing something more here on the Tor. Not just my own blood, but bloodshed, a river of it, tidal and vast, rushing to engulf me. And the baby…the baby Mordred was now kicking again when he'd been so quiet – *embracing* the savagery.

Was this prophecy? The future unfolding before my eyes? Always blood associated with my child! Arthur's blood? And no matter that he was High King, for it was as Nimue had said, *all* men were humble before the Great Mother.

And if he didn't do her work…

I understood Nimue's passion, but was also enraged by it. Arthur was new to his throne – he deserved a chance! And my son was no more a pawn than I was.

It would not be Arthur at fault. He'd been raised in tolerance, was tolerant himself.

It would be Guinevere.

I was about to speak Guinevere's name, *curse* her, when another voice broke through.

"It is done? You've told her?"

A voice that made me jolt, unfamiliar though it was.

A woman in white stepped forwards. Viviane.

I gasped. She'd spoken? She, who'd taken a vow of silence?

"You've made her realise?" she asked Nimue.

Made me*?* Treating me like a pawn indeed, someone to use, and use again, for whatever shifting purpose. Never allowed to just be me. No love for who *I* was.

I'd been right in all my surmises and Nimue was *showing* me I was. For this gifted child was smiling again, and with cause. Viviane didn't know I could see her in this moment. Somehow Nimue, maybe even with the help of the Fay, had hidden me from her sight, drawn a veil between us. If so, it was a veil that had long been in place. Viviane. Distant Viviane. Always so, at least from me. My mother, yet never more than a figure to me, neither flesh nor blood, no layers to her, no depth of feeling. Even her voice, when she spoke, never reached emotion. If it echoed with anything, it was disdain. I might as well have come here seeking a statue.

But Nimue was showing me something else, more damning than Viviane's silence: that she was a liar too, a trickster cloaked in the robes of a High Priestess. Her grand gesture of silence had never been sacred. It was not devotion that bound her tongue, but convenience. For with Nimue, she spoke as freely as she pleased.

Nimue's smile – I hated it! I wanted to rip it from her face, to scream at her that if Viviane didn't care, then neither did I. I'd found others here whose love was truer. I could live without that woman just as easily as she could live without me.

I *belonged* here. Still.

And Nimue – she'd do well to keep out of my way, and out of my son's. *Mordred?* I would *not* call him that! She would not mark him as she'd marked me. He would wear no sigil. If Viviane could deceive us, so too could Nimue. Both were capable of it. Those words at the Dream Tower – were they the voice of the Great Mother, or just another trick? A performance, a lie, in a place where there should be none.

"Come, Nimue, let us away," Viviane continued, "leave them to their frolicking. I've no doubt it'll go on until daybreak. They will, as ever, wring every drop from it."

She was gone. Vanished, as though the smoke or the mist had swallowed her. Nimue remained, though she was beginning to turn from me.

I couldn't help myself – I lunged. I would have lunged for Viviane too, had she still been present. Avalon was sacred, and yet look what they'd done, made a mockery of it with their deceit. In their place, I would never do that. I'd stay true. That was what I wanted Nimue to understand: that she was *not* superior. Nor was my mother.

"Nimue," I screamed, before she could disappear completely.

The mist thickened between us, still bending to her will. My hands found purchase anyway. I could feel her thin shoulders, solid enough, as she struggled against me.

"Morgan! What are you doing?"

She had to see that *I* was flesh and blood at least, not someone to trample on.

Ah, but she was hissing like a wild cat. She was spitting.

"You've always been mad, haven't you?" she said, sneering. "Always...unloved. Because if your own mother couldn't love you, who could? The father of your child? He abandoned you, didn't he? Just as Viviane did. You were a burden to them all. That's why you came to Avalon, begging sanctuary. You think *I* don't belong – that *I'm* a blight. I see it as plain as day in your eyes. But it's you who doesn't. *You!*"

Her words scraped across every nerve. "Hush your mouth!"

She ignored me and pressed on. "You think you're better than me because you're *her* daughter. You think that alone gives you the right to be here – you and that bastard you carry. I *hate* you, Morgan, and I always have. And Arthur – I hated him too. I hated him because your love for him was so…*fierce*. Oh, I should like to do that, you know. Tear down everything you love – for that's what would wound you most. To see you broken, ruined – you, who should never have lived. A High Priestess's daughter? It's me who should have been that, been trained to follow in her wake. My mother was just as revered as Viviane, more so, but too gentle, too gracious to claim it. And in the end, she proved just how weak she was, succumbing to illness the way she did. But I'm stronger. I could make Avalon great again, embracing the new age, not pandering to the past as though I were a slave to it. Viviane – Viviane should have died too that night for all the notice she takes of me."

Nimue… This was supposed to be Nimue. I'd seen her. She'd been standing right there. But these words…

"Arthur… Oh… I can see it now," she continued. "You've grown apart, haven't you? Ah, yes, yes, he is crowned, he has a wife, and soon children of his own will follow. He doesn't…*need* you. Not anymore. Another abandonment, Morgan? That must hurt enough already! Poor, poor Morgan." Her voice dropped to a purr. "That child of yours…what will you call it, when it's born? If a boy, I know a name to suit."

A name? But she'd already said!

"Mallocan," she declared.

Mallocan?

"It means 'little cursed one'. The son of someone as cursed as you."

107

Cursed?

"Hush your mouth," I demanded again. "Shut up. *Shut up!*"

I didn't want to touch the girl in front of me anymore. I wanted to put space between us. An ocean. Leagues. To turn my back on her. *Focus only on the good, remember?* As I'd promised Caireann. A promise I was finding peace in.

She wouldn't drive me out.

She *couldn't.*

I shoved her. Just to get away.

Caught off guard, she screamed as she fell. And then...silence.

"Nimue?" I called.

There was no answer.

I stepped forwards, unwilling to leave her after all. As I did, the sounds of celebration returned – the music, the revelry – masked too, as though far away on the hilltop, and me at the foot of it somehow, spirited there, with only swamps and tall reeds behind me. Loneliness. That's what stretched behind, on and on. Unbroken.

I shook the girl. No response. Her body was limp. Lifeless.

"Nimue!" I cried again.

But it wasn't her voice that answered, it was laughter.

A *child's* laughter.

I turned. Nimue stood there, but in the distance, *far* in the distance.

"Nimue?"

Her smile was unrestrained – victorious.

"Nimue," I said again, this time not a question. "*You're*...Nimue."

And if that was Nimue, then who lay on the ground?

I knew. Of course, I knew. I might even have known all along.

The girl I'd seized wasn't slight like a child would be. She was grown.

Someone who hated me as much as I hated her.

And yet…was her hatred of me ever truly earned? Or had it been born of nothing, a convenient place to pour her venom, then left to fester, unhealed, year after year?

It was the hatred of a woman who'd never known a mother's warmth either. Arienwen, though different from Viviane in many ways, was just as guilty. Seren might have been allowed to remain in Avalon when I had not, but she too had been displaced, told, even if it was without words too, that she was not enough.

I was her target. Her scapegoat. Her mirror. Perhaps even her warning of what she might become if she dared to care too deeply.

I'd never understood her.

Not truly.

But I thought I did now. For only the wounded would lash out as she had. Only the starving tear at another's bread.

Yes. I understood her.

Now that her head had struck stone.

Now that blood spread thick and slow beneath her skull.

Now that the last shreds of her fury had drained away into the earth.

Now that I'd killed her.

Seren.

CHAPTER TWELVE

Still so much night remained, and all around me, the world was occupied.

As I stared at Seren's wretched body, I realised the path ahead had split again.

I *could* stay at Avalon. Confess. Swear it was an accident, what had happened – that I'd been attacked too. *Look at my brow,* I'd say. *See what's been done to me.*

Or I could run again, grab my sickle knife and my horse, and leave Avalon behind.

I'd killed before, yes – but only in battle. Never like this. In anger.

What had she been doing at the foot of the Tor? Had she come seeking me, biding her time, ready to lash out? I remembered the way she'd looked at me earlier, as we waited to ascend, something new in her, something grim. If so, then I'd truly acted in my own defence. Or perhaps she, like me, had been spirited there with no memory of how, and turned on me only because I had turned on her first.

I tried to recall what had passed between us, the words she'd said, the name she'd suggested for my son. But it was already slipping from me, as if the darkness wanted those memories for itself now, hoarding them. All I could remember was how tightly I'd gripped her, my nails biting into her arms as I shook her. Then I'd pushed – driven by indignation, rage, and by something more potent than both: sorrow.

I'd *meant* to hurt her.

Hurt…or kill her.

When I'd flown at her, I'd wanted this: to silence her, properly this time.

But now that moment had passed, leaving in its wake yet more sorrow.

I couldn't stay. I had to leave. Like others here, I'd sullied the sacred ground. Wherever I went, I left a stain: the silent pool, the White Spring – and now the Tor.

Back on my feet, I wondered what to do with her body. Should I hide it? Drag her, if I could, to the swamps, there to submerge her in a watery grave?

No, she might have done that to me, but I wouldn't do it to her, deny her a proper burial, some sorrow from others even, for she couldn't have made enemies of everyone. She deserved at least a few tears for her untimely demise. I'd leave her where she was and she'd be found soon enough. When she was, my absence – and Taran's – would speak for itself.

Nimue knew what had happened. She'd *orchestrated* it; of that I was growing more certain. She could speak of it too…or remain as silent as Viviane. *Why* had she done it? I couldn't fathom that now, nor did I want to. All I wanted was to flee, slip back through the mists, past the swamps, towards firmer ground. But to go where? Who would take me, now that I was of no worth?

Only my child had worth.

The rage returned – swift and familiar. A *mother's* worth, that was all. Not the kind Nimue wanted to crown him with, she who was as cunning and as scheming as Merlyn –

a child on the brink of womanhood, armed with a vision and the ruthless will to fulfil it, no matter who she used along the way. Again, the question begged: why had she brought these events about this night? What would unfold because of it?

As for Viviane – the mother who wouldn't speak to me, who hid within her silence too – avoiding her while I was here had never been enough. Her silence had gnawed at me, day by day, though I'd tried to convince myself different. Her vow was a shield – against *me*. The charms at her dwelling designed to ward me off too. She'd mapped out my life for me, yet perhaps had always known I wouldn't follow what was laid down. Whereas Nimue...

Nimue saw another future. With one more pliant?

My feet moved and my breath came in gasps, my chest heaving. Seren's body was now behind me, but I was certain I could hear her voice still as I continued to run, tears streaming down my face as she tormented me, even in death.

You're cursed – I've always known it. Viviane knew it too, the day you were born. A day you should have died, Morgan. Died! It wasn't life that filled your lung, but the breath of the dark gods. Demons. You don't want to be a pawn? Ha! But you already are! It's their bidding you do. You – the great destroyer. Black Morgan. So yes – run. Leave my battered body behind. Pathetic little thing, aren't you? Run! Run! Run!

By the time I reached Taran – who whinnied at the sight of me, sensing my desperation – I was sobbing loud enough to drown out the lingering drums. Would Wenna find me before I could leave? Caireann? Try to persuade me to stay?

The child needed a home. I knew that. I agreed.

But not *this* one. Not anymore.

It was for his safety I had to go – to get him away from

Nimue's grasping hands. Viviane and Merlyn, they only saw so far. Nimue saw further – *frighteningly* further.

"Taran, Taran, it's all right." Still she was agitated, stepping back and forth as I saddled her. "We're going, you and I. Dear, sweet Taran – we found our way here, we can find our way out. Please, be calm. We have to go, Taran. We *have* to."

She was afraid, and I understood why. Had it only been luck that kept us alive when we first came here? And if so…was that luck about to run out?

Or – and my heart twisted at this – was it demons guiding us now? Not the Great Mother, but darker gods. Unclean. Perhaps Seren had known of them, but I hadn't until now. But what did that matter, when *they* knew of *me*?

My name was Morgan. But to Seren, I was *Black Morgan*.

Her and who else? Guinevere? Because of what I did at her wedding – painting her like a gaudy doll so Arthur wouldn't love her? She'd seen through me, perhaps even guessed the reason why, blaming me for it because she couldn't blame Arthur, not if she was married to him, easier to lay a truth she found abhorrent at my feet. But if I was darkness to her, then she was no less to me. We were *both* blackened.

I led Taran from the stables and cast one last look around. I wouldn't return, though I'd miss Wenna, the ease of her friendship, and Caireann's quiet wisdom.

It struck me then: the only people I called family were not bound to me by blood. They were strangers who'd become something more. Except Arthur – Arthur *was* me, the other side of the coin. But if he was blood too, he'd forsaken me.

Now astride Taran, I dug my heels into her side, and

113

spurred her on. *Galloped* from there. For if I'd tainted this place, it had tainted me in return.

Trust in the Great Mother. Trust in Brigid, in Arianrhod.

And trust in the demons too, if I must.

Soon we reached the borders of Avalon, the ground softening, wetter with each step, but as before, I wouldn't let Taran falter. There *were* paths through the swamps, though the mists hid them. Voices drifted there too – whispers and laughter, like those at Arthur's court, but it was the Fay, not man, responsible. And yet man could be just as ethereal, just as savage, just as prone to whispering.

We plunged on, Taran still nervous but trusting me, when so few ever did.

How I loved this horse!

Where would we go?

Where could we *possibly* go?

The mists parted, not hindering us, but allowing us passage. A certain amount of trust being shown there too. The whisperings grew, words taking shape.

Morgan, they said. *Morgan the Fay.*

Mordred the Fay. The firstborn.

Promise. Promise.

Morgan…do you promise?

PART TWO

CHAPTER THIRTEEN

The storm raged all day and deep into the night. But here, on this wild and wind-scoured coast, it seemed that storms *always* raged. The sea was so close I could hear it from my chamber – how the tides lashed without cease at the shore, whipping sand and pebbles into the air, there to join the howling wind in a frenzied dance.

Cries rode the wind too – echoes of curses and shouted defiance from those who were slaughtered so mercilessly at Ynys Môn. The druids the Romans had driven and trapped there. I'd heard them as they'd made moan on my very first night, while lying in such unfamiliar surroundings, clutching at my belly, exhausted.

Back then, the moans had been soft, scarcely louder than breath, rising as soon as the sun dipped below the horizon, rolling in from the sea towards the tall, ominous walls of this stronghold. *What have I done, coming here?* I'd wondered, as my path twisted further still. Now, on Samhain night – when the veil between this world and the Otherworld was said to be thinnest – the voices returned. They were no longer soft, but layered and raw, a chorus that matched my own.

For in that moment, I too was tortured.

"Morgan, breathe! Just breathe."

It was Teg, a serving woman. *My* serving woman. I had

others, but it was her I liked best. She was older than me, and with the softest brown eyes, reminding me of Caireann, and Priscilla too, my foster mother, both long gone from me now, as so many were. Teg's hand stroked my brow, soaked as it was with sweat.

I clutched at it with both of mine.

"I can't," I gasped. "I can't do this."

In contrast to mine, her voice was steady and sure. "You can."

Nonsense! She didn't understand. The pain was tearing me in two!

"Morgan," she said again, firmer now. "Stop panicking. Listen to my voice and breathe slowly. Breathe *with* me. Aye, 'tis a difficult birth, I know it. The child could be breech – but he will be all right. You *both* will."

I shook my head, fiercely, blindly.

"Morgan!"

"No!" I screamed just as thunder crashed overhead.

It wasn't just Teg in the room. Olwyn was there, and Enfys too, to help her. On blood-soaked sheets, I thrashed, becoming bloodier still.

Teg began to chant. "Ceridwen, Ceridwen, help us this night! Enfys – the fires! Keep them burning. Ceridwen *must* help us!"

All I could do was keep shaking my head. "I can hear whispers," I murmured through parched lips. "Not Ceridwen. The dead…it's the dead. And there's something else too – something higher-pitched than all of them."

I glanced towards the fire, where Teg burned her offering – an animal's heart, newborn, smothered in herbs. An exchange – one heart for another.

"You heard naught of the sort," Teg insisted, continuing

to chant. "Ceridwen, mam Awen – you who stirred the deep cauldron, who birthed wisdom from darkness – the threshold is upon us. Hold fast the breath of the child, and of the mother."

She turned to a cauldron at the bedside, its water waiting to anoint the new child, and her prayers quickened. "Guide us in safe passage – to bring forth in strength, in light." She cast something into the water – herbs, perhaps; water pepper or wild horseradish, both called upon to summon life – and bent low over the rising steam.

"I give you fear, to be quenched. I give you blood, to be weighed. I give you this scream to bear away. Come thunder, come lightning, come *all* the elements of nature. Come the *will* to live. For her lifeblood, for his lifeblood, take what I offer."

Was Teg cutting herself? Blood dripped into the cauldron – hers. She then gathered mine from where it had pooled on the bed and let it fall into that same mix.

"Let that be enough blood for this night," she whispered. "*Please.*"

Further appeasement – that's what our blood had become. But the other sound I heard, rising above the cries of the dead and my own, was still there no matter that she denied it – a keening, thin and sharp, and within it *all* the suffering of the world.

What was she called, the one who'd keened at my birth? The one whose screams Viviane couldn't match? Seren had told me once – Seren, whom I'd killed with my own hands.

This pain!

Teg's offering, her pleading, changed nothing. I couldn't bear it. I *wouldn't.* Seren had said one of us – Viviane or me – should have died at my birth, but we hadn't.

This time, though, a sacrifice *would* be demanded. Blood alone would not suffice.

A *blessed* death. If mine, that's what this would be, if it gave reprieve from this agony that was relentless. Would I cross the bridge to the Otherworld, where Uther and Taliesin waited – one of whom was said to be my father? Ha! If so, I could finally know the truth. Tell them how the mystery of it had shattered my life, ruined me.

My death – that was all I wanted. Not his. Not the baby's.

Ceridwen, hear me, as you hear Teg. Look favourably on him. Protect him if I cannot. Great Mother – don't let him stray too far from your gaze.

He'd be safe here, wouldn't he? On this bleak and rocky outcrop, this place I'd travelled so far to find. An ancient land, untouched, its people an extension of it.

My body arched. I wanted to push, to rid myself of what was within – but voices stopped me. Not Teg's, but Olwyn's and Enfys'.

"Please, my lady," they begged. "You can't push yet – wait…just wait."

Defeated, I fell back. Whatever herbs burned in the room were not enough to mask the bitter tang of blood – the smell of the battlefield I knew it to be. I'd witnessed such carnage twice before, now there was carnage here tonight as well.

The keening… I remembered now who was responsible. The Bean Si – she who belonged to the Fay, yet stood apart from them. A lone wanderer between worlds, a fairy woman who was savage indeed, for her mournful wail was a herald's cry, and if it reached your ears it meant one thing and one thing only: death was due.

She'd been defied once. Could we defy her again?

And if we did…would my son be as cursed as me for it?

Oh, Arthur! If only he were here with me, to hold me, to be the one to wipe my brow, to soothe me. And yet, if this was his child, what could he do? In his world, one that edged so close to the new, I was his sister, not his wife. What we'd done – conceived life together – would be deemed an abomination. If the child was his, it would be his firstborn, as the Fay reminded me when I rode from Avalon. The swamps then no longer the mystery they'd been that first time, when I'd lost my way, wading through water that chilled my bones, clinging to tall reeds to stay upright, and losing sight of Taran. No, when I left, I was shown a path. But it came at a price.

Even now, as my mind reached elsewhere to escape the pain, I could hear the words they'd whispered to me all along that slippery route. *Morgan. Morgan the Fay. Mordred the Fay. The firstborn. Promise. Promise. Morgan, do you promise?*

Promise what? And yet I'd whispered back. *I promise I'll try.*

To defend the Fay? To keep them from fading into silence?

Of course that's what they wanted.

The Christian's One True God must not be allowed to wipe clean what the people of Britannia – Albion, as it once was – cherished, so many of them still, all that had shaped their lives for centuries. Traditions that gave meaning, comfort, and celebration. An *identity*.

Tradition was sacred, to be upheld, honoured.

The Great Mother *was* the truth.

And I was just one woman, no matter how they'd marked me – a woman now made weak. Yet the further I'd journeyed into the mists, the more the whispers had gathered.

Queen.

Be a queen, Morgan.

Queen of the Fay.

Promise. Promise.

As they'd said it, something had stirred – a plan, a purpose.

It was to these shores I'd come, as directly as I could, galloping, but I'd stopped elsewhere along the way. Why? To be certain the past was truly gone?

I could only think it was so.

I was no longer in this chamber, a part of this harsh landscape. Even the cries of Ynys Môn had grown distant, the Bean Si's wail, and certainly the voices of Teg, Olwyn, and Enfys, no matter how urgently they bid me. I returned to the only place I'd ever truly been happy. Before Seren had arrived. Before it all began.

The villa.

My mouth twisted between a smile and a scream as memory pulled me deeper.

Really, it was Taran who'd found her way to the villa – not me.

When we'd emerged from the mists, and were once more on solid ground, it was late, so late. I was tired, overwhelmed, *reeling* from all that had passed. I'd leaned heavily into her neck, drifting into sleep, unable to stop myself.

When I awoke, the sun had risen.

And there it was – before us.

For a while, both of us stood perfectly still, unable, perhaps, to believe our eyes. We'd been gone for three summers, and I'd hoped, in our absence, someone might have tended the place – Cai's parents, who used to visit with him often. Even Anwyn's parents, who'd also visited, or Anwyn herself, with her spouse, Ruach. They had a child now, perhaps even two. It would have made a fine homestead for them.

If not them, I'd feared marauders might have found it. Ransacked it. But though I hadn't yet gone inside, it bore no such sign of violation. Instead, it seemed *no one* had set foot near it since the day we left. All that lingered was abandonment.

"Oh, Taran," I whispered, sliding from her back to the ground.

How often had my feet touched this land – fetching, carrying, and playing?

The tears came, as I'd known they would, but I wiped at them, and sniffed hard.

It was a bright day that dawned as I drew closer, the grass so long now, unkempt, though the edges of the wood that surrounded us still held their beauty, touched as they were with the yellow blooms of celandine and the starry white of stitchwort.

The dwelling, though…the house Ector had built, so proud of his work, following the layout of an older building – ah, look at it now. Would he still be as proud?

The grass was tall around it too, hiding the walls, while ivy gripped every crevice. And yet, though it was overrun by living things, the house itself held no vitality of its own. It was a dead place without the family we'd once been to fill it.

Even so, I was eager to find my way in there. Taran had come closer too, standing just behind me and snorting softly, as if she too wanted to explore.

I forced a smile. "Wait there," I said. "Silly goose! You can't come inside."

She snorted again, petulantly, looked around as if seeking her counterpart, Arthur's horse Baldwine, then lowered her head to graze.

Priscilla had locked the door when we'd left, so I went to a window, meaning to push back the shutters there. Lifting my hands, I tore at the ivy. At first, it was stubborn and resisted my efforts, but I kept at it, until slowly, slowly it gave way.

My belly was round now, though the baby wasn't due until Samhain. We had the rest of the summer to go. I was still small, still agile enough to lift myself onto the window ledge – the one where Priscilla used to burn juniper as an offering to Brigid. I eased myself over it until my feet once again touched solid ground.

A mustiness struck me – neglect, when once this room had carried the smell of comfort, of warmth I'd revelled in. I was in the kitchen, the heart of the home, where Arthur and I had sat by the hearth, Ector telling us stories while Priscilla busied herself. I could see him now – Ector – his gentle gaze, his voice eloquent as he spoke of the land he loved, the history of it flowing from him like song.

He'd told us about the tribes that had lived here long before the Romans came. Of the Roman invasion itself, and what had happened to Britannia when Rome finally left us – how kingdoms had fractured into strife and quarrelling, too accustomed to foreign rule to stand on their own. He'd told us of other invaders too. The Angles, and the Jutes, many of whom had been here so long they now called themselves Britons too, had forged their own kingdoms in the northeast, largely peaceable. But the Saxons – the Sea Wolves – were *not* peaceable. They'd come in their hordes, brazen about their purpose: to wipe clean what had been before.

I'd asked Ector why we had to learn these lessons so intently, for he would insist we heed every word. His reply was this: *Because the greatest battles are yet to come.* Battles that *we* would fight, the young, not the old. But never did Arthur think he would do so as a king, nor I as a princess, nor we as brother and sister.

The hearth was where we'd also learned something else, from Merlyn, the stranger who'd ridden into our lives that other Beltane night.

It was there that worlds had been built. And there that worlds had come crashing down. *My* world, lying in tatters at my feet.

I ventured deeper inside.

Dust lay thick on every surface and cobwebs veiled the ceiling – dark, dense, and clinging. Ivy had made its way inside too, creeping in unchecked through the cracks, trying to claim the inner walls as much as it had the outer. The villa had always been hidden, but now nature seemed to want to erase it altogether. One day, it might be as difficult to find as the land of the Fay itself.

It was to Priscilla's larder I went, where she'd kept her herbs, those used in the art of healing. Memories! I had so many of them. As a child, I would watch her unlock the door, pausing to study the shelves before choosing what she needed – yarrow to make a salve if one of us had tumbled in the dirt, or angelica to calm a restless belly.

As she worked, grinding herbs to powder, there'd be such an intent look on her face – a look I'd loved. She'd catch me watching and explain what she was doing.

"And can I do it too, one day?" I'd ask. "Help you?"

"One day," she'd say, before returning to the task at hand.

And she'd kept that promise. She'd let me help – first here at the villa, then later at Caer Arthur. It was work I'd loved: the collecting and gathering of plants and herbs, learning the power held in petals, stems, and roots. She'd had *so* much to teach me, hoping to make me as great a healer as she was, though sometimes – on the battlefield – there was no healing to be done. All that remained then was easing the soul's swift passage to the Otherworld, while whispering a soft farewell.

Morgan the Healer – that was who I'd wanted to be, just as she was Priscilla the Healer. Was that still a dream I could make come true? Somehow. Somewhere.

I knew where Priscilla hid the key to the larder. I'd seen her place it there one morning when she thought I was busy sweeping, tucking it onto a shelf behind the hearth. Sure enough, when my fingers searched for it, it was there, though rusted.

As I inserted it into the lock, the larder door yielded readily enough. A cloud of dust billowed out, making me cough as I disturbed what had lain still for so long.

There they were – row upon row of shelves, each lined with jars, both glass and clay, some sealed with wax, others stoppered with cork. Within, some contents had surely withered, others though would be potent still, despite the passage of time.

Reaching out a hand, I touched the jars. Each was marked with a symbol, though most had long since faded. What of the symbol on my head, though – the one tied to a promise, no matter how forcibly extracted?

I needed to find a mirror, see what they'd done to me.

Closing the larder door, I picked up speed, flying from the kitchen, heading for the stairs that led to the upper floor – our bed chambers.

Up there, the ivy was bolder still – not only finding its way in through cracks and windows, but snaking across the floor. I kicked at it as I went, not pausing, not even outside Arthur's chamber where he'd slept since he was two. I used to creep into his room if he stirred, my ear always so keenly attuned to the smallest sound of his discomfort, and soothe him back to sleep with a lullaby. Little Arthur. Baby Arthur. He'd always calmed at the sound of my voice, all through the years, until we were grown. And now? Now it was Guinevere's task to soothe him in troubled times.

A mirror – there was one in my chamber, and that's where I went, steeling myself as I entered. A roomful of memories indeed.

There was my bed, my clothes chest, a small table with a hairbrush, and a jar of skin cream Priscilla had made. And the mirror – thick with dust too.

I rushed over to it, eager to see the handiwork of the Fay. As I reached for it, a beetle, black and shiny, scuttled away into the gloom. But something else caught my eye – further movement, quick, in the corner of the room.

For a heartbeat, I froze. I'd thought the house empty. Abandoned. But what if I'd been wrong? What if someone else *was* here, hiding when they'd heard me?

I turned sharply, my hand going to my sickle knife. There was nothing, no one living at least. Just a shadow – that was all. This room had always been full of them.

Returning my attention to the mirror, I scrubbed at its surface with my sleeve. Even so, the reflection remained dull, the glass having become mottled, so I carried it to the window, tearing away strands of ivy to let the light filter through.

There it was – the sigil. Red. Livid. The blood had barely beaded, something that could do with a salve itself to soothe the sting. A pattern, a symbol – with no sharp edges, only curves – covering almost all my forehead, one that would settle with time, but would always be visible no matter how silvery it became.

Morgan the Fay.

Morgan – *Queen* of the Fay.

That's what they wanted me to be.

"A warrior woman."

I nearly dropped the mirror. Someone had *said* those words, not merely whispered them in my head! It took a moment to realise that it was me. Just me.

More than a queen, I had to be a warrior, I had to fight for the Fay – for their existence. That responsibility lay in my hands…and in my belly.

His responsibility.

Like the sigil they had carved, Ector had once carved something too, a warrior woman given to me at Yule. I hadn't taken it when I'd left, so it must still be here, in the doll's house in the corner which he'd also crafted, each room filled with tiny furniture made by his hands, an almost perfect replica of our own home.

I needed her now, to hold her.

Moments later, I opened the doll's house, to find her not lying there on her back, lost beneath dirt and dust, but standing tall, that defiant gaze I'd loved so well still fixed upon her face. Some might call it whimsy to think it, but it was as if she guarded the house, untroubled by her solitude, preserving what memories remained there.

She was so well rendered, every detail flawless – the battle dress she wore, the sword in her hand, the hair flowing down her back, the proud tilt of her chin.

A figure comfortable with who she was.

Who made no apology for it…

"That's it, Morgan! That's it. You can push now. Push!"

More words – this time not from my lips, nor from the shadows.

"Morgan, open your eyes and listen to me. You must do this. Push!"

There was no one at the villa but me. So who was speaking?

No one, yet I felt hands on my shoulders, *rough* hands, shaking me.

"Morgan." The voice, disembodied, was now a growl, commanding me. "Hear me, and hear me well. You *have* to do this. There is no other road. I won't let you give up, do you hear? Now be who you are. Reach deep into yourself and push. Push! By the Goddess, push! You, who are a queen, yes, but more than that. You're a warrior, Morgan. Every woman is. Now seek her. Seek her within. Know her!"

A warrior?

Yes, yes, I must not fail Ector's hopes. Nor Priscilla's. Nor the guardian of the villa, who I would leave where she was, to keep it safe forevermore.

Now was the time. I had to do as the voice said, and

push.

I wasn't in the villa's bedchamber – that had been only a memory, vivid though it was. I was here, in *this* bedchamber, on a barren outcrop, the wind still howling, thunder rolling, the ghosts of Ynys Môn screaming, and the Bean Si keening.

Not today. She'd have no deaths today, either. I would do it – *unapologetically* – and defy her. And her curses? I'd defy those too. Find a way.

Just when I thought the pain couldn't get worse, it did, but now I refused to give in to it. I would master it instead, and push. Keep pushing. The blood beneath me was a river running red, soaking me, painting my skin like woad, readying me for battle.

I screamed, and unlike my mother, I did it. I *outscreamed* the Bean Si!

And through it, a second smile – no matter how small – touched my lips.

Another scream. And another. I was made of them, forged in the fires of agony.

But then – at last – another voice rose to join mine.

His.

My son's.

As furious as the storm.

Pulled from darkness into light, he was lifted up so I could gaze at him.

CHAPTER FOURTEEN

It was Teg who wet-nursed the baby. I was too weak after his birth to do so myself. A mother to four of her own and well-versed in such care, Teg would sit quietly in my chamber while I lay recovering, crooning soft lullabies, soothing his cries, rocking him gently from side to side – and I let her.

Not only from weakness, but because… Because…

"Morgan! You fare better today?"

Another voice – neither soft nor maternal – broke the hush. It was not my husband, Urien, but his son, Agravaine. There was a smile at his lips, though his eyes, as ever, were watchful, intent. I tried not to think it, but how striking he looked. Handsome, even – reminding me a little of Lancelot with his dark hair. Yet as I'd thought before – when he'd come with Urien to Arthur's wedding in Dumnonia and sat quietly at the back of the chapel – he was a rougher-hewn version. I didn't mean it unkindly, quite the opposite. While Lancelot still bore the shimmer of youth, Agravaine had long since shed it. Sometimes, as with his father, I wondered if he'd *ever* truly been young, though in truth, he wasn't much older than me – twenty-six summers, while I was nearing my twenty-first. But even as I tried, I could never quite picture him as a boy, as someone…innocent. He had such a knowing about him.

Here, on this harsh, sea-lashed coast, deep in Cymru – in its own way as hidden as the valley where I grew up – perhaps such knowing was essential for survival.

It was he who'd come to see me this morning, how many days after the birth? I'd lost count. Of course, Urien had visited too. He had perched on the chair beside my bed and taken my hand in his – his skin gnarled, his nails yellowed. His gaze had settled on mine, his faded eyes not just kind, but sympathetic. He'd nodded softly, as if I'd asked a question that only he could hear, and he was offering some silent answer. Then he had whispered my name – *Morgan* – and after a time, he'd left. Asking nothing of me. Simply content, it seemed, that I was still there.

He was a good man.

Good enough to take me in when I'd appeared like a ghost at the gates of his stronghold – begging not only for shelter, but for something more. To be his queen.

Urien had bowed to every one of my wishes, and in the weeks that followed, leading up to my son's birth, I'd grown fond of him, this man so deeply respected across the land – once a fierce battle leader, ably defending his kingdom from raids by both land and sea. A man staunchly of the old ways. As were his people.

His...*loyal* people.

And I was loyal to him. Or so I told myself. To the man who'd reached out to me as I'd reached out to him. The man who had traced the sigil on my brow, who knew what it meant, had *read* it out loud – *Morgan the Fay*. So readily he'd accepted me.

And yet...it was this other I longed to see by my bedside each day. The one whose presence made my breath catch as he sauntered towards me.

I was not as loyal as I thought.

As Agravaine drew closer, Teg rose, the baby as ever cradled against her – Mordred. For if the Fay demanded he bear that name, I would honour it. That it had first been suggested by Nimue was something I'd forced from my mind, as I'd done with so much else. Teg slipped from the room with Mordred, but not before I caught a flicker of displeasure in her eyes, evident whenever Agravaine came near me.

I understood.

She loved her king, as so many did. A man who'd been good to her as well. A steady man, solid. While our pagan tradition did not scorn a queen that took lovers beyond her husband, perhaps it was *who* that person was that irked her.

Agravaine wasn't my lover yet, though. I simply didn't have the strength. But my heart squeezed all the same. A wanton thing, yes, but sad too. Pitiful. All it longed for – stubbornly – was something to soften the ache of what it could never have.

And Agravaine, with days of stubble shadowing his jaw, and black hair as wild as mine falling about his shoulders – a *fire* about him too – offered that. He could *make* me forget. The pain that had led me here, the ruin and the loss.

He made me forget about Mordred, too.

Mordred, with that shock of dark hair so like Lancelot's, and eyes like Arthur's, the colour of sea mist, a mark on his forehead indeed – a birthmark Teg called it – but I knew better. It was a sigil, just like mine. Just as Nimue had said.

Agravaine made me forget that as well, that while Teg loved to hold Mordred, I didn't. Something in me resisted every time I tried.

Agravaine leaned forward, and I flinched – just slightly.

Tiredness, perhaps?

He laughed, a soft, beguiling sound.

"There's a lock of hair near your eyes, Morgan, that's all."

I laughed too, my shoulders easing.

"Sorry," I said. "And to answer your question – how I'm faring – I feel stronger today, thank you."

"You'll be on your feet again in no time," he murmured, "which is good, as we can explore then. I promise you this: it's beautiful here, even in autumn, and in winter. *Especially* then. This is a land that winter suits. There's much I want to show you."

He would show me? But then…yes, for who else?

Urien was able-bodied, but too much exertion, and the strain would show on his face. A great man, but the body he inhabited, as with all bodies, was still journeying towards death. War and disease had spared him thus far, but time would not.

This land required strength. I knew that well enough. When venturing here, when it was still summer – thankfully – Taran and I had had to pick our way carefully through forests so thick with trees they blocked the sun. We climbed hills so steep they tilted the world beneath us, and crossed mountains unlike any I'd ever known –paths so narrow that one misplaced step would have sent us plunging into ravines.

And then there was the coast, which our stronghold overlooked. The sea there was heaving, perpetually in motion. Just beyond it lay Ynys Môn, close enough to see, but too far to reach, not without a coracle and more courage than I possessed. Not even with Agravaine would I dare it. Not after what Ector had said.

Since arriving, I'd been largely confined to my chamber,

first by the weight of pregnancy, then by childbirth and all it took from me. But both chapters were over now. My body had released my son, and soon the time would come to explore indeed – whatever the weather, whatever the terrain. I would learn every path and whisper of this new land, not with Urien, but with Agravaine by my side.

His hand reached for me again, and this time I welcomed it fully. Instead of my hair, he stroked my cheek – gently, deliberately. He'd been here the day I'd arrived – though it was said he was often elsewhere in the kingdom, somewhat restless – and now I wondered: should I have held back, let Urien die, as he surely would, then stepped forwards to marry his son? Why had Agravaine never proposed such a thing? But he hadn't always been this way with me, so familiar, so bold. In the beginning, he'd been…cautious, watching me the way Seren used to – closely, silently, as if to measure me. Urien, by contrast, once his shock at my sudden appearance had passed, had been nothing but willing – eager, even – to take me under his wing. And so, yes, I'd married him. Quickly.

I *couldn't* wait. If Guinevere was a queen, if she had…*stolen* my place by Arthur's side, then I, at the very least, deserved a crown of my own. The Fay had said as much. I would not be a pawn, but a woman of power, the High King's sister, marrying not to unite our kingdom with Dumnonia, for Urien had made that clear – he would *not* bend the knee and become a petty king when he was so much more.

Like Óengus Mac Airem in Demet, on the far side of Cymru's jagged coast, with only Ceredigion between us, another outlier, he simply wanted to rule his land his own way, for it to be as much a bastion as Avalon was. Something that seemed entirely possible, for this was a land apart. A *world* apart. As shrouded in mists as the realm of the Fay.

I was Urien's queen. The Queen of Gwynedd.

But one day I might be Agravaine's. My future taking shape at last.

I lifted my hand and rested it against his – a gesture as daring as his, wanting to feel the smoothness of younger skin rather than the time-worn hands of age. Though it must be said, Urien had *never* forced himself upon me. Whatever I'd done with him, I'd done willingly, because I wanted to please him. And I had. I'd brought tears to his eyes, which slipped into the creases of his weathered cheeks as he whispered my name over and over. "Morgan the Fay. Beautiful Morgan. A jewel."

And I would continue to please him. I resolved to.

It would make up for this – for what I was about to do.

In keeping both father and son content, I would find my own happiness.

Agravaine and I had barely spoken before the birth, but the glances we'd exchanged! Each one more intense than the last. A connection had been forged, without the need for a single word, a bond, once tenuous, now growing stronger.

Could it one day rival what had existed between Arthur and me? Having put so much distance between us, would Arthur simply…vanish from memory? Especially if I refused to look too long into the eyes of my child – to be reminded of him.

A child whose father no one knew.

Not even Urien.

That good man had never asked.

Since Mordred's birth, Agravaine had done more than watch. He'd made a point of visiting me, speaking with me, touching me – as he did now, his breath, like mine, growing uneven. This man who wanted to show me his world and everything in it. And with the baby in someone else's arms, I could do that.

I leaned forward, bringing my free hand to the back of his head so that I could guide him closer. A flicker of hesitation in him surprised me.

I frowned – deliberately – and pulled back. If I was wrong about this, if he didn't want me…then whatever I felt – was it lust? *Of course* it was lust! – I would crush it.

Agravaine. Ah, Agravaine.

It became clear he was teasing me. He smiled again, his tongue darting out to wet his lips, my tongue doing the same.

Then he grabbed me.

Harshly.

And it only heightened the thrill.

Our tongues clashed, his hands lost in the blackness of my hair as he continued to kiss me, until it became as tangled as his. Unruly. Unbound.

Just like us.

CHAPTER FIFTEEN

"Over there, Morgan, can you see it? That cliff, sloping down – the one closest to us, taller, steeper than the rest. That's Craig y Gwaed. An ancient place of sacrifice."

"Sacrifice?" I asked, glancing at Agravaine. "Animals, or…people?"

My question seemed to amuse him. "Both."

I drew a breath, still staring at the cliff. "Why?"

He frowned. "Have you never heard of such things? Dumnonia is a mighty kingdom. The Henge is there, is it not? The ring of stones."

"Stonehenge? Yes. And the stones at Avebury too, where the fairy tree stands." The one Merlyn said Igraine was born beneath – a descendent of Boudica.

Agravaine rubbed the stubble on his chin. "Yes, yes – Stonehenge and Avebury. Sacrifices happened there too – animals and people. So why does it shock you?"

It shocked me because formal human sacrifices were rare now. I'd never known one in my lifetime. Dumnonia was a mighty kingdom, as Agravaine had said, Uther had intended to make it the greatest in the land, and now, with Arthur on its throne – not just as King of Dumnonia, but the High King of all Britannia – it was.

But sacrifices…

We were a civilised people. Or trying to be. We'd found

other ways to honour the gods and goddesses. Hadn't we?

Ah, but here in Cymru, in Kernow further west, and in the wild reaches of Caledonia, who knew what went on still?

"Who was sacrificed?" I asked as he took my hand, and we picked our way along the rocky shore.

The sea, if not calm, was at least more subdued today, lapping rather than lashing at the shore under a sky thick with cloud. Even the cries from Ynys Môn were muted, though a chill rode the air still.

Samhain had passed, and then Yule. We now moved towards Imbolc, celebrating the first signs of spring – a bloom of yellow among the budding green, and that green the brightest it would be all year. A time to honour Brigid and new beginnings.

Mordred was thriving, still in Teg's arms, not mine.

And I – I was often in the arms of the man beside me, any time we could find. Either by day, or at night, when I'd slip from Urien's bed after soothing him to sleep with a small draught tipped into his wine, just enough to ensure his rest.

Thoughts of Urien… Thoughts of Mordred…

No, it was only this I wanted to focus on – these moments with Agravaine, which had become precious to me, a bond between us indeed, different from the one I'd shared with Arthur, for how could it compare? Arthur and I had *always* known each other, in this life and in others. With Agravaine, there wasn't that familiarity. We'd only come to know each other these past few months, and yet I craved him, the touch of his hand, as much as he seemed to crave me.

It was lust, yes, but more than that – something urgent, and alive.

The mountain – Craig y Gwaed – lay only a short distance from Urien's stronghold. It dropped sharply, just as Agravaine had said, down to meet the waiting sea, frothing white at its base – greedy, insistent, needing to be fed.

Very greedy, that sea.

It had already devoured the souls of druids – scores of them – but that was long ago. Even a feast such as that could only satisfy for so long.

Agravaine hadn't answered me, not yet, so I repeated my question. "Who was sacrificed there?" And added another, "By whom?"

Still he said nothing as we walked, hand in hand, our bodies wrapped in fur. He did this sometimes, fell into a brooding silence. He would…contemplate. I understood, I did that too, and so I shrugged and let the silence be.

We were much closer to Craig y Gwaed when Agravaine gave a nod.

"There's a path there," he said.

"Are we going to climb it?" I was further aghast. I'd recovered well from the birth, was in full health again, but was I fit enough to climb *that?*

"It's not as bad as it looks," he said, amused again. "The effort will be worth it." Then more slyly, "For many reasons."

My stomach knotted, as it always did when he spoke like that – my thoughts drifting to how soft the grass might feel at the summit when we lay down upon it…

The path he'd indicated was as rocky as the shore had been, scattered with scree, and slightly treacherous because of it – one step forwards, then a slide back. Agravaine was more sure-footed than me, but proved attentive enough, pulling me upwards when I struggled, higher and higher, insisting we continue.

I was glad the day was dry. In the wet, this would have been impossible. Even now, a part of me thought it was so – that if a victim had once been led this way, their heart might have failed before the offering could be made.

And mercy on them if it did.

"Almost there, Morgan," he encouraged.

How easy he was finding this! A man of twenty-six summers, nearly twenty-seven, and in his prime. Hardened, because a land like this demanded it. Not just a place of rocky coastlines and hidden coves, but of sweeping mountains, wooded valleys, and shadowed wilds where red deer, grey wolves, and boar roamed. A land that might glitter in the sunlight if the sun chose to linger, but – so far – it rarely had. More often, the skies were restless, shifting endlessly, with low clouds and thunder rumbling in the distance, even when the sea lay calm – a constant threat. There was *excitement* in the air, but laced with unease. I'd been born in a storm, as had my son. I shouldn't fear them, but I did. For storms, as everyone knew, could rage out of control.

"Morgan. Morgan! Take my hands, both of them."

Agravaine was hauling me up the last stretch – just as well, for I might have stopped otherwise and tried to scramble back down. It had been steep before, but now it was worse. If I slipped, I might not stop. I might tumble to my death.

Madness!

And for a moment, clinging to him, staring up into the darkness of his eyes, the thought came: Are *you mad? Worse – do you* intend *for me to fall?*

Would I become a sacrifice?

And if so… what for?

"You've done it, Morgan! We're here."

We were there? Thank the Great Mother!

His arms came around me as I caught my breath.

"You're trembling," he said. "There's no need. You're safe. You were *always* safe."

Always?

Still I struggled to speak, though I relished the warmth, the sturdiness of his body so close to mine. For a moment, what I'd feared hadn't felt so far from the truth. My hands were in his and his…hadn't they loosened, just a little?

Now, his hands framed my face, lifting my gaze to his.

"My love, there's a gentler way down."

"Gentler? Then why didn't we take it up!" It was not a question; I was indignant.

He shrugged. "Because I knew you were capable. That's why. I *believe* in you."

He kissed me, and any doubts – any dark imaginings – dissolved.

I was lost in his kiss, willing him to take me there and then, heat rising so rapidly as his touch set me alight, but he pulled away.

"Follow me," he said, and I nodded.

I might follow him forever if he asked.

At the summit, the ground was firm, the grass short and tufted with heather and moss. A faint path wound through it, not quite a trail, more an indentation. Agravaine kept to it, and I did the same. A *ceremonial* path, I realised. The path of the sacrificed, worn by the dragging of heels.

It stretched before us, and with every step, my heels dragged too, until finally we stopped at the cliff's edge – far closer than I would have liked.

Agravaine drew a deep breath, squared his shoulders, and lifted his head high.

"Magnificent, isn't it?" he said, and his voice – his reverence – reminded me of Arthur. Of the day we'd ridden through the meadows, long before the crown, before war. He'd been fifteen, and I seventeen – a *lifetime* ago, it seemed now. Arthur had stopped his horse, Baldwine, and gazed around just like Agravaine did now, whispering a single word as the sun dipped low: *Britannia.*

There'd been awe in him. Pure. Unshakable.

I loved the land too. I'd loved Dumnonia. But, just as Agravaine had promised, I was falling in love with Gwynedd's wild shore, the unpredictability of it.

The unpredictability of *him* – Agravaine.

Was this love I felt for him now not merely the body's craving, but the heart's as well? And this, after I'd sworn, when I left Caer Arthur, when I fled that place, that I would *never* again fall into such a trap…allow myself to be so vulnerable.

But every plan I'd ever made had come undone…and so there I was, on the summit of Craig y Gwaed, staring not at the sea, but at him.

Falling.

Falling.

Falling.

A cry…

A moan…

High and keening, like the Bean Si, and my heart froze because of it. How many times could I defy her? Perhaps here at the cliff's edge our battle would end.

That notion was still forming when I saw it – a kittiwake, perhaps – bursting from the clouds, wings cutting the air as it swooped low before vanishing again.

That was my Bean Si. A bird. Nothing more.

I laughed – loudly, freely – and nestled closer to Agravaine.

"It *is* magnificent," I said. "This land…there's a beauty to it I've never known before. This place – this cliff – tell me its history. Tell me…everything."

About the willing *and* the unwilling, for surely both had stood where we did now.

"Men. Women. Children. Babies," Agravaine said.

"Babies? But why?"

"Because of the gods, Morgan. Isn't that always why?"

"Which gods? Which goddesses? Arianrhod?"

"*All* of them. All need appeasing sometimes." He turned to me then, his eyes catching what little light there was. "Can you see, Morgan?"

"See?" I frowned. "What do you mean? My eyes are open – I *am* seeing."

But before I could speak, even gasp, his hands covered my eyes, steering me closer to the edge. The breeze there struck raw against my face, burning my cheeks.

"Can you see?" he said again.

And this time there was no mistaking his meaning.

The old ways – the ways of the ancient tribes, the first peoples of this land. Children of gods and goddesses, of the Great Mother herself, with sacred blood in their veins.

There was a time, long before any Roman ship touched these shores, before their legions shattered our groves and bound us to their laws, before the new faith came and drove the old rites into shadow…ah, there was a golden time.

A time when the people didn't merely live *on* the land, but *with* it. When they listened to its voice, its breath, its memory – the heartbeat of the earth itself.

And deeper still, in the oldest telling, the people *were* the Fay, and death was not an ending but a turning of the wheel. For if the land was eternal, then so were we, we returned to it again and again, each life carrying with it a shard of wisdom, until at last we could see – *truly* see, the veil between worlds a curtain easily swept aside.

Much has been lost since the Romans.

Four hundred years had passed since they'd first invaded, a hundred since they'd left, and still the people of Britannia were floundering. People lived differently now. They had indeed succumbed to Roman ways, to Christian ways even. Like those once led to the edge of Craig y Gwaed – some willing, others not.

But even among the unwilling, were those who believed the old ways could no longer be maintained – the ways of the Fay, the teachings of Avalon, the worship of the Great Mother – that though lamentable, it was all just coming to a natural end.

But not here. Not in Gwynedd.

Not in places where the Pagans still held dominion, where the land had a grip on them, and gave so much in return. Here, it offered not only a breadth of beauty, waiting to be discovered, but protection as well.

In Gwynedd, the hills and mountains rose like sentinels against marauders and enemy warriors, *daring* them to pass. And where the ground seemed solid, it might suddenly betray, shifting to black sand and mire that sucked men under. A death all feared, for what lay beneath those murky depths? Horrors, surely. There *must* be.

Even the weather was a weapon. Blue skies could darken in a breath, a breeze swell to a tempest, rain lashing the skin like thorns. And then the mists would rise – ghost-like, silent and blinding – swallowing everything.

And so, if the land gave, we must give back.

With Agravaine's hands still covering my eyes, I saw it: a procession. It was different to the one I'd witnessed at Avalon, when priestesses both young and old had wound their way in an orderly fashion to the summit of the Tor. This one was solemn, with faces held in careful repose and eyes cast downwards.

The figures were robed, their garments either black or white, some adorned with green wreaths to honour nature, others wearing bone amulets at their throats.

At the head of the procession walked a man, a woman, and a baby.

The *unwilling*.

The child had been born at twilight, outside the home, in a place deemed impure. He had lived, but never cried, not once – and that silence had unsettled many.

Was he a changeling, a Fay child swapped for a human one? If so, what then? What if the mother came to love him? What if, when the Fay returned to claim him, as they might, she refused? To do so could bring great misfortune, not only on them, but the entire tribe – crops blighted, livestock dead, and sickness spreading like rot.

It was too great a risk. The child must be returned.

Li⊠r, the sea god, would carry him back into the mists.

The Fay could have both children. That would appease them, surely?

They must *all* be sacrificed, mother, father, and child – a baby should be born at home, the woman should not have wandered, and the father should have ensured she didn't. In failing this, they'd displeased the gods, displeased *everyone*.

It was the father who protested.

"We've done no evil," he cried, panic thinning his voice to a reed. "The woman was taken sudden by the pangs of birth."

Ah, by the waters it had happened. *Dark* waters.

"Mercy," he continued, "we're good folk. There's no stain upon the child."

Yet the mother…she remained as silent as the child she clutched at.

At the cliff's crown, while those around her came to a halt, she did not. She leapt into the abyss, the baby still held fast in her arms. I could only imagine the tears in her eyes, mirroring my own, for all they'd endured.

The father no longer pled for their good name, only his own.

"It was all them," he bellowed, turning to a druid clad in white, his face painted like the moon. "They brought the wrath of the gods upon us. My wife would not pray, you see? She danced with the dark ones instead – *here*, on this very mountain she did – beneath storm and rain. A witch, she was! And her child – he was no spawn of mine, but the spawn of shadows. I am clean of it. Clean! A man of honour."

But the druid judged him otherwise.

Two others stepped forwards, robed in black, their bodies as strong as Agravaine's, against whom the man could not struggle. The elder druid – dreadful to behold, his hair spiked with dung – reminded me of the Saxon wizards, strange, prancing creatures, casting curses in battle. He looked like one who might dwell in a cave, as many did, Agravaine had told me – hermits, called upon only for ritual.

The elder marked the man's brow with blood.

Knowing he couldn't avoid his fate, the man ceased screaming. He began to babble instead, words no one could understand – a denial in them still, perhaps. Then, when the elder gave a nod, the two druids dragged him to the cliff's edge.

He followed his wife and child into the sea.

More of the unwilling had been brought here – why, I didn't know. I was no longer privy to such things, nor to when those executions had taken place. How far in the past they lay, or whether – and my body gave a shudder – they were more recent.

And then came the willing. The elderly. The ill. The bereaved. Those who knew they must feed the land that had birthed them, so that it might flourish.

At these processions, there were no screams, no mourning, but always the same solemnity. The sea – ah, the sea – ever rising to meet them.

There was something…holy in it. Even with the unwilling. And though some – the Christians – would call it *un*holy, I understood it. Even though it shocked me still. Even though it could be savage.

Would Arthur ever appease the gods this way, as Agravaine's people did, if he had to, if he was desperate enough? Arthur was gentle, yes, but I'd seen him fight. How bold he was when facing the enemy, sometimes reckless, wielding mighty Excalibur with unwavering intent. He would save this land, whatever the cost.

I'd seen, too, the firm set of his jaw at council, when a

decision was to be made – *his,* not Merlyn's. And I remembered the look on his face the last time we'd seen each other – when I'd told him he didn't love Guinevere but me.

Me.

And yet…Agravaine, whose hands still covered my eyes, treated me as his equal. If he could bear the sight of this, then so could I – though he'd been born to it, and I hadn't. So perhaps he meant for me to see something else: that though I came from the Summer Country, this – *this* – was where my home would be. That though I was married to his father, Urien could not last. One day, Agravaine and I would be wed.

I would live here.

Die here.

In this bleak, barren, beautiful corner of the world.

I would be a queen here, so I had to understand the old ways – fully.

Beneath his hands, the sigil on my forehead throbbed.

I *was* the old way – Agravaine, myself, and my son. Even after Urien, we would never swear allegiance to a court where Christianity flourished. Urien had made that clear, and Agravaine – he didn't need to say a word. I already knew.

My heart opened to him further, my trust returned.

I leaned back, breathing in the scent of him, musky, but laced with salt. The scent of a man, not the boys I was used to, for that's what he seemed in comparison, truly grown. Older than me, yes, but older, somehow, than everything and everyone I'd *ever* known. I was a child beside him, with so much yet to learn, to discover.

He removed his hands from my eyes and wrapped them around my waist instead. Our feet remained close to the cliff's edge, the waters still lapping far below.

"See," he murmured, his breath hot against my ear, his voice with gravel in it. "See how powerful the land is? *Our* land, Morgan the Fay. And ours it will stay."

I kept my eyes closed.

To open them would be to see Ynys Môn as well as the sea.

"Will there be more sacrifices?" I asked, the words tumbling out.

His body stiffened against mine, and he gave a nod. "Yes – if there has to be."

CHAPTER SIXTEEN

Ynys Môn… I was falling in love with so much here, but that diseased isle – offshore, yet still so close – frightened me.

But fear was something Agravaine refused to countenance.

The wheel had turned again. Imbolc had come and gone, and spring had arrived more fully, yet the days at this outpost still insisted on clinging to winter. They remained cold and grey, with thunder rumbling in the skies.

I should have stayed at home today, for I had much to tend to. My child, for one. His cries echoed through the stronghold, not distant at all. Not distant…enough. But Teg had such a way with him. When placed in my arms, he'd only cry louder. The child would thrash, his limbs already full of strength, though he was still a baby. His hair so dark, his eyes so grey…

Sometimes, when Teg left us alone, rushing from the room as though to force us to bond, I'd do it, I'd look at him. Study him. Whisper into his ear as though he might suddenly answer me. *Whose are you?* And, sometimes, a darker thought would come: *Are you even mine? Are you a changeling, too?*

There was nothing of me in him. Nothing. Except…for all his strength, he was delicate. Fine-boned. But make no mistake, if not especially tall or broad, he'd be lethal. That truth hit like an arrow between the eyes.

He'd be someone to fear, just like I'd been warned.

And that's why I couldn't hold him, why I couldn't look at him for long, why I raised my voice as I sat in my chamber and yelled for Teg, for someone – *anyone* – to come and take him. When no one answered the call of a queen, I screamed louder.

"Teg? Someone. Come here – now. Right now! COME HERE!"

It wasn't Teg who rushed back into the room, it was another maid, Donwen. A young girl who was round of face and hips. She arrived in a flurry of apologies, and I thrust the baby at her, muttering that he needed feeding.

He didn't. He was fed well enough – just not by me. Teg and other wet-nurses had seen to that. I'd never given him suck from my own body. At first, I'd been too ill, but then…ah, then came the excuses. And being a queen, no one dared to contradict me, not even Teg, who saw plainly enough the milk that swelled my breasts.

The thought of him hanging off me like that…

No!

I couldn't bear it.

Delicate though he was, the child would drain me of *everything*.

With him gone from my sight, I could think more clearly.

Agravaine *hated* to see any kind of fear in me. His intention was to make me face it. "To be worthy of the title of Queen," he'd said, "a Queen of Gwynedd, Morgan, *Queen of the Fay*, you must vanquish fear."

"I am *Morgan the Fay*," I'd corrected. "Not *Queen of the*

Fay."

"You are the queen of *everything*," he'd countered. "You could be. You *should* be. If Uther's child – his elder child—
"

"And a woman," I'd cut in, angering him further.

"*Women rule!* They used to. The Great Mother is just that – *a woman*! Without her, there would be no Prydain." Prydain was his word for our land. Never once had I heard him call it Britannia. "She who gave birth to it all – to the gods and the goddesses alike. The One True God? He is a travesty! The Christians' treatment of their women is. Never – *never* – demean yourself in front of me, Morgan."

So full of fury. So full of passion.

And it now made me wonder: had I allowed myself to be demeaned before?

Agravaine was right in what he'd said, but the world was no longer what it had been. Did he realise that as fully as I did, I who had lived in Dumnonia, at the heart of it all, when he had lived here, in a kingdom far removed? New powers were rising. Across the land, in caers and fortifications, it was men who thundered to war now, while women held the hearth. No more Boudicas with flaming chariots of their own. But even so, their role remained vital. They raised the young and tended the old, the sick, the wounded. They kept livestock, tilled the land, ensured there was something – *anything* – for warriors to return to. Something worth the spilling of blood. But I was never that woman. I'd ridden into battle with Arthur, insisted on it, as Arthur's mother Igraine had done with Uther. Twice I'd done that. I'd fired arrows, and killed men too.

Killed many…

Killed…Seren.

Ah, I was *grateful* I'd killed Seren. Her death had brought me here, to Gwynedd, to Agravaine, where finally I could see just how *much* I'd been demeaned. Even my brother – he whom I'd loved most of all, and believed had loved *me* best – had demeaned me. He'd *replaced* me, when he'd sworn against it.

Guinevere.

With Seren gone, I had someone new to hate – other than Viviane, other than Nimue. And maybe, just maybe…I could hate Arthur too.

Agravaine was aware of Seren. I'd told him, confessed after too much sweet mead. We'd found a cove and built a fire, our cloaks wrapped tight around us as we'd huddled together. He'd laughed, said she'd deserved death. *Applauded* me.

"You can tell me anything, Morgan. Nothing will change how I feel about you. You're here because it was meant to be – your choice, not your brother's command."

"Half-brother."

Something in my voice gave him pause.

"Of course," he'd said. "My apologies, my lady. Your…*half*-brother."

I'd laughed too, trying to ease any awkwardness I'd caused, then I'd leaned in to kiss him. It worked – Agravaine had responded as he always did, eagerly. He longed for me to lay bare my soul, to bind myself to him with nothing held back, but I couldn't tell him that if I was Uther's firstborn…then Mordred might be Arthur's.

I couldn't tell him because my emotions towards my child were complicated – I barely understood them, let alone enough to explain. Instead, I surrendered to the pull I felt towards my husband's son. Who fathered Mordred was mine to know and mine to keep – a truth I held tight to my chest, since I couldn't hold Mordred to it.

Both his rightful places denied him.

Because Agravaine wasn't privy to the truth of Mordred's parentage, he couldn't grasp my unease – the boy the Fay had marked, just as they had marked me. The sigil on the baby's head? I don't think he'd ever studied him intently enough to notice. Not yet. But he understood my dread of Ynys Môn well enough, of what had happened there, and what might still linger.

And he wanted it gone.

That morning, with Mordred taken from me, I rose from my chair and went to the window. The shutters had been kept closed, but I pushed them wide – not to the gentle blue of a Dumnonia spring, but the steel-grey of Gwynedd.

There it was, framed by the window: the island. Always hovering, ever present. Trees grew thick there, where once its shores had been strewn with blood.

The cries from that island never ceased – at least, not for me, sometimes frantic, sometimes merely a low, grieving wail. I asked others if they heard them. Teg hadn't. Nor Urien. Not even Agravaine, though he looked disgruntled by the question.

Just me.

And perhaps…perhaps Mordred.

For I'd noticed something.

At times, he would turn his head in the direction of the island, just slightly, and focus, as I was doing now – growing quiet, as if straining to hear.

And then, while I felt only sorrow, his rosebud lips would curl into a smile. A giggle, even, that chilled me as much as the weary cries from Ynys Môn ever had.

But I was going there today. I'd finally agreed. Agravaine had asked me over and over – no, *insisted*. I had to face my fears, he'd said. Break them down. One by one.

Was such a thing possible?

It would be a gift, if so.

Either Ynys Môn was a cursed place, diseased…

Or it was just an island, no matter what had happened there.

But first – those other matters. If not my child, then Urien – the man who'd accepted me as his queen. My husband.

I must at least tend to him first.

A smile spread across Urien's grizzled, bearded face as I entered his chamber. Though we were married, we slept apart. He preferred it that way, and, of course, so did I. When it had first been proposed that I take him as my husband, when I was at Caer Arthur, I'd baulked. Everyone knew that Urien, though a respected king of a wild and wind-swept kingdom, was old. Some marvelled he still drew breath at all.

Arthur – or rather Merlyn – had wanted *me* to wed *him*, I'd thought. All for the sake of securing Gwynedd's allegiance. And with Gwynedd, nearly all of Cymru. It had even been hoped that Demet would follow in Urien's wake, Óengus and his Blackshields at last brought into line. What a boon that would have been, for they were hardened warriors – far better as allies than as foes.

But I'd declared I'd marry Lancelot instead – young,

handsome, *virile* Lancelot.

And yet, look where the fates had led me: to Urien, after all.

An old man, yes, but once as fierce as any Blackshield from Éire, his reputation as guardian of this outpost well earned. Time, however, had reshaped the warrior, tempering his might into gentleness – a strength of a different kind.

"Morgan, *cariad*. How do you fare today?"

I smiled at his term of endearment. "I am well, husband. And you?"

He shrugged. "Ah, my limbs ache – as well they might. But I won't complain. At least I can still move them, aye?"

I knelt by his side, beginning to rub his calves and ankles – something he always appreciated. He often insisted my touch made him feel better.

"You've magic in your hands," he'd say.

As I worked, he asked after Mordred. "The boy – is he well this morning?"

I nodded. "Donwen took him. He's away with her."

A silence settled between us, amicable, as I continued to rub life back into his bones. He sat in a chair carved especially for him, a fine piece of craftsmanship, its arms and back adorned with battle shields he'd once carried into war. Woven among them were the swooping images of the birds he loved especially: the goshawk, the falcon, and the white-tailed eagle. They were so lifelike that sometimes I thought they might break free of the wood and take flight, becoming feather and flesh.

The chair was one of many finely made pieces in this stronghold – a dwelling *rich* in detail, with oak beams, woven tapestries decorating the walls, and bright woollen hangings too. And yet, when I'd first ridden up to it and gazed at its harsh exterior, I'd been wary of what I'd find, the reception I'd receive. What Agravaine said was true – fears ought to be faced, shown for the baseless things they could be.

"You've got some ulcers, husband," I said, examining his ankles more closely. "Here, around the bone. I have a salve that will help. I'll fetch it now."

As I made to rise, his hand stopped me. "The salve can wait, Morgan. Just…sit with me a while. Just…talk."

I nodded, rising anyway – but only to pull another chair close. Before us, the freshly stoked fire crackled in the brazier.

Another bout of easy silence followed. Then Urien spoke.

"You know I had another son?"

I started. Yes, I knew – Agravaine had talked of him as well as Urien. A dead son. But in truth, I'd forgotten, and that's what surprised me, that I *could* forget. All I saw was the son who lived. I was blinded by him, just as Arthur had been by Guinevere – when once, even if Arthur had yielded, I'd thought myself incapable of the same.

"Accolon," I said softly. "His name was Accolon."

Urien nodded. "My eldest son. Barely fifteen summers when the gods took him."

"A long time ago now," I murmured.

For a moment, Urien seemed bewildered. "Is it? Aye…I suppose you're right. And yet somehow, when you're old – at least, as old as I am – time becomes something other. A trick. That's how I think of it, now and then, you know? A cruel trick…but also kind. Do you understand, Morgan, that something can be both?"

"I…I think so," I replied. "Yes."

His smile turned wistful. "You've a wise head on those young shoulders."

"Husband," I began, unsure whether I deserved such a compliment – uncertain, even, if I deserved *him:* this kind and gentle man who'd given me so much, who'd never begrudged me anything since the day I came to him – not even his son, if he knew of us, though we tried to be discreet. But he hushed me and went on speaking.

"You are…a gift," he said. The sincerity in his voice brought a sting of tears to my eyes. "If only I were a younger man. If only it were I who could keep you satisfied."

Now I wouldn't be quieted. "Urien, it's *your* satisfaction I care about!"

It wasn't a lie, for after his quick acceptance of me, never questioning, never demanding to know why I'd run to him, I'd vowed it, that I would make his life as comfortable as possible, until the gods took him too.

I knew the healing power of plants. Alongside the salves that eased the swelling in his legs and any old wounds that continued to grumble, I'd made tinctures to lighten the heaviness in his bones, to soothe the cough that sometimes seized him, and to bring rest when sleep seemed to elude or trouble him.

A vow. An oath. They were the same thing – and I would not break it.

Urien, though, turned further into the past. "Accolon was like his mother," he said. "Aye, he had her fair hair, and the same green eyes, *light* green, the green of the ocean at dusk. A beautiful boy, as Rhianinfelt was a beautiful woman. But when he died – despite everything she did to keep him breathing, in whatever way she could – something in her died too. She was never the same. She never shone like before, and I was powerless to change it. Not I, nor her younger son, Agravaine."

"Agravaine has spoken of her," I said quietly. "He loved her deeply."

"*Everyone* loved Rhianinfelt," Urien murmured, "but she loved Accolon most of all. I wonder, though, if he had lived, if the winter chill hadn't turned to lung fever, what kind of king might he have become?" He looked towards the fire, the light catching in his worn eyes. "This land is the land of the people, but as you've come to discover, it can be harsh. You think me gentle – you've said as much – but there are times when gentleness has no place. And yet, when I am gone, you will be Queen of Gwynedd if you choose. There is gentleness in you, too, Morgan. But something else besides. Tell me – *will* you stay here? Will you rule?"

"Agravaine—"

"The strange thing is," Urien interrupted. "I've never been certain Agravaine *wants* to be king. And so, when you came, it gave me…an opportunity. I could test him."

"Test him?" I echoed, unsure of what he meant.

Wry laughter escaped him. "I am old, Morgan! Some say too old to rule. But there's life in me yet – though I know some grow impatient. Could it be… Was Agravaine among them? Waiting for me to die? Hoping for it?"

"No! He loves you!"

Urien laughed again, not unkindly. "I do not doubt that. But minds wander, and hearts are such complex things. When I asked you to marry me – because of who you are, Morgan, clever and beautiful, a jewel as I have said – not because it was Merlyn's wish, or Arthur's…I watched to see what Agravaine would do. Because if we wed, *you* – not he

– could rule after me. As would be your right."

I swallowed. "And what did you see? What was his reaction?"

"He didn't seem troubled at all."

"Good news!" I exclaimed. "For men's ambitions can be poisonous."

"You know that well?"

"I *have* lived at Caer Arthur," I said, arching a brow.

That earned another smile from Urien. "Indeed. Or perhaps he wasn't troubled because…he knew the two of you might rule together. Eventually."

And there it was, in his eyes – a knowledge. No matter how careful we thought we'd been, Urien knew I was his son's lover as well as his.

"Urien—"

He raised a gnarled hand. "I've never questioned you, nor will I. Nor judge. But I *will* say this – Accolon was open, easy to read. With Agravaine, it isn't always so."

"You think him dishonest? Your own son?"

"I think I've never truly known what he wants. And at times, I suspect *he* doesn't either. He is clever. Curious. Deeply devoted to this land…"

"*Fiercely* proud," I added.

"Aye, but he's also restless. Searching, always searching, and barely here before you came to stay. Can somewhere as small as Gwynedd truly hope to contain him?" He didn't wait for an answer. "It was he who wanted to go to Arthur and Guinevere's wedding, even though he knew what it would signal – our allegiance to Dumnonia, when we had no such intention. Not when Caer Arthur has become so devout."

"Arthur isn't a Christian."

"His wife is."

His wife. Those words still stung.

"He needs the Christians," I said, "to raise an army strong enough to face the Saxons."

"Words Merlyn told you?"

They were. Perhaps the only words of his I still believed.

"If Arthur's queen is Christian," Urien went on, "a woman who looks as she does, who is so...*beguiling*, it won't be long before others follow."

"She bewitched you too?"

I said it low, bitter – so bitter, he asked me to repeat it.

When I did, he shook his head. "It was only *you* who did that. Even so, we left his court quickly, Agravaine and I. We saw the tide turning. Powys and Glywysing have already followed Arthur. Soon, all of Cymru might. Even Ceredigion. Even Demet. *Unthinkable.* Once. And I'm angry about it, Morgan, but Agravaine...is angrier still."

"This land is yours," I said. "It doesn't have to follow. It can remain as it is."

"Because we are hidden? Tucked away from the world?"

I nodded. "Yes. In a way."

Urien's eyes – faded now, though once surely as green as the sea too, like Accolon's, like Rhianinfelt's – closed briefly, as if in pain. "If that were so, I'd be content. All I've ever wanted, all I've ever fought for, was to keep this kingdom safe, the memory of what the Romans did here leaving a scar still. Now the Christians may do the same...*infest* us. This is what Agravaine wants to prevent, what he will fight for. But fight against Arthur's might? One kingdom against many?" He paused. "Agravaine hides much, but his fury when we left Caer Arthur was unmistakable. It is *bigger* than Gwynedd. It festers too. How that fury will manifest – how his loyalty will – I cannot say. But loyal he is. That much I see now." Another pause. "Morgan, I've asked the gods for guidance, but they've been silent of late – strangely so. And I wonder, is it *only* him they guide now? If so, then perhaps I *should* let go, take my last breath, allow fate to play out as it will. Perhaps it lies in his power, and yours, rather than mine, to keep this land from every new scourge that threatens it. And in doing so, remind other kingdoms that it *is* possible – we can resist. We have history, a rich history. It should be cherished, not forsaken."

We'd been sitting apart, but at those words, I knelt before him again.

"I don't want you to die," I said, clutching his hands. "And neither does Agravaine. You must understand we are *both* loyal to you."

I reached up and touched his cheek, brushing my fingers over the grooves there.

"Do you love him?" he asked, his gaze steady on mine.

I faltered. "I…I love you," I said instead, which was again the truth.

"But do you love *him*?" he pressed.

"I… Why are you asking?"

His pale eyes darkened.

"Enjoy him, Morgan. In that way a young woman enjoys a young man. *Satiate* yourself – you have my blessing. But do not love *either* of us completely."

"Urien—"

"Morgan, let me speak. You must keep room in your heart for another."

"Another?"

He nodded. "For the one who needs it more than us."

"*Needs* it?" Then it struck me. "Urien!" I laughed, trying

for levity. "You're talking of Mordred. *Of course* I love him!"

Urien's gaze didn't waver. "If I've heard anything from the gods of late, *that* is what they've told me: a child needs their mother's love. Rhianinfelt may have loved Accolon best, but she loved Agravaine too. Without it…" He hesitated, as though choosing his words carefully. "Morgan, to be denied a mother's love completely is a terrible thing."

I swallowed hard. He knew who my mother was, but not that I'd been to Avalon. Not what had happened there. Not with Seren, Viviane, or Nimue.

"Grave words, Urien," I said, still trying to jest, for hadn't I made peace with Viviane's indifference? She may not have loved me, but others had.

That *had* to be enough.

Yet all that Seren had said, as children and when we were grown, still echoed in my dreams, sometimes night after night. Hadn't it *broken* me how Arthur's love had vanished so swiftly? Wasn't I *still* broken, despite Urien? Despite Agravaine? Despite even my own child? And wasn't the root of that brokenness *always* Viviane – the one who should have loved me most, but who'd cast me out instead? Treated me as something…repellent, even while using me.

And as for Urien – was it that brokenness he saw, besides the gentleness he spoke of? Was it all so obvious, despite my efforts to bury it?

My thoughts spiralled as I knelt there, silent before him, and Urien leaned forwards – not to take my hands this time, but to cradle my face in his palms.

"Do you see?" he whispered. "The damage it does to a child when a mother withholds her love. It isn't just terrible, *cariad*, or unnatural. It's…dangerous."

164

CHAPTER SEVENTEEN

On Ynys Môn, I learned so much.

And it was Agravaine who taught me.

The day we first crossed, the water was choppy, yet still he insisted we go.

"Morgan," he said, steadying me as I stepped into a small round coracle, two oars secured on either side of it, "don't worry so. Look how short the crossing is!"

And yet, despite his reassurances, my stomach fluttered. My hands trembled.

Ynys Môn.

Soon I'd set foot on it – leave one shore for another. And once there…would we truly be able to find our way back? Or would the mists, as they so often did, rise suddenly and enclose us, *trap* us among the dead, until death came for us too? Our cries mingling, indistinguishable, with those of long-past slaughter.

Such fancies, and I would scold myself for them, but the fear never quite faded, not *all* the times I visited.

But that first time… It was seared into memory. Both terrifying *and* magical.

An island, but once, Agravaine said, it had been a part of Gwynedd's mainland, until the sea rose and claimed it back. Cradled by salt winds, it was lusher than I'd anticipated – an *emerald* isle. The crown of Gwynedd, then and now.

Though the sea churned beneath us; the sky had lightened somewhat from its usual grey, and for that I was grateful – and for the light that drifted down towards us. I'd expected the whispers, the cries I would hear from this direction to grow louder as we neared, but they quieted instead, as though *appeased* by our presence.

Diseased land? That was always how it had been described to me – by Ector and Merlyn both, he who would also give a shiver at its mention. And yet, as I finally stood upon its soil, surrounded by the sea, I felt something else entirely.

Not dread.

Empowerment.

Agravaine took my hand. "Come," he said.

The shingle beneath our feet formed only a narrow strip, soon giving way to turf and grass, and then to trees rising tall around us – the mighty oak, revered by the druids, and the rowan too, which also grew here in abundance.

Rich land. That's how I redefined it as, with Agravaine explaining that we'd pass the remains of hillforts and settlements on the way to wherever he was leading me.

"Until the Romans came, until they…*butchered* here," he said, "there was such life on this island, Morgan. Even before the druids set their mark upon it. There were farmers and blacksmiths, weavers, potters, and carpenters – all of them called this island home. Bards, too, set foot here. Aneirin came. Taliesin did."

"Taliesin?" I gasped as we crunched over woodland.

"That's right," Agravaine said, oblivious to my awe.

For a moment, I couldn't understand why. Then I remembered: Agravaine – like Urien – believed Uther was my father, just as Merlyn claimed, and I'd never said otherwise. There was so much I kept secret. But like his father, Agravaine never pressed, so secrets they remained.

But *Taliesin* – who might have been my father instead – the mysterious Taliesin, whom no one I knew had ever met. What had he been like? If a bard, a poet, an archdruid, then surely gentle. Sensitive. A man attuned to both pain and beauty.

According to Agravaine, he'd walked this very land, not afraid of it like his successor, Merlyn. And now I was here as well.

"Do you know any songs Taliesin crafted?" I asked.

Agravaine, still pulling me along by the hand, stopped and turned to look at me.

"Why, yes, Morgan! He sang of my father, for one."

"Your father?" I echoed, astonished further. *My* possible father sang of my now husband? "What did he say, Agravaine? What words?"

"He called him a flame against foes. The bravest of men. A defender of our land."

"Urien," I breathed, joy rising in me at the thought – imagining him as he used to be, every bit as noble as Arthur. If only we'd been together then.

"Unlike many kings, my father never fought for greed," Agravaine continued. "Only for the survival and honour of his people. That's what's mattered most to him."

"You're very proud of him," I said.

Agravaine nodded, his dark hair even more tangled because of the salt-laced air. "Of course. We should *all* love our fathers."

"And yet…" I stopped myself, biting back words before they could sour the magic of the moment, of learning more about Taliesin especially. Like him, Merlyn was an archdruid, but a bard? I'd never heard of a single song he'd composed either.

"Morgan?" Agravaine asked, his brow furrowed. "And yet what?"

"And yet…" I swallowed, changing course. "Your father knows about us, Agravaine. He's given his blessing."

"I know," he said simply.

My voice lifted in surprise. "You know?"

"Yes, do you think I'd defy him so easily? Without care?"

"I… No, but…"

"Morgan, I'd never do that. As you say – I'm proud of him. I want to be a son he can be proud of too. To carry on his legacy."

"Fighting for Gwynedd to remain Gwynedd."

He nodded. "My father is *not* the petty king Arthur would make of him."

"Merlyn," I corrected, albeit softly.

Agravaine looked puzzled. "My lady?"

"When Arthur learned the truth of his lineage, he only ever expected to rule Dumnonia. It was Merlyn who told him he must be High King."

There was a flash of something in his eyes when I said that – hatred, perhaps. The man before me was certainly passionate, but how deep was that other well?

"Merlyn," he spat. "Arthur is High King because one man said so. *One man.*"

There was so much I wanted to say, to remind him that, yes, while the Saxons might seem like a distant threat here in the far west, they were real enough. That though the raiders from Éire had long been a danger – and Urien and Agravaine had fought them off time and again – the Saxons *would* come too. Eventually. They wouldn't stop until all of

Britannia was theirs. That was their aim. Even Kernow. Even Caledonia. They were as stubborn as those they sought to conquer.

But more than any of it, I wanted to ask what truly burned behind his eyes.

Do you feel for me as I feel for you? Do you…love me? After Urien – for his death was a truth to face as well – *would you be my king? Would you rule beside me? Or would you seek to usurp me, take the crown, but only for yourself?*

My thoughts, such as they were, wouldn't stop, but tumbled over each other.

What do you *plan for the future, Agravaine? You who want to keep your world the same in one that is ever changing. I want that too! Though I didn't carve the sigil on my head, it proves that. I believe what you believe. I fight for what you fight for.*

You wouldn't betray me. Would you?

Another betrayal…

Perhaps I might have summoned the courage to speak all this – alone as we were on Ynys Môn – but he'd turned again, was tugging me along once more, as though that flicker of hatred had never been. He was excited again. It was a *boyish* excitement, though he was a man full grown, inciting a girlish excitement in me.

We trampled through the woods. If there were foxes nearby, or boar, or even wolves, they kept their distance, though I was certain I heard the scuffle of such creatures in the undergrowth, felt their curious eyes upon us before they slunk back to their dens. At times, the canopy overhead grew so thick it turned day to night. Then suddenly – light again. Dappled, golden light filtering through.

We'd entered a clearing, a grove I recognised it as, again thanks to Ector and all he'd taught Arthur and I as children.

A place where the veil was always thin.

A carpet of soft moss covered the ground, and ivy curled up the trunks of the trees that surrounded us, tangled with ancient vines – twisted and gnarled.

It was sacred. I could *feel* how sacred, a place where the druids had worshipped.

My gaze swept over it all, then stopped – held fast by what stood at the centre of it: a flat-topped stone, resting atop two upright slabs. An altar, stained dark in places.

Blood?

Another place of sacrifice?

Agravaine had released my hand. He stood beside me, waiting for me to speak.

At last, I did.

"You're a druid?" I asked.

To which I sensed rather than saw the smile that crept across his face.

"Morgan, just like you, I am *many* things."

It was the blood of beasts, Agravaine assured me – creatures native to the island: foxes, wolves, hares…but most often, ravens.

"Why?" I asked, feeling as green, as new to all this, as I had when I'd first set foot in Caer Arthur. "Why them?"

"You know of the Morrigan?"

I nodded. I did.

"She favours the form of a raven because of what the raven is. Ah, Morgan, they are such creatures! They dwell on the borders between life and death, the known and unknown. Ravens can move *between* worlds. They bear messages too."

"So…this is where you commune with the Otherworld?" Something the more learned at Avalon also sought to do – with Annwn, they called it.

"With the *gods* in that Otherworld, Morgan."

"And…what have they told you?"

"They told me about you."

I started. "*Me?*"

"That you are significant. That you have power."

I shook my head. "I don't."

But Agravaine only smiled, undeterred. "Morgan, you can *see*. That day on the cliff, you knew what had happened without me needing to say it further."

"I *think* I saw," I amended. "It could have been imagination."

"Your imagination *is* your power. And now we must use it. We must understand what the gods meant by their message – how you can help to achieve a dream."

"A dream?" *His* dream? Was that why he was so interested in me – because of what the gods had told him? The *only* reason?

If I had any doubts – as I *always* did – they were swept away by what he did next.

Still in the grove, which others had worshipped at before him, doing as he did, divining sacred messages, he reached out, and swept me off my feet.

As he swung me round, there was such radiance on his face, such joy, that I couldn't help but feel it too. I wanted to soak it in, for it to banish all else within me.

"You're here," he said, beaming. "You're here!"

In that moment, I felt sacred too. As though I were a

goddess. *His* goddess, when once I'd thought I was Arthur's. I'd been wrong, but perhaps this – *this* was right.

"I will teach you, Morgan," he said, now smothering my face with kisses. "I will teach you *everything*."

"When?" I said, as breathless as him.

"Now! We begin now. And then…then we'll see what messages the gods bring next. But, Morgan the Fay, know this: it is *you* who will keep the old ways alive. The Great Mother works through you. *You* are her vessel. The highest priestess of all."

I'd felt empowered simply by stepping foot on Ynys Môn, but at his words – his conviction, how absolute it was – I was *infused* with yet more power. It was such a strange feeling, when powerlessness had defined me so much of late.

Seren – she'd been a sacrifice too. It was just as I'd thought before, my slaughter of her had driven me here. Forced me to come. The gods never rested, were always at work. Plotting. Guiding. Pushing. And I should believe in them, as Agravaine did.

His gods, though he hadn't yet named them.

I was here with him for a reason. I was as vital to the future of Britannia – or perhaps I too should call it Prydain – as Arthur. *More* so, even. I was the balance needed, for with Guinevere as High Queen, the scales could tip too far.

To be *integral* – that notion made me as giddy as when Agravaine had spun me round and round. As heady as apple wine; I was perhaps…drunk on it.

But above all, I wanted to learn. To see more. To commune with the gods as Agravaine did, as Merlyn would have us believe he could. They were darker paths, undeniably, far removed from the gentle ways that Priscilla cherished, and those that Avalon was supposed to. A *dual* path, but one could inform the other.

Was that my purpose here? To tread where light and shadow met?

To learn…*everything?*

Agravaine intended to find out.

For both of us.

CHAPTER EIGHTEEN

The wheel was turning quickly. Warm days and rain-soaked nights, hours and minutes blurring. It was not an empty time, though, but filled with meaning.

Agravaine, true to his word, taught me diligently, a man more learned than I had realised, with a depth that continued to surprise me. His knowledge of plants and herbs surpassed that of any wise woman in the village – perhaps even Priscilla.

Where she'd been reluctant to go – teaching me the darker side of the Great Mother's bounty, the realm of nature's killers: belladonna, hemlock, henbane, and foxglove – Agravaine was not. I'd used poisons before, but only for good. Priscilla had made me swear it, though why she thought I needed to had always baffled me. The only reason I'd *ever* wanted to learn of such things was to ease the pain of those left behind on the battlefield – the ones death passed by, though they begged for it.

Unlike Priscilla, Agravaine treated all plants with equal reverence. He *trusted* me with them. And perhaps that was the difference: a trust that gave me confidence.

So *much* confidence.

The confidence to learn things I'd only touched on in Avalon – rituals.

We *both* slaughtered hares, foxes, ravens, our hands and

the altar slick with blood as animals' eyes glazed quickly over. We chose their bones with care, guided by some instinct I hadn't known I possessed, then consigned the rest to earth or fire.

With those bones, Agravaine would chant in an archaic tongue I could not comprehend, just as Nimue had done through Viviane on that Beltane night on the Tor. Or perhaps…better to say it was *dissimilar*. These words sounded harsher, syllables scraping the air like dry leaves over stone. He told me it was a language preserved on scrolls I had yet to see – scrolls hidden deep within the stronghold.

He taught me what to seek in the bones, the curve of them, the cracks that split their length, scorch marks or strange patterns like sigils burned into their surface – each one a possible message from the gods. At times we took the organs as well, peeling them from bodies still warm with departing life, studying their hue, their texture, the twists and swellings, a warning in every deformation.

Different deities were entreated – Taranis, the god of thunder and storms; the Morrigan, of course, she who was also the raven; and Liⵧr, god of the sea, who could ferry you through the mists into other realms – letting you die a thousand small deaths along the way, only to bring you back again. It was he, I learned at last, whom Agravaine favoured most. Gwyn ap Nudd was another – Lord of the Wild Hunt, a guardian of the shadowed boundaries between worlds.

I was enthralled by it all, but most of all by the ancient tongue, trying to learn it: *brun* for power, *tagne* for fire, *vasir* for prophecy and *thar'gulenn* for come to us.

"Deaun Môrath Ruven Talmaris, dareth gulenn traen nuveth," Agravaine would say, lifting an offering high – an animal struggling in his grasp, sensing its doom. *God of the*

Sea, King of the Ocean, guide us through the mists. That was the meaning of his words, and I would echo them after him, shaping my breath to match his cadence, his inflection – the tongue of the Briton, Cymru, and Éire woven into one.

Nuvren was the sacred grove. *Alduwen* the Otherworld. It was all written, Agravaine said, and he would teach me to read it. He would show me where the scrolls were kept, the hidden chamber down a long dark corridor that could be mine as well as his. A place to continue our workings of magic, for Ynys Môn – though close to the mainland – was not always within reach. Not even in summer.

"Nothing will stop us from understanding what the gods want," Agravaine declared. "What our purpose is – and how we may fulfil it. We are a small kingdom, but sometimes, Morgan, the smallest kingdom can shatter an empire of giants."

An empire of giants? *Arthur* stood at the helm of that empire, as Agravaine called it. Whatever had passed between us, I didn't want any harm to befall him.

Did I?

Again, I had to ask myself what it was I *truly* wanted. If Arthur could betray me, could he not also betray an entire country? Yes, he would save it from the Saxons, but only to deliver it into Christian hands – they who would *silently* devour us.

Arthur… In the wake of Agravaine, he was indeed beginning to fade from my mind, for I was secretly beseeching the gods for something too: to consign him to some deep, unreachable hollow within me. I asked this for two reasons – so I wouldn't have to feel the ache of his betrayal any longer, but also if the gods *did* demand of me – something difficult, given our past – I might be able to do it.

For it was the gods, not man, who held the greater purpose. A truth I repeated to myself until it was etched into me as deeply as it was into Agravaine.

More time passed. Beltane was nearly upon us – the festival that heralded the beginning of summer – when I would see a Gwynedd transformed. I was excited about it. Everyone was. The stronghold buzzed with talk and preparations.

Urien wouldn't attend the hill fires, though many would gladly carry him there if he wished it, his own son among them. But it was the smoke that deterred him. It would aggravate his cough, and no salve then able to soothe it, at least not straight away.

But I had his blessing to attend, to experience it fully.

The day before the fires was all sunshine. I was *supposed* to be with Mordred. I'd promised myself I would be, especially after what Urien had said. More and more, I took him from Teg, trying to form an attachment, doing my *utmost*. He was becoming so bonny, everyone said so. A lusty child, Teg called him. Yet in my arms, he'd wiggle still, was restless, discontent, as if the sight of me, the smell of me – *everything* about me – unsettled him every bit as much as he unsettled me.

I'd persevere, though. "There, there," I'd soothe, just as Teg did. "If you're hungry, I'll fetch you some pap. If you're sleepy, sleep. But don't fuss like you do. I know! We'll go for a walk. Yes, let's do that – take the air. Come little one – *Mordred*."

His name always caught in my throat. It had been *her* name for him – Nimue's – and the Fay's too. Perhaps…perhaps it would be easier if I changed it. To what, though? Medraut? Similar, but just different enough. I tried it. Even told Teg of my intention. She'd only looked at me strangely and then, not even an hour or so later, I heard her call him *Mordred* again – whether deliberately or not, I didn't know.

So today was meant for mother and son. Another chance. But then Agravaine knocked at my chamber door and begged me to come riding.

"My son," I said. "I was meant to be with him."

"You've told him that?" Agravaine asked. As I frowned, he laughed. "Morgan, even if you did – he is but a baby! He won't know. He has his nurse, doesn't he? Teg. Give him to her. Come on – it's too fine a day to waste."

Soft, subtle, persuasive – it was as though he cast a spell with his words.

And so, once again, it was Teg, not me, who Mordred found comfort with. And I – I raced across bright meadows with Agravaine, chasing him down, surging past on Taran, only for him and his steed to thunder beside me, fierce with intent, as though a horde of Saxons were at his heels. Them, or Arthur's men. I imagined that, too.

There was a purpose to our ride today, though, beyond pleasure. We were hunting. My bow and arrows were slung across my back, and Agravaine's spear was at his side. Tonight marked the traditional night of darkness before the blazing fires of Beltane – a night of restraint, of reflection, of sitting with shadows. But tomorrow, before we climbed the hills, there'd be feasting, and it fell to us to provide the boar.

Ahead lay woodland, the place we'd been racing towards, our horses coming to a swift halt just before we crossed into the trees.

I'd never hunted like this before, so Agravaine called out to me. "Stay close."

"I will," I replied, catching the gleam in his eyes and feeling it spark in me too.

"And arrows at the ready," he added, moving ahead.

The forest closed around us, the trees as gnarled as Urien's hands, thick with green moss that cloaked their bark. All too soon, the blue sky was gone, along with its warmth, a damp chill finding its way into my bones instead. It was quiet – so still I could scarcely believe *anything* lived within it. Even the birds withheld their song.

We rode deeper, our horses stepping carefully through the undergrowth, wary of roots that might seize a hoof. Was this truly the best place to hunt boar, I wondered? The wood was too dense. Too cramped.

"Agravaine…" I began, my voice edged with doubt. I was ready to challenge him – there were other forests, less tangled than this, that were more bountiful, surely. Because this place was not merely untouched, it was…forbidden.

Yet Agravaine pressed on.

He had schooled me in the hunt – how we must move in silence, he and his steed, Taran and I. How to breathe lightly, keep watch in all directions, and brace for the charge. Breathing lightly was no effort for me; I was scarcely breathing at all, the force that gave life to my limbs ebbing. I felt faint because of it, gripping the reins tighter. If there was such a thing as a sacred grove, this was its contrary – not a place of offering, like the cliff, but a place where deaths had taken root nonetheless.

A place of slaughter.

Human slaughter.

My breath caught.

179

The Romans and the Druids again? Those who never reached Ynys Môn, who were cut down before they could? The children of druids, the frail, the seeresses…

So much blood. So much loss.

It was getting easier to see it now. To feel it.

To take it into myself.

That Fay-sense Agravaine claimed I possessed was stirring, rising unchecked. It was he who'd drawn it out in me, yet as we continued, he still seemed unaware.

Did he even…*know*?

And if he didn't, while I did, was his power truly so great?

Unlike Ynys Môn, which called to us, this place didn't. It wanted no one. The grief here – it was simply too vast to surrender, too heavy to share.

We had to turn around. Leave.

If we stayed, we would choke on it. *I* would.

My hands, tight on the reins just moments before, loosened.

My body, once rigid, slumped.

A darkness crept into the edges of my sight – slow and deliberate. The sorrow here wasn't merely felt, it was…known. Not something to fear, I began to realise, but to recognise instead. Ah, yes…it was the ache I carried too, the loss that shaped me.

Unlike so many moments in my life, there were no whispers. No cries. No voices calling my name – neither Morgan nor Morgana. Yet I was slipping from my horse.

Even if no arms reached to catch me, I would find them, whoever lingered here. And when I did, I would tell them: *I'm one of you.*

A kindred spirit.

Capable of grieving forever too.

"Morgan!"

A voice – *at last*. Male, panicked.

"Morgan, stay upright. Your bow! Your arrow – shoot!"

Shoot?

At what? You couldn't kill ghosts. They were already dead.

"Shoot, Morgan!'

The man – Agravaine, *of course* it was Agravaine – called out again, but it was my horse, rearing and whinnying in terror, that had more effect.

I had to shoot.

Bow and arrow.

But at what?

Something was coming – rushing straight at me. The forest was alive after all.

Taran had reared, and I'd let go of the reins. I wasn't just slipping, I was falling. I hit the ground with a brutal thud. In the same moment, I heard something else, the deep grunts of a wild beast. The pounding of hooves, thundering towards me.

Closer.

Closer.

I cried out as I landed, as a series of small fires erupted across my body. The beast was nearly upon me. I couldn't reach my bow and arrow – not in time.

Agravaine was my only hope.

Why hadn't he thrown his spear? Was it still strapped to his side?

This beast – it would make a feast of me, not the other way around!

I didn't want to do it – to join the dead in grief – even if moments before, I'd felt I belonged among them, could imagine, if not see, the chasm I'd fall into, and how endless that fall would be, one without cease. Perhaps it was what I deserved, to fall like that, for what I was, for what I'd become. A murderer. A creature of shadow, when I should have been light. But the light had been stolen from me. *Arthur* had taken it – he, who had so much of his own. And there it was again: a flash of hatred. Not for him, though I willed it to be, but for her, who'd taken from me too. Guinevere.

Artful, conniving, *Christian* Guinevere.

Every drop of bitterness, of resentment, of long-simmering loathing surged like fire too. And I vowed – this time, it would not fade. Like this cursed place, it would live.

Even if hidden.

It would live!

The fury was enough to galvanise me.

No one was going to save me but myself.

Pain lanced through my arms, my back, and my legs as I moved. But move I did. Swiftly. *Lightning* quick – my hands already reaching behind me.

Quickly!

Quickly!

Or it would be too late.

I swung the bow forwards, braced my heels against the earth, drew the string, notched the arrow – *shot*.

Hoping.

Praying.

Calling on the gods, if not Agravaine.

Help me!

The arrow flew, the creature no longer grunting, but releasing a full-throated squeal. Still running, though, but with an arrow straight between its eyes.

As I pushed back further, my hands scrabbling in the dirt, the creature landed just shy of me – barely a hair's breadth between us. Laughter spilled from behind me, and I whipped my head around as quickly as I'd thrown my body aside.

Agravaine stood there, not having shifted so much as a toe.

"I knew you could do it," he said, the words as smooth as a blade's edge. "I've told you – you're special. You have a destiny to fulfil. The gods won't let you die."

CHAPTER NINETEEN

Since my arrival in Gwynedd, I'd kept mainly to the stronghold I now called home. There was no bustling village at its foot, no market stalls or children laughing and running as there had been at Caer Arthur. My days passed in the company of Urien, Agravaine, Teg, Mordred, and the ever-busy servants who fetched and carried. At times, I thought there *were* no other people nearby. But Beltane proved me wrong.

At midday, they came – villagers from all around. Men, women, and children, all clad in linens dyed green and brown, their faces, arms, and legs daubed with green as well – plant dyes made from nettle or crushed leaves, then smeared in swirls or handprints across their skin. Some were crowned with oak leaf laurels, others were adorned with stag's antlers. There was not just one May King and Queen, but many.

We're all *Kings and Queens of the May*, Agravaine had told me. That was how it was done here, where the day was still called by its older name, *Calan Mai*. Agravaine was one who wore the antlers, joining the throngs who climbed the highest cliff, Craig y Gwaed, to prepare the fires.

I stood at the window of Urien's chamber, watching it all unfold with a mix of awe and quiet longing. Laughter and music drifted up on the breeze, full of life and anticipation. For a time, I let it fill me, and then I turned away – to Urien.

I'd returned from the hunt to find him unwell. His cough – always troublesome – had deepened. A man once broad-shouldered and strong, with long hair and a thick beard, was now frail, growing weaker with every moon since I'd come here, still not a full turn of the wheel. I'd spent the night with him rather than alone in my chamber or with Agravaine, had treated him with all the usual tinctures, but nothing had helped.

I so wanted to attend Beltane. To be queen to Agravaine's king, if only for one night. To pretend it was us, *just us*, who ruled here in Gwynedd, then swiftly berating myself for the thought. I didn't wish Urien ill – never that. But I couldn't help wondering when the inevitable would come. And if I ever wished for it to hasten, it was only for his sake – for the pain that wracked him, and my own frustration when I *couldn't* ease it. I was not black enough in my heart to desire it for selfish reasons. Yet...*something* inside me was shifting. And I knew not in which direction.

I loved Urien, but as yet another father rather than a husband. How could I, with good conscience, leave him today, or tonight, even if others could care for him?

I felt...responsible. More for him than for my own child, ironically. But Mordred...he was happier with Teg, that's how I always justified it, whereas Urien, when he was like this – vulnerable – wanted *me* close.

I'd been denied a true Beltane – twice.

I didn't want to be denied it again.

So as I sat with Urien, holding his hand or smoothing his brow, I resolved to go through with a plan already devised. The daytime festivities could wait; I didn't need to be there.

Mordred was with Teg – she'd dressed him in shades of green and had also placed a leafy crown of his own on his head, his chubby hands immediately reaching up to yank it off, but she'd persisted, placing it back there.

"You're a prince," she'd told him with a smile. "You must act like one."

On hearing it, I'd smiled too. He was a prince indeed; either way, I'd ensured it. A *handsome* prince, it couldn't be denied. That tingling in me – was it pride?

Urien was slumped in his carved chair, eyes half-closed, and lips moving faintly.

I leaned closer. "What is it you say?"

I think it was *thank you*, followed by *sorry*.

I patted his hand. "There's no need for apologies, husband."

"Please."

On that occasion, I heard him clearly.

I nodded, for he knew I'd help as much as I could. I'd administer a draught to bring sleep – *deep* sleep. When I made it, I'd measured the dose with care, enough to quiet his aches almost completely, to douse the fire in his lungs.

All I wanted was for him to rest.

In the chamber Agravaine had shown me, the one filled with scrolls, I'd begun to gather herbs and plants. Already, it was a finer collection than Priscilla ever kept at the villa. Part of me longed to show it to her, to have her by my side to advise me, as Agravaine now did, but I wished in vain. She was lost to me, as were all at Caer Arthur, and Avalon too. No one knew whether I was dead or alive. I'd insisted on it.

For now.

There was no need to leave Urien again, no need to

return to my chamber as the tincture was already in my pocket.

I released his hands, crossed to the table, and poured water from a jug into a cup. Handling the tincture with due reverence, I carefully broke the seal and let a measured amount drip into the water – a dark, bitter distillation of hembane, as thick as resin. Finally, I stirred in honey to make it at least a little more palatable.

I hadn't always been so cautious. I remembered a Beltane past, when it was Ector and Priscilla I'd meant to lull into sleep. And sleep they had – and woken again – but even now I shuddered at the risk I'd taken. It was so new to me then, all of this, guided more by instinct than knowledge. That night had ended in a way I hadn't foreseen, but it could have been worse, far worse. I'd been so desperate to be with Arthur…but desperate enough to risk everything? Other lives even – *blessed* lives?

Urien. I must think only of Urien. His comfort. *Never* his harm.

This was a moderate dose, stronger than the draught I'd once brewed from poppy seed for my foster parents, perhaps the strongest I'd dared to make so far.

I returned to him and held the cup to his lips.

"Here," I said. "Drink this."

He did, obedient as a child. Just as trusting. *'There's magic in your hands,'* he'd said that to me more than once, calling me *cariad,* his beloved, and I'd laugh, chide him gently. But now, with Agravaine and all he was teaching me, I could believe it.

With the tincture gone, I helped Urien to rise. He leaned more heavily than I'd expected, his limbs already slackening. At the bed, I eased him down onto the pellet, then drew a light cover over him, adjusting the bolster behind the grey of his head.

Then I waited.

Soon enough, his eyes drifted shut and his breathing slowed. Became slower still. The lines of his face softened as all tension faded. Peaceful, but...too still?

I leaned in, listening. Watching. His chest was barely moving.

I touched his skin, it was damp and cool, then pressed two fingers to his throat. There was a pulse, surely? A flicker, a beat. Faint, yes, but there.

"Urien?" I said, as if he could hear me.

I knelt, placing my ear at his chest, listening for breath. I hadn't guessed the ratios when making the tincture, I'd been precise. Careful. So careful.

"Urien," I said again, my voice now holding a tremble, and then, just as my own blood roared in my ears with panic, he reacted. He snorted, then belched, and in doing so, seemed to clear something. His breathing steadied, falling into an easier rhythm. There was even a smile on his lips, as though he was dreaming of his own Beltane, one from long, long ago, his first even, when he was the young stag.

With a sigh of relief, I climbed back to my feet. He'd be all right. For *hours*, he'd be all right, though I'd fetch someone to sit with him until I returned.

I was now free to prepare myself.

If Agravaine was the stag – the Horned God – then I would wear the face of the Goddess for him. Cast a spell if I could, by moonlight, so that – unlike with Arthur – he would never look away, never set me aside.

His Queen.

Tonight.

And always.

Smoke and fire, the pounding of drums, and above us the sky – black as jet, yet with a scattering of stars. The children had long since been taken home, and those with old bones had slipped away too, returning to their hearths. Just as Arthur and I once had, in the days with Priscilla and Ector – hurried off before the night grew too wild.

But there was no Priscilla and Ector now. No Arthur. No Viviane. No Nimue.

No one left to stop me, to hold me back from tasting all the glories Beltane had to offer – the sheer magnificence of it, the exultant pulses that matched my own.

Mead sweeter than ever flowed past my lips and down my chin, poured by a stranger, straight into my mouth. I laughed as the man claimed my lips next, his tongue pressing eagerly between my teeth, his hands roaming freely.

There was no hierarchy tonight. No one was off limits – not if you wanted them, and they wanted you. It was a night for *living*; death held no place here. And though I'd once broken that rule – however unwittingly – I need not fear it happening again. I was home. Where I longed to be. With those I longed for too.

I was *heady* with happiness, laughing as the man kissing and touching me grew more ardent, until at last, I pushed him away – gently – seeking the one I'd come for.

More hands reached for me as I crossed the clifftop, all strangers, yet I felt at ease among them. Smiles were exchanged, if not kisses, and bursts of laughter too.

A woman approached me then, stroked my hair and gazed into my eyes. She reminded me of the Fay woman who'd done the same, the one who had cradled me while another carved the sigil into my brow. A beautiful woman.

"Bendithion," she now whispered – *blessings,* in her native tongue.

"Bendithion," I replied, before her mouth was on mine.

I was tempted to let her kiss me further, to taste her, *devour* her, my smile wide, even as she kissed me, as wide as hers, but it was him I truly ached for.

Agravaine.

Only he could satisfy me this night, so I left her behind and carried on.

There were bodies everywhere! Naked, most of them, their clothes long since discarded. Dark shapes that writhed and rutted, the air thick with unbridled joy.

This was love in its rawest form, open and honest. Many babies would be sired tonight, blessings from Brigid herself. Not a sin. Never a sin. Curse the Christians for branding it so, for *condemning* our ways only to replace them with what? Their so-called virtue? With rules so rigid that joy itself might perish – for women especially, not only ruled over, but restrained entirely.

How could *anyone* deny the presence of one such as Brigid on a night like this? Or the Great Mother? They were here, at the centre of us all.

Beltane would not be banished, as the Christians willed – it would endure. A night that bound our people together – not only in body, but in heart and soul.

Agravaine was still lost to me. Was he even searching for me, as I searched for him? If not, I found it hard to mind, too caught up in rapture, wondering which deity had taken up residence within me. Arianrhod perhaps, rather than Brigid. It would be fitting, for as Caireann had told me, she was the goddess of the stars, the moon, and of fate – all present tonight. The embodiment of the feminine, and of feminine *power*.

My feet quickened until I was running, past more heaving bodies, laughing women and men who grunted like the boar I'd slain in that strange woodland just the day before. Soon – all too soon – they were behind me, the fires also.

I ran until there was only me, the stars, the moon, and the darkness. They urged me on, guiding my steps, until other cries rose ahead – those from Ynys Môn.

How I wanted to ease them, this night of all nights, as I'd eased Urien.

Hush, I told them. *Hush, I'm coming. Please don't cry anymore.*

If it was Arianrhod that lived within me tonight, she'd awakened the mother in me, the most divinely feminine of all, the caretaker. For hadn't I always been that? At least with Arthur. As children, I'd mothered him – there by his side whenever he was upset, angry, or afraid, holding him close and murmuring words of comfort. Yet my own child – *our* child, as I was growing more certain of it – found solace only in Teg. Still, I knew I was capable of it, Arthur had proven that. And tonight, I could prove it again, with the spirits – the many spirits – that haunted the isle still.

"Hush," I whispered again. "I'm here. I'm…yours."

Tonight, they moved within me too.

I was the champion of the dead, the slaughtered, the banished. Morgan the Fay. The defender of those deemed savages. *Black Morgan.*

191

I'd hated that name when Seren first spoke it, but now, I *grew* into it, with every passing moment, my breath turning ragged, thick with the realisation. The blackness, the dark, the night, the shadows – all the things I'd once feared, I feared no longer.

For if I was champion of those others, if I nurtured them, then they nurtured me.

Soon, I'd reach the cliff's edge. If I didn't stop, if I kept this pace, I'd plunge over it – tumble past the rocky outcrops into the churning sea. A sea that waited for someone – *anyone* – to wander too far from the fires, drunk on lust and mead.

Would I misjudge it too?

I could barely see what lay ahead, and so I should stop.

Or – I could do as Agravaine had in the woods yesterday and let the gods decide.

If they spared me, it would be further proof I had purpose. Proof that the night – and Agravaine – were meant to nurture me further.

More laughter – mine. A sound *rich* with pleasure, a burst of it that drowned out any lingering cries, from behind me, or from Ynys Môn.

I'd come to Gwynedd, *hidden* in Gwynedd, and being here had changed me. I would never again be that girl from the valley, deep in the woods, innocent of so much – the one who rode to Caer Uther in Merlyn's shadow. A girl so desperate for recognition from her birth mother she'd gone to Avalon to force a meeting, only to stir yet more turmoil. Nor was I merely someone's lover, to be cherished or cast aside – someone who stood at the edge of the battlefield because she'd been told to.

She'd be told no more.

Neither would she always hide. The Queen of Gwynedd. She who should have been High Queen. And her son – he who should have been High King.

After Arthur…

When Arthur fell…

In battle – for there were *many* battles to come.

No more laughter.

My feet skidded to a halt – just in time. The cliff edge was close – *too* close. Stones crumbled beneath me, breaking free from the rock face. But instead of stepping back, I stayed there, teetering as I was, listening to the sea.

And then, after a few breathless moments, I cast my hands wide.

I *roared*, not at the sea, but with it – felt it churn, not below me, but inside me. A bird swept past, low and fast, just as one had before when I'd stood here with Agravaine, but this one was as black as the night itself. It was a raven, of course.

She who comes from the sea was the meaning of my name. A child born on an isle, the most sacred of all. And yet, Avalon was something else besides. A place of lies, of deceit, of fear. It wasn't as sacred as here. Not in this moment.

Liⓧr was of the sea. Tonight, I could be his goddess too – commanding the waves, like he did. For hadn't the Fay foretold it? That for me, the waters would part.

Such was my power.

I had only to imagine – and believe.

With arms still outstretched, I did as I'd learned to do at Avalon, and breathed. Inhaled through my nose. Exhaled through my mouth. Again – deeper this time – drawing air into the pit of my belly. Exhaling slower, for longer. Breath after breath, as stones continued to crumble at my feet, the cliff as eager for sacrifice as the water. And I *would* feed it, but with life not death, as befitting Beltane.

My hands clenched as I breathed, as though I held the power of the sea itself within them – its hunger thrumming in my palms. But I felt too how ready it was to feed me in return. When I exhaled, I drove it back. When I inhaled, I drew it forwards. Commanding the tide– in and out, in and out. Each time, it retreated further. Each time, it crashed back harder, my body swaying to and fro in rhythm with it.

And the spirits, I commanded them too.

To hush.

To quiet now.

To rest.

Finally.

They were *all* at my behest.

The tide drew back, *beyond* Ynys Môn – no coracle needed now to reach it. Then it surged forwards, flooding the isle, *cleansing* it.

To commune with the gods. To commune with nature. I was learning both.

It was not only the sea I commanded, but the sky too, if I wished. At a whisper, the rain would come, pouring as though a vein had been slashed. Thunder would answer like warring gods, their fury and all their might colliding. I could split the night with lightning, just as the thorn was once split – a jagged wound unable to heal. Earth, water, air, and fire – Morgan the Fay was born of them all.

They bowed to me when men would not.

"Morgan! Morgan, what are you doing?"

If I'd been entranced, caught up, the voice shattered it – broke the spell I'd been weaving, swept away the power I held, *old* power, like that poured into Excalibur.

My head turned towards the sound, and my foot slipped. More stones gave way – larger ones now, a ledge collapsing.

Falling.

Was I falling?

And if so, the sea below, would it welcome me? Buoy me? Carry me to safety?

Preserve me?

Was this real? Or dreamwork? Or worse…mere fancy. Imagination *was* a power, but it could be a curse, sometimes for you, sometimes against.

It was Agravaine who'd called my name, searching for me after all – and now he'd found me. As I fell, I wondered if he would only watch, as he had in the woods when the boar charged from the undergrowth. Trusting in the gods.

Too much trust.

Was there such a thing?

I'd roared before, but now I screamed, high and piercing. My arms flailed at my sides – just arms now, no longer instruments of power.

I slipped further. The ground was gone. There was *nothing* to cradle me. Nothing to save me. The gods were laughing again.

"I've got you. I've got you, Morgan. Stop! Don't struggle."

I was still falling – but backwards – strong arms locked around my waist.

Agravaine and I thudded to the ground, his grip like iron as he dragged us back to solid ground. He hadn't stood by, he'd saved me. So…his faith, it was not absolute?

When it was safe, he released me and turned me round to face him.

"Morgan, what were you doing? You could have died!"

"I was…" My voice faltered. What could I say? The truth? "I was at one with the sea," I said, exhilarated, unable, in that moment, to speak anything *but* the truth. "With the night, with the stars, the gods and goddesses, every one of them. Agravaine, I *commanded* the night and all in it! I *was* the elements."

"The elements?" he echoed, and excitement sparked in his eyes too, a wonder that I relished, and something else besides…something I couldn't quite define, or perhaps…didn't want to. But something, or *someone* – a ghost, perhaps – refused to let me dwell in ignorance. They wanted me to know *exactly* what it was.

A memory that wasn't mine seized me just as Agravaine had.

A vision. A *seeing*.

Another woman had stood here, on this very spot, watching as sacrifice after sacrifice had taken place. Rhianinfelt. Agravaine's mother. Fair-haired, with light eyes. Beautiful, and desperate too, trying to save her eldest son stricken with an illness no wise woman could cure, so she'd begged the gods instead, offered other children in his place, again and again, believing that with each sacrifice her own might be spared. A terrible act. Those cries I'd heard weren't just the slaughtered of Ynys Môn, they were the cries of the bereaved. But that wasn't what Rhianinfelt wanted me to understand. There was no guilt in her because of what she'd done. What she wanted me to know was *why* she'd been so desperate.

Accolon had been good. Like his father, he would have made a fine king. She knew that, could map it out, see it. But the son she bore after Accolon, Agravaine – yes, she loved him, Urien had been right about that – yet she couldn't read him, not the way she could read Accolon. She couldn't be...*sure* of him. What he might...*do*.

She sensed it even then – a downfall.

Because of him.

And with that downfall the death of everything.

As more and more mothers begged her to spare their children, she turned away, finally realising that no matter what she did, it was all in vain.

The gods took Accolon, and whatever this world would become without one such as him, she wouldn't stay to see it. She tumbled from the cliff edge, too.

All this passed through me as Agravaine took my hands, kissing them with such fervour before reaching inside his jerkin. If he had worn the antlers, they were gone now – torn away by whom in the throes of ecstasy?

"Close your eyes," he said.

"What is it?" I asked, feeling him sweep my hair aside, then move his hands to the back of my neck, fear stirring, just for a moment, at the intent behind them. Then something cold touched my skin. A chain. A clasp. A pendant.

When he was done, I reached up. "What is it?" I asked again.

"A moonstone," he said.

"A moonstone?"

I'd always loved them, ever since Anwyn, my childhood friend, had come to visit wearing one, a precious heirloom from her mother. Arthur knew how much I loved them, and promised he'd gift me similar, but never had.

"You...had this made?" I continued.

"I had it fashioned for you, yes, and I wanted to give it to you tonight. I was searching for you – everywhere – and finally, finally, I found you here. Thank the gods I did, Morgan! You were falling. Actually falling."

I smiled. "You know as well as I do, I would *not* have fallen."

A smile from him too, one that was beguiling, enough to make me forget the whisperings of a ghost.

If Accolon had died, it was because he was meant to.

If Agravaine and I had found each other, that too was meant.

I couldn't see the jewel, not yet, not without a looking glass, but my fingers kept tracing it, feeling it already moulding to me.

"Is it milky white?" I breathed. "Like the moon?"

"No," he said, *capturing* me with his smile. "It's black. Like you are, Morgan."

CHAPTER TWENTY

The weather was such that no one should venture outside, but stay as close to the hearth as they could, keeping hands and feet warm, *dozing* beside it, for even animal furs and the arms of a lover might not keep the chill at bay. It was only *I* who wanted to brave it, who intended to venture beyond the safety of our stronghold that day.

Three summers had passed since I first came to Gwynedd – *three!* – and this, yet another winter, was upon us. We were in the brutal thick of it, with snow piling in drifts, and the wind howling, carrying with it the sorrowful cries from Ynys Môn. No longer subdued, those voices were raw, more pitiful than ever, riding the wind like the lament they were. Agravaine and I hadn't been able to reach the island in some time. And yet I'd often tried to calm the tide, *both* of us had, me teaching Agravaine now, how to breathe in, breathe out, to let breath flood his body, until it pulsated through him, something tangible that could be worked with, used, *harnessed*. Not magic, at least not as I saw it, rather an understanding that though we were small, we were part of something vast. If it *was* magic, then let it be called natural magic.

But Agravaine, he who could master so much – who could commune with the gods, speak their tongue – couldn't master this. Each time we stood together on the shore, our hair and our cloaks whipped by the wind, his frustration grew. The sea...*refused* him. If he had the ear of the gods, the elements were deaf to him.

Was it frustration...or was it more akin to anger?

Certainly, his mood would sour after, and it would take time and coaxing to draw him back into my arms. When I wasn't cajoling Agravaine, I was with Urien – maintaining our closeness – or trying to soothe Mordred when he continued to struggle in my arms, looking beyond me for Teg, *always* for Teg. He could toddle well enough now and would wander off in search of her, his screams echoing through the halls if she happened to be gone too long.

His rejection wounded me, but it also reminded me who had rejected whom first. Such worries, such upset, but there was much to distract me, my hunger, my thirst for knowledge so rampant it teetered on the brink of something else...obsession.

So, even on a night like this, I wouldn't shrink from the elements. I'd embrace them, let them drive me forwards. If word reached me that I was needed, I'd go, wrapped in my warmest cloak and my boots laced tight. I didn't always bring Taran. With head down and scarves drawn tight, I'd trudge alone instead. It wasn't as if tonight's journey was far, but in weather like this, even short distances could prove treacherous, so I'd have to slip from the castle like a thief in the night, though with a more noble purpose. And it *was* that – noble – even if things took a darker turn...

A child needed help.

His name was Naw, meaning 'nine' – fitting, for he was his mother Gruddieu's ninth. Three summers older than Mordred, and prone to illness, I'd treated him before, as I had so many now in the nearby villages and dwellings. Since my first Beltane here, I'd made it my purpose to walk among the people, to let them know I carried knowledge of herbs and healing, that if they needed me, I would help.

How surprised they'd been to learn that a queen could be a healer too, but how could any woman master such arts without practice? And if, on occasion, a dose was misjudged…well, such moments were rare, and easily laid at the feet of the gods. I was skilled, growing more so, driven by a need to stand at the pinnacle of *all* arts.

Perhaps…perhaps when you've been made to feel worthless, that becomes the fire that fuels you. And yet, when the remedies worked – when healing came – the joy and gratitude in my patients' eyes bolstered me like nothing else could.

I could bring life. I could bring death. For me, the pendulum swung both ways.

Ah, but Naw…poor child, with lungs that burned.

It was his elder brother, Blaen, who'd brought word – arriving at Urien's stronghold near frozen, his face as pale as the snow that fell. We'd brought him in, sat him by the fire, and given him hot drinks. Once I'd heard what he had to say, I made ready.

Agravaine then found me.

"Morgan," he said, "the weather is foul! Not even you can hold it off tonight."

Not even me? Was that sarcasm rather than concern in his voice?

I loved Agravaine. My love for him was…*blistering*. And I believed he loved me, as much. But lately…

He closed the gap between us, arms slipping around my waist, his mouth at my neck. The gesture surprised me, made me question, as it always did, my suspicions.

He pressed closer. I felt the hardness between his legs, the urgency of it.

"Morgan, Morgan…stay with me, here in the warmth. My father sleeps, I take it?"

"He does," I murmured. "Comfortably."

Sleep was all Urien wanted these days, as though halfway across the bridge to the Otherworld already. But I loved him too. Dearly. I couldn't let him go. Not yet.

Was it cruel to keep him here, tethered to life by my own selfishness? Perhaps. But his gentleness – I needed it. It reminded me of Arthur. Of whom Arthur had once been. Urien *had* to stay. Just for a little while longer.

Gentleness… It was something Agravaine lacked, sometimes.

He was pulling me now, and I knew where, a path well-trodden, one that led to his bed, his breath becoming ragged, laden as it was with desire.

"It's Naw," I said, trying to steady my own. "Remember I told you about him?"

He frowned as if confused. I *had* told him – several times. About Naw, but others too, so I shouldn't be surprised he couldn't recall.

"Agravaine, he's just a child—"

"A child?" Agravaine scoffed. "Morgan, children get sick all the time! It's nothing. He'll recover. Leave him, for tonight at least."

He was right, children and those with old bones were prone to winter illness. Mordred had fallen ill more than once during these bitter months, but Naw's lungs were already failing. Blaen wouldn't have braved this storm unless it was truly urgent. Gruddieu wouldn't have let him.

"He may die," I said.

Agravaine shrugged. "Let him."

I shouldn't do it, grow angry, push him away, storm from there into the night because Agravaine…I knew he had no love for children. He'd never shown any interest in Mordred, never once spoken of having a child of our own.

Of course, he was perfectly aware I took the necessary herbs to prevent conception, or to end it if it had just begun. I worked spells, too, chanted incantations, *implored* my body to be as barren as stone until I chose to call life back into it. But would I ever? Mordred's birth had nearly killed us both. I didn't even know if I *could* carry a child again. Even so, I kept a womb stone tucked beneath my bed, smooth and round, and under Agravaine's too. Not for conception, but for prevention.

No, Agravaine had no love for children. And mine…mine had not come easily either. But those words – *let him* – spoken so dismissively, the words of someone spoiled and entitled, did not merely dim the desire he'd sparked in me.

It died.

I stepped out of his arms.

"I *will* go," I said, meeting his eyes.

If Blaen had made it here, I could make it there.

Agravaine didn't close the gap between us again. He simply glared, then did as I'd wanted him to and turned away. *He* was the one who stormed from *me*.

And though I'd meant to stand firm, it tugged at my heart just a little to see it. Until I thought of Gruddieu's face, and how relieved she'd be to see me.

There was someone else under her roof, though, who would *rue* my arrival.

And it was for that reason – more than any other – I

pressed on.

Even though it pained me to admit it.

"Oh, my lady, my queen, you're here! Truly here. I can't thank you enough. I lit a candle to Brigid, I did, prayed she'd guide your steps through that wicked storm. Please now, come in, ah, come in, won't you?"

Gruddieu was just as desperate as I'd thought she'd be when she opened the door to me, my body shaking from the cold no matter how tightly I was wrapped.

"Come close," she continued, immediately fussing, "to the fire now. Sit by it. It's burning bright, it is. Oh, you're a goodly queen! I am as low as moss before you."

I took the seat she offered. The room was meagre, more of a hovel than a home, another room beside it, in which the family all slept, tucked like birds in a nest.

"My queen—" she began again, but I interrupted her.

"I've told you before. When I come for this work, call me Morgan. Just Morgan."

My Lady. Princess. Queen. They were titles that many would covet, and I had – I'd come to Gwynedd *because* I wanted to be Queen, a title I'd been born to – but even so, in these humble dwellings, where I went door to door, I preferred to be known just by my name. A healer. And if a healer, then a healer of *all* ills.

As the cold eased from my bones, and I wondered if I might make it back this night or need to sleep here too, my eyes adjusted to the gloom.

The walls were wattle and daub, the smell of the dung

used to make them still clinging, at least to my nose. Above, a sagging thatched roof teemed with all manner of creeping, nesting things. There was good stone in this part of Cymru, and some houses – however crude – were made of it. But not this place. This…wretched place.

My eyes adjusted further, so I could see more than just the brazier and the smoke that curled from it. I saw the pots that were set all around it, one full of broth still, a cupful of which Gruddieu pressed on me, but I refused. I accepted instead a warm drink made from nettles, light and sharp on the tongue, reviving me as I swallowed.

Eyes peered from the dark – one, two, three pairs of them. Children still awake.

Their father, Meurig, lay in the next room, snoring loudly. It was only ever Gruddieu who would stay up, fretting over any child of hers who was sick, standing vigil through the long, lonely nights. Naw was in there too, no doubt nestled among his remaining siblings. His cough echoed well enough through the thin divide.

Now that I could feel my limbs again, I stood.

"Take me to Naw," I said.

She led me at once, my nose wrinkling further at the stench. It wasn't just the sourness of unwashed bodies or the rank of stale breath, there was something else beneath it, deeper, heavier. A smell I knew all too well by now.

Death.

Naw was there, cradled by his siblings indeed. They were clutching at their little brother, as desperate as Gruddieu to keep him anchored to this world.

"It's all right," I said softly, attempting to soothe them, though Naw's body heaved with each cough, wracked and restless. He murmured faintly in his sleep – if sleep it was.

Fevered. Delirious. A bad sign. The only other sound was the continuing snores of the father, smacking his lips too as he rolled his bulk from one side to the other. In a bed that was *fully* his. Not shared. Though sometimes – *oh, sometimes* – he'd share it. With whomever he pleased.

"It's too dark in here," I said. "We need to bring the child to the fire."

"Yes, yes, surely," Gruddieu said, motioning to her children.

"Go – all of you," I added. "I'll need every one of you by the hearth with him."

She glanced towards the bed. "My husband?"

"Drunk on ale?" I asked.

She nodded as my lips pressed into a thin line.

"He can stay. Now do as I say. We don't have much time."

With one of the bigger boys gathering Naw into his arms, they shuffled past me, leaving the room empty but for Meurig.

I followed soon after, back to the hearth. Carefully, I drew back the blankets wrapped around Naw and pressed my ear to his chest. I heard it plainly – the wet crackle in his lungs, like a stream gurgling through stones.

"I would have come sooner," I said to Gruddieu.

"The weather…"

"Weather is just weather. It doesn't deter me."

"Aye, and it's a wonder it don't," she breathed. "*You* are the wonder."

There it was, what people thought of me. Gruddieu and others I'd healed too, that I – Morgan of Gwynedd – was not just a healer, but a wonder. Word had carried across the kingdom. Whether I could work *this* wonder, though, I couldn't say.

Naw's heart was weak – weak as a lamb in winter – and the cough too deep, too strong. He should never have been pressed on Gruddieu, worn down by nine births already, but beneath the rough skirts she wore… I saw it: a tenth on the way.

Someone like Meurig would go on and on, rutting without care or consequence. Whether his wife's body could carry another meant nothing to him. He would kill her with his selfish desires. And Gruddieu…she'd let him. She'd do so because she knew no other way, because she thought she had no other choice.

She was trapped here, pregnant again, and not the only one either – one of her daughters was too, something I'd seen earlier when they'd left the room, her eyes so downcast, so ashamed that I had shuddered to look into them.

The same father for both.

But first – Naw.

I opened the pouch at my waist and drew out the meadowsweet I'd brewed as strong as I dared, thickened with elecampane into a dark, heavy syrup. I dripped it carefully between the child's lips, his head resting in his brother's lap. Then I pressed into Gruddieu's hand a small bundle of thyme, gathered last summer and dried.

"Burn this in a dish," I said, "but first, open the door. Just a crack. The air here has become too close. The Great Mother, but this child needs to breathe!"

He was struggling more with each breath, his ribs trembling with the effort.

It was as I'd thought – tinctures alone would not be enough.

I leaned in and placed my hands on his chest, seeking the

heat, the infection – then began to work, drawing it out, and driving it away.

My lips moved swiftly, murmuring words that, to the ears of those around me, must have sounded no clearer than Naw's own fevered whispers. But they meant something to me. I was calling on the Great Mother, as all would expect – begging for her mercy, but I also spoke the language of the scrolls. I pleaded with whatever gods had written them to spare this child's life. An innocent, a boy who deserved to see another summer, *many* summers. To run in the sunshine as he grew.

But there was one who *didn't* deserve to see another day. And so that was what I offered, for the gods must be appeased. A life for a life, *human* life.

My chest was heaving painfully too as I breathed in and breathed out, but for reasons other than illness – with the weight of what I was doing.

As my hands continued to work over the boy's chest, my voice grew hoarse.

"Amarc orum! Ná gelthe é!" *Look upon me! Do not take him!*

"Is éon annam doberfad duit an áit." *There is one soul I will give you in his place.*

"Clúmaim mé!" *Hear me!*

My arms were weakening. In fact, my whole body was – work like this took its toll. The gods demanded a price. A life, yes – but they took a piece of your own as well.

I fell back into my own tongue, into raw pleading.

"Please. Please. Please."

I was fervent. I *had* to save this boy, because this boy…he was good. But weren't all children? What about my own? If this night the choice was between a child I barely knew and

Mordred, who would I choose?

Who would harm this world *less* by living?

A howl tore from my throat – deep, guttural, terrible.

Around me, the other children clung to each other and wept. What was their queen doing? She was meant to be a healer. But this…this was something else.

Something…other.

Possession, they might whisper later.

But then – another sound. Naw coughed, but it was different now, less strained. The fire in his chest was faltering, his lungs beginning to clear, no longer so clogged, no longer as tight. His breathing eased as he clung to me – despite the fearful howl I'd emitted – small fingers digging into my arms with something akin to ferocity.

He was reviving. Which could mean only one thing.

There was movement beside me – not Gruddieu, and not the children.

It was Meurig. Roused at last. But then pain had a way of doing that, allowing no rest. Something his child knew well enough.

As Gruddieu gasped, we all turned to the doorway. There he stood, framed within it, a man I'd loathed from the moment I'd first entered this dwelling to treat Naw, back in the summer. A child who was sick in every season, no matter how warm the sun. But he wouldn't be anymore. From this night on, he'd be stronger.

I'd made certain of it. I'd bargained.

Meurig stood sweating and panting, his chest heaving as both hands clawed at his belly. His eyes were wider than his son's, than any of ours.

"What is it…?" he rasped. "What's…happened…me? I was well… I…"

209

Each word cost him.

"Husband?" Gruddieu – loyal Gruddieu, even if that loyalty was sorely misplaced – stepped timidly forwards, but I stayed her with my voice.

"Wait!"

"But—"

I turned to her. "Who would you rather see live? Your husband…or your child? I can save only one."

"Gruddieu," Meurig tried, but the name barely escaped his lips. Shock struck him dumb as, with a thunderous sound, his bowels voided.

The further stench that filled the air, even as the child breathed easier beneath my touch, forced bile into my throat, but I swallowed it back. Around me, the children still clung to each other, though I thought I heard a giggle, no matter how nervous.

"Who do you want to live?" I asked Gruddieu again. "Of the two of them?"

"Gruddieu!" Meurig said again, as his legs gave out and he vomited too.

"You can say it, Gruddieu," I told her, and then more gently, "The Great Mother, Arianrhod, Brigid, they already know your heart, so you can say it. It's all right."

As Meurig writhed on the floor, his lips mumbling other names now, those of his children, barked as commands, I could see, in the light of the fire, the tears on Gruddieu's face. Her husband was dying, in front of her eyes, but they weren't tears of grief. She was relieved. Relief *filled* this sordid room, as thick as any smoke.

After today, with Naw thriving, the light could return to this dwelling when a man like Meurig had only ever invited the darkness in. He was a man who bullied, who beat, who raped, and I cared nothing for his reasons why. Whether unloved, broken, or wounded himself – it didn't matter. What mattered was this: it ended now. His wife and children deserved a future, all of them, a chance to begin again.

Gruddieu's voice came, faint at first.

"Naw," she said.

It wasn't enough. She had to own it.

"Who?" I asked.

"Naw," she repeated, firmer this time.

And then, as Meurig glared at her – as much as a dying, convulsing man could glare, a man whose lips I'd also dripped tincture through earlier, when all had left the room and I'd lingered behind, belladonna, of course – she did as I wanted. She *bellowed* her son's name, straight at the man who could rule her no longer, her teeth bared and her eyes blazing. "Naw! Naw! Naw! Not you, Meurig. You can *die*!"

Oh, how his body thrashed, but I'd give him this: he was determined. Somehow, he dragged himself forwards on all fours, bit by bit, towards me.

I glared at him too as I spoke, as I cursed him further.

"May the gates to the Otherworld be sealed against you forever, for you deserve no welcome there. Your soul is doomed to wander, hungry and lost. And, Meurig, others who wander too, just as cursed, just as desperate, will find you. They will hunt you down. *Devour* you. Then spit you out whole only to begin again."

His hand reached for me, fingers thick like knotted roots, nails chewed and blackened. Spittle and bile sprayed from his throat as he groaned.

He was close now, almost at my feet, but I didn't step back. I wanted his wife and children to see they *never* needed to fear a man like this. A *weak* man. Ultimately.

It wasn't help he was pleading for. He knew he was beyond help.

And when the final breath left him, it wasn't the word *healer* on his lips either.

But something else entirely.

CHAPTER TWENTY-ONE

The wheel had turned twice more. Mordred was five, and through him, the gods continued to tease me. So much of Arthur lived in him, but at times he would grin like Lancelot, or tilt his head with that same careless charm.

Under Teg's guidance, he'd grown into a happy child, not the tempest I had braced for – he was sweet, even, his tantrums now rare. And yet, did that very quality – that treasured trait – soften me towards him? I wanted it to. It *should* have, but something in me resisted still, even as I reminded myself his fate wasn't Nimue's to command, nor the Fay's – it wasn't anyone's but his own. It made no difference, and so I buried myself deeper in my work, in the endless pursuit of knowledge. Knowledge that, as Caireann had once told me at Avalon, had no boundaries. A truth I sometimes met with awe, and at other times, with something closer to despair.

Agravaine knew the same frustration. His gods teased him with signs but never gave him certainty, no matter what he did. He *knew* he had purpose. That *I* did. And, in his eyes, mine was not to be found simply in the healing of the sick, nor administering justice when it was needed – *quiet* justice, more bargaining taking place, saving a life that deserved to go on by offering one that didn't. A sacrifice? Yes. But if it pleased the gods, if it was the way of things –

the *old* way – I accepted it. And never, not once, was it met with anything but gratitude.

Morgan the Healer could also be Morgan the Destroyer. No arrow, no sword needed, but it was destruction all the same – never wanton, though, but measured.

Yet if I needed no armour, elsewhere in this land there were others that did. Arthur had fought more battles against the Saxons, and each time word of them reached me, my heart would clench as if caught in a vice. Still it did that, despite everything.

Emissaries had come to Gwynedd, of course, seeking Urien – a man who lived only because I ensured it. They still wanted his allegiance, but Agravaine would intercept them before Urien ever became involved, without revealing my presence either, declaring instead that Gwynedd would remain as the gods intended – a kingdom in its own right, not one beholden to a crown in Dumnonia.

Though I feared such staunch defiance would not be tolerated, that allegiance might be forced on us, as it had been on Lot, no such march had come. Not yet. Put simply, Arthur's men were needed too much elsewhere. The Saxons, though defeated, never stayed that way for long. They regrouped with frightening speed.

There'd been the Battle of the River Glein, the one I'd fought at alongside Arthur, loosing arrow after arrow from the edge of the field as we were charged at. Then there'd been a second, a third, and a fourth, all at the River Dubglas, far to the south, near Kent. *Dubglas* meant dark waters, though by now I imagined them running red.

I'd heard tales of the tactics Arthur had employed, how he'd driven his cavalry straight into enemy ranks, the Saxons *quaking* at the sight of so many horses thundering towards them. It was the stuff of legend. So too was the story of how he'd flanked their lines – Cerdic's army that time, who was younger than Aelle, and likely twice as ambitious. They crumbled almost at once. But now, a fifth battle loomed, and the Saxons were learning, growing wise to the ways of the Britons.

Soon, Dubglas would run with blood again. It was only a matter of time.

There was also news of how increasingly Christian Arthur's court had become, of the promises made, with chapels to be built everywhere it seemed. More priests on councils, more missionaries pushing into every corner of the land. But not here, not in Gwynedd. Urien, even as his health failed, remained as resolute on that matter as his son – just as I was. Guinevere's religion was not mine. *Nothing* of hers was.

"It's the Christians who remain the greater threat," Agravaine would say, his dark eyes fixed on mine. "And the gods will show us a way to defeat them. They *will*."

Scrying was another of the arts my lover had taken up of late. Though reflective, the black moonstone he'd fastened around my neck wasn't the one we gazed into in the confines of our hidden chamber, but another stone – quartz, more easily sourced. It took many forms: clear, milky white, dark grey, even black.

The quartz and the moonstone – both had stirred something in me from the first. It took time to place that familiarity, and then, with a start, I remembered, not just why, but where I'd seen their likeness. It was at the silent pool, a place as rare as any jewel, undisturbed save by nature. Its waters held hidden depths, were fathomless in places, as Igraine had once told me. It was there I'd seen the future –

effortlessly, vividly. I'd seen not only my son, but myself, as the Triple Goddess.

The Maiden, so innocent, unmarked.

The Mother, who was the caregiver – and in many ways, I *was* that.

The Crone, older, wiser, or meant to be.

As both the Mother and Crone, I'd worn at my neck a black stone that caught the light, though none had existed. Back then, I'd believed Arthur and I were the ones fated, but remembering the vision now, I understood its truer meaning, that in this life, it was Agravaine and I who were meant instead.

In the chamber, only a single candle was permitted to flicker as we approached the slab of quartz mounted on the wall. Agravaine went ahead to gaze into it – to see...*dimly* in its reflection. For to scry was to *de*scry, to glimpse what the gods allowed, yet it was never shown plainly, but veiled, requiring interpretation.

The night, for once, was calm. The worst of another winter had passed, and there was no wind to rattle the shutters, no ghostly cries echoing through the air. The spirits were as silent as we were, as if equally absorbed by all that was unfolding.

Agravaine stood before the black quartz, which earlier he'd polished to a mirror's gleam. His breathing was shallow, as was mine. Though I'd learned some of the language he used, I still wasn't as adept as he was, so I listened intently, trying to catch even fragments of what he spoke. His voice was low – so low I could barely hear him, let alone decipher his words. What I could feel, though, was the power that gathered around us, several jars rattling on their shelves behind me because of it.

Moments passed. Long moments. His voice, though it was still low, grew steadily more fervent, until it no longer sounded like chanting but something more animalistic. I wondered then: were the gods silent not out of mischief, but because they sensed a desperation in him – and disliked it?

Of course Gwynedd couldn't go to war against Dumnonia. And both Agravaine and Arthur knew that. It was why Arthur had never wasted men or time on us. He might send emissaries, but even that had dwindled to a formality. He was likely aware, too, how frail Urien was, and perhaps found no honour in challenging a dying man. But what if he learned *I* was here, despite the stronghold's oath of secrecy?

Arthur was busy with war, *winning* it, keeping the Saxons not only from our kingdom but from all of the West. I'd severed myself from him, cut ties, yet I couldn't help but wonder further: what would I do if he faltered? If something befell him?

Urien, I think, had little sense of his son's dealings. Rhianinfelt had been the last to offer sacrifice, for he had no stomach for it. In truth, I think he was…*blind* to the talents Agravaine possessed, for Urien, though an advocate of the old ways, was a simpler man by nature, plainer of soul. Like Arthur, he preferred to deal with what he could see with his eyes, not what there might be – communing with men, not gods.

But if you *did* speak with them, it was perhaps best not to argue, to rant or rail, to demand of them. If Agravaine knew so much, then surely he knew that too?

I stepped towards him, afraid that all he'd do was encourage their wrath.

"Agravaine," I murmured, placing my hands gently on

his shoulders.

Immediately, he shrugged them off.

"Wait!" he hissed.

My hands by my sides again, I did as he asked. Was he seeing something at last?

Even if he was, I sighed.

All the rituals he performed – the incantations, the spells he wove with herbs and water, not seawater but spring water from a well, that which a spirit or a deity would inhabit, blessed by them. All the stones he cast, each carved with symbols; the bones of animals and birds he threw; the patterns he tried to read in fire and water; even dreams, another conduit…

And still – *still* – he didn't know how to thwart the rising tide of Christianity.

But tonight…tonight might prove different. The energy was mounting, undeniably. Even the usual fluttering in the rafters above had gone still. *Something* was coming. We would finally receive what we sought. *He* would. His reward.

If only he'd let *me* scry…

The quartz – though he'd placed himself in front of it like a barrier– wasn't fully obscured. I could still catch a glimpse of its surface.

I stared at it, just as intently, murmured words of my own so low he wouldn't hear them, beseeching, but…and I had to be honest, I had to be clear…this was more for his benefit than anything other, because it was *him* I wanted to appease. Those moods when a ritual hadn't gone to plan? They were becoming more wearing.

"Speak to us," I breathed. "Whoever is present this night, hear us. We are your servants. We will do your bidding."

The Christians – ah, the Christians. Word had come from those Agravaine sent across the borders into other kingdoms that even the sacred springs, once ours, were being claimed and declared holy wells, no longer dedicated to our goddesses but to their saints, the likes of Gwenfrewi, Cadog, and Ninian. Agravaine's fervour was not misplaced. This trampling had to end, the insult just too great.

"Please hear us," I continued. "Tell us what you require. We will do it."

The candle that had been flickering beside us went out, having either burned down naturally or been snuffed by the breath of the gods. We remained there – still, so still – one behind the other, in a darkness that had grown vast. The quartz shard seemed to have expanded too, no longer just a sliver, but resembling the surface of a pool, one that glittered faintly. We were speaking in two different tongues, but somehow, in some way, our voices had merged, the meaning the same, the promises we gave, again and again. *We will do what you require of us.* All *that you ask.* There could be no hesitation, only devotion. We would give our souls if that was the price to preserve the old ways. The ways of Prydain. Of Albion. A land of tribes before the Romans came, before any Christian ever walked here. Sacred and beloved by the Great Mother, by all the gods and goddesses she'd birthed, and we her faithful children, who would be shown the path – if only we persevered.

Something stirred in the quartz, shifted, like clouds forming in a night sky. My voice faltered, but Agravaine went on – growling, seething.

I longed to touch him again, whisper his name, *tell* him. *Something* is *happening, Agravaine! See… See…*

Couldn't he see?

Like I could?

This man who couldn't control the tide's ebb and flow.

Like I could.

He was older than me – my guide, my teacher. And yes, he *had* taught me much. But now… Was the student surpassing the master?

And if so – would it be allowed?

The clouds within the quartz were thinning, and I at least had fallen silent, waiting. What would be revealed? A clear path, perhaps, rather than yet another riddle.

And then…

A face.

There was definitely a face within the mist.

Familiar.

A breath caught in my throat, so hard I struggled not to choke on it.

Familiar since childhood…

Cai!

The moment his face became clear, his…*worried* face, I sensed rather than heard a commotion elsewhere in this stronghold. More demands being made.

She's here. I know she's here. Get her. Get her now. I must see her. I've news!

News of what? Of whom?

In the quartz, Cai's face had shifted from worry to anguish.

Such anguish.

I turned from the stone, from Agravaine, and bolted from the chamber.

Questions crowded my mind.

How had Cai found me? Had one of Arthur's emissaries caught sight of me, a woman resembling Morgan? Or had a servant spoken out of turn?

And how did Cai fare? Dumnonia to Gwynedd was a long road. While there'd be dwellings along the way where he'd be welcomed as one of Arthur's men, it was still a dangerous passage to take if he'd come alone. Had he done so? In the vision, I'd seen no one else, only him, eyes straining, as if desperate to see me too.

Question after question plagued me as I swapped one dark, twisting corridor for another, heading for the great hall, where *all* visitors were brought, the guards swords drawn until their intent was known, whether they were friend or foe.

So many questions…and yet only one face truly haunted me now, as vivid as any vision. A man with fair hair and the greyest of eyes.

His eyes weren't open now, though, they were sealed shut, and his skin beneath the stubble that covered his face was sallow, his cheeks sunken. His lips were parted too, but the breath between them was not something that flowed with ease.

It was hard-won.

And getting harder.

It was his face, of course.

Arthur's.

PART THREE

CHAPTER TWENTY-TWO

Arthur had been wounded during the fifth battle at Dubglas, against Cerdic in Kent. The cut wasn't deep, but the blade had been tipped with poison. *Fresh* poison. To coat a weapon in such a way was an old battlefield tactic, wolfsbane used, or hemlock, either one of them enough to stop a heart. It was *not* an honourable way to kill, though, it was deemed cowardly, frowned upon not only by our gods, but likely by the Saxon gods as well – those whom they called Wodin, Thunor, and Tiw.

A warrior of reputation ought to deliver death with skill, but if we called the Saxons' tactics filthy because of it, then perhaps they saw ours – fighting from horseback – as no better.

"Arthur *was* on the ground this time," Cai said.

"At the helm of the shield wall," I'd replied. Not a question; I knew it to be true.

In Gwynedd's Great Hall – he'd told us this. That Arthur, *my* Arthur, was dying. Cai had stood there, almost as wretched as I imagined Arthur to be. His red hair lay flat against his skull instead of standing in its usual wild tufts, his frame diminished somehow, his green eyes with no shine. Time and warfare – *events* – had worn him down. The boy who'd once delighted in pranks and laughter barely discerned.

"He was part of the shield wall, yes," Cai continued, "though he'd been advised to stay mounted. But that's the thing with Arthur...sometimes he can't help himself. He has to be in the thick of it – the fray."

"That's where his men are. He would never ask them to face what he would not."

"Yes, yes – that's it, Morgan, that's it. He was marked, singled out, as any king would be, as he knew, so he must have become distracted. Ah, it was a weak blow. Weak! Yet it broke the skin. And now the poison is in him, *killing* him. Not even your foster mother – nor your birth mother, for she was called to his side – can cure him."

"What makes you think Morgan can if Viviane can't?"

It was Agravaine who asked this. Whatever trance he'd been under had shattered the moment I fled the chamber. He followed, storming into the Great Hall not long after me, still seething, not with frustration, but hatred, having quickly assessed the situation. For if Arthur died, why should we care? It would be the gods' will, surely? Arthur was *not* the saviour of Britannia. He and his realm could destroy us.

Before I could interrupt Agravaine, desperate to hear more about Arthur, further commotion broke out. *All* had been roused by Cai's sudden appearance in the night, it seemed. Urien was brought forwards, servants supporting him as he was placed on his throne, and Teg arrived too, with Mordred – a Mordred who clearly hadn't slept. He was squirming in her hold in a way I'd never seen before, and Teg looked as flustered and as confused as me by it, hence, perhaps the reason she'd come to find me. The moment Mordred spotted me, he wrenched free from her grip and ran towards me, a rare occurrence – if it had ever happened at all.

I was at my throne, beside Urien, though, like Arthur with his in Dumnonia, I seldom sat there. But after hearing the news, my legs had weakened beneath me, and I'd staggered to it. That was where Mordred found me, climbing onto my lap.

He was the strength I needed – I didn't know how much until then, and I clutched at him too, felt something tighten between us when it had been so slack. A bond?

"Morgan," Cai said, ignoring Agravaine while eyeing the child, a frown creasing his brow, which I wondered at, "your reputation has spread."

"My reputation?" I asked as Agravaine thundered to a halt beside me.

Cai nodded again. "You are skilled indeed. Priscilla taught you the beginnings of the healing arts, yes, but now, you're…gifted. People have said it, Morgan!"

I frowned as I tried to work it out.

I hadn't changed my name when I came here. I was Morgan, always Morgan. Lately, I'd taken Taran and ridden nearly to the edges of Gwynedd, where you could look across the hills to Powys – *Brochwel's* Powys, he who'd bent the knee to Arthur long ago. I warned those there not to speak of what I'd done, but perhaps some couldn't help themselves, especially if they believed they'd witnessed a wonder.

They talked.

Always they talked.

I thought I'd wanted to remain hidden. For so long I'd believed that, emerging only when the time was right, when the path was clear and straight instead of mired. But maybe I'd been fooling myself, for sometimes…hadn't I *forgotten* to remind them?

When Cai said this, I glanced at Agravaine even as one arm loosened around Mordred so I could reach out to Urien. I saw the fury there, on my lover's face.

"It doesn't matter how you knew," I said. "Just tell me about Arthur. When did it happen? How quickly has he worsened? If Priscilla can't help... If Viviane can't..."

Two great women.

If I'd surpassed Agravaine, could I surpass them?

Cai's voice cracked, reminding me how much he loved Arthur – like a brother. "They say now there's no hope. But, Morgan... if there's you, there's hope."

Agravaine could restrain himself no longer. His hand went to the sword at his side as he stepped forwards, and so, with Mordred still clinging to me, I rose.

"Agravaine! No!"

Cai had entered Urien's fortification unarmoured, a clear sign he came in peace. And alone. He was indeed alone. If Agravaine raised a blade against him now, then Arthur's army, even if Arthur himself couldn't, wouldn't hold back any longer. They'd march on us. Powys and Glywysing would too, all the Cymru kingdoms bound to the High King. We'd be slaughtered.

"Agravaine, I am queen here, and Urien is king. Step back!"

Oh, how Urien longed to speak, but he was weak, so weak, his voice was lost to him that night, so I had to act for us both.

Agravaine stayed where he was, and Cai hadn't retreated either. Around us, our warriors had gathered, their hands on the hilts of their swords – but whom would they strike? Cai, on Agravaine's command? Or Agravaine, on mine?

It was Mordred who broke the tension.

He slipped from my arms, and, with a burst of high laughter, darted towards Cai – further bewilderment in my eyes to see it. Cai just as surprised by it too. A child of five, but as small-boned, as delicate as I'd been at his age, looking more as though he were three or four. Reaching Cai, he lifted his arms, wanting to be picked up.

Cai hesitated, still uncertain if he needed to defend himself, but I gave him my consent while Agravaine encroached no further, though his bones remained rigid.

Mordred, stubborn as ever, would not be denied. Cai scooped him into his arms, and the child gave another bright laugh, poking at his cheeks and nose.

Cai murmured something then, quietly, almost to himself.

"Guinevere and Arthur have a child too."

Another frown. *They had?*

"A…boy?" I asked.

"Yes," Cai replied, letting out a soft laugh at Mordred's antics, which only encouraged him further.

I was the one to step forwards.

"A boy?" I repeated, swallowing hard. "Arthur has a son? How old?"

"Four summers."

"Four?" I echoed. "Almost as old as Mordred, then. He…he is five summers."

My voice cracked, just as Cai's had – Cai who was studying Mordred now.

"Dark hair, yes," he said slowly, "but by the gods, this child, he has Arthur's—"

I'd reached them. "I'll take him," I said sharply.

Arthur's eyes, that's what he'd been about to say. But he

mustn't! Not here.

I'd never told anyone – not Urien, not Agravaine, not a soul – who Mordred's father might be. A mistake, I realised now. I should have said something. I should have claimed Lancelot, for what would that matter if he were? Lancelot, though a king's bastard son, was not a king. Not Arthur. Yes, I should have said it long ago.

Because…

Because…

Again, Mordred came to me easily enough, still laughing as I turned – not to Urien, as it wasn't his reaction I sought, once again it was Agravaine's.

He was no longer tense, no longer furious, his head had tilted, and eyes narrowed. As if…intrigued. As if…calculating. As if realising the mark upon my child's forehead was *not* something as benign as a birthmark, but resembled my own.

"The child is Lancelot's." Though I said it then, it rang false, even to my ears, rushed, breathless, a lie scraped together in haste. "You can tell, can't you, Cai?" I was almost pleading with him. "Because of the hair. Dark like mine, but like his too."

Cai looked from Mordred to me, then back to the child, and I told myself he had no notion of what he was doing, the seeds he was planting in another's mind.

Even now, as we raced across the plain, with dawn breaking, I clung to that belief.

He has Arthur's eyes. Agravaine had divined what Cai was about to say. He had asked the gods for a sign that very night – for guidance, for clarity, for something more, something…special. He wanted to fulfil a promise to them, but also to himself.

His pride demanded it.

Oh, he was proud. Cunning. And patient, so patient.

He *deserved* to be rewarded.

And now he knew. Guinevere and Arthur's son was *not* Arthur's firstborn. Mordred was. The child Agravaine had never taken an interest in before, just as he'd taken no interest in any children. The child *I'd* barely taken an interest in, and yet, when Mordred climbed onto my lap, something had shifted – *truly* shifted this time. A love I hadn't known I was capable of surfaced. A need, at last, to be a mother. *Me*. Not Teg. To take back what I'd so freely given. Agravaine knew something else too: that I'd go to Arthur, even if I couldn't save him. That I would ride as fast as Taran and the wind could carry me, across kingdom after kingdom, stopping only when I must.

If only to say goodbye.

Goodbye.

It was the cruellest word I'd ever known. In any tongue.

I would return to Caer Arthur…and leave the High King's son behind in this lonely corner of the world because I couldn't take him. To do so would slow us down too much. He'd be left in the company of a man who wanted the High King dead.

Though Agravaine hadn't taken a blade to Cai, would he harm Mordred in my absence?

No. Of that, at least, I was certain.

He wouldn't kill him.

He would use him.

Oh, the gods! They had answered him indeed.

I would go to Arthur, and Agravaine would do nothing to stop me, when once he might have. He would have said, 'Let him die.' And then, more joyously, 'Morgan, let him die!' But as swift as I was riding, I'd return swifter still. I would come back for my son. Without me to tend to him, Urien would surely die. Agravaine might then press his claim as King of Gwynedd, but even so, I would remain the kingdom's queen. I'd done more for the people than he ever had. There were many who loved me, who were grateful – so grateful – and they would rally to me, do whatever I asked. I wouldn't run again, as I had run from Caer Arthur, and from Avalon.

Was the heart I'd thought healed by Agravaine's love breaking again? Everything I'd said... Everything he'd said... The promises we'd made. Even the lies.

I didn't know.

All I could think about was Arthur, the man Agravaine had wanted me to hate as fiercely as he did – yet it was plain I never had, and never could. My half-brother. I'd always insisted Agravaine referred to him as that. And now he understood why.

I'm almost with you, Arthur.

I sent the words flying ahead of me, straight to his ear.

Hold on for a while longer. Please. You have *to hold on.*

And not just for my sake.

CHAPTER TWENTY-THREE

We raced across fields and meadows, Cai and I, as hard and as fast as I ever had – either with Arthur or with Agravaine. Taran was as sure-footed as always, and so was the horse carrying my former childhood friend, as dark as Merlyn's, but taller, a fine beast, perhaps even the finest in Arthur's cavalry, for its purpose was as great.

After days of near constant travel – when it seemed the road had seeped into my very bones and made its home there – we came at last to Caer Arthur. Priscilla was the first to greet me. She'd kept watch from the parapets, she told me, and the instant she spotted Cai and me – two pale and weary figures – she flew to meet us.

At the sight of her, I dismounted and ran as fast as I could into her waiting arms.

My mother. My *true* mother.

How had I stayed away from her this long?

"Morgan," she murmured. "Oh, Morgan…Cai was right. He'd heard rumours you still lived, while I wasn't so sure, fearing something terrible had happened after Avalon. All the emissaries we sent to Gwynedd, and not once did Urien or his son let us know you were there. That you were Urien's queen! But Arthur… He knew you weren't dead. He said…" She broke off, swallowing, though still she held onto me. "He said he'd have felt it in his bones. He never stopped searching for you, Morgan. Perhaps…perhaps you don't know this, but emissaries were sent *everywhere*."

Arthur knew I wasn't dead. He would have felt it in his bones?

And what did I feel now, standing once more on the threshold of this place I'd called home for two summers? Was his death – his *impending* death – something that pressed upon my bones as well? The inevitability of it.

I couldn't say.

"He lives still?" was all I asked, though I already knew the answer – not from my bones, but from the sight above: Arthur's standard, the Pendragon, flew high from one of the parapets, and beside it, the Christian cross.

There was no sign, though, of Igraine's Pictish beast, the emblem Arthur had adopted to honour his birth mother. What had become of it? Had it been banished by Guinevere? Why? Because it was *too* pagan, and therefore, in her eyes, barbaric?

I couldn't dwell on that now. Two standards flew, and that was enough. If Arthur had drawn his last, rasping, *agonised* breath, they wouldn't be raised at all.

How quiet the caer seemed as Cai dismounted too. Servants hurried towards us, taking the reins of our horses and leading them to the inner courtyard to be stabled there, while we remained where we were. Even the village at the foot of the hill was devoid of its usual liveliness, I noticed, no children at play or hawkers calling out.

Though the fifth battle at Dubglas had been won by the Britons, elsewhere in this land, things wouldn't be so subdued. The Saxons, despite their losses, would be feasting, raising cups sloshing with ale and mead to toast a victory of sorts.

For as much as we knew it, so did they – Arthur was the hope of this land. If he died, hope might well die with him, his son far too young to take up his mantle.

Anger surged. Why did he still insist on doing this? Arthur. Putting himself in so much danger when he knew he'd be singled out? A king should command in battle, not lead the charge! And now this, because of it. Treachery of the worst kind.

It was treachery that felled Uther, too. A well that Saxon spies knew he drank from had been poisoned, and though he'd ridden into battle one last time – 'the half-dead king' as they'd called him – though he'd won that battle despite their mockery, he'd died soon afterwards, before they could even reach camp in Londinium. Arthur, though, still lived, younger and stronger than his father had been. But for how long?

It had been five summers since I'd last seen him. What further changes had those years wrought? As much as I feared his death, I dreaded something else as well: that though he lived, there'd be *nothing* left of the man I knew.

I drew back from Priscilla.

"Mother—"

"I've done everything I can," she said, weary herself, her back stooped. "But it's not enough. Viviane came and tried as well, but still there's been no improvement."

"I heard. And another with her? A child named Nimue?"

Priscilla nodded, the gravest of gestures. "We know you went to Avalon, Nimue told us, also that you left…that it did not…"

"Suit me," I finished for her when she faltered. "Is that…*all* you heard?"

Her look of confusion told me it was so, that Nimue

hadn't mentioned Seren.

"It didn't suit me," I repeated, "but I learned there still, though more so in Gwynedd. And I will do my best."

She nodded. "I know you will."

I glanced past her. "Father?"

So quickly her eyes filled with tears, and I knew then she'd already wept enough to fill an ocean. "Ector died this past winter. I failed him too."

Oh, that my heart was numb instead of this – so tattered and raw. It swelled with fresh pain, with memories of the man who'd loved me as a father should.

Ector, who'd carved toys for me in the barn near our villa, who'd taught us the history of our land so diligently, spinning tale after tale by the fire. Once one of the greatest warriors in Britannia – Uther's general – he'd urged us to dream, to imagine a bright future filled with light and joy, and to reach for it however we could.

His deep laughter would rumble through our kitchen, his eyes gleaming with pride when he showed us how to parry, how to hold the line in a shield wall, and finally – *finally* – we got it right. He'd prepared us for so much. But not this, the loss of him.

"Morgan, Priscilla…" Cai was beside us, speaking gently. "Shall we enter?"

Enter the caer, where not only Arthur was, but Guinevere, Lancelot, *Merlyn*.

When we'd fought against Lot in the North, I'd likened entering his garrison, Barr Dubh, to walking into a viper's nest. This felt no different. Priscilla and Cai I could always count on, but what would my welcome be among those others?

Cai coaxed me again.

"The caer isn't as full as it should be," he said. "Many of our men have been posted to the eastern borders of Dumnonia to keep the Saxons at bay."

"Because they gather, don't they?" I said it dully. "The Saxons gather and they wait, ready to swoop in again, emboldened by what's taken place. A siege upon us."

Cai nodded. "Yes. Even now, Lot's men in the north, the warriors of Powys and Glywysing, the men of the Middle Lands – they're all ready to make march. But…"

His voice faltered, and I turned to him.

"But what, Cai?"

He swallowed hard. "I don't know, Morgan. They *will* come. Oaths have been sworn, and a man doesn't break such things lightly, not if he values his soul. But…"

"Cai, just say it." My voice, like his, was gentle now.

A tear slipped down his cheek.

"It's just a feeling. A foolish one maybe, at least I *pray* it is. But…it's as if the heart's gone out of everything, and this despite our last victory, despite *all* the victories, for it was only ever Arthur who remained certain we could hold back those bastard Sea Wolves. Even Merlyn falters. He hides it well, but I've seen it. They're relentless, Morgan! You know it too, even though you've been so far from here these past few years. Everyone does. Nowhere's safe. They'll invade all four corners, achieve what even the Romans couldn't. That's the fear that persists among us all, but when Arthur spoke, when he said it *wouldn't* happen, that the Britons would overcome them, that again and again we'd do that… Ah, when he spoke, those fears vanished! It was *easy* to believe him. To rally again. To ride to victory. And now…"

My own tears came – tears for Arthur, for Ector, for Priscilla, for all that I'd missed since that morning I'd left.

When I'd run away.

Should I have stayed, even if it meant torment? I'd sworn an oath too – my *first* oath – to protect Arthur, come what may…come betrayal, even.

But I was here now, a part of this world again, if only for a while.

I could help him. Arthur. The light in *everyone's* heart. In mine.

Removed from Gwynedd, I could see it more clearly. I could understand that, even if Agravaine hated him, I never had. I *could* hate – hate hard – just not Arthur. Had I been all shadow, it might have been possible. But I'd left Gwynedd in time.

"He won't die," I said, taking my mother's hand and walking forwards. As the guards at the entrance moved aside to grant us passage, Cai fell into step beside us. "You both know I've learned much where I was. And he will *not* die."

CHAPTER TWENTY-FOUR

Merlyn.

He hadn't come to greet me. He had, at least, allowed Priscilla that courtesy, but I should have known he'd be there, waiting, just inside the caer, in the outer courtyard. He appeared before me exactly as I remembered him: no older, and no younger. *Timeless.* The black robe he favoured hung from his shoulders, its hem, as ever, trailing in the dust. His staff – made of elder – was in one hand, the symbols carved into it thrumming faintly with the magic he'd woven into every curl and line.

But I bore a symbol of my own, worn upon my brow, and he saw it, no matter how silvery it had grown in the years since, despite that I wore my hair to half conceal it.

His eyes widened, as well they might, for if he hadn't changed, I had.

When I'd fled Caer Arthur, I was a girl still, even though a child grew within me. An innocent, though I'd taken lovers, Arthur among them, of course, the man Merlyn claimed was my brother. I was angry then, or thought I was, but it had been a child's anger compared to what flared in my chest now – a *woman's* anger.

This man – the Archdruid of Britannia – revered by all, even the Christians, even if grudgingly, had snatched my dreams from me and crushed them so casually beneath his heel, his staff. And not once had he uttered a word of remorse.

Because of him, I'd had to build new dreams – dreams I'd dared to nurture again, right up until days ago when I'd realised that they, too, were built on shifting sands.

He knew my anger well enough.

Knew, too, what the sigil on my brow meant as I pushed my hair aside.

And still, he walked towards me.

"Greetings," he said. "*Morgan the Fay.*"

His eyes then drifted lower. My cloak had fallen open, and I hadn't yet removed the black moonstone at my neck, or decided if I *would*. It was this that held his gaze.

"Or should I say, greetings, *Queen Morgan*. The necklace – a gift from Urien?"

He understood its power, the rarity of such a stone, brought from distant lands, and never given lightly. Even though he stared at it rather than me, I felt the way it shimmered at my throat, how it resonated. Who'd given it to me was not for him to know, but oh, how I longed to see the look on his face if I told him the truth.

"Arthur," I said instead. "I want to see Arthur."

Needed to see him. We'd lost so much time already.

Merlyn nodded. "Guinevere is with him at present. His *wife*," he added pointedly. "She and their son, Lumiel."

Lumiel?

I hadn't thought to ask Cai for the boy's name, and nor had he offered it.

Lumiel – I'd never heard of such. What did it mean? Merlyn, ever the mind-reader, hastened to explain. "It means 'light of God.'"

"Light of God?" I repeated. I spat. "Such a…*Christian*

240

name?"

If he, too, was disappointed – an archdruid, a pagan, a supposed keeper of the old ways – he gave no sign. He simply nodded. "He is the finest of boys."

"Is he indeed? I'm glad to hear it."

His eyebrow lifted. "Do *you* have children, Morgan?"

He didn't know, then. I'd always expected him to know everything, but that was pure fancy. No one knew *everything*. Not Merlyn, not Agravaine, nor the gods whispering in their ears. He hadn't even known where I was. It was Cai – hearty, sometimes oafish Cai – who'd proved more perceptive. He'd heard rumours of a healer in Gwynedd, a *great* healer, and recalling my interest in the craft, in the teachings Priscilla had begun to pass on, had pieced the puzzle together.

If Merlyn *had* known – about Mordred too – if he'd bothered to listen to others, rather than mostly to himself, might he have also solved it? Or had he simply hoped that if it *was* me in that far-off kingdom, I'd stay there and rot. Forgotten.

Maybe I'd hoped for that too once. But that's all it was – hope. To remain in Gwynedd was not my fate, and it should *never* have been Mordred's.

Merlyn was still watching, still waiting for my answer, so I lifted my chin.

"I have a son," I said.

"You have a son *too*?" He glanced from me to Cai and back again – a flicker of something across his face, so fleeting I barely caught it.

"His name is Mordred," I continued.

I was *not* mistaken – he was somewhat shaken, the colour draining from his face.

"Mordred," he repeated, as if testing the name on his lips.

Just as he'd told me the meaning of Lumiel, I now told him what Mordred meant, as defined by the Fay, my eyes flashing as I spoke, perhaps. "His name means ruler. It means defender. *Righteousness*. His name means that, too."

"And you…you bestowed that name upon him?"

"I think you know who did, Merlyn."

He stood before us – an archdruid, a man, my nemesis, a barrier between me and Arthur. Cai shifted beside me, uneasy. Priscilla too had caught the change in the air, for I could hear it in her breath, which had become shallow.

Cai had sought me out, but Merlyn, he didn't want me here. When I was Morgan – just Morgan – I was no threat. Even with the title of princess, I was a tool he could wield. But now? Now, he was confused. I saw how much. Maybe – just maybe – his gods were whispering to him this very moment, and if not about me, then Mordred.

I tilted my head, imagining I could hear their whisperings every bit as clearly as he could. *Mordred. With black hair and grey eyes. Arthur's eyes, Merlyn. Arthur's!*

Lumiel is not *his firstborn.*

His fists clenched – just slightly.

Everything he had striven for was falling apart. Arthur the Invincible was dying. Excalibur, the sword forged in the hills by the ancient people, imbued with all their might and magic, had failed him. The Saxons pressed on, undeterred by any fleeting victories. And there was no balance either between the old ways and the new. The scales were tipping – swiftly, irrevocably – in favour of the Christians, as rabid as Priscilla had once called them. Intolerant of any worship but that of their One True God. Guinevere, right here in the heart of the High King's kingdom, had welcomed more and more to her court while Arthur had been away, fighting.

Ah, but she was beautiful. The kind of beauty bards would laud for centuries to come. Even so, was she worth the fifty horses that had been traded for her? A daughter of Leodegrance, the man who'd insisted a chapel be built for Arthur and Guinevere before he would consent to the match.

Could Merlyn truly not have seen how that might unfold, just as he'd never foreseen what might transpire between Arthur and me if placed with the same foster parents? The love that could blossom. How deep it ran – for one of us, at least. And if so...was he more arrogant than wise? Like Agravaine. Every bit as desperate.

Arthur *had* to live.

He wanted it, and so did I, though not entirely for the same reasons. And no matter what he thought of me, I might be the key. Priscilla couldn't save him, not even Viviane, or Nimue. That gifted child not quite gifted enough.

But perhaps I was.

And if there was even the slightest chance...

"Take me to Arthur," I said again.

"I've told you—"

"Merlyn," I cut in, my voice sharp, unwavering. "Take me to him. *Now.* As much as you may try to deny it, it's *me* that Arthur needs."

As Merlyn had said, Guinevere was there with Arthur, but

not with Lumiel, as he'd claimed, perhaps even believed. She was by his side with Lancelot.

In the corridors on the way to Arthur's chamber – not the one he'd once shared with Guinevere, but another far removed from their marital bed, about as far away, perhaps, as she could force it, I recognised the smell of death again, something dank and sulphurous but with a sickly-sweet edge to it. My heart dropped like a stone to realise it, growing heavier with every beat. But I had to fight against despair, harder than I'd fought against anything. For I'd sworn it: death would not steal Arthur away.

At the threshold, though, I'd faltered.

The last time I'd seen Arthur, we'd argued. I'd been so angry, so jealous, hurt and bewildered. Because Arthur and I were not just kin – by blood or fostering. We weren't just lovers. Lovers came and went. We were *meant*. Fated. When we were together, we were whole. He used to believe that as much as I did. He used to say it as often as me, and yet Guinevere, with her bright beauty, had blinded him.

Agravaine – oh, Agravaine. Rugged, beguiling Agravaine. If Arthur hadn't turned from me first, I would never have sought another. But he had – and I did. And I was blinded too. I let myself be swayed, wanting so much to believe in him. I could not – or would not – see him for what he truly was: vain, ambitious, and ruthless. Every word, every gesture, every kindness he offered part of a bigger design.

Nor could I see how like him I'd become.

Almost.

And if I had, ironically, his love might have been what I'd wanted all along – truer.

Arthur and I, we were both guilty. But what did guilt matter now?

What did *any* of it matter if he died?

It would matter to some – eyes turning towards Lumiel. Others, though, in distant corners of this fractured land, would look to someone else.

Mordred.

I'd hesitated, though I knew I shouldn't. Two urgent tasks lay ahead of me: heal Arthur, then return to Gwynedd. But return to what? Urien dead, almost certainly. Agravaine had been content to let me keep his father alive while he waited for his gods to reveal his purpose. But now that he'd found it, would he ensure Urien received the strict regime of tinctures he needed as strictly as I did, or be too consumed by that other purpose to bother with anything beyond it?

Urien! My heart ached for him. Too old to be a husband, but a man I'd cared for all the same. Someone *incapable* of betrayal, who clung to his beliefs, who'd cherished his wife before me with all his heart, and gave me the love that remained.

I would miss him. I already did.

I *grieved* him.

There was no room in my heart to grieve another.

I'd pushed open the door and saw them first: Guinevere and Lancelot. Her in his arms, his lips pressed to her hair, and whispering.

Hush, my love. My love. Ah, Guinevere, my dearest love.

I'd seen this devotion take root the day she wed Arthur. In the chapel, as she recited her Christian vows, her eyes had found Lancelot, and his had found hers. The sigh that escaped her…the gasp from him…they collided with such force, their hearts knowing before they themselves did that they must be entwined.

I'd seen it – felt it – but in my last meeting with Arthur,

I hadn't spoken of it, even though to do so might have made him see sense, might have made him realise that Guinevere, his queen, was neither perfect nor truly his, nor ever would be.

Why hadn't I told him?

This was a time for truths indeed. I hadn't told him because I was cruel. That dark, shadowed part of me – so hard to silence – had risen. I'd wanted him to find out in my absence what it was like to be on the receiving end of betrayal. To love someone so deeply, only to have them forsake you. I wanted him to feel like a fool. To wail. To curse – both the gods and himself. Because that's what he would have become.

Cursed, like me.

His queen and his dearest friend – both would betray him.

And the sting would never fade. Just as mine never had.

All that dark conniving, those heinous wishes… They'd crumbled too now, along with our broken dreams of youth. Ah, life, it was never simple. Paths never straight.

I wanted Arthur to live. Did the two in front of me want the same?

I coughed to interrupt them, and Guinevere stepped back at once, slipping from Lancelot's arms. Though the room was kept dim, with the shutters drawn, I could see well enough how she paled at the sight of me, just as Merlyn had.

But it wasn't she who spoke my name.

"Morgan!" Lancelot breathed, blinking as if in doubt. "You're here. How?"

"I'm here," I said, offering no further explanation. "And it is *Queen* Morgan."

"Queen…" he echoed, his voice then trailing off.

Guinevere said nothing as I approached.

"I see you're being consoled well, my lady?" I said.

"I…I…" Her chest rose and fell in sharp, shallow breaths. One hand fluttered to her throat to clutch at a pendant there – a moonstone, white, not black like mine. She was the one Arthur had given it to, a stab in my gut because of it.

I stopped just short of them. "It is truly I," I said, as the pair continued to stare at me in disbelief. "Flesh and blood, Lancelot, Guinevere. No apparition."

"A queen," Lancelot murmured again, in shock, or was it…admiration?

We'd been happy once, he and I. Content, in our own way. We'd suited each other – in the bedroom, especially. It was there we'd connected most of all.

Was it the same with Guinevere now? Or something different entirely?

With Arthur it had been different, not rough and tumble, more tender. Yet a woman could enjoy both, and Arthur…he would have learned.

Ah, such musings at a time like this!

"I am Queen of Gwynedd," I clarified.

"Gwynedd…in Cymru?" Lancelot's interest deepened. "You went there?"

I nodded. "And now I've returned. Because Arthur," I would not call him *brother* again, a word forced on me, "needs me." I turned to Guinevere. "Leave us."

"You cannot…" she began, before indignation almost strangled her.

"*Leave us.*" This time I barked the command, pouring every ounce of my will, my power, into it. I *dared* her to defy me. She knew what I'd just seen.

247

Lancelot took her arm. "Come," he urged gently. "If only for a few moments." When she resisted still, he added, "My lady, please."

How tight the beautiful Guinevere's voice was as she stood there, clothed in ivory, with her golden hair tumbling and her white moonstone glowing – the very vision of purity. And I? I was cloaked in black with the dust of the road still on my boots.

"I will leave," she said, "but for a few moments only. *Morgan*."

Just Morgan.

To her, I would never be a queen.

CHAPTER TWENTY-FIVE

I laughed. "Do you remember that, Arthur? Oh, you must! And how Priscilla chided us. We were meant to use the flour for bread – we'd ground the grain ourselves – but *you*, and I swear it was *you*, threw the first handful. What choice did I have but to retaliate? By the gods, the mess we made! And we'd just washed, too, in the troughs behind the house. We covered the kitchen in flour; every surface was white, the walls even. You were laughing so hard I thought you'd collapse. Both of us doubled over, holding our sides for fear they might split. But Priscilla – Priscilla was *furious*. She dragged us out of the kitchen by our ears and dunked us back in the troughs. But I saw it, Arthur. She was pretending at fury, hiding a smirk behind all that scolding. Our laughter, yours and mine, ah, she loved it, how it would echo through the house. She and Ector both. Happy times, Arthur. They were such…happy times."

I'd rushed to his bedside, *flung* myself towards him after Lancelot and Guinevere left, and seized his hand – limp, the skin so cold – pressing it to my lips, covering it in kisses. The hand that would wield mighty Excalibur. The same hand that would hold mine, just as I'd held his, time and again through the years. Whenever he was afraid, whenever he was happy, whenever he just needed me, I was there.

Did he know I was here now?

Did he realise how much *I* needed *him*?

More memories of our childhood spilled from my lips.

"That day we saw the sea – surely one of your finest memories, just as it is mine – our first glimpse of it together. We didn't know then that Priscilla and Ector had strict instructions not to take us far, to keep us safely closeted at the villa, where in truth we were happy enough to be. Among the barns and the soft green grass, the deep, dark woods that encircled us, the sky always so blue overhead. But Ector… Ector told us stories by the hearth. Among them tales of the sea and how vast it was, how magnificent. And in telling them, he set your imagination on fire! You *had* to see it. You begged, again and again. And really, who could ever refuse you, Arthur?"

Still holding his hand, I let my mind drift further back.

We hadn't known, that morning, that we were going. The day had begun like any other: we woke, wandered down to the kitchen, and breakfasted on oats and dried fruit. It was another beautiful morning – the kind that earned the Summer Country its name – the air already warm, the light tinged with gold. At the window, a lacewing had fluttered, and, as always, I'd called it to me, to admire the shimmer of its wings.

We'd just finished breakfast, and Priscilla was clearing our bowls, when Ector appeared.

"Are we ready, family?" he'd asked.

Priscilla had smiled at him. "Yes, Ector. I think we are."

I'd frowned. "Ready for what?"

Beside me, Arthur had simply tilted his head.

"How old were we then?" I now murmured. "Eight. That's it. I was eight, and you were six."

There'd been another exchange of smiles between

Priscilla and Ector, decidedly conspiratorial this time, then Ector couldn't contain the secret any longer.

"We're going to the sea!" he'd blurted out.

"The sea?" I'd echoed, at first unable to believe it. "But...what about our chores?"

There was always so much to do at the villa. We kept chickens and pigs then, so there were eggs to gather, animals to feed, and pens to clean. Water had to be hauled from the well, floors swept, bedding shaken out, and laundry scrubbed. But before I could voice any of this, Priscilla had raised her hand.

"It's done, Morgan," she'd said. "Everything that needs to be."

Arthur had had no such worries. Once the news settled in, he'd leapt from his stool, bouncing up and down with his fists in the air.

"We're going to the sea!" he'd shouted. "Morgan, did you hear that? The sea!"

His laughter had rung out, bright and infectious. Priscilla had urged us to hurry, to head outside and climb into Ector's cart. She said it was a long way, so there was no time to waste. We'd obeyed at once, though I half-feared it was a jest, that the promise would be snatched away, for if we ever went anywhere, it was only to the local village. But no, our foster parents would never let us down in that way.

It was a long journey to the coast, just as Priscilla had said, the paths often bumpy, jolting us from side to side, but this had only made us children laugh harder.

"We held hands even then," I whispered to Arthur now, though I was lost in the past, quite lost. "And I remember thinking...there was no one I'd rather share this first sight with than you. I wanted *all* our firsts to be together."

The journey had passed as journeys do, Priscilla handing us pouches of water to drink from and fruit to nibble on. As a growing boy, Arthur loved his food. The only time he ever truly grumbled was when his stomach was empty, but Priscilla knew that as well as I did, and she hadn't wanted anything to mar the day.

Magic.

I've heard people question the truth of it – earthly magic; the magic bestowed by the gods, and the darker kind too, that was steeped in sacrifice and bargaining. I'd known all of it so far, and could say, with certainty, it wasn't all myth. There was substance to it, if not always understanding. But this – a simple day shared with family – was when magic was at its most powerful.

When it was rooted in love.

At last, we arrived. We were at the coast, Priscilla assured us, but if so, there was no sign of it, though the ground had changed below us. It was no longer just mud, baked hard in the sun; there was a softness to it now, a granular texture. Arthur bent down, scooping some into his hands, then letting it pour through his fingers.

"That's sand," Ector said. "And it means the sea is near." He then raised a finger in the air, held it for a moment, then brought it to his mouth and licked it.

"You try," he said to Arthur and me as we watched. "Tell me what you taste."

We mimicked him, curious, and I answered first. "Salt."

He nodded. "That's right. The salt of the sea. Another sign we're close."

Arthur was beside himself now, fidgeting and impatient. "But where is it?"

"Come," Ector said. "You'll hear it before you see it."

And he was right. We did.

It was a sound unlike any I'd heard before – not a roar, as the sea is so capable of, a wrathful thing, crashing against the shores – but the gentlest of whispers. Perfectly rhythmic. Soothing. Punctuated only by the cry of a bird overhead.

The ground beneath us was all sand now, soft and shifting, and the horizon shimmered with a silvery-white glow. There was no one else that we could see; the world as we knew it had vanished. Gone were the green fields, the trees, the clutter and noise of our household with its horses and livestock.

This was…serene. Vast. Still.

The promise of the sea pulled us forwards, Arthur and I scanning the vista.

And then – we saw it.

There it was, as if hiding in plain sight, an *expanse* of sea, its briny scent sharp and clean. Salt on our lips, yes, but also clinging to our skin, and tangling our hair.

Priscilla had my hand, Ector had Arthur's, and now they let go.

I turned to Priscilla.

"Go," she urged. "Go closer."

We didn't just run towards it; we kicked off our shoes so we could feel the sand beneath our feet. Until then, I'd only ever known the grass of home or the mud of the riverbank, but the sand was as fine as the flour we ground, prompting an urge to coat myself in it from head to toe, to truly be something the sea had spawned.

We ran as fast as we would gallop on horseback in later years, never once breaking stride. Unstoppable. Straight to the water's edge.

And there we stood.

Side by side, we stared at the sea, ablaze in the sunlight, its shifting colours, green and blue, the silver-white clouds mirrored in its surface. The *lazy* sea, I thought of it then, waves rolling in at such a leisurely pace, soft and constant.

Whispering. Whispering. Whispering.

It spoke a language without words, though like Ector it told a story. One of distance, and depth, and time. Of secrets long since drowned.

Arthur and I at the edge of the sea.

At the edge of *everything* – the precipice.

A magnificent moment shared, and the desire to share many, many more.

"And we have, haven't we, Arthur?" I said, returning again to the present, though I longed to stay where I was – in that place where Arthur was something bright, and full of life, not so diminished. I longed for Arthur the baby. Arthur the boy. The young man. The king. The warrior. Invincible – though I knew no one ever truly was.

I sat there, recounting memories, his hand held tightly in mine, but what I hadn't done yet – not truly – was look at him.

I hadn't dared.

I had to summon up the bravery, examine his face.

He was frail. Frailer even than Urien, though so much younger. Twenty-four summers, that was all. So many more should follow.

Oh, how I wanted to look away! To tell another story instead, not only of those rare, exceptional moments from our childhood, like that visit to the sea, but also of the mundane as well. For I saw it now: there'd been magic in that too. In the ordinary. The everyday. But my task was to measure how close to death he'd come.

His long golden curls – his bright, boyish halo – were gone. His hair had been shorn in the Roman style. It should have made him look every bit the war leader he was, but instead, he had shrunk before me, and with each shallow breath, seemed to shrink further. There was no expression of pain. Would that there were – some grimace, some tension, anything to show he was in there still. Still fighting. But his brow was smooth, and his skin as white as bone. As white as death could be.

As if…as if he'd…*accepted* his fate.

"No!"

Arthur could do many things to me – but not this.

Not die.

If only his eyes were open. If only I could see the grey of them, just once more.

"It's me," I said, repeating what I'd said when I first arrived. "It's Morgan. I'm here now. It's all right, Arthur, I'm here, and I won't leave you. I won't do that again."

Priscilla believed the blade that had struck him had been laced with wolfsbane. If she was right, it would have begun with a burning at the wound, then a tingling. Numbness would have spread as the heart slowed, leading to muscle weakness, to paralysis – and finally this: a sleep so deep you could not be woken from it, the poison spreading further with each day, each hour, each moment.

In truth, I was surprised. His death should have come sooner. It was likely only because he was so young, his body strong from being trained in warfare, that kept him clinging on. But it was there – his final breath – waiting, as determined as I was.

I should act. Prepare poultices of dried mustard seed and garlic for his chest and feet, to stir the blood, and keep it moving. Drip a tincture of angelica root between his lips. The room was warm, but I could make it warmer, hot enough to *sweat* the poison out. I could invoke the Great Mother, and Brigid, Arianrhod, Ceridwen – all of them – begging and begging them to spare him. I could circle the bed with juniper, sharp and clean as salt, to chase out the stink of death, refusing to countenance it.

I could do all that, but it had been done before. Priscilla had told me. She'd tried it all, and still he lay there. Unmoving. Unchanged. Not even stirred by me.

I had no time to waste. I *knew* that. But my body had become as rigid and as helpless as his. I continued to clutch at his hand, my vision swimming, blurred with tears. I didn't just want to weep; I wanted to scream at him, to *make* him hear me.

"I'm here! Doesn't that mean anything, Arthur? Give me a sign. *You.* Not the gods, not the goddesses. It has to be you."

As memories had tumbled from me, so now did words – spilling in a torrent.

"I can bear it now. Truly, I can – if Guinevere is your true love and not me. If you fill this court wall to wall with Christians. If, when you wake, you never wish to see me again because you believe it was *I* who betrayed *you* by leaving – without even a goodbye. I can bear all of that," I repeated on a sob. "But I cannot bear this: your death. Your death will be the thing that breaks me. For the love of all we once had – and Arthur, it was a great love, it was – do *not* succumb." A breath, a silence, and then I leaned closer, my voice trembling now. "I will do anything, Arthur. *Everything* possible. Just don't leave me." Then the truth wrenched itself free, naked and raw. "I...I can't live if you don't live.

I… Arthur… I'm scared without you."

I squeezed my eyes shut, clinging to him, afraid that the flood of tears I'd unleashed might not swamp only me but him too. Wash us both away.

Would that be so terrible?

Perhaps that mournful tide would carry us back to the shores we once stood on together, with no one else around, not even Ector and Priscilla. Just the two of us, children again, innocent again, our hearts full of joy and wonder. We could take a step forwards, then another, and another. Become the sea. Let time and tide take us.

Vanish.

Dreams. Just dreams.

Imagination.

"Oh, Arthur," I cried, my own heart caught in paralysis too. Let the world, the wars rage on without us, for we both knew it: fate could be cruel.

And then, in the midst of my misery, I heard it. The door. It creaked open behind me, and footsteps approached, quick and determined, not tentative in the least.

I was about to turn, to face Guinevere, to say what, I didn't yet know. Perhaps I'd bark at her again, demand more time. I was Arthur's kin before she ever was. I had a right to be here. Maybe – just maybe – I'd do with her as I had with the tide at Gwynedd and force her back by sheer will alone. Expel her from this room, slam the door behind her, and let it open only when *I* said so – not a moment before.

I was about to do all that…

When I felt as well as heard something.

The slightest something.

Barely discernible.

Arthur's hand was in mine. Lifeless. Limp. Or it had been.

As I stared at our clasped hands, I realised it still appeared lifeless. But a moment before – a *heartbeat* before – something had changed.

His hand had squeezed mine, however briefly.

He *knew* I was here!

He was…*glad* I was. That I'd come. Ridden out of the mists, as I'd once vanished into them. And if I was here…then he wanted to be here too.

He wanted to live.

"You've had long enough with him. He needs to rest. Morgan. Morgan, do you hear me? He is my husband. *Mine*. You must do as I—"

I turned to Guinevere, viper-quick.

"Hot water," I demanded. "As hot as you can make it. Scalding."

Her brow creased, marring her loveliness.

"Hot water? He's been bathed already today! Morgan, you must heed—"

"Bring bowls. Bring cloths. A stack of them. Open the shutters at the window, but keep the fire stoked. We need warmth *and* air. And call Priscilla too."

Her eyes, the colour of cornflowers, locked onto mine, while behind her the shadow of a man lingered – Lancelot, of course. Ever hovering. Always near.

I released Arthur's hand, though it pained me, and laid it back at his side.

Morgan the Healer.

Morgan the Destroyer.

Morgan, Arthur's Saviour.

I'd done it before, saved him. I would do it again.

Guinevere trembled in the face of my resolve, as uncertain as she'd been when I'd first met her here at the caer, before her wedding to Arthur, when Merlyn had insisted on introducing us. Then, she'd been timid, tearful, or had appeared to be, but underneath it all, cunning and wily. But now, any guile she'd had was gone. She was as scared as I'd been just moments before. As well she might be, if Arthur lived.

"What…what is it you're going to do?" she said, her voice barely a whisper.

I told her plainly. "Cut the poison out of him. That's what."

CHAPTER TWENTY-SIX

Guinevere was hysterical. Screaming. Protesting. Having to be restrained.

"She will butcher him," she shrieked. "That's what she intends! Unhand me – stop it. We can't let her do this!"

"Or what?"

It was Merlyn who spoke, who was the calm beneath the chaos, as Lancelot held Guinevere as gently – but as effectively – as he could, keeping her from flying at me as I held aloft the knife I'd secured, its blade red-hot from the fire.

"Or *what*?" Merlyn repeated, his voice unshaken. "Guinevere, we have tried *everything*. Arthur is dying. That he even breathes still is a miracle, but miracles run dry. And he is not meant to die. Not yet. It is a travesty what the Saxons have wrought, but we will rain fire and arrows down on them for it, hound them from this island once and for all. *Arthur* will. Because that's what's been foretold. What the gods have decreed. Perhaps..." and I saw how hard it was for him to say this, "Morgan is right. Cutting the poison out may be our only chance. Draining it from him. Our *only* chance, do you understand? All we have left."

"God will save him," Guinevere cried, still struggling. "God! No one else."

"But He hasn't, not yet." It was Lancelot who dared to

voice it. "And we need Arthur, my Queen. Without him...we *all* fall."

"Remove her," I said, cold and clear. "I need to focus."

Guinevere – who'd once clung to me on her first night at the caer – now reviled me. But I didn't care. All that mattered was Arthur. Priscilla had arrived and now stood beside me, ready with a bowl to catch the blood, her eyes urging me onwards, for Arthur's breathing, since all had entered the room, had become more laboured, a rattle in his chest that would only become more pronounced if Guinevere didn't dispense with her screaming.

"If Arthur dies," she went on, refusing to be silenced, "then it is *God's* will! We cannot set ourselves against it. No, this isn't what we foresaw – what *you* foresaw, Merlyn – but doesn't that prove something? That the gods you cling to are nothing but smoke and air? Arthur's soul must be consigned to the One True God. He needs the bishop, not *her*. Someone to anoint him, to guide his soul to Heaven. *Heaven*, Merlyn – not the Otherworld. And yet here he lies, surrounded by those who will imperil him. Hear me, all of you. You must! I am queen here. The High Queen."

The blade was hot enough. I needed to cut soon, to take advantage of the heat before it faded, but Guinevere's hysteria, her insults, were making my hands tremble.

I stood abruptly, the stool behind me crashing to the floor.

I turned to her, took a step forwards, the knife still raised.

"Is there any reason – *besides* the supposed will of your God – that you don't want Arthur to live? Something, perhaps, that we should *all* know about?"

Deliberately, my gaze shifted – from her to Lancelot, then back again.

She knew what that look meant, exactly what I was implying. Whatever existed between them might be secret, but not from me.

Lancelot…how hard he swallowed. His grip on Guinevere slackened in shock, then tightened again as he no doubt tried to master his racing heart as much as she struggled to master hers. She wanted a Christian court. All sanctity, all piety. *Hypocrite.* For in the eyes of her own faith, adultery was a grave sin. Some leniency granted to men, perhaps, but never to women.

I stared harder at her, watching her weigh my words, the threat in them.

It was a dangerous game she was playing. And so was he – my former lover – who stared back at me with pleading in his eyes. *Don't hurt her, Morgan. Please.*

Oh, how he loved her! He was besotted. Blinded. But there was something else too – he was torn. His love for me may have died, reduced to ashes in the wake of Guinevere, but his love for Arthur? *That* still lived, for I read something else in his eyes. *Do it. If it will save him, do it. Even if my own ruin follows.*

Even if hers did too? Guinevere's?

Merlyn, who'd watched the entire exchange in silence, with a look as wily as any Guinevere could conjure, came forwards.

"My Queen," he said, addressing Guinevere as he reached for her arm.

She shook him off. Shook off Lancelot too.

"Heathen," she said, aiming the word solely at me before turning and stalking from the room, as I held the blade still, as it glinted in my palm.

Rain lashed outside as I worked.

Earlier, after Guinevere left, Priscilla gripped my arms and looked into my eyes.

"You said you've learned much while you've been away?"

"Yes, Mother," I'd replied.

"At Avalon *and* Gwynedd?"

"Yes."

She'd frowned at that. "Taught by *whom* in Gwynedd?"

She was right to be concerned. She was Arthur's foster mother as much as mine. The thought of losing him – after losing Ector, after years spent grieving me – was almost too much to bear. Her eyes brimmed with sorrow, but there was hope there too.

It was as Merlyn said, this was the only path left. All the tinctures, the herbs, the prayers – whether they be fervent or whispered – none of it had been enough. If we were going to save him, we had to go further.

"I wouldn't hurt him," I said. "Mother…you know that."

She'd nodded. She did know.

"Then I'm here to help in whatever way I can. *You* guide *me*, Morgan."

I smiled. Once again, the student would become the teacher, though I'd never done *this* before. But desperation…it can summon all manner of braveries.

We'd had to reheat the blade, for it had cooled somewhat. The only other person allowed to stay was a boy, ordered to keep the fire stoked. The rain had brought with it a chill, a gloom descending too, as clouds blotted out what little sun remained.

The room was still.

So still.

A hush thick with anticipation.

The wound, as Cai had said, was not deep, but it had fully closed, sealing the poison inside. The skin around it had putrefied, was blackened and swollen, a map of raised veins pulsing beneath the surface. Now it had to be cut open again – carefully, cleanly – the blade I held had not just been reheated but sharpened enough to slice air. Dipped too into a concoction of vinegar and rosemary.

Priscilla held the bowl as the blood flowed, as I forced my hands to stay steady, even as the sight of it churned my stomach. Arthur's life blood, ebbing away.

The stench filled the room, stinging our eyes. It was the smell of death *and* venom – worse than anything I'd encountered on a battlefield.

Now came the time to change tools. I laid down the knife, Priscilla handing me an obsidian shard instead. It was as sharp as the blade, but more than that: sacred – something magnetic, able to draw the poison to it, as my hands embedded it deeper, then deeper still. How far had the poison spread? There was no way of knowing.

My mouth opened, and I called on every deity I knew to lend me their strength, to work with me. The words I spoke were drawn almost entirely from the scrolls – the gods' own language, ancient and solemn, used only when I needed them to hear me most. Words I doubted Priscilla had ever heard before, perhaps not even Merlyn.

"Bréssan na craven, voscaíl an belach. Tarran na'nim vo bronnan na feloch. Le fuil, glaneth; le peyn, eilith."

Whatever Priscilla might have thought of their strange

cadence, and the weight that trembled beneath them, I couldn't stop. *Break the skin,* I'd said. *Open the path. Draw the poison from the womb of flesh. With blood, be cleansed; with pain, depart.*

"Imrech! Imrech! Imrech!" *Begone! Begone! Begone!*

I called to the Fay as well. "Ossan na Sídhen, camhara é. Camhara é." *Breath of the Fay, keep him safe. Keep him safe.* "Marai!" *Please.*

If I thought Arthur might at least flinch with all that I was doing to his body, he didn't, but I had to hold on to faith. The gods worked in ways we didn't always understand. The path, even towards healing, as crooked as any.

One bowl of blood filled, then another, and another, and still it ran dark, not bright as healthy blood should be. It was still tainted.

Would it ever be anything else?

"Morgan…" Priscilla breathed, but I dug deeper.

"This is the only way," I told her. "A purge. It *has* to be a purge."

What chants fell from my lips now, what incantations, what frantic, desperate pleas, I no longer knew. The language tangled in my head, but no matter. The gods *would* hear, so I continued to weave words around him, *spells*, as the blood poured.

"Arianrhod, silver wheel, hold him in your stars! Do not let his thread be cut. Bind it, weave it, keep it whole. Brigid, pour your fire into his veins, let your bright source quicken him. Morrigan, dark sister, not yet – not yet. Turn your raven's eye away!"

There was so *much* blood!

Not just filling bowls, it soaked the garments I wore,

coated my hands to the elbows, and spilled across the floor in deepening puddles.

Priscilla would be quieted no more.

"Enough," she said, seizing my arm. "Morgan, it is enough!"

Outside, the rain fell harder than ever.

She was handing me something – a mixture I'd prepared earlier from moss, honey, and pine resin, to pack the wound and ward off further infection. Taking it from her, I did as she bid. After I'd finished, she asked me to step aside. She'd stitch it herself, her fingers swift and sure, working a thread of sinew through torn flesh.

Arthur… What he'd endured…

All for the sake of healing. It had to be. A tincture brewed from many plants, mandrake root among them, was dripped between his lips, in case he felt any pain.

I *wanted* him to feel pain – not be this, a hollow shell.

Had our efforts been in vain?

"Believe," Priscilla said.

I nodded. She was right. I had to.

And you, Arthur, you believe too.

We'd done what we could.

All that remained now…was to wait.

CHAPTER TWENTY-SEVEN

Everyone in the caer waited.

Lives – like Arthur's – held in suspension.

Guinevere had left his chamber, but when she returned, she made a show of it.

Servants scurried ahead of her, bringing all she needed to settle in: bedding laid beside his, a comfortable chair by the fireside instead of a stool, everything arranged to suggest she meant to dwell there indefinitely. All so the people could say: *Ah, she is always there, do you see? At Arthur's side. Praying for him. Utterly devoted.*

What they wouldn't do, what they'd conveniently forget, was to ask: *Why now? Why not before?* Yes, she'd visited him. As his wife, she was duty bound to do so. But always with Lancelot. Her gallant champion, supporting the queen in her grief. Why, though, had she never stayed? Why return to her own chamber each time?

I would have stayed.

They'd forget because she was a queen. And no one must question the queen.

Except me.

I questioned her, not aloud, but with my eyes. *Why, Guinevere? Why, why, why?*

She'd sit by the fire, stiff-backed, resolute, but defensive too. Defensive because she knew I understood that the *why* was because of me.

This overt gesture wasn't about devotion. It was performance, a quiet denunciation. A message to the caer that she didn't trust me – Arthur's so-called sister. She didn't condone what I'd done – the 'heathen' rites, the blood, the blade.

And if Arthur died…

It would be my fault.

In her eyes, I'd given no one hope, rather I'd snatched it away.

So we sat – she and I – in that sometimes stifling room with Arthur still lying silent on the bed, and we *both* watched. We *both* waited. Lancelot kept away now, making a show too of absence rather than presence. Aside from the servants, only Priscilla and Merlyn were allowed to enter. And then Lumiel, Arthur and Guinevere's child, came too. And when he did – when I first saw him – he stole my breath.

It was Merlyn who ushered him in. The boy entered hesitantly, his steps small and uncertain. Guinevere's eyes were closed at the time, lightly sleeping, and I was grateful that she couldn't see my face, couldn't witness my reaction.

My child, Mordred, was dark-haired and grey-eyed. But *this* child – ah, his curls were as fair as Arthur's had once been. And though the room lay dim, candles softly spluttering, I could well imagine his eyes were grey too. There was no doubt here whose son he was, for he bore Guinevere's extraordinary beauty as well. A child that was…perfect. That if he were mine, I could not help but love.

Arthur's second-born.

"Mama," he said – at first a whisper as he and Merlyn

stepped further into the room, but then childish excitement outweighed the gravity of the moment. "Mama!"

Guinevere's eyes snapped open. "Lumiel!" she exclaimed, her expression, always pinched when in my company, softening at once. "Son, come here. Come to me."

He ran straight to her arms, her smile widening as she gathered him close. It was plain – in the way she ruffled his hair, in the soft words she murmured into his ear – how much she loved him. Just as plain was how he basked in that love. *Easy.* It was so easy for her. When it had been so difficult for me. I should have felt further bitterness then, let hatred flare deeper. But, for a moment, I didn't. All I wanted was to bask in that love too, because like knowledge, it seemed boundless. Not a threat, but an answer. Something that raised Guinevere higher than any man could.

He was the love of her life. Not Arthur. Not Lancelot. Her child, Lumiel.

Lumiel, who'd seemed so fine, as Merlyn had said, so strong, but who now began to cough.

"He is ill?" I asked, more to myself than to Guinevere.

"Have you not been given your tincture this morning?" she checked.

Lumiel nodded, his curls bouncing. "Yes, Mama! I had two spoonfuls!"

Her eyes widened in mock surprise. "Two? Ah, then you are being spoiled!" Quickly, though, her brow furrowed. "It doesn't seem to have eased it, though."

"I *am* well, Mama," Lumiel insisted, coughing again, though only slightly. "I was promised a honeyed drink too, after my visit with you," and then with mischievous laughter he added, "with an *extra* spoonful of honey."

Guinevere laughed with him. Even wily old Merlyn in

the shadows smiled.

I came forwards.

"Arthur," I said. "I'll need to tend to his wound again. Soon."

I couldn't do it with Lumiel in the room, for the smell of infection was ripe still, barely tolerable to the grown, let alone to a child.

Still in his mother's arms, the boy whirled around.

"Who's she?" he asked, pointing one finger at me.

"She…" Any joy on Guinevere's face quickly faded. "She is—"

Merlyn came forwards too. "She is Morgan," he said. "Arthur's sister. Your aunt."

"My aunt?" Lumiel repeated, clearly surprised. "I have an aunt?" And then he glanced at his mother, the same frown as hers on his face. "Mama, *what* is an aunt?"

Guinevere's chest rose and fell. I could see it well enough beneath the bodice she wore as she tried to explain. That I hated her was something I could understand. That she hated me so much…why? Did she truly believe I would say something about her and Lancelot – stir rumours, sow discord?

Was I *that* convincing?

Again, Merlyn intervened.

"Morgan, come. Let Lumiel visit with his father. We will go for a walk; some fresh air will do you good." When I hesitated, not wanting to leave Arthur's side, he insisted, though his voice was surprisingly gentle. "It's just for a short while, Morgan."

At last I moved, Lumiel then slipping from his mother's arms and rushing to Arthur's bedside. "Father! Father! Will you wake now? I've so much to tell you. I've learned my letters – yes, letters! The priests have been teaching me."

I nearly baulked at that, but Merlyn was already guiding me to the door.

When out in the courtyard, I couldn't deny the fresh air *was* welcome. I drew it into my lungs deeply, purposefully, a bid to cleanse myself as I'd tried to cleanse Arthur.

"You're exhausted," Merlyn said, watching me closely.

"I'm fine," I replied.

"Morgan…" He reached into his cloak for a small leather pouch. "Here. Take this."

"What is it?" I asked, not reaching for it.

He sighed and gave a small, impatient shake of his head. "It isn't poison, Morgan. Think of it as a tonic, something to revive you." Still I hesitated. "It's made with nettle leaf," he continued, "wild thyme, willow bark…and a splash of elderberry wine."

I raised an eyebrow. "Ah. The secret to your youth, Merlyn? A…*vital*?"

He laughed. "It is merely a pleasant drink I've grown fond of. Go on – take some. Who knows, you might grow fond of it too."

Relenting, I took it and drank. The cordial was potent, sending a burst of fire rushing through my limbs when they had felt so slack, so heavy.

He was right, I was exhausted. It had been two days since I'd cut Arthur. Two days, and still no change. He should have shown some sign of improvement by now.

If Guinevere had moved into his chamber, if she'd dozed on the cot beside his bed, or curled in the chair by the fire, I'd barely closed my eyes. And when I did, it was only to dream of blood. Rivers of it. *Oceans.* Not waves lapping at my feet, as they once had that long-ago day on the shore with Arthur, but blood – drenching us.

I must have swayed slightly on my feet, as Merlyn took my arm again, steadying me as he led me further towards the rear of the caer, to a place I used to roam with Lancelot. Where my young love had kissed me. And I'd kissed him back – harder.

Memories clung to the air here. They were everywhere, all I had left.

"How fares Urien?" Merlyn asked, his tone light, almost casual, as though we were two friends passing the time of day.

"Old," I said. "It's likely he'll be dead by the time I return."

Did he flinch at that? At how plainly I'd said it?

"And before you ask," I went on, "Gwynedd – even with me at the helm, should I choose to remain – will not bend the knee to Arthur. In that respect, Urien's will shall be honoured. His kingdom is not the property of another."

"Urien was – *is* – a fine man," was all Merlyn said in response.

"Yes," I replied firmly.

A strip of stone, half-claimed by moss, lay nearby, and he gestured towards it. We sat together, gazing out over the hilltop, its slopes flowing softly into the valley below. To the left stretched woodland – the same woods that hid the silent pool.

For a while, we said nothing, just admired the vista, then I broke the silence.

"Much is the same here," I said. "And much has changed." Before he could respond, I turned to him. "How Christian a court has this become, Merlyn?"

His gaze stayed fixed on the horizon. "What should

concern you – what concerns *me* – are the Saxons. Their threat."

I couldn't accept that deflection. "There are two battles being fought, and you know it. The Saxons, yes. *Of course* we must rally against them. But we fight them for the very same reasons we resist the Christians, because in the end, they will both take everything from us. All that this land is, and all it has ever been, will be lost – washed into the mists alongside the Fay, never to return – if we don't."

As tired as I was, there was still passion in my veins, I was glad to note. But if mine burned, his seemed to have faded, despite whatever cordial he liked to sip.

"This land is fractured, Morgan. It has been for so long. *Centuries.* The darkness is…so dark. So hard to see a way through it sometimes—"

"Merlyn—"

He turned then, his voice a rasp. "Listen to me! We do what we can. Do you hear? *What we can.* What we can get away with. I'm the Archdruid of Britannia, but I am still just a man. *One* man, who is growing older by the day. I fear what this world will become if we *don't* act, using whatever means are left to us, *whomever.*" He shook his head, his long white hair rippling. "The Christians, their One True God, their sanctimony, I despise it! But for now, they remain the necessary evil. The Saxons, though, are an evil we *cannot* countenance. And you know the reasons why." His gaze bored into mine. "And so, Morgan, it is as I've said, we do what we can."

Mere moments ago, I'd thought him lacking in passion. I'd been wrong.

"Guinevere," I said.

"What about her?"

"You hate the Christians, so do you hate her?"

"Morgan—"

"Was she worth the price we paid for Arthur's cavalry? Their Christ, nailed to his wood – He is *everywhere* in the caer. We're lost, Merlyn. Lost already!"

He stood, and not with the slow creak of age.

"Don't do that," I said.

"Do what?"

"Look down on me." I stood too. "You underestimated the power she could wield. You thought Guinevere a pawn, as you once thought me. But have you considered, Merlyn, that *you* are the pawn? That *we* might one day use *you?*"

I'd spoken to him curtly before, but not like this. He was the Archdruid of Britannia! But I could feel it, rising in my chest, not the fire of the tonic, but something deeper, the power that was there, that had been in my blood since the day I was born.

I was speaking to him as an equal.

And he knew it.

He knew it, yet there was no anger in his face. Only sorrow.

"You don't listen, do you?" he said, and it was that sorrow that finally *compelled* me to do as he asked, and truly hear him. "We do what we can, and we face the consequences. The *wrath*. Your battle is not with me, Morgan, and it never was. You must learn to accept that. If we do what we can, what we believe the gods demand of us, then it can't be wrong, not if it's done for the greater good." He turned from me then, when I wanted him to stay, to explain himself further, to teach me, only feeling his equal when angry, never in this – this sorrow, this weight. For as heavy as my grief was, his was heavier. As burdened as I felt, he carried more.

His suffering was greater.

I reached out, desperate to stop him. To say what? To apologise?

"Merlyn," I began, but he shook me off – gently, yet firmly.

I tried again, but it was no use.

"Save him," he said, already walking away, his black cloak trailing in the dust. "Save Arthur. It *has* to be Arthur. No one else – not even his son – can save us. The gods have been clear on that, at least. Save him…or the darkness will be absolute."

CHAPTER TWENTY-EIGHT

Another day passed. And then another. Days I cursed.

Despite everything I'd done – every deity I'd invoked, the Great Mother even, laying this at her feet – Arthur showed no sign of improvement. He was alive, yes, but still only just, my tears barely restrained as I watched over him. Guinevere's too.

She grew paler by the hour, just as Arthur did, thinner beneath her gown than I'd realised, her hands red and raw from constant wringing.

She loved Lancelot. And Lancelot loved her.

But did she also love Arthur?

It was possible to love two men, I knew that.

I'd loved the *same* men.

In Arthur's chamber, Lancelot, Peredur, Uwaine, the twins Balin and Balan, Lot and Morgause's sons – Gaheris, Gawaine, and Gareth – noble Sagramor, and Cai, entered one by one to gaze upon Arthur. To whisper their farewell into his ear. If some had been away, patrolling Dumnonia's borders, then they'd ridden back in haste. These were his most trusted warriors. His companions. Above all, his friends.

Another had joined them now – Tristan, the son of Mark of Kernow.

I remembered him from Arthur's wedding day. A

striking man then, with dark hair and dark eyes, just like Isolde's, Mark's wife. Mark, as grizzled as Urien, and almost as old, had stood between them like a pillar of stone – those at Avebury or the Henge. But even so, they'd exchanged glances... *Heartbroken* glances.

Tristan was to remain here, at Caer Arthur, to join Arthur's circle. Isolde would return to Kernow with her husband – her rightful place. They'd been distraught at the parting, but now...now Tristan looked *haunted*. His eyes were sunken, his pallor almost as wretched as Arthur's. What had happened? What was his story? It was clear he had one – one that amounted to more than just missing his love. *Far* more.

It was a flicker of curiosity on my part, no more. It was Arthur's continued decline that consumed me, as it did Guinevere. She too was having to steel herself. For we all loved Arthur, no matter what. But more than that, she was also doing her utmost to push me aside. Not only was her bed close to his, she'd now moved her chair closer too, claiming my space and refusing to move. Worse, she'd had a wooden cross hung over his bed, so that he lay in the shadow of it.

She blamed me, as I knew she would. And when the dice was finally cast, she would strike. If she did, though, it would be nothing compared to the attack I'd already launched on myself. Was it the wrong thing to do, cut him open as I had, trying to drain the poison from him? Was it, as Guinevere had insisted, a heathen act? I'd been so careful not to introduce more infection, taken every precaution I could, used every potion before, during, and after, every incantation I could summon.

Had I only made it worse? Was his body just too weak to

take any more?

His companions had filed in, then out again – in silence. Perfect silence.

Curse this silence!

The smell in his chamber wouldn't lift either, the clutch that grim death had on him. Guinevere insisted the room stay dark, with the shutters almost fully closed, and the fire burning low, but I wanted light in here. Me! Not her! The irony of it.

And that cross gone.

It was the three of us again: me, Arthur, and Guinevere.

She wouldn't leave. I wouldn't either. Who knew when his last moment would be?

She sank into her chair, and I wandered over to the fire, again and again asking myself what more I could have done. Whatever Guinevere believed, I'd acted within the bounds of recognised law. But now – should I step beyond it?

The bane in his blood still surged with every ebb and flow. Could I do as I'd done with the tide in Gwynedd – push it back and keep pushing? Push it *out* of him?

It was as though his very spirit had been poisoned, not just his body!

I could try. I could only try. But not with Guinevere watching. She would countenance no more from me, and in the end, this was her realm, not mine, and so I couldn't force it. But my realm – it was a shadow realm. A realm of pleas, of bargaining. His life, his purpose, they mattered more than mine ever had. Not just in recent years, but always. Arthur was what this land needed. What these unsettled times demanded. And I? I could fade away. I already had – for five summers. I could do so forever now. It wasn't me the world would mourn.

A sacrifice.

Like some who'd stood at the edge of Craig y Gwaed, I'd be willing.

I would draw the poison from his body and into my own. Trade places. His blood becoming mine, and mine his – truly, this time. Reminding myself of something else too, that I'd realised only recently while sifting through old memories, that magic was at its most powerful when rooted in love. And this would be. Oh, this would be.

Even as I thought it, my hand reached for the black moonstone at my neck. It hummed at my touch, as though it sensed the righteousness of the act.

Mordred. He would be my only regret in doing this. That I would not be returning to Gwynedd, to his side – that happy child, happy at least in Teg's company, and, perhaps, at last, in mine. I wouldn't be there to shield him from Agravaine, who now, having guessed the truth, had the weapon he'd long sought.

I must make provision.

Arthur would be that provision.

He had to know about Mordred. Had to acknowledge him, even if it was only in private, send warriors there to remove him from Agravaine, by whatever means necessary, and have him placed into gentler, more trusted hands.

Hidden, as we once were, to live the life we never could. Our son.

Definitely, our son. I had no more doubt.

I had a plan, a sense of purpose once more. Guinevere must leave me alone with Arthur, and so, a plan *within* a plan was born. One that Cai could help me with.

On leaving Arthur's chamber, I raced through corridors and courtyards until I found my childhood friend, my *best* friend, other than Arthur, the one whom I trusted without reserve. He was near the Great Hall, deep in conversation with Lancelot.

Both turned as I approached, Cai clearly surprised as I'd been cloistered away for so long, Lancelot's expression closer to embarrassment.

He spoke first, not Cai.

"My lady," he said.

"Lancelot," I returned.

"Arthur—"

"Still lives. Still breathes. Just as he did a short while ago, when you last saw him."

"Thank the gods," he whispered, tears welling in his eyes. "When you appeared... Lady, how do *you* fare? You look so weary. You're as wholly devoted as Guinevere."

I was surprised by how sincerely the words tripped from his tongue, an untruth, essentially. Guinevere was *not* wholly devoted, and no one knew it better than him.

I couldn't help but frown as I looked at him. His grief – like mine, like Cai's – was real. Palpable. The queen's champion. I think he truly believed that that was all he was in this moment. In the shadow of Arthur's impending death, he seemed to have forgotten all else. *Convinced* himself of Guinevere's pious devotion, and of his own.

Arthur, once so besotted with her – besotted enough to forsake me – surely would never have tolerated sharing her. He still didn't know of their betrayal. Not fully.

Lancelot spoke again. "Would you walk with me, Morgan? It's been so long since we last talked. *Properly* talked."

"Where would you have us go?" I asked, my gaze steady. "Through the outer courtyard and onto the hills, as we used to? Or would you prefer somewhere more…*dreunach*?"

He tried to echo the word I'd used from the scrolls. "Dreunach?"

"Hidden," I said. "Or perhaps…secretive. Do you know of such a place?"

I cursed the way the flush rising to his face was, absurdly, quite becoming.

"No. No," he said, with a laugh a little too forced. "Why would I?"

I remained deliberately nonchalant. "Just a thought." Then I turned to Cai. "It's you I've come to speak with. You I'd like to walk with."

Lancelot, unable to stifle a sigh of relief, stepped back, vanishing into the shadows, just as I was so used to doing. Cai, meanwhile, looked nothing short of baffled by the exchange. Before he could question me, I took his arm, casting a glance around to see who else might be near – what ears might be listening.

Whispers were rife at Caer Arthur – I remembered that well. Tongues wagged on all manner of subjects, but never about Guinevere and Lancelot, it seemed. In all the time I'd been there, I hadn't heard a single rumour about the closeness they shared. And no one – but *no one* – must hear what I had to say to Cai.

We seemed to be alone, and so, reaching into my pocket, I took out a small vial.

"Lumiel," I said. "Do you have access to him?"

"Lumiel?" Cai repeated, clearly growing more confused. "Why, I…" He shook his head. "No, not me, personally. The boy has maids, though. Several."

"Any maid in particular?" When he hesitated, I cajoled him. "Cai, I haven't had a chance to ask, are you married yet?"

"Married?" he spluttered. "No! These past years…the wars we've fought…"

"You've been kept busy. But not so busy you haven't got to know a maid or two."

Like Lancelot before him, his face flushed, almost matching the red of his hair. "I've known a few, yes. And yes, one of them has tended to Lumiel in the past, or will know of someone who does now. That vial in your hand…what does it contain?"

"Lumiel has a cough?"

He nodded. "Yes."

"A bad cough?"

"It can prove troublesome at times, certainly."

"And can do so again. It could settle on his chest, and once there, affect his lungs. And when the lungs are involved – lung *fever* – we know how serious that can be."

Cai gasped. "Are you saying…his life may be in jeopardy too? Arthur's *son*?"

"He needs this tincture," I said, holding up the vial. "It will ease the cough. Do away with any…danger. But Guinevere, she doesn't see things the way we do. You know as well as I how effective these tinctures can be, but what would she do instead? Have a priest say a prayer over him?" I snorted for good measure.

"Who knows what will work anymore?" Cai said, sighing, and as much as I baulked to hear it, at perhaps the truth of it, I kept my composure.

"This *will* work. Lumiel needs it. And...we may need Lumiel. If Arthur... If Arthur..."

It was just as well I didn't have to finish, for they were words too abhorrent to utter, let alone hear, as Cai took the vial.

"I'll see it reaches him," he said.

"Tonight?" I said. "A bedtime draught is best. Then it has the night to work."

"Tonight," he confirmed. "Leave it to me."

"And, Cai?"

"Yes?"

"Don't tell anyone about this, will you? And make sure the maid says nothing either. As I've said, Guinevere..."

"You're a great healer, Morgan. I will impress that on her too, though she follows the old ways well enough, *respects* them, as much as we do. The Christian girls," he said with something of a shrug, "I tend to avoid them. Too much like hard work."

I smiled at his jest, but my smile faded as I watched him go, as I wondered at myself – just as I'd wondered at Lancelot earlier – at how easily I could lie too.

CHAPTER TWENTY-NINE

It was late into the night when the rap came at Arthur's door – urgent, sharp.

"My Queen, my Queen, come quickly. Lumiel…"

I was already awake, waiting, but Guinevere had been dozing, snuffling softly in her sleep, and murmuring too. Calling out for someone, as if beseeching them. Her god, perhaps? Or a lover? And if the latter – which one?

At the mention of her son's name, her eyes snapped open.

"Lumiel?" she cried. "What's wrong with him?"

A young woman entered the chamber then, her eyes darting nervously around, tongue flickering across dry lips. "He's coughing," she said. "Badly."

Without so much as a glance in my direction, Guinevere rushed from the room, leaving me alone, at last, with Arthur.

The tincture I'd arranged to be given to Lumiel would do him no lasting harm. It contained coltsfoot, enough to irritate the lungs, not soothe them as I'd claimed. But only briefly. By dawn, he should be well on his way to recovery. If what I'd done was ever discovered – if the maid spoke, or Cai did – there'd be consequences. *Severe* ones. But if Arthur lived because of it, when all around me were abandoning hope, then perhaps Cai, at least, would see it for what it was: a necessary act.

There was no time to waste. The path I walked now was untrodden, and who could say how long it might take?

Before approaching the bed, I crossed to the window and flung open the shutters. Cool night air swept in. I then went to Arthur, candle in hand, and set it on the table beside him. Unclasping my cloak, I let it fall to the floor, gathered my skirts, and climbed onto the bed to tear down the cross that hung over him. Tonight, it would only be me who hovered there, his body so wasted beneath mine.

Swallowing hard, and at the tail end of a deep, ragged sigh, I placed my hands on his chest, closed my eyes, and said nothing. I only imagined. For wasn't it as Agravaine had said – had *taught* me – that imagination *was* my power? And hadn't Caireann echoed something similar too, that it was only disbelief that bound us?

His blood churned like the sea did, broiling within him, fed by a poison that spread and kept spreading – black as the ocean at Gwynedd. And the air…it was thick. Not just with the sharpness of herbs, but with sweat, glistening on his brow and on mine.

I shut my eyes in furious concentration.

My breath – so unlike his – was steady, deep and full, drawn in through my nose, sinking through my body before spiralling into the tips of my fingers.

I pressed it into his chest and let the current flow, envisioning the tide rising with each exhale – gathering strength, hunting the poison, driving it upwards, as it had done with Naw, and with various others since. Forcing it out of the body, through his lungs and throat, lips and nose. *Expelling it.*

Nothing had worked before – Priscilla's touch, Viviane's,

mine. The venom had continued with its journey, devouring him from within.

Ah, but they would pay for this – the Saxons. Every last one of them. As Merlyn had said, Arthur would see to it. And I imagined that too: more battles, Britons and Sea Wolves clashing face to face, their features twisted, taunts flung, and cries ripped from their throats. Cerdic, Aelle – *all of them* – slayed without effort.

The Morrigan herself would swoop low, plucking souls from broken bodies and carrying them far, far from the gates of the Otherworld. For they had no place there – not cowards such as these, not among the great warriors in the feasting halls. Their fate was Meurig's: a place of torment, where no glory could ever reach them.

My chest rose and fell, the sound of life filling the chamber with the utmost determination. With each exhale, my vow carried forwards. I would drive the poison from his body, but it had to go somewhere. Into me. I would draw it in, hold it fast, lie in his stead until something as simple, but as powerful, as breath finally failed me.

A bargain. The gods *loved* a bargain, their appetite without edge.

Out. Out, foul tide. You belong to me, not him. Skath! Skath! Out!

Ah, but the poison was stubborn. It clung to its victim like a leech would.

The sea within him surged, each vein an endless river, and I was cast among its currents, my hair crazed around me as I raised my arms to summon the fiercest wind, the gales that would so often batter Urien's stronghold, the kind no one could withstand – unless you were me. Unless you were Morgan. I *was* the sea. I was the wild wind. The storm-bringer. Not just Morgan, but Black Morgan. And I could do this – I could! – draw the poison from another, scour the rot from such sacred shores.

At first my back was rigid, my spine unyielding, but now, sweeping my hair aside, I bent low and pressed my lips to his. Cold, shockingly so. I forced his mouth wider with my tongue, forging a channel between us through which the tide could rush.

By the Great Mother, who bore the first breath.

By Arianrhod of the silver wheel, keeper of fate.

By Ceridwen of the cauldron, shaper of transformation.

By Brigid of the Flame, healer and guardian of the sacred well.

This poison is mine!

I am the sacrifice, not him.

The land does not need a storm-bringer.

It needs a storm-breaker!

I breathed. I pulled. I willed. I commanded. The tide may resist Agravaine, but it would not resist me. I would take whatever part of Arthur I could, and if that part was only this, the poison that sought to undo him, then so be it. It was still something.

It was him – only him – in my mind. No other existed. No other ever would.

Out! Out! Out!

I am your host. LEAVE HIM BE!

A jolt beneath me, slight at first, barely there. But then…as I lifted myself up, as I opened my eyes and watched, there came another, this one more marked.

He gave a cough, just as his son coughed, a hoarse sound, something else at his lips where mine had just been: a foamy blackness, thick and viscous. I touched my own mouth and felt it there too. The magic had worked! The poison had come!

I shifted off him, hurling the chair back as I'd hurled the cross earlier so I could return to his side and kneel there. I continued to watch, my gaze as sharp as a hawk's, as his body stirred to life again. A battle hard fought, but won.

Arthur, as ever, triumphant.

I reached for his hand. There was a semblance of warmth now. *Glorious* warmth. And *that* would be the thing to spread next, flowing through him, even as I whispered in his ear. "It is done, Arthur. You're healed! You will live!"

It was I who would feel the wolfsbane soon, for it was already creeping through my blood. No pain yet, though… Nothing. Had I thought it would be different, that it would strike instantly, the gods wasting no time?

Soon… The effects would come soon. A bargain had been made. A sacrifice that must be fulfilled. And yet…was it possible we'd *both* been spared?

I shook my head.

Of course I wouldn't be spared. So, while there was life in my limbs, while I could still move, I had to leave Arthur, though as always, I was loath to do so, because look! His breath was more regular too! But I had to go, run through the corridors, find the others, and *tell* them. *Your king lives! He is poisoned no more! Arthur LIVES!*

He would still need tending; it would take time to regain his strength, but Priscilla could do that, nurse her son to full health, her hands always so tender.

Soon he'd be strong enough to deal with *anything*.

One more kiss.

One last, lingering kiss.

My mouth touched his again, no matter what lingered

there, our lips brushing.

"Wherever I go, I will wait for you," I promised. "Don't forget me, Arthur. And if I have ever hurt you, I'm sorry. I forgive you, too, for any hurt you gave me. In this moment, there is nothing but love in my heart for you. Arthur, you *have* to hear me." For there was more I had to say, though I hesitated. I stuttered. "We…we have a son, Arthur. Mordred. He is but five summers old. And he is *yours*. Yours – with my dark hair and your grey eyes. Once I'd healed you, I was to return to him. He is in Gwynedd. Agravaine has him – Urien's son. He knows the truth, that Mordred is yours, he is your firstborn, not Lumiel." My voice faltered again, but I persevered. "I…I don't know what he'll do with that knowledge, but I fear it. Agravaine is a proud man, a keeper of the old ways, as passionate in his convictions as you are in yours. He will do anything – *anything* – to preserve them. So what I fear is this: that he will twist Mordred…*poison* him. Not with wolfsbane, or hemlock – no. There are subtler ways. And I won't be able to stop him, so you must. You must go to Gwynedd and take him from Agravaine. Hide him, Arthur. As soon as you are able." I drew a shaking breath. "Though I struggled to love the child at first, he is sweet nonetheless. Just as you were, he is happy and curious, always running here or there. A *good* boy. Whatever he becomes, remember what I've told you of a little boy so like you. Not Lumiel – *Mordred*. His name is Mordred. Think of him as he once was, and think of me as I used to be too, when we were young, when we would race across meadows together and planned our Beltane. Oh, Arthur. Dear, dear Arthur."

There was no sign he heard me, but I had to trust.

I drew back. Nothing seemed amiss with me yet, either,

but the gods would surely choose their moment, no doubt watching as though it were sport, waiting for me to fall, to writhe upon the ground, more black foam spilling from my lips.

What I'd done, some would call it spellwork, others sorcery. An act as dark as the poison I'd purged, even if the outcome was desirable. If so, let them. They could say whatever they liked, whether out loud or behind their hands in whispers. He lived!

Without further delay, I rose, turned sharply, and bolted for the door. In the corridor, I picked up my skirts and ran, the corridors eerily empty. I shrugged it off. Soon, with Arthur at the helm, the planning would begin anew, what measures to take against the Saxons, even as they plotted in their strongholds what measures to take against us. We'd always known they'd grow more cunning, and though they preferred to fight on foot, they would likely secure horses too – match us, adapt.

Fire against fire.

I could only hope that Arthur had learned something too – that it was simply too dangerous to be at the forefront of battle. He'd have to fight differently now.

Along with his care, *all* such matters were in the hands of others. The Fay had once marked me as their champion, but they would have to find another. And they had. They had. *Mordred the Fay.* Would that he might grow to become his own man, not theirs, and certainly not Agravaine's. Would that I could protect him, nurture him, when once I'd never wished to. How strange it was that that longing *burned* in me now in place of the poison, but too late. The bargain could not be undone.

At last came the sound of life, from just up ahead, in a

chamber close to the one Arthur used to share with Guinevere. Lumiel's?

If so, Guinevere would be in there, and it was her I needed to tell. *His wife.*

I flung the door open, a storm of emotions in my chest – elation, excitement, grief, and yes, fear. For though I would travel soon to the Otherworld, none who still lived could say what that passage truly required, whether it was easy to find the bridge between two worlds, or if the mists were as thick there as they could be here.

I should be dying. Work like this took its toll, regardless of any bargaining.

And yet...I'd never felt so alive!

When I'd handed the stoppered vial to Cai, I'd made it clear what he must tell the maid who'd administer it. "Just one drop. A single drop," I'd said. "Do you hear? There's little more than that in there anyway, but just make sure they know, Cai. Make them understand. With medicines, we *always* err on the side of caution."

He'd nodded solemnly and assured me he'd do just that.

I was sorry to irritate Lumiel's cough further, but it was, as Merlyn might say, for the greater good. The elation I felt that Arthur would live would surely be felt by the child too, for I'd seen it, when he ran to his father's bedside, his love for him, how tenderly his small hand had stroked Arthur's cheek.

As for Guinevere, there was love in her, too, for Arthur, even if it had been eclipsed by her devotion to Lancelot, though how it would all transpire, I didn't know.

"Guinevere," I said, on sight of her. "The gods have listened. Arthur...he will live."

Startled by my voice, she turned, her eyes red-rimmed,

her entire body trembling.

"Guinevere?" I echoed.

She didn't respond, only turned back to the bed.

Merlyn was there too, his face cast in shadow, even as he looked at me.

Why weren't they reacting to what I'd just said? What occupied them instead?

Lumiel, of course.

All elation drained from me. "What is it?" I said. "What's wrong?"

I grew cold, began trembling too – the effects of the poison at last?

Or something else?

Not just fear now. *Terror*.

I crept closer even though I wanted to run from the room and go back to Arthur, feel his body next to mine as I lay close to him, listening to each breath as it grew stronger, wishing mine would diminish. *Willing* it to be so.

A bargain has been struck!

The gods. The goddesses. The Great Mother…

Why did they do this? Continue to tease and torment me?

I'd offered my life for Arthur's. *Mine*.

And the dose given to Lumiel had been small. So small.

Yet I knew, as Guinevere sank to her knees beside the bed, as I gazed down upon Lumiel, who was pale, paler than his father had been, who had coughed and coughed, his lungs irritated again, who was now not merely asleep, but had slipped into unconsciousness instead, that it was not me who was wanted. To return Arthur to us, the gods would demand someone of equal measure, someone who burned as brightly as he did. And though I burned indeed, it wasn't in the same way.

One drop.

Just one drop of tincture.

But it had been enough.

The excuse the gods needed.

As though it were yet another vision, as though I was gazing into the quartz mirror in my chamber at Gwynedd, with only a candle flickering beside me, I could see it as clearly as I could see Lumiel. As Arthur continued to draw breath, getting stronger and stronger indeed, Lumiel's would become fainter and fainter, until it ceased.

And there'd be *nothing* I could do to stop it.

CHAPTER THIRTY

I'm here again—

At the edge of the sea, standing on the sandy shore, staring into the vastness.

The last time, Arthur had stood beside me.

But Arthur…he's elsewhere now.

I turn my head – right, then left. There is nothing but sea and sand, stretching on and on. Even if I look behind me, I'll see nothing. All has fallen away.

It's just me and the sea.

And the sea is calling. "Morgana… Morgana…"

A siren song – soft, enticing – though I haven't yet stepped forwards.

At my feet, the water is warm. It laps tentatively – a gentle caress.

'She who comes from the sea'. That's what my name means. And yet, as a child, I saw the sea only once, so my mother meant the waters around Avalon when she named me – that sacred isle, reached by coracle, through reed beds as thick as woodland in parts, or paths slippery with moss and shrouded in mist.

There are voices in that mist, too, and they have also called my name. They guided me – I must remember that. I waded through shallows and over hidden depths, and the waters bore me up, lifted me so high I felt I was walking on them.

My crooked path was always meant to lead me there.

What happened with Seren… It was no accident. It was manipulation. I'm not evil, though I understand how I might be seen that way, and how that shadow might cling.

Despite everything — despite the welcome I never received from Viviane, my own mother, the High Priestess of Avalon — I miss it. I miss Caireann's sweet smile, Wenna's bright laugh, the thrum of power in the earth, the song of centuries.

Avalon. A haven for the Great Mother when She grows weary of tending to Her children. A thankless task indeed sometimes, for people are just so…wayward. Continually forsaking Her, turning to another, though it was She who gave them life.

I have given life.

That too I should remember.

I am not just *a bringer of death.*

There are no paths before me now, they've all been washed away.

There is only the sea.

The world behind me…can I ever return to it? Will it…allow me to?

I don't know.

And oh, the sea — it is beautiful. Rippling green before shifting towards blue.

Whispers rise again, clearer now. "There is a world beneath these waters too…and there, Morgana, you are *welcome. You who has the tide in your blood."*

Imagination. Wishful thinking. But when you've never belonged anywhere, not truly, even imagined voices can be a comfort.

"It is here you're meant to be."

Rumination. I've always been prone to it. Priscilla used to say so, chiding me gently for allowing thoughts to gnaw at me, to pierce my soul.

Those I've loved are gone.

Even him. Even Arthur.

He is fading, as I too shall fade. Surely no one's remembered forever.

I can only hope that is so.

No more ruminating.

No more turning the blade inwards.

I take one step forwards, then another, and another.

The sea coils around my legs now, as if suddenly remembering something: it's hungry. And it can never be tamed, no matter my belief.

Perhaps this is my atonement. My apology for being untameable, too.

Here it comes – the ice to chill my bones. The water is warm no longer, and unseen hands – not the current – grip and pull.

Soon, I'll discover what lies below.

What creatures.

What madness.

Perhaps death is the best I can hope for.

Soon.

Soon, I'll be under.

I shouldn't look back. I know what I've lost.

And yet…my head turns. My shoulders follow.

The horizon…

It isn't empty.

It's lined with people! Shoulder to shoulder, watching.

Those I've loved.

Those I've despised.

Those I've killed in battle.

Those I've saved.

And those I've murdered, one of them small, so small.

All of them stare, but only one raises a hand.

Is he calling me back?

Telling me to save myself?

Or simply waving farewell.

Arthur.

It is Arthur.

My Arthur.

All others remain still.

Oh, Arthur – if anyone could persuade me, it would be you. But the sea is more demanding than either of us. It wants back what is part of it – to feel whole again.

And what I want?

It doesn't matter.

I can't change anything now.

Powerless, powerful, then powerless again.

As I turn back to the sea, I understand, finally: I'm in too deep.

The maid had gone, bolted, and the vial – unstoppered, bled dry – found.

I'd rushed to Cai, and he to me. We collided in the outer courtyard, and he pulled me into the shadows.

His cheeks, usually as red as his hair, were drained of all colour. "You've heard?" he said.

"Of course. The maid—"

"She isn't stupid," he insisted. "I gave her your instructions. She would've followed them. A drop. Just one drop. You said… You *said*…"

If only I could close out the world again, seal it off as I

had before.

Earlier, in Lumiel's chamber, with his mother stricken by his sudden collapse, fear hollowing her – that *oldest* of fears, the loss of a child – I hadn't collapsed, but I had managed to lose myself. Merlyn's eyes were on me, and I'd simply just…slipped away. Drifted far from that room where death had found a new home, back to the seashore of my childhood, there to drown myself – the sacrifice I should have been. I'd screwed my eyes shut, then opened them, and Merlyn was still watching – silent, unblinking, and so I'd fled again, in body as well as mind, desperate to find Cai, and piece together what had gone *so right* this past night…and so terribly wrong.

Dawn was upon us.

"It was just one drop?" I asked, needing to hear it again and again. "Cai, there was barely more than that in the vial!"

"But, Morgan," he said, his lips trembling, "just how potent can one drop be?"

"I…" My voice faltered, even as my mind screamed what I knew to be true: *Not so potent as to cause death!* "I must confess," I whispered. "I have to!"

"Confess? To poisoning Lumiel? Morgan, there was no intent! Was…there?"

I shook my head fiercely as we stepped further back, deeper into the shadows, just so fearful someone might see us, might overhear.

"Where could the maid have gone, Cai?"

"I don't know," he said miserably.

"She couldn't have gone far. Is a horse missing?"

"I haven't checked. I still…I'm *reeling*."

"Frightened. Yes, I know. I am too." For we were both complicit. "I wouldn't mention you, Cai. You know that, don't you? I wouldn't betray you."

"Yes, Morgan," he said, tears brimming now, slipping down his cheeks, "I *do* know. But if Lumiel worsens… If… Do you know what they'll do to us?"

"*To me*, Cai! You have to swear it! Only to me."

He was indignant. "Where's the honour in lying, Morgan?"

"Where's the honour in murder? This was my doing – my idea. You and the maid…" I hated saying it, but it was true, "…I used you. Because Arthur… Arthur…"

"What of Arthur?" Cai latched onto his name like it might anchor him.

"He will live, Cai. *Arthur will live.*"

Wonder in his eyes, and more fear. "But how, when he was so close to death?"

"Because I've ensured it. And hear me now: if Lumiel is taken instead of him, I'll confess – me alone. If you try to intervene, to share the blame, I will curse you. Do you understand? In both this world and the next. I will hunt you down there!"

Harsh words. Words meant to terrify.

And Cai – brave, beloved Cai – was a simple man at heart, the kind who'd believe such threats, no matter how hollow they rang to me.

As he held my gaze, I softened, just a little.

"When Arthur recovers – and he will – he'll need you. Not just as a friend, but in battle too, to protect him, or, Cai…he will fall again."

There!

That was enough to seal his lips.

"Fila," he said. "The maid—"

"Never mind the maid. She's gone – what's the point in

dragging her back? But yes, because she fled – though I don't blame her, I might have done the same – and because she left the vial behind, the hunt for the saboteur will begin soon. And, Cai, if they can't find her…they'll need someone else to blame."

"*If* Lumiel worsens. For he has always been a sickly child."

My brow creased. "Has he? You said a cough worries him—"

Cai nodded. "He's fallen ill many times in his short life. Though lately – and oddly, despite the cough – he's seemed a little stronger."

"Who treats him? Priscilla?"

Cai shook his head. "Guinevere has her own advisers and medics."

"She doesn't trust our ways at all."

"No. Especially after Viviane failed Arthur, and Priscilla too."

To her, their failure was all just further proof against our beliefs, that our rites and offerings were nothing more than foul superstition. Even so, what he'd said had given me hope. Perhaps the gods weren't mocking me after all, teasing me, laughing at my constant attempts to outrun fate, the lengths I'd go to. The poison I'd ingested might still be in my veins, lying in wait, biding its time, ready to overwhelm me when I least expected it. And Lumiel, perhaps it was merely an unfortunate coincidence what had happened. Yes, the potion had affected him, worse than I'd anticipated, aggravating more than just his lungs, but he'd recover, along with Arthur.

In time.

Hope is as easy to believe in as the gods.

It was hope that made me nod when Cai grabbed my shoulders, when he shook me, when he forced me to look into his eyes when I was losing myself again, in that same ocean as before, but now clinging to driftwood there.

"We wait," Cai was saying, his breath hot against my face. "We wait and see what happens before we do *anything*. And you…you saved Arthur. You! The rumours of you being a great healer – they're true. There's something about you, Morgan. I've always felt it. A magic." Even as I recoiled at that, tried to deny it, he continued, refusing to let me. "You healed Arthur when no one else could. When all of us, even Merlyn, thought he would die. I was certain he was hours from death – just hours. That last time I kissed his brow it was so cold. And now…now there's warmth in his blood again. You put it there! And soon…" Ah, such hope in him too. "Soon, Morgan, there'll be fire! The fire of old. Because of you." He pulled me into his arms, tears still streaming down his face, as they streamed down mine, *both* of us clinging to driftwood. "And fire will return to Lumiel's bones too. You'll see. And one day – ah, yes, one day – he'll be as great as his father. He'll lead *armies* of Britons towards further victory, greater than any Roman legions. Arthur's firstborn."

"Arthur's firstborn," I whispered. "Yes, his firstborn will rise, Cai. He will rise."

Cai released me, green eyes fierce with resolve. "There. That's it then. No more talk of anything else. You saved Arthur, and despite Guinevere, you'll save Lumiel too, bring him back to full strength. Banish the last of his childhood weakness – for good this time. As I helped you with Arthur, I'll help with that."

"But you'll speak of it to no one. Not a word. Because–

_"

"You have my oath," he said without hesitation.

"A *warrior's* oath."

"Yes."

"Sworn before Lugh?"

"Before Andraste and Belatucadros, too."

I heaved a sigh. "Then we wait?"

"We wait. And we watch. You'll find a way, Morgan. You always do."

CHAPTER THIRTY-ONE

You'll find a way, Morgan. You always do.

There was *no* way Guinevere would let me tend to Lumiel. Now, at all hours, his chamber was heavily guarded, her priests the only ones allowed to enter, and Merlyn too, for she dared not go against him. Not yet, anyway. As for Lumiel, his health was *not* improving, while at the opposite end of the caer, Arthur grew stronger by the day.

I wasn't allowed near Arthur either. Not even Priscilla was. His chamber, too, was under constant watch, again only Guinevere's holy men permitted within.

Bishop Elwyn, who'd presided over their marriage rites and was revered by the Christians as something close to a living saint, had been summoned from his monastery in the southern reaches of Cymru. He had come before, when Arthur had first fallen ill, for something the Christians called the Last Rites, a set of prayers to prepare a soul for its onward journey, wherever that may be. I would watch him as he emerged from Lumiel's chamber, and his expression was always the same: grim.

And so, once again, all we could do was watch and wait.

Of the maid? Still no word.

Warriors had been sent to track her, but hadn't yet returned with news. As for Merlyn, his gaze remained just as it had been when I'd first entered Lumiel's chamber.

Stern, watchful, and accusatory, yes, but he was also trying to determine what magic had been worked. What bargain struck.

If I'd thought the poison might still be active in me, still searching for its stronghold, I no longer harboured that illusion. And yet…if I *could* reach Lumiel, be alone with him, perhaps I could bargain again. Convince the gods I *was* worthy of being taken, that I'd do *anything* for them, suffer for them, bleed for them, be cast among shadows for eternity, because I would *never* want this, the death of a child. But even as I told myself this – over and over – that other part of my nature denied it.

It was *Arthur* I'd do anything for. He was the one I truly worshipped.

And that was the problem. The gods could see through my lies.

Watching and waiting. Watching and waiting. The days passed, and each one was slower than the last. We gathered in the Great Hall, aimless and anxious.

On one such occasion, Lancelot joined us there, sitting across one of the long trestle tables from me, his face so changed from the boy I once knew. That grin of his, always wide, especially when it turned my way, the careless tilt of his head – it was all gone. Time and war had marked him, but so had something else, something quieter, more insidious: deceit.

Ah, the shadows…the shadows. They never sat well with some.

A noble warrior. Even in Gwynedd, tales of his heroics had reached us – how he would charge into the breach once the shield wall broke, his sword rising and falling, felling Saxon after Saxon. Limbs severed and heads rolling.

They said he would lift a head aloft afterwards, roaring like a beast.

Battle fever. I'd seen it before in more seasoned warriors, how they whipped themselves into a frenzy, a lust for blood that cast all fear aside, because, in the end, it had to. To tear a man apart, you must convince yourself first that you *wanted* to, leaving no room for doubt. But the doubt always came – after. Boys were sent into battle, and sometimes it was boys you split in two. The blood that splattered might be washed away by time and tide, but not the stain. That never quite faded.

Plenty had taken its toll on Lancelot, on all Arthur's warriors, but when I'd known him before all this, he'd been so…light. Unencumbered. His thoughts only for me. *In love* with me. Now it was love that tore him apart, binding him in a war of its own.

Cai had left us, wandered off, perhaps to find Peredur, or Balin and Balan, for the hall was nearly empty today, aside from me and Lancelot, everyone losing themselves elsewhere it seemed, seeking some respite from this watching, this waiting. We were all caught in it – not just Cai and me – and there'd been so much of it lately. Those absent could be out in the fields, engaged in battle training, or simply idling away the hours. Maybe some had ridden back to the border to patrol there.

"Lancelot," I said. When he didn't respond, I called his name again, softer.

He lifted his head as if surprised by the sound of my voice. "Morgan?"

"How do you fare?"

"Me?"

I reached out and his eyes dropped to my hand. He

305

swallowed, uncertain.

"Take it," I urged. "I can see well enough the toll this is taking on you."

He hesitated a moment longer, then grasped it tightly.

"Morgan," he whispered. "What's happening? I can't tell anymore."

"Come," I said, rising. We couldn't speak here. The people were few, but there were still too many for that.

He rose too, and we walked into the quiet of the day, towards the back of the caer, the very place I'd first pledged my maidenhood to him.

We didn't sit as I had with Merlyn, we kept walking, the day a clement one.

He was lost, Lancelot. Walking beside me, but lost. Or he wanted to be – because to lose yourself in the mists meant never having to face what waited beyond them.

There was no point in dancing around the edges. As I fired my arrows straight, I did so with my words. "You and Guinevere…Arthur doesn't know, does he?"

No reply from him, not at first. He simply continued to put one foot in front of the other, his head bowed, and his dark hair, ever lustrous, catching the sunlight.

"Is there anybody here who *does* know?" I persisted, and then when I was still met with silence, I thudded to a stop, and grabbed his arm. "Lancelot!"

His eyes were shining, and he was trembling too.

"Morgan, I… Oh, Morgan."

His arms closed around me, *crushing* me to him, holding on as if he was trying to stop himself from falling apart. "Why did you do it? Leave? Was it because of me?"

Because of him?

He was continuing to murmur, feverishly almost, his lips

brushing against my hair while he did so. "If you hadn't done it… If you'd stayed…"

Being this close to him again stirred something in me. Lancelot had loved me, and I'd loved him, even while loving Arthur. The touch of his hand and his skin against mine had always brought joy. Besides, it was I who'd betrayed our love first, not him.

For a few seconds, as he clung to me – *needed* me – I wanted him to keep doing so. And to cling to him, in turn. Lancelot, one of Arthur's finest warriors, could protect me. And I might need that protection – soon. But what he'd just said…

Was he…*blaming* me for what had happened between him and Guinevere?

I pushed him away.

"If I'd stayed, would it have been different?"

He was taken aback by the edge in my voice.

"Morgan," he said, reaching for me again.

My hand went instead to the sickle knife I kept at my side.

His eyes widened. "Morgan?"

"It would have made *no* difference, Lancelot," I continued. "To you or to me, to anything that's happened. Now answer the question. Does Arthur know about you and the High Queen? Does he even have the slightest notion?"

The wretchedness returned to his face – whatever spark of hope had flared between us was gone, extinguished for good this time, perhaps.

"I love Arthur," he said, gnawing at his lip in between words, so harshly I thought he might draw blood. "Arthur is…everything to me. But so is Guinevere." His voice cracked as he thumped a fist against his chest. "I didn't expect to feel this way. How could I? But the moment our eyes met, mine and hers – *the moment* – it was done. Even though she was marrying someone else, we were helpless in the face of it. But we tried, Morgan – I swear it's true – we tried so hard to stay away from each other. To deny what had blossomed. Because she loves Arthur, too, just as much as I do."

Impossible, I wanted to cry, but it would have been a lie. The heart, as I knew, wandered its own road, a rebel that could drive you to madness, make you long to wrench it from your chest, just to feel – no matter how fleetingly – sane again.

Oh, to be sane again!

Lancelot pressed on. Now that the secret had been spoken of, he couldn't seem to stop. "War kept us apart for many years, and I was grateful for it. I wanted more war. Can you imagine, Morgan? How desperate a man must be to *wish* for the battlefield?" He shook his head, breathless. "I took lovers, woman after woman, but none of them – *none* – could quench the fire she'd stirred in me. And that's why I said what I did, about you staying. Because…there's something between us. Even now. We called it love once, but maybe…maybe it *transcends* love." There it was again – hope – flaring in his eyes. "It was only you who could have saved me."

I understood him. Every word he said, but my teeth gritted.

"Whatever's between us does *not* transcend love."

Lancelot faltered, then shifted course. "You mustn't blame Guinevere. She's virtuous. Devoted. To Arthur, to Lumiel, to the land. The love she has for Lumiel… I've never seen anything so pure. If anything happens to him…"

He, like so many others, like me, could not bear to contemplate it.

"She fought against our love as bravely as any warrior. This…this is *not* her fault." His defence of her was so impassioned, so raw, I could easily believe it. "What will you do," he asked, softer now, "with this…knowledge?"

When still I said nothing, trying to make sense of it, to decide what I *could* do, he dared to touch me again, took hold of both my arms, our faces close.

"Arthur needs to recover. Fully recover. They're keeping the news of Lumiel from him until then. Consider, just for now, keeping this from him too. Morgan, I beg you!"

"I shall do nothing with it," I said at last, Lancelot so aghast, having not dared to believe it, that his hands dropped back to his side and he stepped backwards.

"Nothing?" he echoed.

I nodded. "You're right. Now isn't the time. And it's not for me to decide when it will be. Arthur…does he love Guinevere? Truly?"

I swallowed hard as the words left me.

"He does," Lancelot said. "But none can love her the way I do. And if she were not a princess of the Middle Lands, if her father hadn't had horses enough to give to Dumnonia for Arthur's cavalry, if we were just two simple people, we would be together. And life…ah, life would have been perfect."

Again, he was right. What had happened – or hadn't – was because we were *not* simple people, and these were *not* simple times. They were the dark ages, an age of chaos, of change and confusion, and dread that there was worse to come. Everything could be lost if those like us refused to bend to fate.

"So you won't breathe a word, Morgan? Our secret is safe with you?"

"I've said so. But know this, Lancelot, it isn't for your sake, and it isn't for Guinevere's. If I stay silent, it is only ever because of Arthur."

His expression darkened. "He is much loved. Whatever has happened."

"He is. And you must never hurt him."

"My lady, you have my oath," Lancelot said, his voice steady now. "And thank you. Truly – thank you. We know the danger of the game we're playing, and that we play it still should tell you how real our love is, how deep. But we will be more discreet. What you saw in Arthur's chamber…that was a moment of weakness. We will try again and again to deny our love, we've sworn this to each other. Guinevere will devote herself to Lumiel, and I'll go to war, fight until the Saxons are broken. We'll put time and distance between us, in whatever way we can. Because…even though she is High Queen, so exalted, there may still be a price to pay. Poor Tristan…"

My ears pricked. "Tristan? What's happened to him?" I remembered the way he'd looked when he came to bid Arthur farewell – ashen, hollow-eyed. "What is it?"

"It didn't happen to Tristan," he said at last, a dullness entering his tone now that I was forcing him to recount it, filled with yet more despair. "It happened to Isolde."

My skin went cold. "Isolde? Mark of Kernow's wife? Lancelot – *tell me!*"

"It was discovered – the love between them, his own son lying with his father's wife. He was here when it came to light. He had come to court to fight beside Arthur. A good man. He is *such* a good man, Morgan. They call me a fine

310

SHANI STRUTHERS

warrior, but the way he wields a sword – 'tis like a miracle in motion. That's the sole reason he still lives, because of his talent, his skill, what he can do for us. Mark was ready to see him dead, but Arthur intervened. He insisted. He *threatened* Mark. And it worked. Mark relented, but Isolde, she was *not* allowed to live, for to Mark the offence was too great. He'd wanted his bride from Éire solely for himself, had made that clear, and still she'd gone against him. Arthur had to concede to something, or the whole of Kernow would have turned against him. Mighty Kernow. And it *pained* him, Morgan, so deeply I believe it distracted him – this was just before the last battle, why we were *all* distracted, allowing the Saxons too close to him, the news of it haunting us.

"Isolde… She was so young, so beautiful. What she endured! All because she loved Tristan, who'd ridden back and forth between Dumnonia and Kernow just to see her, who couldn't find it in himself to stay away. Such was their love, that they risked everything, for Isolde knew all too well how jealous Mark could be, and so did Tristan, what it was he was likely to do. She was dragged naked through the village – *a queen*, Morgan, treated like that – there to be tied to a stake and burned alive."

A silence fell between us, colder than the fields hereabouts in winter.

"I went to her execution," Lancelot said at last. "Tristan would be killed if he set foot in Kernow again – that was Mark's decree, and it still stands. So I swore to him I'd go in his place. I'd stand in the crowd, to let her know she wasn't alone, that there was someone there who understood all that had happened, and didn't condemn her for it." Tears filled my eyes as much as his as he went on. "And, Morgan…she saw me. I *know* she did. She found my gaze

311

and held it. And I didn't look away, not when the flames caught the hem of her dress, when she opened her mouth to scream. Not even then." He looked away now, though, having to blink his dark lashes hard. "But the fear that Guinevere might suffer the same fate, that I too might be put to the sword, with Arthur powerless to stop it despite being High King, because we need the Christians, or we *all* burn – none of it lessens what's between us. It only grows."

Everything else Lancelot had said – *everything* – paled into insignificance in the face of this. All I could think of was Isolde.

I'd once thought of running to her instead of staying at Avalon. She'd been losing Tristan to Arthur's army, just as I had lost Arthur to Guinevere. I imagined we might have found solace in each other's grief, forged a friendship even.

If I'd gone…could *I* have stopped it? Summoned a storm from the edge of the horizon, drawn down the ever-waiting mist, called lightning to scorch the earth – anything to send the crowd fleeing while I stole her away, not for death, but for life.

No. Because I couldn't have done then what I could now – not before Gwynedd, before Agravaine even. I would have been as powerless as Arthur, as powerless as I felt in that moment, for all I'd learned. Because sometimes all power was – though fed by the staunchest of beliefs, even when it leaned towards the gravest of dangers – was nothing more than illusion. Guinevere's smoke and air.

Lost in sorrow, in grief, in the sharp bite of that realisation, it took a few moments to realise there was a commotion elsewhere – the rising clamour high-pitched and frantic. Women's voices, men's too, and one above all – a girl's, shrill with fear.

Lancelot and I exchanged a glance, his frown a perfect mirror of mine, and then we turned as one and, swift-footed, made our way back to the caer, to the courtyard.

A crowd had gathered when only moments before there'd been barely anyone.

As we drew closer, the crowd began to part.

"What is it?" I asked. "What's happening?"

Then, as two warriors stepped aside, one young, one more grizzled, I saw her – a girl whose clothes were caked with filth, as though she'd been dragged through mud.

"Who is she?" I demanded.

The girl opened her mouth, even as she lifted a hand – pointing straight at me.

"Her!" she bawled. "She gave me the tincture. She said it would help Lumiel, not harm him. She…she *bewitched* me into doing it. Because that's what she is – not a queen, but a sorceress – and for her own foul reasons, she wants Lumiel dead."

CHAPTER THIRTY-TWO

If I thought my shrieking voice might rise to meet hers – a protest, a denial in it, an *outrage* – if I was drawing breath to cry out, the moment was stolen from me, drowned as surely as if we stood submerged in cold, deep water.

And in its place rose another.

Guinevere's.

It was her voice – and hers alone – that rang through the caer, that stopped us all in our intent, that rendered us still as statues.

It could only mean one thing.

Lumiel was dead.

By my hand.

My legs threatened to give way. Lancelot was still beside me, his head turned towards the cry, and so I made good use of him. I leaned into him, grasped his arm, and clung to it, forcing myself to stay upright, not to fall, to admit my guilt that way.

Whatever had happened, I hadn't meant it!

It *shouldn't* have happened. I'd made the tincture countless times before, though always to soothe, not to harm. This time, yes, it was meant to irritate, but only mildly, so I'd made it stronger, but only a little. And I'd given clear instructions: one drop.

One.

Had Lumiel's maid ignored that? There it was – the variable I couldn't control.

As I turned back to her – Fila, I remembered Cai telling me her name was, fear twisting an otherwise pretty face into something grotesque – I saw it all too clearly. The tincture *had* worsened Lumiel's cough, as intended. So, thinking it a mistake, that more might help, she'd given him what remained in the vial. Hardly any, as I'd said, another drop, perhaps two, three at most, when one – one was enough!

There was good intent in her actions, just as there'd been in mine. Lumiel was never meant to die, only to suffer briefly. Just long enough for me to work on Arthur undisturbed, to ensure Guinevere remained at his side. Then both would recover.

But intent no longer mattered. Hers or mine.

Men moved towards me. None that I recognised.

On seeing them, Lancelot stepped in front of me, his sword already drawn, and Cai, pale and breathless, hurried to join him.

"Step back," Lancelot demanded. "Step back! Morgan is the High King's sister – a queen in her own right."

Merlyn – where was he? Still with Guinevere, with her priests and the bishop? If so, then all their power combined hadn't been enough to save her son. Not the old gods, and not the new one. They would all have what they wanted, without mercy.

Cai, with his strong, lumbering body, was now in front of me, while Lancelot had moved to my side. Though the warriors who'd rushed towards me outnumbered them, they held back – for now. Would they wait on Guinevere's command? Or even then, might they hesitate? Lancelot had spoken true – I was Arthur's sister. A queen. Would they truly take the word of a maid over mine?

I had to speak, open my mouth, form words. Counter her.

She'd only named me so far, not Cai. There was love between them, then? She didn't *want* to name him, perhaps. For why do so, if blame could be laid solely at my feet? Save her lover *and* herself. But what of me? Lumiel was dead. *Dead.* And he had no surviving siblings. Guinevere had just had Lumiel, just as I only had Mordred.

Mordred – who was not just Arthur's firstborn, but now his *only* child.

I should fight, if only for his sake. He bore Arthur's traits – could be sweet, and loving. If he continued to grow into that, and not into the shadowed thing the vision at the silent pool had warned me of, what the Fay had hinted at, and Nimue too, what even my own instincts had whispered, then he could be a worthy successor.

Curse the Christians again, and all they would have to say about it! Why should I hold back because of them? He had a right. A claim. He deserved a chance as well.

Speak, Morgan. Speak. Lie!

Cai had turned his head towards me while Lancelot stepped forwards, forcing the crowd to fall back. Lancelot – heroic Lancelot, beloved by so many. If they rushed him, he'd do damage. Great damage. But eventually he'd be overwhelmed. One man – two – they couldn't stand against so many, though if Sagramor should ride in, if Lot's three sons appeared, if more of Arthur's companions emerged from the crowd, not so idle now, they might not be as certain. And Tristan too – dark, brooding Tristan – his fury barely contained. Was he prepared to see another queen burn?

"Morgan," Cai was whispering, trying to gain my attention, to shake me free of the stupor that had me gripped. "Morgan, say something!"

At his urging, I tried. Truly, I did. I opened my mouth, but the only words that came were these: "Remember your oath, what you swore. Remember to keep it."

His expression twisted – not just pained, but agonised.

"Morgan…" he said again.

You're not to blame, I mouthed, stepping forwards and lowering his blade.

Lancelot turned to me then, his dark eyes full of confusion, though the questions that raged within them were easy enough to read: *What are you doing? The maid is mad. You're innocent of this. Aren't you, Morgan? Aren't you?*

He'd been willing to believe in my innocence. He'd wanted to – desperately. And something in my heart – my beleaguered, troubled, treacherous heart – that I thought had long since burned itself out, still loved him for it.

"Lower your sword too," I said, just as a fresh commotion rose from the back of the crowd – more of Arthur's companions arriving, stunned by what was unfolding.

"Morgan—" Still Lancelot pleaded with me, his eyes glistening.

"Do as I say. Both of you. Let me pass."

When Uwaine, Peredur, and Sagramor lifted their swords in response, Lancelot held up a hand to stop them. He did as I said, and so did Cai, though tears shimmered in his eyes as well. He would lie, if he had to, but I couldn't. Not for myself, not for anyone. A child had died – a beloved child – at my doing.

"Secure her," came a voice from the crowd.

No one moved, all stood frozen, as though I'd cast another spell.

"Secure her!" the voice boomed again.

The moment broke, and two warriors stepped forwards. Wide-eyed and with mouths gaping, they feared they'd be poisoned too, just by touching me.

"It's all right," I told them. "I am but a woman."

And they were boys, caught in a game of war, of sides.

I had to coax them further. "I won't harm you, you have my word, but your commander will, if you don't do as he says."

Finally, they bound my wrists, as quickly and as tightly as they could, and only then did their commander, older by far, come forwards.

As they led me away, the maid found her voice again, shrieking in triumph, certain she'd saved herself.

With a shout and one clean stroke, Cai silenced her.

Poor girl. A pawn of the worst kind. She couldn't have saved herself. She was the one who'd administered the tincture, bewitched or not. What Cai did was a mercy for Fila, though others would deem he'd done it for Guinevere's sake alone. Because it was not worth drawing out her punishment, only mine.

The architect of it all.

"Morgan. Morgan! Wake up. You must wake. You have to leave – now. While all are asleep. Morgan, rouse yourself. We've so little time."

I hadn't slept for days, and now – now that sleep had

finally come, heavy and dreamless – I was being dragged from it.

I groaned. "Go away. Leave me."

That sleep had been a gift. A dark, silent oblivion. Exactly what I craved.

But the hand shaking me grew more insistent, hard enough to wrench further protests from my lips. "Stop it! Unhand me. Do as I say – leave me be, or…or…"

Cai.

It was Cai.

What was he doing here, in the cells? This was a part of the caer I'd heard whispers of, but never seen. Every fortress had them: damp, stinking hollows dug into the earth, a stark contrast to the grandeur above. No straw covered the floor, only mud – hard and compacted, fouled by years of filth. A place where the very walls screamed suffering and despair. I'd tried to stay clean, but was given no water for washing, barely enough to drink – oatcakes sometimes, too hard to chew.

Hour after hour I'd lain there…forgetting, in my misery, how blue the sky had once been, and how green the fields. Wondering if I'd ever see either again.

Sleep. I wanted it to hold me under.

But if Cai had come…

"You must get out. Tonight. This very hour," he urged.

"Out? But…how?" I rasped as he helped me to sit up, every joint screaming with the effort. "The guards at my doors… Where…where are they?"

He gestured over his shoulder, to where another stood – Sagramor, the Numidian. Tall and regal, as though he were a prince himself. Perhaps, in another land, he was exactly that, with a tale as tragic as Tristan and Isolde's. If so, would we ever know? In the darkness, only the whites of his eyes gleamed, fixed not on us but straight ahead, while two men lay at his feet.

My guards.

"You…you've killed them?" I whispered.

Cai tried for nonchalance. "It could be they've killed each other," he said. "A game of knucklebones gone wrong, perhaps."

Killed each other? Though Sagramor's eyes didn't so much as flicker at his words, I knew it for the lie it was. The guards had died at the hands of Arthur's companions, and though I studied their faces for guilt, there was none.

My breath caught.

Cai believed me still, and Sagramor did too.

They believed in my innocence, when Guinevere had not.

Oh, the day I was brought before her…

That wretched day.

I'd always thought Guinevere beautiful. Even if there was no light inside her, what lay on the surface shone so brightly it could sear the eyes. But what an appetite grief has! It devours everything in its path, no respecter of beauty at all.

Guinevere. Poor Guinevere. Aside from our very first meeting long ago, I'd never felt warmth for her. Yet hypocrite though she was – so rigid in her devotion to the Christian faith, but behind closed doors refusing to live by its principles – I pitied her now. She had loved her son. It wasn't just Lancelot who'd told me that; I'd seen it with my own eyes, in Arthur's chamber, when the boy ran to her and she wrapped him in her arms and held him as if she would never let him go. A mother's love, with such purity in it. It was perhaps the *only* pure thing about her. And I'd destroyed it.

I'd had no chance to say how sorry I was, to say anything at all.

What the maid had said was quickly carried to her, and when at last she could bear to look upon me, I was dragged before her in chains.

Lumiel's body was not burned on a pyre behind the caer, as his grandfather Uther's had been, in the Pagan way, but buried deep in the earth – the Christian way. The guards told me this, had *delighted* to tell me. They said Arthur hadn't attended either, still too weak, and at that, I'd shrunk even further into myself.

Lumiel's body. That little body. I couldn't bear to think of it trapped beneath the soil, as I was. I had prayed, wept, keened for him, wrapping my arms around my legs and rocking back and forth, begging that his soul might claw its way up, up, up through layers of cold, unyielding earth – black as my heart surely was – and fly free.

"I'm sorry," I kept murmuring that too. It was *all* I could say. "Sorry. Sorry."

I'd wanted so much to say it to Guinevere as well, to force the word past my lips, to make her *see*. To tell her the truth – all of it – from the very beginning. But the moment had passed. She stood before her throne in the Great Hall, no longer in ivory but in the blackest mourning silks, ringed by her priests, with Bishop Elwyn as grim as ever. And Merlyn – where was he? Why did he not stand there, gloating with the rest of them? Since that time we'd spoken outside the caer walls, he'd kept his distance. He had simply…let me be. Alone in a storm of my own making.

Oh, what did it matter if he were there or not? And it was Guinevere who was the storm, not me. She needed no guidance from him to carry out her vengeance.

"You're a fiend. A devil!" she'd cried, her voice as sharp as a whipcrack, carrying through the Great Hall and beyond. Around her, her priests nodded, eager disciples to her wrath. "A heathen queen of a heathen kingdom. A kingdom that won't bend the knee. Had we all forgotten that? You took my son's life, the throne's successor. A *precious* life. He wasn't the one who was meant to die. It was Arthur!"

I flinched as if struck. My hair hung wild and tangled around my shoulders, my skin surely pale and drawn, my eyes as feral as a hunted animal's – red-rimmed. *Neither of them was meant to die.* I should have said it! *It was me. Only me.*

"Sorceress," Guinevere hissed, foam gathering at the corners of her mouth, animal-like herself. "I see what happened, Morgan. I see it *exactly*." She thrust a hand towards her priests. "They've uncovered your foul treachery, pieced it together, bit by bit, every blasphemous fragment. You wanted time alone with Arthur, when I knew – *I knew* – you couldn't be trusted with him, kin or no. I was sent scurrying to...to my son's room. Distracted." Her voice caught. "So you could... You could..."

Bishop Elwyn stepped forwards to fill the void. A living saint, they called him, but I saw a man as old as Merlyn, though with no hint of youthfulness about him. A man who wore the tonsure, his balding head polished, just as furniture might be, his eyes too small for his head, his mouth too mean, and his body too rounded. An indulgent man, who fed on the reverence of others, had grown fat on it.

A man who knew of the old gods as well as the new, the bargains we could strike.

He finished her sentence. "All so you could save Arthur

in exchange for his son, an Arthur you thought you could perhaps…manipulate for your own warped ends, when with Lumiel that would have been impossible." Until then, I'd only ever heard him speak the Christian vows of marriage between Guinevere and Arthur; now, as before, his voice boomed like judgement. "And though we rejoice Arthur's recovery – who will surely stand strong against you, sister or no, queen or no – it was never your decision to make." His eyes bored into mine. "It was the One True God's, and no man – *no woman* – may thwart Him. You will burn in hell for your treachery, Morgan of Gwynedd, for your vile interference, but first we will see you burn at the stake. For witchcraft, like murder, is the gravest of sins."

Murder.

It was that one word that rang the loudest of all. Not witchcraft. Not even the fire and damnation they promised me. Just that word. *Murder.*

In response, I only bowed my head and let them lead me back to my cell, before Guinevere could lose what little composure she had and lunge at me shrieking, priests and guards having to restrain her – not for my sake, but for hers.

Isolde's fate was mine.

Whatever Cai was doing, and Sagramor too, releasing me, aiding me, she who was condemned, I couldn't obey. This cell was where I belonged until the stake was raised, whether in the courtyard of the caer or in the village below. Until I was led to it, wearing only dung hurled by the crowd, voices rising, shrill with disgust.

Witch. Witch. Witch.

I would fight off Cai, even as he tried to hoist me to my feet, having to swallow against the stench of me. I would fight off Sagramor too. Why should they believe in me, when I didn't? I was infuriated by their temerity. With whatever will I had left, I would drive them back, slam them into the wall with such force the breath would leave their lungs. Then I'd find the jailor's keys and lock myself back in.

Breathing in, breathing out, steeling myself, and then someone else stepped out of the shadows. One who'd decided to show himself at last.

"Merlyn!"

Had I ever thought of him as youthful? Powerful, even? I'd been so in awe of him. Now, he looked…smaller. Shrunken with weariness. Diminished.

My enemy. I'd always believed it. And yet, just as I'd felt pity for Guinevere, another I had blamed, and hated, and named enemy – I now felt the same for him.

For all of us cast into roles that demanded so much of us.

And it seemed my role was not over yet.

"Do as they say, Morgan," he said softly. "You have to go. Now."

"But—"

"You saved Arthur. And it was…the *right* thing to do."

"But… I didn't… I didn't…*mean* to hurt Lumiel. To…kill him." The words finally came, and his reply – like his presence here tonight – was wholly unexpected.

"There are other forces at work, Morgan. Forces…" he winced a little as he admitted it, "…beyond our seeing. Beyond *you*."

"The tincture—"

"The tincture may have had nothing to do with his death." He shrugged, though gravely. "That is something we will never know. And I'm sorry for that, truly, for that uncertainty will torture you all the days of your life, as so much uncertainty already has. But this I do know: you must go. Your own son…"

My ears pricked further. "Mordred? What of him?"

"Find him."

"Find him? What do you mean? He's at Gwynedd!"

"Morgan…I don't think he is. Not anymore."

"But where… Who…?" Then I understood. "You've sent emissaries?"

Merlyn nodded. "News has come from Powys." *Arthur's* Powys.

"And?" Already I was climbing to my feet, though I knew the answer. "Urien is dead, isn't he? And Agravaine – he's gone. Taken Mordred and vanished."

Merlyn had only one concern. "Whose son is he, Morgan?"

It didn't matter that I never answered.

"Yes, let me go," I breathed instead. "Let me go and I will find him."

A mother's love… Surely it bound me to him? A thread that had always existed, even when I hadn't known it. Error after error after error. How many mistakes could one person make? I was damned. The Christians were right about that.

But not yet.

Not yet.

The fear rose again. What would Mordred become in the hands of Agravaine? What threat might he one day pose to Arthur? Agravaine, who clung so fiercely to the old ways, just as I was meant to, both of us the champions of that fading path. But curse it too that I could see, due to my upbringing, what others refused to, that the old and the new *must* find a way to coexist. Even Igraine had seen it. When she'd left Caer Arthur, unable to stay after Uther's death, she hadn't vanished into the wild, but gone to a convent by the sea, news that had come as such a surprise to me. When I'd asked her why, she'd simply said: *Not all Christians are bad, Morgan. And not all prayer is, either.* She had a friend there, someone waiting to welcome her. To her, it would be a place of peace, where she might find solace, even if she remained pagan, through and through. Uther, too, had been tolerant, in his way, and now it was part of Arthur's role to ensure a realm where there was room for both the sacred grove *and* the chapel. Time wrought change, no matter how much we resisted it. Yet Arthur had been wedded to Guinevere, who possessed no such tolerance. Who appeared to *loath* the old gods, and all they stood for. A woman who would tip the scales far too soon.

And that – *that* was Merlyn's error.

Again, that flicker of pity for him, even if he'd never held any for me.

Men were fallible. It seemed even the gods might be.

But Agravaine…Agravaine believed himself *infallible*.

And worse – he would teach Mordred to believe it too, about them both.

I would return to Gwynedd, to see for myself whether Merlyn spoke the truth. And if he had, I'd begin the search there, seeking clues, scrying for them, casting bones, *anything*, for to ask, even Teg if she remained and hadn't been forced to go with them, would likely yield nothing, not if Agravaine had threatened them. If he had, then any threats of mine would pale in comparison. But I'd persevere. I'd save Arthur again by saving his son, the boy who, against all prophecy, *was* him: bright and cheerful, yet who, under different tutelage, might become something else entirely.

Arthur's shadow self. Fulfilling some dire prophecy after

all.

Guinevere – how she had loved her son. Her only son. She'd loved him so fiercely because…she could *not* have another…

There in the cell, that knowledge flashed before me, as certainly as my own damnation. Birthing Lumiel had been as hard for her as birthing Mordred had been for me. Her cries had sounded just as shrilly the night of his birth – though in Dumnonia, it had been a still night rather than a stormy one. Like Mordred and I, they'd both survived, but Guinevere barely. She must *never* bear another, that's what she'd been told by the women who'd tended to her, with Priscilla in agreement. Not if she wanted to live.

Arthur, terrified, had never risked it. He sought to please her in other ways, never daring what might lead to conception. And so – even if the warning had been wrong – she *could not* conceive again. Because if she did, the lie she lived would unravel.

Arthur… Mordred… His son. His *only* son.

Ah, yes, I would do what needed to be done, whatever it took, my full truth guiding me at last. I *would* leave this place, but not before seeing Arthur.

They'd take me to him, no matter how they might rage or resist.

Even if Bishop Elwyn was right, I couldn't leave again without saying goodbye.

CHAPTER THIRTY-THREE

No more deaths that night. At Merlyn's request, the guards stationed at Arthur's door were dismissed with grim warming instead, Cai and Sagramor taking their place.

Once they were gone, I stepped from the shadows, just as Merlyn had in the dungeons earlier. Merlyn, who was angry indeed at what I'd insisted on, fearful time was running out, that we'd be discovered. Before I entered, he seized my arm.

"Be quick," he hissed. "Moments only, Morgan."

Moments. But when everything else had been stripped from me, my dignity even, those few moments were what I needed if I ever hoped to embolden myself again, if I was to gather the will to face what was coming – yet another storm I'd wrought.

Arthur was sleeping. There was more colour in his face now, his cheeks not so hollowed, flesh returning to bone as life recalled him. There'd be no need to learn the deeper Mysteries of Avalon just to commune, and perhaps I never would, for those who *had* gone – Seren, Lumiel – their truths would be hard to bear.

Though I touched his face with the gentlest hand, he stirred. And the name on his lips – even before he opened his eyes – was mine.

"Morgan."

"Arthur!" I breathed as his eyelids fluttered open, as his gaze found mine at last and held it, adjusting, blinking, until he was certain I wasn't a dream, or a ghost, or a wistful fragment of memory. That I was real. I was there.

His cry was as raw as mine. "Morgan! You came back."

I nodded. "Because you needed me. Because...*I* needed *you*."

I couldn't hold back the tears as he struggled upright, just far enough to pull me into his arms. Unlike Cai, who'd recoiled at the sight of my wretched state, having to swallow hard at the stench of me, he showed no such hesitation – only eagerness.

"I'm sorry," I whispered, burying my face against him. "For Lumiel. So sorry."

Arthur shook his head, his hand stroking my hair like he used to, so many moons ago. "I've heard," he murmured, "and Guinevere is wrong. You wouldn't harm him, Morgan. Ah, but poor Lumiel. He was ever frail, though she would never see it. He'd rally, yes, seem robust, but it never lasted. And next time he'd be frailer still. They won't harm you – her people. I'll never give the word. *Never.*" His voice cracked. "Would that I had the strength to stand! It is I who should be sorry, for what I did, for letting you go so easily. I *must* stand. Help me. Help me, please."

I tried to stop him. "Arthur, no. I can't stay—"

His grip on me tightened – stronger than I expected. "Excalibur. Where is it?"

I frowned. He wanted his sword. Why?

"Fetch Excalibur!" he said, and I saw it then: a will far greater than my own.

The sword, bestowed on him at Stonehenge at the dawn of his reign, stood nearby in the corner of the room. I'd noticed it before, of course, but could hardly bear to let my gaze linger on it, something as forsaken as I was without him.

Now I turned fully towards it. Though it had gathered dust there, the jewels on its hilt – jet and moonstone among them – burned with sudden light, though I could have sworn they never had before. They reminded me of the gem at my throat, left untouched by Arthur's guards, who dared not lay a hand on it, and, perhaps because of it, dared not touch me either. It had glimmered on when I could not, exuding a power I lacked. Reason enough to keep it, despite who'd gifted it to me.

I left Arthur to do as he asked. When I turned back, with Excalibur heavy in my hands, I saw he'd done it, swung his legs over the side of the bed.

"Arthur!" I cried. "No! You've said it yourself – you're too weak."

He shook his head, then almost growled his next words. "I've been weak for too long. It's as clear to me now as if I had the Sight. Weak from the moment you left."

As I crossed the space between us, I felt the will in Excalibur too – a death-bringer, yes, but in bringing death to some, it gave life to many, many others.

Holding it out to him, I wondered: could it truly be that Lumiel was never meant to live? And of his parents, only Arthur could accept that. Whether or not his birth had left Guinevere barren, Lumiel had been her only chance – her one child. She would *always* blame me for what happened to him, and I would never begrudge her that. I'd accept her hatred, carry it without protest. For a mother's love runs deep.

As I was learning.

"Arthur," I said, and though I longed to fall at his feet, to take his face in my hands and lose myself in him – I didn't. I wouldn't. My tone was resolute. "I will go now."

He agreed. "You will, Morgan. And *I* will escort you. You leave here as a queen – the queen you should have been." Then, more pointedly, "As the mother of a king."

My heart lurched. "You heard, then? About Mordred?"

"That he is your son?"

I could only nod.

"That he is mine too? Yes, I heard. Every word." He swallowed. "I was close to death, Morgan, as you know. So close I could see the bridge of swords, right there before me. Ector stood on the far side, and Uther with him. They were smiling, pride in their eyes, yet they didn't call me closer. And though I rejoiced to see them – *all* those who've fought and fallen for us, for surely they were there too, the bravest, most selfless warriors I've ever known – I didn't want to cross. I *understood* why they didn't beckon; it was simply not my time. Ah, my love, my love," he went on softly. "There is such light beyond the bridge, such a wonderful calm. But another reason I didn't want to cross was that *you* weren't there. If you still lived, so would I. And then…then you were here. In this very chamber. And somehow…you breathed life back into my bones. You would sacrifice yourself for my sake, yes – but Lumiel, you would never do that."

Tears slid from his eyes as he reached for me, as he drew me close again. Excalibur was the only thing between us – *infusing* us with its ancient energy, binding us further. When he finally pulled away, he was different. Not as broken.

"Your hair," he said, touching strands that had become matted. "You need to wash it. Wash yourself too, and change into clothes, not the rags they've left you in."

"But, Arthur—"

He silenced me with a look. "Not just as a queen, Morgan, you will leave Caer Arthur with your head held high. And I…I would come with you if I could, if there was any way, but…" His voice grew rough again. "There are more battles coming."

"The Saxons will not fell you again, Arthur!"

The words were out before I could stop them.

He gave a wry smile. "You know this?"

"I…"

Somehow, I did. It had come to me the way other truths had lately – swift, unbidden, and without source, and it should have filled me with relief, this glimpse of Arthur's survival – but it didn't. Because if not the Saxons, then who?

Oh, Mordred, Mordred.

Prophecy could be denied. It *had* to be so – even if it brought consequences, ruin of another kind. *Any* ruin but the one we were bound for.

As I'd sworn before, so many times, in so many ways, through rage and love and grief – I swore it now: I'd save Arthur. Even though, in Gwynedd, I'd stood on the edge of a very different vow, close – *so* close – to making it, *believing* in it. Doing as Nimue had wanted, she who I now knew had steered me there, with Seren's death, into the arms of Agravaine, who'd been waiting for someone like me.

She was a more artful tool of destruction than Merlyn or I could ever be. And still a child, as Mordred was, both destined to grow stronger, to become yet more formidable. The two of them together? Would she do it? Seek out Agravaine and Mordred, reach them before I could? She, who saw further than any of us.

More battles were coming indeed, but the moment was now, all that remained in our grasp. And before I could save Arthur, he was intent on saving me.

He'd risen; there was no use in protesting further against it, though I saw the toll it took, the way his hands trembled, how his breath came short. I feared it might undo all the progress he'd made, but as he'd said, the time for weakness was gone.

He asked who stood guard outside his chamber, and I told him – Cai, Sagramor, and Merlyn. How they were helping me.

"To find Mordred? He's gone?" He reached again for Excalibur, his fingers tightening around the hilt. "Then by the gods, Morgan, I will find him."

"No!" The command in my voice surprised him, but he took notice of it. "That task is mine. Agravaine is like Merlyn, as wily, as cunning, but he has taught me much over the years, and I will learn more still: how to outwit him."

Him *and* Nimue.

Arthur gave a slight pause. "Agravaine... You were close to him?"

"Was he my lover, you mean?"

Arthur had the good grace to look abashed. "Yes."

"He was," I said simply.

"Yet he has stolen your child? Why?" Then he remembered more of what I'd whispered before. "Ah, because he is ambitious. That's why."

I confirmed it. "More so than Lot of the North ever was." Lot, who now fought at Arthur's side, ever since Arthur had risen against him.

But you couldn't rise against a shadow. And that's what Agravaine had become.

And in shadows, much could be wrought.

Agravaine, like my son, was not only ambitious, but susceptible.

If Nimue did reach them first…

"Arthur, I will strive to put this right."

"*We* will," he corrected. "Even if apart."

"For Britannia," I said, words I'd uttered to him once before, when we'd first come to the caer and stole a moment in the darkness.

"For Britannia," he repeated, as if recalling that memory too. Then he drew a deep breath and turned towards the door, his voice rising. "Cai! Sagramor!"

They burst into the room, stunned to hear him – *more* stunned to see him standing. Merlyn, too – ecstatic.

Arthur continued to bark orders.

"Fetch a maid – no, fetch two. Have them bring fresh water, combs, brushes, and clothes fit for a lady. For a queen." He turned to me. "*For a goddess.* Go! Now!" Before either man could turn, eager to obey, Arthur smiled, a wide smile, the smile of the man I'd known long before we ever came to court. "Thank you," he said, and this was what his men loved him for, how he always acknowledged everything they did, how he was always so grateful for it. "Thank you for trusting her like I do."

The thick of night had passed, another dawn was rising.

The wheel of time – night into day, day into night – turned on, yet not all days were born equal. Some never faded, not from your own memory, nor the memories of others. Some were joyful. Others, tragic.

And some – some were marked by triumph, however dubious.

I should have been grateful for the Christian influence at Caer Arthur. Without it – the law that placed a man's word above a woman's – Guinevere would have had me burned already. As it was, only Arthur could decree such a fate. And so I remained alive, not yet reduced to ashes, scattered at a crossroads, at the edge of a village, or on some forsaken boundary of land – those cursed places meant to bewilder a spirit.

The maids had come. They'd bathed me, washed and untangled my hair, brushed it until it shone like the raven's wing it was. They'd dressed me in clothes that were indeed fit for a queen, the cloak draped over my shoulders not black, a colour I tended to favour as much as Merlyn, but red – as bright as a ruby I was glad to note and more than a match for the garments Nimue wore.

Arthur had even seen to it I was equipped with a sword, nearly as fine as his own.

"It was a gift," he explained, "for Guinevere, at our coronation. From the kingdom of Glywysing, though she never touched it. She isn't the type to wield a sword."

"But I am?" I asked, half-teasing.

"Bow and arrows, a sword – you may need them all, Morgan. Use them well."

"I'll stay safe," I promised. "As long as you do."

"I swear it."

"Your son will be safe too."

He nodded. "When you find him, bring him here. To me."

"You would raise him? Acknowledge him?"

Another nod.

"But what about Guinevere? You would…put her aside?" When he hesitated, I pressed him. "Arthur…do you still love her?"

"I cannot put her aside, Morgan, she's suffered enough already. As for love…I don't know what lies between us. For my part, it was always little more than infatuation. I knew, the moment you were gone, how pale it was compared to what we had. And yet, I still see glimpses of the good in her. How she was with Lumiel…"

His voice trailed off as I considered his words. Guinevere was like me – a woman who could love, and love deeply. But Lancelot…Did Arthur truly not know?

"Arthur—" It wasn't me who spoke his name, but Merlyn. He'd entered the chamber, clearly deciding he'd waited outside long enough. "As ever, rumours have spread through the caer," he said. "One of the maids, it seems, is quite the tittle tattle." He gave a shrug as he said it, a somewhat exaggerated gesture, and raised an eyebrow. Those rumours he was talking of, they'd been *meant* to spread. "Quite a crowd has gathered outside," he went on, "despite the hour, to see the…" He tilted his head, as if searching for the word. "…spectacle. Shall we?"

Arthur turned to me. He was freshly washed too, his fair hair bright again no matter how short the cut, though I alone, perhaps, saw the weight of effort behind his eyes, how much his body still longed for rest. Rest he'd deny it, now and later.

"Are you ready?" he said, offering his arm.

"I'm ready," I said.

We left the safety, the sanctity, of his chamber. There were guards outside again, in among them Cai and

Sagramor as well as others from Arthur's inner circle, those he trusted the most. Lancelot was there. And Tristan. But if there was only sadness on Lancelot's face, and a quiet dread that Guinevere might see his presence here as betrayal, wondering too whether she'd ever forgive him for it, there was only relief on Tristan's. I was right: another queen burning was something he couldn't endure.

As we passed, they fell in behind us, then flanked us as we stepped outside. Just as Merlyn had said, a crowd had gathered in the courtyards and beyond, more people than I'd ever seen outside a battlefield. At the sight of them, I nearly staggered, Arthur having to tighten his grip on me.

A king and a queen.

For a moment I sought refuge in that imagining – Arthur as king, and me as his queen. That this was how it could have been, if not for Merlyn.

If not for him, *all* this might have been avoided – the death of Lumiel because he would never have existed. Only Mordred. And I'd have loved him from the start.

Arthur. Morgan. Mordred.

Three forces of nature.

The vision crumbled as quickly as it had come with a hiss from the crowd.

"Witch!"

Whoever had spoken was quickly silenced, but by whom, and how, I didn't know.

As the crowd parted to let us pass, like the mists would part for me sometimes, like the sea would, I saw what waited. Taran, pawing the ground, as impatient as ever. Beyond her, the day wasn't a bright one, but that wasn't what I focused on.

It was Guinevere I sought.

Surrounded by her priests, by Bishop Elwyn, her face was hewn from stone.

Again, I faltered, just a step, but Arthur kept walking, so I had no choice but to follow. *Witch. Black Morgan.* That was all some would ever see me as. A sorceress. A murderer. An enemy of the crown. But hadn't Caireann said it? Nothing was *wholly* black – not the night sky, not the shadows, not Guinevere, or Merlyn. Not even me.

In time, perhaps we'd come to understand that better, all of us.

Perhaps we'd be…easier on each other.

I'd taken the life of one child, but I would deliver another.

I promised that – to myself, to the gods, to all who watched, however silently.

That Guinevere remained silent too surprised me, and that she was even here at all. Perhaps she wanted to witness my departure. For even if it wasn't death by fire, it was exile all the same. I couldn't return – not until I had reason, until I had purpose.

That would be her solace. That she kept Arthur. Arthur *and* Lancelot.

So many eyes grazed my skin. The whispers grew louder, multiplying, but I became deaf to them, as Arthur had forced himself to be, at least he had for now.

Taran was closer, the mists rising behind her like the veil they were, alive, always so alive. Soon, I could disappear into them. Breathe again. Because now – surrounded by all these people, all this judgement – I could barely breathe at all.

Priscilla! There she was, smiling at me, despite everything.

A mother's love endures indeed.

I smiled back, sending all the love I had rushing towards her. Her hair was so grey, her back so stooped. This might well be my last sight of her. After this, all I'd have left were memories. *Good* memories, though. Enough to last.

I couldn't resist another glance at Guinevere.

Her hatred was cold, but as I had with Priscilla, I met it only with warmth, with silent words. *Please know that by whatever measure Lumiel died, I'm sorry.*

Our gazes held, and I saw them – the tears she only barely held at bay. Tears that would follow me, haunt me, *punish* me, exactly as Merlyn had said, no matter where I went or how long I lived, through any storms, or any victories I could bring about.

In that moment, I would rather have burned.

"Here," Arthur said. "We're here."

Taran whinnied.

I turned to Arthur, wanting to fling my arms around him, to bury my face in his neck, but of course I couldn't. Earlier, I'd asked what this would cost him, releasing me and in such a way, so publicly, not only with Guinevere, but with the Christians, those you could pick out in this crowd for their pious glares.

Determination had entered his eyes, quiet but indomitable.

"Leave the Christians to me," he'd said, and so I must.

It was his fate to unite them. Mine was to preserve the old. But not blindly. That's what some would never understand. I was of the Fay, yes, but I was no Agravaine, no Nimue – I was the balance between them, and between Guinevere as well.

The middle path was mine, hard to walk already, and it would only get harder still.

I swept my cloak back and mounted Taran.

Some would cheer my departure. But there were some here that would miss me.

And some would wish me back as soon as possible.

Merlyn would. As long as I brought Mordred with me, *for the greater good.*

"'Tis a misty day," Arthur said, looking up at me. "You'll be safe in it?"

"I will," I replied. "I've navigated them before, many times."

He gave a sad smile. "One day I want to know everything. From the beginning."

"One day," I promised.

"That mark on your head... You'll tell me about that too."

"Yes," I said. "Everything, as you say. There'll be no more secrets between us. And Arthur...thank you."

He gave a nod as he stepped back, though he struggled to do so, torn between duty and desire. Behind him, the crowd surged, a tide ready to reclaim its king, some intent on moulding him further, bending him, using him – not just Merlyn, but Bishop Elwyn, and Guinevere too, not realising like I did that he was becoming his own man.

"Go," he said, his voice rough-edged. And then again, "Go...Morgan of the Mists."

I did as he asked, turning Taran outwards. And again – just as he would have wanted – I didn't gallop from the caer, didn't flee like something hunted.

I was no victim anymore. I'd been victim enough.

We rode at our own pace, queen and steed. The red of my cloak and my raven hair the last things the crowd would see of me – for now. Perhaps even the silver flash of my sword as I raised it in final defiance. And then I became what he had named me. Not queen, nor witch, nor Morgana, not even plain Morgan – the girl who'd indeed burned to ashes – but something ethereal, something savage too.

For like the Fay, she had to be.

Morgan of the Mists.

A NOTE FROM THE AUTHOR

As much as I love writing, building a relationship with readers is even more exciting! I occasionally send newsletters with details on new releases, special offers and other bits of news relating to the Psychic Surveys series as well as all my other books. If you'd like to subscribe, sign up here!

www.shanistruthers.com

Printed in Dunstable, United Kingdom